What Delderfield did for the country gentry
of England,
what John O'Hara did for the first families
of Gibbsville,
Eloise Weld now does for the Pennsylvania
fox-hunting aristocracy in the smash
storytelling triumph of the year—

ENGAGEMENT

*"Beneath the facade of neatly manicured fields
and forests and of debutante balls and social
teas, here is a world throbbing with passions
and alliances that are not neatly manicured
at all!"*—BURLINGTON FREE PRESS

*"The descriptions are beautiful and satisfying
. . . the knowledge of how men and women
feel and act is deep . . . Eloise Weld is a
master writer!"*—FORT WAYNE NEWS-SENTINEL

*"A splendid novel . . . a genuine
American version of* Upstairs,
Downstairs . . . *exactly right with its
descriptions of the homes, the servants,
the families, and most especially the male-
female relationships."*—DETROIT FREE PRESS

Have You Read These Big Bestsellers from SIGNET?

Eloise R. Weld

ENGAGEMENT

A SIGNET BOOK
NEW AMERICAN LIBRARY
TIMES MIRROR

SIGNET TRADEMARK REG. U.S. PAT. OFF. AND FOREIGN COUNTRIES
REGISTERED TRADEMARK—MARCA REGISTRADA
HECHO EN CHICAGO, U.S.A.

SIGNET, SIGNET CLASSICS, MENTOR, PLUME AND MERIDIAN BOOKS
are published by The New American Library, Inc.,
1301 Avenue of the Americas, New York, New York 10019

First Signet Printing, July, 1976

1 2 3 4 5 6 7 8 9

PRINTED IN THE UNITED STATES OF AMERICA

Contents

1 • Calling 1

2 • At Finchwicke 36

3 • Hunting 62

4 • Accepting 122

5 • Presenting 148

6 • The House 178

7 • Rehearsing 194

8 • Wedding 243

ENGAGEMENT

1

Calling

IT WAS only a flat mile between Co-Eden and Finchwicke, but Miss Faith Meddleton Hoagland, barreling down the Stone Mill Road in her cream-colored phaeton, was in no hurry to get there. She shortened the reins with a sharp turn of her wrist. Trooper, the old dock-tailed hackney, feeling the nervous tug in his hardened mouth, took the bit in his teeth and stepped out faster. Quinn, the coachman, riding along beside her, wrinkled his nose in a worried sniff as puffs of dust rose from Trooper's hooves and settled in a gray veil behind them over the lavender asters and the goldenrod growing on the side of the country road.

She was on her way to pay a condolence call, and a death in one or another of the best families always threw Quinn into a black gloom, as though he feared for his own future. He scanned the sky and shook his head. The cloudless blue held no promise of rain at all. Fine for corn maybe, but very poor for fox hunting. Hard going, and no scent at all. "Be careful he don't run away with ye," Quinn said, "or we'll both be dead too."

It was fall in Penngwynne, Pennsylvania, and plowing was underway, turning the stubbled sod from gold to dark, re-patterning the fields into new designs of squares and neatly fitted triangles, getting ready for winter wheat. The faintest movement of air loosened the gold coinage of the trees and floated down the bright, dry leaves. Walnuts fell to the ground with a thump. Baskets of apples stood in the orchards. Barns overflowed. Doves feasted on the spilled grains of corn. The satisfied smile of the harvest was spread across Chetford County in October 1914.

But Quinn could see no good in it. "The flies is hangin' tre-rible," he said, as Faith expertly flicked a greenbottle from Trooper's glistening black rump with the tasseled end of her whip. "That old one kept pace with us all the way from our own gatehouse."

1

"Don't worry, Quinn. I won't keep the horse standing any longer than it takes to leave the cards. Mother said it won't be necessary to go in. Dr. Walding won't feel like seeing anybody so soon after his wife's funeral."

Quinn drew back his lips in an unsmiling grin and blew out his breath through the crack in his teeth. "All the best people is dyin' it seems." Ever since Faith's father had died four years ago, Quinn was given to moods of longing for the past. "I miss the Judge, I do. Them days is gone forever. The gentlemen takes the railroad now, gettin' back and forth to town. With the Judge, 'twas always the coach and four."

Faith gave another twist to the reins. She was nervous about having to call on Dr. Walding alone. She had been sent because the relationship between Mama and the dead Mrs. Walding had been so painfully strained. The Judge used to say he couldn't understand why two such wonderful women couldn't get along, particularly since the Doctor was an old friend of his. But it wasn't just coming alone that made her nervous. Mama had given her so many instructions about the proper way to pay a call that she was sure she was going to get the dos and don'ts all mixed up and disappoint her mother again.

As the road dipped down to go under the railroad trestle, Faith let Trooper have his head. It was horrible to be caught in the dark tunnel when a freight rumbled by overhead, on its way from the mining country into the city. The horse stretched out willingly, his hoofbeats echoing against the dank stone walls.

Out in the sunlight again, on the right stood the Penngwynne Station, an Elizabethan cottage covered with sooty rambler roses. Next to it was Winkler's General Store, which also contained the post office. A few carriages were already waiting for the afternoon train to discharge its quota of businessmen from the city. Faith's brother Bellwood would be arriving on the train too, bringing his fiancée, an actress, home to meet Mama for the first time. Mama had never received an actress before—no one had—and Faith was supposed to complete her call at the Waldings and be back at the station in time to pick them up and drive them to Co-Eden so that Mama would not be left without help at tea. Another reason to be nervous!

"People are already waiting for the train! Look, Quinny!"

"They're all early," Quinn said. "With this fast horse, we'll be back in time to see the locomotive come round the bend."

2

"There's the Finchwicke trap!" That meant that Chugh Walding would be arriving. Nothing would be more embarrassing than to be caught seeming to pay a call on *him*. He was a bachelor. And futhermore her brothers had laughed at him since their football days at Chetford Hill Academy. They had called him Carrie behind his back. That had been his nurse's name, who had washed his football pants after each game until they were gleaming white. But the Hoagland boys and all the other boys had worn their uniforms right through to the end of the season—the dirt and grass stains a badge of honorable service.

Mama had said, "You will leave two cards of mine, one for Dr. Walding and one for Chugh. But you will leave only one card of your own, because you will be calling only on the old gentleman. Chugh is a bachelor, and young ladies never call on bachelors. Besides, he has a reputation for—well—for being experienced!" Faith knew that meant more than just being a dandy; but even though she found the idea intriguing she had not dared ask further questions as Mama had relentlessy continued with her instructions. "Turn down the right-hand corner of each card to show that it has been delivered in person and not mailed or handed in by the coachman. And turn down the left-hand corners of my cards, but not yours, to signify that the call is on all the members of the family. But on no account go in."

As they left the station behind and drove through farmland again, Faith handed the reins to Quinn. Her mother had told her not to act like a tomboy for once, and to let Quinn drive her like a lady. But she had disobeyed in this one small thing because not driving made her feel suffocated. "I have to do something, or go crazy. So don't tell her," she had begged of Quinn at the outset.

Now she pulled off the loose chamois driving gloves and reached into her beaded reticule for her tight-buttoned glacé kid gloves and the brocade card case. More of her mother's words echoed in her ears. "You can't expect to spend your life just fox hunting and going to church. You must make an effort, and I have tried to teach you what to do. You must call on every hostess who invites you to her house whether or not you accept, or she will be mortally insulted and think that you do not wish to be invited again. You must be the first to drop a card on new neighbors. You must pay regular calls on your friends. How else will you keep in touch? How else will you keep from being on the shelf? This visit to Finch-wicke will be good practice."

Quinn kept a tight hold on Trooper as they came to the in-tersection of Stone Mill and Station Road, and they turned right. Here, on either side, lay the fat lands of Finchwicke. A team of handsome Belgians plowing on the rise came into view and then disappeared. A shower of yellow butterflies joined the carriage as Quinn turned Trooper in between the narrow stone posts and their white picket gates that marked the Finchwicke drive. Quinn cheered up with the precision of his maneuver. "I could thread a needle with this old horse," he hissed, as Trooper settled down to his best slow prance up the driveway.

Faith had a sensation of having entered a territory foreign to time, a magical world where nothing ever changed, where this moment of autumn would shimmer and glow forever. There had been a death in the family, but peaceful Finch-wicke had simply folded it in without leaving a trace. Chugh Walding's Appaloosa hunter ran up to the fence to greet them as they made their way up the long drive. A foal at the side of a chestnut mare kicked up its tiny pointed feet and then, with neighs and squeals of joy, galloped away. In the middle of the pasture an enormous beech grove burned, the color of new copper.

Another pair of gateposts, topped with urns of ivy, an-nounced the driveway turnaround in front of the eighteenth-century house and it famous gardens. Columns of white wood cut into the mansion's façade of weathered, square-cut stones. The front door stood between two long windows with iron balconies, and two low wings in perfect proportion extended out from either side of the central house. Huge sycamores shaded the wings, and clumps of boxwood flanked the circu-lar front steps. A wisteria vine was trellised up at one corner to the second floor of the house.

Quinn held the horse's head as Faith unbuckled her driving apron and stepped down, her heart beating hard against whalebone stays. Clutching her bag in one hand and lifting her long skirt with the other, she climbed up toward the white double front doors. With only one sharp rap of the brass lion's head knocker the door opened, and a maid, in ruffled apron and cap, appeared. Faith inquired if Dr. Wald-ing was at home. To her dismay, instead of saying that he was not, the maid said that she would go and see, if the lady would step inside. "And who should I say?"

4

"Miss Faith Hoagland from Co-Eden."

The maid held out a small piecrust-edged silver tray. Faith extracted from her card case one of her own plain white cards and two of her mother's large cream-colored ones, the black edges of which were now very narrow, reduced to the point of permanent mourning for her husband. Immediately the maid withdrew the tray and flounced away, leaving Faith standing in the great hall of Finchwicke, the first time alone.

There was absolute silence in the house. Faith's fingers tapped lightly on the hall table, whose high polish reflected the flowered Lowestoft bowl, filled to the brim with the cards of those who had already called to express their sorrow at the passing of the mistress of the house. Two tall glass hurricane lamps with their wicks trimmed and ready to be lit stood at either end of the long table, and between them hung a tall mirror, topped with gilt sprays of flowers and wheat. At the end of the hall, a Dutch door stood open, leading the eye from the terraces out to the distant countryside. Above this door the flying staircase rose to an arched Palladian window. Huge pots of bronze and yellow chrysanthemums stood on the brick floor, banking the carved arched doorways which led to the other halls on either side. It was through one of these that the maid now reappeared.

To Faith's intense relief she said, "I'm sorry, mum. I can't find the master. He's gone and stepped out in the garden somewhere." Without further ceremony the maid dumped the cards from the tray into the overflowing bowl without giving Faith a chance to turn down the corners as instructed.

Maybe I should have done it before I went inside, but it's too late to fish them out now, especially since the maid is being so rude. But at least we didn't mail them, Faith thought as she ran out the door and down the steps to where Trooper was stamping with impatience, swishing his tail against the flies. She hopped in and took the reins. Quinn refastened the checkrein, and they were just about ready to leave when a man came through the gate of the walled garden on the right and started rambling across the lawn toward them.

Thee was no mistaking that this was Dr. Walding himself, his head bent sideways on his neck as though he were permanently inquiring into the nature of things. (In reality, he was suffering from a creeping arthritic condition.) He wore a frayed shooting jacket and heather-colored tweed knickers with green stockings up to his knees and soft leather tramping boots. He held up his hand in a gesture of greeting.

Removing his tweed cap, bowing, and beaming through his steel-rimmed spectacles as he approached, he said, "It's Miss Hoagland! A charming young lady who has had the unusual good sense to come without her difficult mother! You've come to pay a call, supposedly with the intention of giving sympathy to a neighbor, but secretly hoping to get away without being caught."

Faith, quite confused by such honest speaking, blushed and laughed. "Not at all, Dr. Walding. I was most disappointed not to find you in. I come not only for myself, but also for Mama, who finds herself with a sick headache. But she wishes me to say that she will come in person very soon."

This was a lie, and they both knew it.

"Ah, then do let me press you to come in. I'm lonely, and it's time for tea, and I've had no company at all today. That is, of course, if you can spare the time to chat with an old man for a few moments. And Chugh will be along soon."

"But I'm afraid I must go to meet Bellwood at the afternoon train," she said, turning scarlet with embarrassment. "He's coming out from town just to have dinner with Mama and pass the night."

"As you wish, of course. But come to think of it, you could send your carriage to the train, and allow me to take you home. Do come in, Miss Hoagland. Your father was a great friend, you know. No Hoagland has been to Finchwicke since he died. Do come in, I beg you."

The mention of her father, coupled with her own resentment at having been forbidden to be friendly, made her suddenly decide to defy her mother and accept. After all, I did have another parent, she thought.

Last week, on her way to Mrs. Walding's funeral she had gathered the last of the yellow roses from the garden at Co-Eden and placed them on the Judge's grave, on top of the hill right next to the church. The Judge had bought part of the old Jaspar farm and given it to the church to enlarge the cemetery. He had wanted to be buried with a good view of the surrounding farms, where the Redcoats had once battled the Revolutionary Army on their way to winter quarters at Valley Forge. It was not only that he wanted the plot with the best view, the Judge had said; also he didn't want anyone else's bones dripping down on him.

Faith had tried to evoke her father's presence by speaking to him softly as she bent to lay flowers at his feet. "Papa, this is Twinkle," she said, using his private pet name for her.

6

RICHARD HALLOWELL HOAGLAND
1850–1910
Mark the perfect man,
and behold the upright:
For the end of that man is peace

But it had been impossible to imagine him there, lying under the polished red granite stone.

Now, however, it was as if he were pushing her from the basket phaeton, urging her to accept Dr. Walding's invitation.

"You are irresistible, Dr. Walding," she said finally.

And so Quinn and Trooper were dispatched back to the station without her. Dr. Walding enveloped his young guest with a gesture of his arm, sweeping her back into the house, through the hall archway and into a small, high, book-lined room with one long window looking out on the drive. He yanked hard on the needlepoint bellpull.

"The butler's probably asleep," he said.

"It's a charming room." Faith looked around at the rich colors of the gleaming leather books against the gray-gold of the fruitwood paneling. In the twin arched niches over the bookcases were two busts, one of George Washington in green marble and one of Benjamin Franklin in white. Over the mantelpiece hung a portrait of a young gentleman in a yellow silk coat with ruffles at his wrist and a white neckcloth, his brown hair puffed at the temples and tied back with a black ribbon. He had large, brown, popping eyes and his lower lip stuck out in a speculative pout.

"The portrait," she said. "I feel as if he were following me with those extraordinary eyes."

"As indeed he is. It's been a long time since he's had a pretty girl to look at, and he wonders why you've never been here before. He's very rudely taking pleasure in positively staring at you. He's Percy Walding, the builder of Finchwicke. As you can see, he has draped back the red curtain by the window and he is showing you an aerial view of Finchwicke as it was then. Of course it's an imaginative bird's-eye view. Very bare. All the newly planted trees in neat rows, and the box gardens laid out in geometrical designs."

"It's not at all the way it looks today, is it? It has grown up so the house is nearly hidden by the trees."

"Exactly. The straight lines are all blurred. The only big tree you can see there in the portrait is the Guardian oak. It still stands out there on the terrace. And it may be the oldest

7

tree in this part of the world to have had a picture painted of it. And now that book he's holding. That's something rather interesting, you know. It bears the inscription 'Before him lie the fruits in their season, and the lovely gardens: around him float the messengers of love.' " Dr. Walding let his lower lip protrude as though he were copying the man in the portrait. "The messengers of love, you know. I would tell my wife, Thessaly, they were wasps. It used to make her furious. 'Butterflies are the messengers of love,' she would say, 'not horrid stinging bugs.' " Dr. Walding gave Faith a beaming fatherly smile.

"I agree with Mrs. Walding. How could wasps be the messengers of love?" (He was a "talker," she realized, who would keep going with very little encouragement.)

"Well, if you studied them the way I have, you'd know how like humans they are. I must give you a copy of my book, *The Life Cycle of the Great Cerceris*, which has been published by the Academy of Natural Sciences."

"How wonderful!"

"Well, it's really not wonderful at all because I'm president of the Academy, and they had to publish it. Couldn't get out of it. But then I've spent hours studying wasps. I have some particular friends at the back edge of the vegetable garden in a pile of rotten logs—which is where I've spent the afternoon."

"Oh my! Don't you ever get stung?"

"Never. But at this time of year one has to be particularly careful because the wasps get quite drunk—if you'll pardon the term—on the fallen apples. One has to sit very still and make no sign to disturb them. And I've gotten to know these particular wasps rather well because they've been living for years in this same pile of logs, which I've given orders shall not be moved, unsightly as it is. It happens to constitute their ancestral home, which they will never desert. Wasps are very loyal."

He was interrupted by the appearance of the butler in the doorway, an old man with a white unhealthy face and a paunch sticking out through his rumpled coat, looking indeed as if he had just woken up.

"Tea, Bunce. And bring some cakes, or whatever we have. And send word to Sweeting that when he comes back from meeting Mr. Chugh at the station, he is to wait and take Miss Hoagland back to Co-Eden."

The butler gave a wheeze of assent, and left the room.

8

Faith and the Doctor smiled at each other. She picked up the threads of the conversation for him. "Wasps are like humans, the way you describe them."

"Ah yes. Exactly. Ah how I used to make Thessaly furious by telling her that she reminded me of a Great Cerceris! A Cerceris will tap her foot when she is annoyed! Just as Thessaly would." He illustrated with a gesture of his large boot. And Faith laughed. "Ah! How Thessaly hated to wait in line for anything. How unladylike she could become, pushing to the front! And she was very intolerant of other insects who blew into her special zone. Each zone, my dear, as you know, has its own assemblage of insects—those who got there first. But should new ones arrive by wind or tide, they multiply very rapidly and become pests, seeming to upset the balance of nature. For instance, like Catholics and Jews! Darkies and Democrats! Ah, how Thessaly hated Democrats. Most of all, I think."

"My mother is a Democrat, of course. As you say, she blew in from the South, another zone."

Dr. Walding twinkled. "You get the point exactly. The Cerceris of course are very cosmopolitan. Found everywhere. And they understand only each other perfectly."

"Unlike Democrats and Republicans!"

"Quite, dear Miss Hoagland! But I shouldn't be surprised to find a resemblance in you to Cerceris! What a huntress she is! Her victim dies without any struggle, completely paralyzed by the sting to the one vulnerable point on the abdomen, the nerve ganglia to the wings and legs. There lies her prey, the great sacred beetle, twice her size, completely pickled by her poison so that he doesn't stink after she drags him all the way home and salts him away for the future. A delicious menu indeed, all waiting for the young family which will emerge in the spring from the apartments she has dug for them. Ah yes, Thessaly used to feed us very well."

The Doctor's voice broke, and he pulled a large red silk handkerchief out of his pocket and wiped the mist from his spectacles. Faith thought that if he broke down she would put her arm around his shoulder, the way she would have done had he been her own father. But he recovered, and continued, "Ah yes. After she has dug her burrow, the beautiful female sits in her portico, polishing her antennae, while clouds of males circle about, waiting for her to choose the one to light upon her back. Watching their courtship is very entertaining. The hum and thrum of an autumn afternoon is rather pleasant. I hated to pack up and come in, but the sun was no longer warm. But sweet are the uses of adversity, for I was just in time to catch the lovely Miss Hoagland about to escape away!"

"Oh no indeed! I wasn't escaping! It was just—just—"

"I know, Miss Hoagland. I forced you to come in, because the truth is I was unable to bear the thought of coming back into the empty house alone. This is the first day that Chugh has gone to town. It was high time to go into the office to attend to his affairs. As for myself, I thought it was a bit too soon after Thessaly's death for me to face the members of the Philadelphia Club at lunch as is my habit. It's damned quiet here without Thessaly! She was always stirring things up, you know. And I had somebody to talk to!"

Faith was afraid he was going to weep again. But he busied himself with his watch chain, hung with a Phi Beta Kappa key, a Masonic emblem, and a penknife which he opened to clean his thumbnail. Then from the pocket of his needlepoint vest came a large gold onion. He unsnapped the cover.

"If Chugh has caught the four o'clock, he should be home in a few minutes now. But, by Jupiter, I have been thoughtless! Here I have kept you standing all this time in front of the portrait. Do take off your wrap. Do sit down while we wait for tea. Would you be comfortable here?" He beamed at her through his Ben Franklin spectacles, head on one side, pointing to a stiff, high-backed chair covered in a frayed red Chinese brocade. He attempted to help her off with her coat, but she said, sitting down, "Thank you, I'll just keep it on. Mama says, 'Never remove your cloak and gloves when paying a call.'" They both smiled. "But what a nice room. All the books. One can almost feel the people who have set here through the years."

"Ah yes. You are referring to Finchwicke's ghosts, so you are a very perceptive young lady. All friendly ghosts, you know. But the atmosphere here is very congenial to spirits. For instance, this library has always been the province of the man of the house, and the matching room on the left of the front door as you came in has always been the private parlor of all the Mrs. Waldings who have lived here. There have been four of them. And then, of course, Miss Walding, my Aunt Sarah, who lived here until she was ninety-one. She collected china dogs, and Thessaly used to say if she moved so much as one spaniel the ghost of Aunt Sara would put it back by morning."

They were both laughing as the butler appeared carrying the Chinese bamboo tea table followed by the sullen maid carrying the heavy tray, her bosom straining at the tight seams of her uniform, dark stains beginning to show under her arms.

The butler unfolded the legs of the table with a loud snap and started to set it up in front of the Doctor's armchair by the fireplace, but he was waved off toward the guest.

"Do be so kind as to pour my tea, Miss Hoagland. I still haven't got used to doing it. If I'm here alone, Delia does it for me." He beamed the same tender smile at the stony-faced maid as she maneuvered onto the table in front of Faith the heavy mahogany tray with its pierced silver gallery.

The Doctor continued. "Now that we're having tea, won't you change your mind and take off your coat?"

But she refused, and inquiring how he liked his tea, poured it with her gloves on.

She felt very foolish, but Mama was going to be furious, and so while she was here against orders, her behavior would be exemplary. She did push up her veil so that it caught on the tip of her nose, permitting her to sip her own cup of tea, but her gloves forced her to refuse all the delicious food which Bunce now brought in on a tiered mahogany cake stand. Buttery muffins on the top, tiny cakes covered with raspberry icing in the middle, on the bottom thin curly molasses cookies. The Doctor helped himself liberally, and drank his tea in big gulps. "The best meal of the day. *De gustibus non est disputandum!* You don't know what you're missing, young lady."

"I really only care for the tea, thank you. And such a pretty pot. It must be an old family one."

It was a squat white china pot, deeply fluted and painted with a wreath of violets. She held it up.

"It was Thessaly's pot. Something she had treasured as a girl. But everything else in this room is pure Walding. Thessaly had developed a passion for the history of Finchwicke. It was her idea to catalogue everything here that was authentic. The house was a terrible jumble when she came, but she found all manner of treasures in the attic, and put them back in their proper places. She even found the original plans for the house and gardens in an old trunk. They are now in the archives of the Historical Society for safekeeping, together with the geneaology of the Walding family. That man you see there over the mantel, Percy Walding, even though he was the builder of Finchwicke, was *not* the original Walding in the American Colonies. That was his father, Sir Charles. He came over from Wales in 1684 in his own ship, the *Blue Quail*, with the land grant to most of Penngwynne in his pocket."

Faith was surprised to hear he was a "Sir." Mama was always saying how ordinary the settlers in this part had been, giving themselves airs as first families. But Mama prided herself on being descended from both the Lords Proprietors of Charleston and from French Huguenot aristocracy.

"Sir Charles knew Billy Penn, who personally converted him in England to the quiet religion. So, of course, being a Friend, he had to drop his title when he arrived in the Colonies. But his son Percy was enough of a snob to decorate his silverware with the coat of arms. He had the right to fifteen quarterings, and you can see his tankard there." The Doctor pointed to the shelves of the tall mahogany secretary which held a collection of china and silver behind its reeded glass doors.

The whistle of the train sounded as it rounded the bend half a mile away into Penngwynne Station. Mama was going to be livid.

"I hope I'm not boring you?"

"Oh no, indeed."

"Just a little more tea, to finish up the sugar and cream, you know." Dr. Walding was holding out his cup. "But Finchwicke is one of the very few places that has remained in the same family up to the present day. It's not simple to keep a house in one family, although you may think so."

"Oh I know. Mama is very bitter about The Mount. That's her grandmother's plantation in South Carolina. It was burned to the ground, you know, by Sherman's men."

"Ah yes, but in that case the house was destroyed. I meant that the house and the people have to have very special qualities to stay together through the generations. The house must take hold of the people, become the most important thing in their lives. It must overcome a natural wanderlust. Thessaly was very conscious of that and left some provisions about it in her will. Then, there have to be adequate finances over the years. An old house is forever demanding. But most important, the family has to pass the house on. And to do that

12

they must have children—sons, of course—to carry on the name."

"Yes. I have three brothers! Marshall, Bellwood, and Richard."

The old man ignored this, bent on his own line of thought. "Chugh is not married. But even that can be overcome, if there is a will. There was one generation of Waldings that produced nine females only."

In the driveway, visible beyond the red curtain with its ball fringe pulled back to one side, exactly as in the portrait of Percy Walding, a station trap was pulling into the circle and Chugh Walding was getting out. He looked very elegant in his pearl-gray suit, a black morning band on the left arm, his pearl-gray bowler hat, his short gold beard.

"One good thing about this room," Dr. Walding observed, "one can see everything that is happening in the drive." Then he cleared his throat and went back to his subject with renewed speed, as if trying to finish before his son should fatally interrupt him.

"As I was saying, there was one generation, not so far back, which produced only females. So that when the eldest of them married she had to persuade her husband to take the name of Walding, in order that the name would not die out. But having gone to all the trouble of changing their name, they only produced one daughter, Aunt Sarah. And when she died, she left the place to my father, who was her second cousin. A male Walding, a *rara avis*."

Chugh was standing in the carved arch of the doorway. "I see we have company. I hope you're not boring her with the family history, Father." He stepped forward to shake hands. "How very kind of you to come." He smiled at Faith, and she thought, His eyes are dark blue like his sapphire stickpin. That's why he wears it. He's vain. I like that.

However, now that Chugh was here, Faith realized that she must leave immediately. Setting down her half-filled teacup she rose, smiling up at him. "I really must be going, I shouldn't be here at all. Your father was kind enough to say he would send me back to Co-Eden in your trap as soon as you arrived."

"I'm sure he didn't say you had to go as soon as I arrived, Miss Faith. If you have an extra, do let me have a cup of tea."

"I persuaded her to come in, very much against her will. After all, her father and I were very closely associated for

13

many years on the board of the hospital and the university, the Farmer's Club and the Fish House. So, dear Miss Hoagland, do stay one moment more."

She smiled. She wavered. She twinkled. She sat down again. "My mother told me not even to come in!" at which they all laughed.

After receiving his tea, Chugh hypnotized her into taking one of the buttery muffins, which she now ate, making little dark grease stains on her gloves. But much as she longed for one, she again refused the cakes with the raspberry icing, thinking that she would not be able to lick her fingers.

"Had a good day in town?" Dr. Walding asked his son meaningfully, as though looking for a coded answer, something that would not betray the day's business in front of their visitor.

"Fine," Chugh answered coolly, not offering any hint. "And, Miss Faith, what have you been up to on this gorgeous day?"

"I've been playing tennis up at the club with Mariette Pardue. She beat me, but only because she was wearing bloomers and I was wearing a long skirt."

"Bloomers are horrible things," Chugh said, "most unbecoming. Better to be beaten than to wear them."

"But they look so comfortable. All the girls at Bryn Mawr wear them now for hockey."

"Do you attend Bryn Mawr College?" Dr. Walding asked with interest. "Thessaly was a trustee . . ."

"Oh, no, Mama wouldn't hear of it. She said all her friends would think it funny if I wanted to leave her before I was married. And that bluestockings and bookworms never get husbands. And that a man doesn't want a wife who knows more than he does." And then she stopped in embarrassment, feeling that she had revealed too much. But she couldn't stop herself from adding, "I have a pair of bloomers, but Mama doesn't know it."

Both gentlemen seemed delighted by these disclosures, and made another attempt to prevent her from leaving. But this time when she rose she was in a small panic to get out and would not be deterred. So the bell was rung for Sweeting.

"Thank you again for coming," Dr. Walding said, rising from his chair and bowing to her as best he could. "We're very dreary here, just the two of us. Many come to the door, but few come in. Do drive by again. Finchwicke loves people. Chugh will see you out."

On a sudden impulse she offered him her cheek, instead of her gloved hand, which he brushed deliciously with his mustache.

"I did so much enjoy our conversation. Good-bye!"

"Good-bye. And come again."

Walking down the steps, Chugh took her arm. Faith realized that this was the first time she had ever been alone with him, ever touched him. He never danced with her at parties, never visited at Co-Eden. He did greet her politely when they met in the hunting field, although they never really talked about anything. But he was talking to her now, looking down at her as if seeing her for the first time. His hand was tucked under her elbow pressed close to her side, causing an electric current to run up her legs and root itself somewhere in her whaleboned center.

"It was really very thoughtful of you to call on Father. He's quite shy with all but a few people, and with them, he opens up and talks them to death. Please forgive me for saying this, but when I came in and saw you sitting there on the edge of my mother's chair, holding her teapot just the way she used to do, for a moment I thought I was seeing a ghost. You were smiling at Father happily. You were enjoying each other's company. The light was behind you so I couldn't see your face at first, but you look extraordinarily like the pictures of Mother as a young girl. I hope you don't mind my saying that, but the whole sensation was so unexpected. Of course I knew it was you. Sweeting had told me you would be there. Then, of course, you have on that charming hat with the wings decorating it. And you were pouring tea with your cloak and gloves on. My mother never did that!"

He was still squeezing her elbow as she stood there deliciously confused. Was he only being polite? Was he teasing her? She hoped he would not let her go too quickly. And now she felt that she must make a serious explanation of her unorthodox visit. It was embarrassing.

"Your father is charming. He reminds me a lot of mine. That is the reason I came. I know what it is like to lose someone you love. But on the other hand, I don't really feel my father's gone very far away. He comes back to help me when I need him."

Then they both looked down and stood a moment, scarfed together in sad intimacy. But since Sweeting was standing there swishing flies away from the back of the stamping horse, the moment did not last.

"What a handsome horse."

"Yes. Her name is Emmeline. Emmeline Pankhurst. Mother was a suffragette, you know, and naming the gray mare that was Father's idea of a joke!" They both laughed. Then Faith said, "Well, I must be off." Chugh handed her up into the seat of the trap. "The flies hang on so at this time of year. Will you be hunting in the morning?" she asked.

"Indeed so. The meet is at our back gate. Will you be out?"

"I plan to." And they smiled at each other. Faith lifted one small greasy glove to wave as Sweeting flicked the air ever so lightly with the tassel of his whip, and then the trap moved off around the circle.

Perched on the seat beside Sweeting, Faith was whirled off in a dream down the long driveway into the autumn twilight. There was a lavender haze over the fields. The sudden cool made the horse swing along, rhythm rippling down his back in tune with the beat of his hooves, the slight jingle of his harness, the crunch of the high thin wheels on the dirt road. Inside her long tight corsets, Faith still tingled from a slight touch on the arm by Chugh Walding. It was as if an orchestra had just burst into the first waltz of the evening and a handsome stranger was walking toward her across the ballroom to ask her to dance—to dance away from her mother—to dance in new patterns. Chugh Walding. Chugh Walding, Chugh Walding, beat the horses' hooves in the lengthening shadows.

The station trap from Finchwicke entered the Co-Eden gates and wound up the hairpin turns of the steep drive, twisting through thick groves of Douglas fir, white birch, oak, honey locust and tulip poplar. A low stone wall of square-cut granite topped by a pointed edge of chipped stones like dragon's teeth bordered the road as it rose into a curved bridge across a brook. The drive cut through a wooden glen, passed a miniature Japanese teahouse, and then, a few yards further on, the service drive branched off. The main drive went straight up the hill to the house itself.

In the midst of a countryside of eighteenth-century stone farms and strictly balanced manor houses, Co-Eden was a folly. A shingled gothic summerhouse. It was kept warm all winter by three large furnaces which had been installed in the cavernous cellars. Stoked with anthracite from the family mines, they sent hot steam through banging pipes to hissing, stand-up radiators in front of the odd-shaped windows. The elaborate roof rambled into gables with rafters carved into dragons or ocean waves hiding bedroom balconies between their many levels. It rose into towers encrusted in bands of square, diamond-shaped and round shingles in a complex design and capped with Oriental-style minarets. The gothic porte-cochere arched over a portion of the pear-shaped turn-around into which the Finchwicke trap now pulled. Emmeline Pankhurst flattened her ears at the sight of Rick's Pierce Arrow standing there. Rick home from Princeton. Perhaps Mama had not been left alone with Bellwood and his actress-fiancée, after all.

Faith thanked Sweeting for driving her home, tipped him out of the depths of her beaded bag, and with increasing trepidation went up the granite steps to the front door. Not only would Mama be angry with her for having disobeyed, but because she was not well enough to go out very much herself, she would demand a full description of the events. She had a way of absorbing the doings of others and then recounting them with a special witty twist of her own at the next gathering, usually the boys or the boys' friends who always ended up being her swains, instead of Faith's. Faith dreaded having to tell about this experience. She wanted to keep it private, to have a chance to relive it until it had become indestructibly her own to save it from being just a new part of Mama's repertoire to be served up like Virginia ham and beaten biscuits.

Faith pushed open the heavy front door with its porthole of vaseline and milk glass. The oak-paneled vestibule smelled of the large open cloakroom on the right, a mixture of old raincoats and carnation soap. An assortment of fancy canes and umbrellas stood in an antique leather firebucket of Volunteer Company One of the Hand-in-Hand. And beneath the light of the green Tiffany chandelier was Bellwood's derby, hanging on the sword hilt of the suit of armor, where he always left it.

Three broad steps led up into the great hall, the largest room in the house. It was paneled in golden oak and rose two stories high to a beamed ceiling painted with a copy of a garden scene by Alma-Tadema. A broad staircase led to the landing, lit by arched, lead-mullioned windows of stained glass, and then beyond to a heavily balustered gallery onto which opened some of the bedroom apartments.

Downstairs from the hall, which was itself a sitting room with a big sofa placed in front of the granite hearth, a door opened to the smoking room, which in turn led into the gun room. Across the hall was the dining room which was connected to the basement kitchen by a complicated series of pantries and passages and back stairs. One of the towers rooted itself in a corner of the great hall, forming a small round conservatory jutting into a porch which was always filled with greenhouse flowers. And from this hall opened the French doors to the drawing room, whence came her mother's voice, like bells, attended by male laughter: Mrs. Hoagland was talking to her sons.

Faith entered. An Aubusson carpet of pink flowers led the way back past stiff groups of statues and palms, small chairs, sofas, and tiny tables supporting collections of semiprecious treasures to the focal point of the room, the woman who sat at the far end in front of the drawn curtains of the bay window, in the light of a rose quartz lamp with a fringe shade. Her red hair, in an elaborate pouffed coiffure, flamed against the French gray walls and curtains. She sat in a tapestry-covered gold armchair, her tiny pointed slippers crossed in front of her and displayed on a cushioned footstool. She was wearing, as always, a black taffeta dress with a high white lace collar that rose stiffly into the tendrils of red curls at the nape of her neck.

She was crooning to the circle around her, "How too, too delicious, my dear! How I would have loved to have gone myself to call on *two* gentlemen. But I'm simply not able to get about much anymore."

Diamonds and rubies circled with more diamonds flashed on her plump white hands as she plied her needle in and out of a piece of silk held stiff in a wooden embroidery ring.

Bellwood's fiancée, wearing a tight, dark town suit and a high feathered toque, was perched on the edge of a straight chair, her back to the door, holding a teacup tentatively, as if she had been wondering for quite a while where to put it down. Bellwood was coiled in the wing chair, his head hidden. And Rick sat a little behind his mother on a low bench, his red curls and reddish face radiating good nature as he fiddled with his pipe, knocking it gently against his tweed-knickered knee. He was the first to see Faith.

"Here she is! Here's the straying damsel herself. Hey, Sis!"

Her mother looked up, letting her sewing drop into her lap. "Where in the world have you been? We've been worrying!" The voice retained a lilt of amused exasperation, but her eyes, like pale aquamarines, fixed sharply on her daughter as she advanced into the room.

Bellwood's fiancée cocked her head like a small bird. She is more frightened than I am, Faith thought.

Bellwood unwound his length and turned to watch his younger sister. His long nose reflexively twitched from side to side as though scenting amusing sport at her expense. He got to his feet and stood erect, the toes of his boots pointed out, one hand behind his back. He bowed low, displaying the thinning hair carefully combed over the ridge of his skull.

"Ah, dear Sis. Becca'd been wondering if you had been devoured by dragons!" Bellwood had always called his mother by her first name, as though he were more lover than son. His voice was unexpectedly high for so large a man, his accent slightly British, having spent two years studying at Oxford making up his mind whether to be an actor or a bishop.

"Vivi, this is my sister Faith. Faith, this is Vivienne Curle."

The young woman rose and extended her hand, cool as water. "I've heard a lot about you," she said, implying great intimacy with Bellwood. "All good."

"And I've seen you on the stage. I did enjoy *Lady Windermere's Fan*. And I think it's nice that you're engaged to Bellwood. You'll have so much in common."

"Actually, Sis, Vivi is already my wife. We've kept it a secret. Better for Vivi's career, you know. But now, the circumstances are such that we think it best to announce it."

Faith was stunned. What would people think? A forced marriage was a stigma that would follow Vivi all her life. No one in Penngwynne would really be friendly to her. Faith looked at her mother to see how she was taking it. But Mama had evidently already been told, and being a bit of an actress herself, was giving no hint of the shame and displeasure which Faith knew must have been boiling within. Mama was playing her part admirably for Bellwood's sake. Anything for Bellwood.

"It's too, too delicious," Mama trilled. "I once had hopes of being a concert pianist myself, you know. I used to sit in the moonlight, draped in a white silk shawl embroidered in peacocks and palm trees, and dream of playing to vast European audiences."

Vivi's black eyes were bright with apprehension as she waited for Faith to say something.

"I think Bellwood's very, very lucky," Faith said finally.

What could be better than a sister-in-law like a frightened bird? She was sure they could be friends. "I've always wanted a sister. Why, it's thrilling, Bellwood." She gave her brother a kiss, reaching up to his pock-marked cheek.

No one had thought that Bellwood would ever marry, because of the shock it would be to Mama. But now, here Mama was, accepting it calmly—other than taking it out on Faith.

"What in the world took you so long," her mother repeated with annoyance, as if she had not been heard the first time.

"Mama! You told me I shouldn't go in, but Dr. Walding caught me in the act of leaving and insisted on my having some tea. After all, he was a dear friend of Papa's."

Mrs. Hoagland raised her delicate red eyebrows in disapproval. "Well, what can't be helped can't be helped. Did he inquire about me? He must have thought it very odd that I didn't come with you."

"I explained you had a headache."

"Did he seem very sad?"

She's beginning, Faith thought uncomfortably, to rub my thoughts and feelings over the washboard, holding them up to the light to see if they are clean. She parried, "Very sad? No, I wouldn't really say so. I mean, not sad on top, just down underneath."

"Well, who could blame him for *not* being sad." (Faith realized she had said the wrong thing.) "Such a dreadfully rude, common woman."

"I mean Mrs. Walding just simply wasn't talked about. And they're not common, Mama. The first Walding to come to this country was a noble."

"So that's what he talked about! That's what I've been trying to find out! Noble ancestry! I hope you told him about ours?"

Papa, had he lived, would never have allowed the war of the ladies to develop. During his lifetime the ladies had confined themselves to very polite dislike. And now that Mrs. Walding was dead, why couldn't Mama drop it?

"When and where *was* the wedding?" Faith switched subjects, turning back to Bellwood.

"Vivi had no church and no family, and so one day, a few months ago, we just got married quietly, before a judge." He spoke the lines as though he had memorized them for a play.

Mama had evidently already heard this piece too. "All I ask is that you let me know exactly when it was, so that it can be properly announced in the paper. Otherwise my friends will think it's most peculiar. They'll think I didn't know anything about it, if you understand what I mean. These things must be done properly."

"Becca! Of course. We'll write it out any way you want it." Bellwood bowed and kissed her fingertips.

"I do wish it could have been in the church out here. I'm sure Mr. Fitzjoy at St. Jude's-under-Buttonwood would have liked to have done it. He's new here and such a nice young man," Faith said, blushing earnestly. "I mean he's been such a help to you, hasn't he, Mama?" He was the only male who ever came to call on Mama who seemed to prefer talking to Faith. But then of course he was engaged to be married, so it meant nothing.

"A nice enough young man. But he'll never make bishop as Bellwood might have done."

"Not I, Becca. I'm too irreverent. A believer, of course, but irreverent."

"It's kind of you to suggest a church wedding," Vivi said, turning toward Faith. The room grew very still to catch what she was saying in her quiet, studied voice, every word enunciated. "But you see I'm not a believer. Even though I was brought up in a convent, I don't believe there is a God. So it was better the other way."

Such words had never been said out loud in the Hoagland house. Faith was shocked. The Judge had been a strong church man and any mention of the subject of atheism would have met with grave disapproval. Mama had become a backslider recently, but Faith made up for it by being very active in the Altar Guild, and by visiting the two poor old ladies she had adopted in Chetford Hill with baskets of chickens and vegetables from the garden. Faith was shocked, but it was more important to gain a new friend than to show it.

A lapsed Catholic! Faith would save her soul. She would somehow persuade Vivi to come to services at St. Jude's-under-Buttonwood right after the wedding was announced. Vivi wouldn't be able to resist Mr. Fitzjoy in the pulpit, and the neighbors simply couldn't snub a churchgoer, even if they did disapprove.

"I can see you're thinking of taking her to church!" How could Mama read her mind like that! "Well! Being an actress she's not required to be religious, or play hockey, or indulge in blood sports, or any of those things you do, Faith. For my part, she's only required to be entertaining. I can't stand a bore!"

"I'll guarantee she won't be a bit like old Thessaly What's-her-name," Bellwood added.

Mama beamed at him. "As soon as the news is out, I'll give a tea to introduce Vivi around. Just a few close friends."

"Yes, but better make it soon. Vivi tells me we're planning a large family."

There was a small silence after this indelicate remark.

Faith thought it might be very bad luck to tempt fate in this way. Some people never were blessed with children. Like her oldest brother Marshall's poor wife, Hebe, who had lost a baby boy and then had to have some dreadful operation. She stole a glimpse at Vivi's waistline. She was such a tiny creature, but—but could she be? Nanny Jaspar was having, and you couldn't see a thing yet either.

"I'll bet Carrie was at Finchwicke for tea," Rick said. There didn't seem to be any subject they could talk about for long.

"He was," said Bellwood, his lose nose sniffing a good tease. "He was on the train with me, and looking more than ever like a worried white rabbit. He didn't expect me to be on the business train with a pretty girl, so he hid behind his paper and pretended not to see us."

"Tell now, Sis. What did you talk about? You, and Carrie, and the bug doctor?"

"Bugs."

"I asked you before, did you actually go in and take tea?"

"I told you, Mama. Yes I did. Dr. Walding spoke so kindly of Papa. He was just coming in from wasp-watching, so we talked about that. When Chugh got there, I left *immediately*."

"How too delicious! Watching wasps! I suppose he compared me to one."

"No, no, Mama! It was Mrs. Walding he said—" She realized her mistake too late as Mama went off into peals of laughter.

"Mrs. Walding! A wasp! Of course! It explains —Oh dear me—" She dabbed at her eyes with a lace handkerchief as her merriment subsided. "But I can't believe you actually took tea?"

Faith felt that the attack by repetition of this question could only be met by refusing to answer it again, and she stared hard at the tapestry behind Bellwood: two wild boars in a death struggle deep in a leafy forest, a troupe of knights

22

and ladies on horseback approaching from the distant turret-
ed castle.

"Don't stand there staring at the tapestry and looking so
glum, Faith. If you had used your wits a bit, you might have
avoided going in. Where was the tea served?"

The tapestry showed a medieval hunting scene. There
would be a hunt tomorrow, and she would see Chugh again.
The blue lake in the tapestry had not changed color on account of the cloud over the mountain. On account of Chugh's
sapphire-blue eyes, she thought, neither shall I change color.
On account of Chugh I'll stand up for myself. Otherwise I'll
find myself permanently stuck on the shelf, stuck at home,
taking care of Mama's whims. Bellwood is married. And
Nanny Jaspar is having her second baby.

Bellwood came to the rescue of the deteriorating moment.
"At least Sis sent the carriage for us, for which I was grateful. I've had a dreadful week of rehearsal problems and I
couldn't possibly have managed the walk with Vivi's
suitcase."

"But to have allowed herself to be sent home in the Finchwicke carriage! I knew I shouldn't have allowed her to go
alone."

Rick now got up, a short, broad-shouldered man, the calf
muscles bulging through his golf stockings. He put his pipe
decisively in his pocket and shook himself, as if the room
with all the little bibelots, cloisonné bowls, tiny Battersea
boxes in glass-topped gold table-cases, and the embroidered
conversation was suffocating him. He said he was going to
hunt up Paddy Monaghan and arrange to shoot pheasants in
the early morning before going back to college. That was
what he had come for: to work his new dog, Major, that
Monaghan was training for him.

He bent to kiss his mother's marble forehead. She smiled
with pleasure, patting his tweed sleeve. She loved to have her
men go shooting, as had all her family men in her youth in
South Carolina.

"The hounds aren't coming this way, are they, Sis?"
Wouldn't want to shoot the fox by mistake."

"They might," Faith said. "They're meeting at Finchwicke."

"At Finchwicke!" Mama's voice rose to a high soprano.
Faith waited for the paralyzing sting to the abdomen, to the
nerve ganglia of the feet and the wings. It came. "I forbid
you to go hunting in the morning. After what happened to-

day, what will they think if you chase over there again at dawn? You will not go!"

At this injustice the memory of the Judge residing in his daughter spoke up. "They won't think anything, Mama! Of course I'm going."

"Of course they won't think anything!" Vivienne said, suddenly quite imprudent, and by that one remark cemented her friendship with her new sister-in-law. But Vivi had also deflected to herself a share of the enmity which Becca Hoagland had hitherto reserved for her daughter. This was sensed by everyone, although nothing was said as the moment trembled in the air. Becca always insisted she could get on with everyone except her stubborn daughter. But then there had been Thessaly Walding. And now there would be Vivi. Becca's face became a shut mask.

"Which room will Vivi have? Maybe she would like to rest before dinner," Bellwood said in his best bishop's voice, commanding an immediate return to good manners.

"The downstairs blue guest room. I hope Mademoiselle has already put her valise there. But let her stay and talk with me just a moment," Becca said, drawing off the ruby ring from her little finger—the one she had always said would be for Bellwood's wife—disguising her dislike in a display of generosity and regaining her pedestal in Bellwood's eyes.

Faith then excused herself to go and dress for dinner.

"At least try to be careful and not fall off and be carried into Finchwicke unconscious," Becca trilled angrily as Faith started from the room.

Faith turned back to answer, but then decided not to. In a sidelong glance she saw Vivienne Curle put down her teacup. No one had noticed her holding it all this time.

As Faith started up the wide, red carpeted staircase, Rick was just coming through into the front hall with the pair of Purdy shotguns that he had inherited from the Judge and a leather shoulder bag of shells. She paused.

"Don't you just love her, Rickie? Vivi, I mean?"

He raised a thick, sandy eyebrow and shrugged. "I suspect she'll boss him around. Beware the small brown mouse who nibbles away at your beard while you're asleep! But how about yourself? You're not going sweet on old Carrie, are you? The lily of the field?"

She stood on the landing in front of the stained-glass window, stunned by this bit of telepathy on the part of her favorite brother. "What makes you ask that?" she choked,

24

knowing that no secrets had ever been possible between them.

"I can tell by the look on your face. You're no actress."

"The lily of the field!" What a killing name to call Chugh.

She wanted to say, "Yes indeed, I certainly am," but all that came out of her mouth was a high, foolish laugh, as holding up her long skirt with one hand and gripping the pierced oak balustrade with the other, she fled up the stairs, the kettle-shaped hat with the bird's wings now tipped over one ear.

To get to her room at the far end of the gallery, Faith had to pass her parents' suite on the south side of the house. The door to the large corner bedroom with its Chinese lacquer doubled bed was open, as was the adjoining door to her father's dressing room. There, everything had been left exactly as it had always been. Not even one cuff-link box had been moved. Papa's suits still hung in the cupboards. His shirts and handkerchiefs were still in white piles in the drawers. And his many pairs of silk socks were there, all neatly mended by Ma'selle. Next came Mama's huge bathroom with a polar-bear rug in front of the open fireplace and a huge green marble tub in the middle of the floor. French doors led from the bedroom out to the gingerbread balcony, where her parents had slept together in a squeaky double bed on hot summer nights. A window from this same balcony looked into Faith's room, which was the last family room on the south side and ended in a tower.

On the north side, the staircase continued up to the boys' rooms on the third floor. Under the stairs was Ma'selle's room in the northeast tower just before the hall ended in a green baize-covered swinging door to the back hall. Ma'selle jealously preserved her station in life, as symbolized by the location of her room, halfway between the family and the servants. She had her meals served to her there on a tray, with the same napkin for a week rolled up in a silver ring. And on Sundays, if there happened to be no guests, Ma'selle ate dinner in the dining room with the family, when there would be huge damask embroidered napkins for all and an opportunity to make conversation in French (not very successfully) as she had in the old days when she had eaten all her meals with her charges. Her services as a governess no longer necessary, Ma'selle acted as lady's maid to Faith and Mrs. Hoagland, hooking and lacing and buttoning up in the back, mending and marking and rinsing out in order to justify her continued residence at Co-Eden, where she hoped to stay until she died. She often said to Faith that she knew she ought to leave, but she was too old to take on another family, and the thought of going back to her village in France was impossible, now that her sisters were both dead and a favorite nephew had absconded with all her earnings.

Luckily, Ma'selle was a little deaf and did not detect Faith as she crept past her room and peeked inside. Head bent over her work basket, open under the lamp on the table beside her, Ma'selle's wispy black hair was screwed in a knot on top of her narrow head. A thick gray sweater covered her hunched shoulders, and her knees were spread wide apart to make a receptacle for the various colored wools scattered on her brown serge lap. She was reweaving a hole in a heather-mix wool golf stocking, pulled tight over the thrust of a darning egg. It was probably one that she herself had knitted for Rick and which she had come upon while rummaging through the suitcase full of dirty clothes he had brought from Princeton. *"Mirabile dictu,"* as the girls at Springbank School had enjoyed saying to each other, she was thoroughly absorbed. Jesus on His crucifix bled at the head of her narrow brass bed.

Faith slipped into her own room and shut the door. Faint click of the latch. Silent sliding of the bolt. She shivered and turned. Nothing had changed in her private castle. The tower on the southeast corner made a lovely window-seated bay with a view over the lily pond to the roof of the stables. There was her small bed, the head and foot curved like the dashboard of a mahogany sleigh, covered with a thickly woven white fringed spread. Reposing on the flat pillow was Woggy, her rag doll which already had had three new faces embroidered on by Ma'selle as the old ones had disintegrated. The afghan which Ma'selle had knitted from leftover wools in squares of serviceable tan, red and marine blue all crocheted together in a border of black lay neatly folded on the end of the bed. Her King Charles spaniel, Tiddy-Boom, rising from a dog basket with a matching afghan, shook all over and then rolled onto her back, thumping her ginger and white tail in greeting on the red oakleaf-patterned carpet. With the pointed toe of her buckled shoe, Faith scratched the pale pink freckled stomach. Then she tossed her beaded bag, her grease-stained kid gloves, and her pongee duster onto the black bamboo armchair.

The lamps on the dressing table sent columns of light upward through their pea-green glass shades, picking out fat pink and yellow roses on the trellised wallpaper. Casting pools of light downward, they caught Faith's monogrammed silver toilet set, her brushes and mirror, the pin tray, the powder box and the square jewelry casket gleaming on the dark mahogany. Also on the dressing table were pictures of the family, framed in ornate silver frames. Her mother, full-bosomed and wasp-waisted with a long train streaming from her bare shoulders and three ostrich feathers in her pompadoured hair, was being presented to Queen Victoria at the Court of St. James. Her father, wearing his tall gray hat, sat atop the road-coach with his four famous grays. Looking very pleased, he was surrounded by pretty ladies in large hats all swaying together. A tiny round picture showed Rick and herself as babies, posing in their goatcart in the grass circle in front of the porte-cochere.

Faith stood like a deer transfixed, but no sign came that Ma'selle had heard her come in. Darling Ma'selle. She too liked to hear a full report of the family news, and since the window in her tiny round room gave her full view of the driveway, she would have noted the strange comings and goings and undoubtedly would want to know why Faith had arrived in the Finchwicke carriage. Faith would tell her all about it—but later, after she had had a chance to wipe the excitement from her face.

She leaned over the table to look into the heart-shaped mirror. Hat over one aquamarine eye. Deep flush on sallow cheeks. She pulled out the long hatpins, so that her loosened hair, clean and slippery, fell in a black shawl down to her waist. It was her father's hair. Why in tarnation couldn't his only daughter have inherited her mother's red curls instead of his straight black Indian hair? Proof of the existence of the archfiend, to play such a trick, the Judge had said. But what would Chugh think if he ever saw her with her hair down? Oh, he couldn't possibly like it, Faith thought, comparing unfavorably her dark stubbiness to his tall, slim blondness.

Her corsets were constricting her, forcing her to breathe with her upper rib cage. One whalebone was sinking unmercifully into the flesh under her arms, another pressing into her stomach. But without the help of Ma'selle she could not manage to get out of her black and tan silk dress. She could reach the velvet sash and unfasten the bunch of black silk roses under her pressed-down breast but that was all. She felt her life rising and boiling within her bonds, escaping with her breath, pouring down into her thighs.

Fully dressed, Faith lay down on her narrow young girl's bed. Her body pressed against the rag doll, as she filled with desire to do that which she knew was very wicked. Ma'selle said it was wicked and had slapped her hands for it. But Faith hadn't been able to stop, not since that long-ago night when she had been awakened by her mother's cries through the window that opened from her room onto her parents' sleeping porch.

She had been having a nightmare. She was being run away with in the station buggy pulled by a huge chestnut horse, mane flying and tail straight up, spume flying from his mouth. His crazy white eye turned to look at her as they dashed headlong under the railway trestle, the wheels of the buggy squeaking faster and faster as they approached the sharp corner. Then suddenly she had awakened. "Ah no! No! No more, for God's sake!" her mother was crying out. The springs of the bed squeaked inexorably faster and faster, and then suddenly stopped, and there was no sound except her mother softly whimpering. Faith had jumped up to see what was so terribly wrong, but she was stopped by the Judge. He was standing stark naked on the polar-bear rug, silhouetted by the moon. Scooping her up in his hairy arms, he had held her so close that through her thin white nightie she had felt the soft feathers on his barrel chest. Her mother had had a bad dream, he crooned, depositing her back in her own bed and carefully shutting the window before he had padded out.

Now her corsets were pressing. Life itself was pressing—pressing—until a quick flash of lightning brought relief and she lay softly panting, thankful that no tap on the door had come, her mind gone blank and white.

Faith stared at the pictures on the wall beyond the foot of her bed, dark blots against the flowering wallpaper which were so familiar that they no longer recalled the past. But now that the past demanded to be reexamined from Chugh's point of view, she considered them again.

There was a Kodak of her graduating class at Springbank. A small oil painting of the white columns of The Mount done by Granny Huger from memory. And a large sepia photograph of the Judge standing in front of the gleaming marble steps of the Spruce Street house, in the old days before soft coal, when everything could be kept clean . . .

In the Spruce Street townhouse, the upstairs nursery had been a nest in which the little birds, Twinkle and Rickie, grew and where her little brother had held sway, enslaving both herself and Ma'selle. Rickie had always been the apple of Mama's eye, and it had been Twinkle who preempted Papa's knee. That had been a time of complete security and comfort, she remembered. The affairs of the outside world were only dimly heard; distant wars took place with no effect on their lives. The Spanish War. The Boer War. The war between Japan and Russia. President McKinley was assassinated. President Teddy Roosevelt set out to ruin people of property, but property still seemed to amass. And a dreadful coal strike threatened the family mines but was settled without too much damage. Life had been orderly and quiet.

Across all this the death of her father had fallen like the black stroke of a whip, changing everything. She had been a schoolgirl, sixteen, walking home with Ma'selle and a group of girlfriends. She had waved good-bye to the girls once in the sunny street and again from the top of the front steps. Then she had rung the bell.

Mary Quinn's face through the open door had looked terribly swollen. The darkness of the hall enveloped them like a pall; Mama was right there in the front parlor, visible through the wide doors. She was dressed in a light green suit, ruffles at the high throat. And she stood beside a heavily framed Dutch painting of black and white cows and a brown stream. One white hand gripped the edge of the high mantel for support.

Two gentlemen in black coats had stood before Mama, strange lawyers who had come to tell her that the Judge was dead. He had been stricken by a heart attack in some mysterious house not far away, where he had been visiting for some inexplicable reason in the middle of the day.

No, ma'am, it had not happened in the courtroom. Yes, ma'am, he had a particularly difficult case that morning which had been a great strain. True.

Carefully arranging her long skirt, Mama had moved very slowly to seat herself on a straight chair. Her face white, her green eyes dry, she dabbed at her lips with a crushed wisp of handkerchief as if she wished to stuff it into her mouth. Her red hair seemed to go dull.

When she spoke her voice had been tightly choked. "You tell me that my husband is dead, but refuse to tell me where he died? I find this impossible to accept. I want to know where, to see it for myself."

"Regrettably, ma'am, it is not a place which would be

suitable for you to visit, and we are not at liberty to disclose the address."

"But I must know where my husband died! Surely you have no right . . ." Becca's voice had broken with sadness, as though she realized the futility of arguing the point further.

"You may wish to consult your lawyer, ma'am."

"Never mind for now. As you say, the Judge is dead!" The grief in her mother's voice had a terrible finality. That much Faith had understood before Ma'selle firmly hustled her out of the room.

All that afternoon, Faith had been kept upstairs with Ma'selle and Rickie. He had come home from school just as the box containing their father's body was heaved up the front steps from the hearse, and placed by the undertaker's men in the front parlor. Rickie had been hustled up to the nursery, where Ma'selle first broke the news and then comforted him and then insisted that he and Faith keep hard at their lessons until teatime, when Mama sent for them. She was, as usual, in her cozy chintz sitting room, which was entered from the landing between the first and second floors. Here each day the grown-up world briefly existed for Faith and Rickie; washed and starchily dressed they would be sent down to bow and curtsy to Papa and Mama's friends taking tea there. They had not been supposed to speak, nor to listen. "Little pitchers have big ears!" Mama would caution when the conversation got too interesting.

This day there had been no one there but Bellwood. Hastily summoned home from college, he was standing red-eyed behind Mama's chair. She beckoned Rickie to sit on the footstool at her feet so that she could stroke his hair while she explained.

"Papa was a very famous judge. He had been working late nights on a very difficult case. Today he died suddenly. We must all remember how hard he worked, and work hard ourselves to draw closer together. You and Bellwood must take his place," she had said to the little boy, "and learn to take care of Mama."

"But Mama," Faith had asked, sitting alone on the hard sofa facing them, "where did Papa die?"

"He died in his chambers, doing his duty."

"But I heard the men say something about they couldn't tell you where he died!"

"You heard wrong, Faith. He died in his courtroom and that is what you are to tell people if they are so bold as to

.ask. That is what will be printed in the paper, and that is the truth."

Faith had never seen Mama so angry. Bellwood looked stern also and what Mama had said was the truth for Rickie. Faith later realized that over the years she had come to believe it too.

Papa's body had been taken by special train to Penngwynne Station where it had been unloaded by the undertaker's men onto the buckboard with the two back seats taken out, and driven by Quinn wearing his tall beaver hat, to St. Jude's-under-Buttonwood. Here the coffin had been unloaded by all the men who had come from Co-Eden in their best clothes to carry him into the church. Mama, shrouded in a black crepe veil, had been waiting just inside the vestibule with Faith and the boys. She had walked up the aisle alone behind the casket, head bowed, face covered, followed by her children.

The Judge's funeral was the largest ever held there, crammed with friends and dignitaries the Judge had known from his very active involvement in the social and civic life of the city and in the church. The Judge had been chief vestryman of St. Jude's and had just enlarged and remodeled the historic old church in memory of his mother. He had also just completed the landscaping of the top plot where he and his wife were to be buried side by side under one huge headstone like a double bed. The stone had been bought on a trip to Italy and shipped to the tomb-carver's shop, where it had waited to be inscribed with final dates under each name. So Papa's had been filled in, and he lay there beneath the stone, seemingly waiting for Mama.

After his death the atmosphere in the house changed abruptly. Life swung entirely with Mama's moods. She who had always kept slightly distant like a queen now became omnipresent in her demanding grief. Abandoning her long dresses of lace and embroidery, she wore only shrouding black. And she gave insistent orders: Do this; Don't do that. As Mama came to the foreground, Ma'selle receded to the mending basket. Mama arrogated all sadness to herself, refusing to share it with her children or to permit any discussion of happy memories of the Judge or their life as it had been.

However, there had been agonizing discussions about money. Instead of leaving everything to his widow, the Judge had left half his income to be divided among his children, so certain economies had to be made. Marshall had thought of purchasing the townhouse from his mother, since he was engaged to be married to the beautiful and statuesque Hebe Pardue and was planning to practice medicine in the city. But Hebe had not liked the changes taking place in the no longer fashionable district and they decided to move to Rittenhouse Square. Bellwood persuaded his mother to sell him the Mews for a very small sum, and he had turned it into his Little Theater. Never mind that Papa had always counted on Bellwood being a bishop, or that he would have hated to have had his stables used for a theater. Besides, with the clanging of the trolleys, it was almost impossible to keep spirited carriage horses in town. And with the convenience of motor cars and the railroad, all the best people were moving out to the country all year round. So the townhouse was sold to a Russian Jew to be used as a boarding house, and the Hoagland family packed up and moved to Penngwynne.

Rick was old enough for boarding school and followed his brothers to St. Paul's. Faith lived at Co-Eden with Mama and finished off her education at Springbank in Chetford Hills, taking the ten-minute train ride back and forth from Penngwynne. She had developed a deep loyalty to the school and to the friends she had made there. For at home, no matter how hard she tried, there was nothing she could do to please Mama. The sight of her mother's back, huddled in a cashmere shawl in front of an ever-burning open fire, chilled Faith. It was only when her brothers had come home from school that Mama took on the warmth that no amount of loving attention from Faith could supply. Since the death of the Judge, only the boys could do no wrong. Only the boys could make Mama turn and face the room. So that it was really Faith's friends from school who had saved her life. She would never give them up.

She wondered how Chugh would like them. Would he think Gee was a frump?

Gee was her best friend, now and forever. Faith remembered how they had "come out" together, and also how Mama had worried about the money for the parties and worried about having to appear in public—she felt ill so often. But Mama had managed to give a tea dance at the Walnut Club, after making financial arrangements with Welch Seabreese, the president of the bank and the man Papa had designated as trustee of his estate. Welch Seabreese was the one who decided whether the bill for the occasion would be paid out of the custodian account or out of Mama's own pocket, and Mama resented this. In addition she made a point of telling Mr. Seabreese that she took it ill that Papa had not left her all the money. Mr. Seabreese suggested that she speak to Papa about that when she got to the next world. With asperity, she had replied that she intended to, but she doubted they would meet.

In the year she was presented to society, Faith had been taken by a cousin to the St. Cecilia Ball in Charleston and the Cotillion in Baltimore, and escorted to the Assembly by Bellwood. Gee and the other girls had had their fathers there, and Faith had missed the Judge bitterly. Still she had never indulged her feelings openly until this afternoon when she had bared her heart in blessed relief to Chugh. She had spoken to Chugh of beloved Papa who stood there in that photograph, one shiny boot on the pavement, one on the steps, his tall hat cheerfully tipped, his mustache waxed, his gloved hand on the knob of his cane, dapper in his morning coat and striped trousers.

Tiddy-Boom now put her paws up and scratched on the bedspread wanting to be picked up, but Faith pushed her down. It was time to get ready for dinner. Getting up, she smoothed out the pillow and rearranged the long legs of Woggy.

On the bedside table lay her well-worn Bible and the pale-blue Morocco-leather Prayer Book and Hymnal which Uncle Bishop Hoagland had given her when he had come to St. Jude's to confirm her Sunday School class. "Defend, oh Lord, this Thy child." In a weakening moment of guilt she sank to her knees by the bed and prayed.

"Oh Jesus, forgive what I have done.
I have desecrated thy holy temple, and there is
     no health in me.
Miserable offender.
Miserable sinner.
Help me never to do it again.
Enter my bedroom and make it Thy temple.
Oh Jesus lead me not into temptation, and
Deliver me from evil. Forgive . . . Forgive!"

For a long time she waited on her knees for grace and forgiveness, for Christ to enter her heart as He sometimes did. The face of Chugh Walding with his searing blue eyes kept swimming across her mind, so that when Tiddy-Boom began to scratch at the door she gave it up. She rose, collected her

33

towels from the washstand, and slid back the latch as noiselessly as she had closed it. Crossing the hall, she entered the bathroom she shared with Ma'selle. A single light bulb illuminated the green walls, the copper tub standing on its mahogany base, the toilet with the mahogany seat, a mahogany box holding the water up near the ceiling, and a heavy brass chain hanging down with a mahogany handle on the end. Faith dumped the towels on the chair and checked in the mirror to make certain the flush on her cheeks had subsided.

"Yoo-hoohoo! Mazzy darling!" she called.

"*J'entends ta voix? Eh bien, chérie! Ma petite! . . .*" Ma'selle appeared instantly in the doorway, sparks in her eyes.

"Unbutton me, please."

"*Oui, oui. Patience, patience.*" Ma'selle dropped the black rubber plug into the drain and started to draw the bath water. Then she began undoing the long row of tiny buttons on the back of the tan and black striped silk dress. Tinier buttons closed the guimpe of white net that filled in the low square neck and rose to Faith's ear lobes. Faith knew that Ma'selle was also anxious to strip her of the day's news as she removed her camisole with pink ribbons threaded through the top; her petticoats with ribbons threaded through the bottom; her long embroidered handkerchief-linen drawers from Paris, lace-edged, with buttons up the back; her corsets laced up from behind; and her ribbed cotton undershirt edged with lace and ribbons. The hot water gurgled merrily, and not until Faith was seated in the steam, with nothing on but a gold cross on a gold chain, and was having her back sponged off did Ma'selle begin to divulge her own private news. Of course Monsieur Rick had been up to see her with oh so much mending. But also Monsieur Bellwood had come to her room with special news. But probably Faith would have to wait until dinner to hear it. Unless of course, she had been told?

"Oh Ma'selle! You mean *il s'est marié!*"

"*Avec quelque chose comme ça!*" Ma'selle said in scorn, and launched into a tirade about how the Hoaglands shouldn't get themselves mixed up with people from another class.

Faith got out of the tub, and while Ma'selle rubbed her back dry and dabbed at her soft underarms with a huge powder puff out of a silver box, Faith described her visit to old Dr. Walding. She did not mention Chugh at all, even though the memory of his closeness, the way he touched her arm, was present in the steamy room redolent of violet-per-fumed soap.

After an uneventful dinner, the young people gathered around the player piano in the central hall. A fire burned in the huge rough stone hearth. Wrapped in a Spanish shawl, Vivi sang like a canary, following the words printed on the piano roll, while Rick pumped. Bellwood sprawled on the worn leather sofa. Faith, enchanted, joined in the choruses until Mama, who had retired immediately after dinner, sent for her to brush her hair for an hour and thus prevent a threatening headache.

2

At Finchwicke

WHEN THE cat's away the mice will play, Bunce thought as he sat on his butler's stool in the semicircular pantry that connected the Finchwicke kitchen to the main house. Across the shadowy expanse of cobbled courtyard, a semicircular sun loggia connected the opposite wing including the drawing room downstairs and the nursery, now Mr. Chugh's apartment, upstairs. All was dim there, as the gentlemen were in the library of the main house. Bunce, in shirtsleeves, scratched his balls under the dark blue apron tied around his swelling middle; he looked like a robin in spring, full of worms. He was waiting for Delia to appear to help him set the table for dinner. This chore was usually accomplished while there was still daylight, but today he had been caught catnapping when the master rang early for tea to entertain the young lady visitor. Then Delia, not feeling well, had disappeared to her room in the attic. The big clock on the pantry wall was ticking away; it was already six-thirty and yet here were the tea things sitting next to the tin sink just as they had been brought out from the library, with tea leaves and little puddles of tea in the bottom of the porcelain cups making a ring stain that would be impossible to wash away. Madam had always insisted the cups be washed by the parlor maid immediately, and now because it hadn't been done, those particular cups would have to join the other chipped and stained ones hidden in the back of the long, china-laden shelves, and other cups would have to be brought forward to hang on the hooks for everyday use.

Opening one of the cupboard doors as if to inspect the situation, Bunce removed a small crystal shot glass, slightly cracked. Then, checking both the kitchen windows and the backstairs doors to make sure that no one could see, he filled it from a whiskey bottle that he kept for himself in the silver-polish box under the sink. Inconveniently, at that moment the 'tween appeared with a mop to clean up a large puddle of water, left no doubt by the stable bitch, which had followed the gardener in. Bunce wrapped his large white flabby hand around the shot glass, making it disappear.

He was in charge, really in charge. Even though one might say that he had always been in titular charge, the reins of the household had always been very firmly held by Madam. After her death, the house had continued to bumble along under its own momentum. The cook continued to materialize the familiar three meals a day with five- to seven-course dinners. The leftovers of those dinners continued to be served by the kitchen maid to the servants in their own dining room. The laundress washed and ironed as usual, the gardener brought in fresh flowers and fruits, the coachman fetched the mail and papers in a leather pouch. In fact, there had been no need for the butler to assert his authority. But now the increasingly hoity-toity behavior of Delia and the sight of the dirty tea things still in the sink so annoyed him that he resolved to do at once as Mrs. Bunce had been urging. Take charge! Bottoms up! He raised his hand to his mouth, and in one quick motion drained the shot glass.

Only this morning he had caught Delia coming out of Mr. Chugh's bathroom after Mr. Chugh had gone to the city. Bunce had gone in to hang up the riding breeches that Mrs. Bunce had just washed and boned (a special art she had leaned from her English mother). Delia had no business coming out of Mr. Chugh's bathroom into his strange bedroom with all them animal heads hanging on the wall— mountain goats and moose he'd shot out West on his boyhood trips with his mother. Madam hadn't wanted to have them hanging anywhere else. And Mr. Chugh had all the rest of his boyhood trappings in there too. Framed pictures of little boys' football teams. Silver sailing cups he'd won. Anyway, cleaning and dusting it all was entirely the purview of the chambermaid or the 'tween. Delia had no call to be in there, none whatsoever. But Bunce had been too surprised to mention it before she managed to duck away. Now, having thought it over all day, he certainly intended to bring it up, along with other things.

For instance, a horrid suspicion had been growing in Bunce's mind while taking his afternoon nap in his apartments. Why was it that Mr. Chugh never seemed to bring any nice young ladies to the house? Madam had always begged him to. She had wanted him to get married, of course, and fill Finchwicke with children. But Mr. Chugh had always laughed it off. "First I have to fall in love, and when I do, you'll be the first to know," he would say. When Madam asked him how she would know when he never invited any young ladies home, he answered, "You'll know, Ma. I'll give a sign—I'll shave off my beard. Yes. When you see me clean-shaven like the Hoagland boys, you'll know I'm going to get married."

"It's unnatural," Mrs. Bunce had said. "A young man like that home alone nearly ever night with his mother and father."

"Never you mind, Bertha," Bunce had assured her. "Never you mind where he's getting 'it,' but getting it he is." Bunce just assumed that Mr. Chugh went to the Fancy House in the city in the afternoons.

But then he had begun to wonder because last week on his day off, Mr. Chugh had asked him to procure some of the necessary covers at Rex's Drug Store in the city. Bunce had never bought the damn things before, as it was difficult enough joining himself to Bertha without adding that. She was so short and compact, and he had grown so large and low in the stomach. He had consented however, because he thought he just might like to try one out. But it hadn't worked. He hadn't been able to get it on.

Bunce reached into the silver-polish box and poured himself another half shot. He had to decide right now what he was going to say to Delia about having been in Mr. Chugh's bathroom. If Mrs. Bunce thought he had been winking at any goings on, he would never hear the end of it. She knew all about "goings on," having once been a 'tween herself, saved from her master's advances only by the young footman, Bunce himself. But before he had thought out just exactly what he was going to say, Delia edged through the swinging door carrying the tablecloth, starched and ironed without a fold and rolled up on a long bamboo pole.

"Where have you been, girl? You're an hour late, and the tea things aren't washed!"

But Delia didn't answer him. Looking like green cheese under the pantry's hanging electric globe, she brushed past him into the dim caverns of the dining room.

She had already lit the crystal girandoles on the demilune serving tables and was trying to close the long garnet velvet curtains when Bunce appeared. He gave the stubborn curtains a contemptuous jerk, and then stood aside, waiting while Delia removed the asbestos silencer from the long serpentine drawer of the sideboard. Then together they unfolded its panels to fit over the mahogany table so that no hot dish should damage the intricate inlaid border of rosewood. Together they unrolled the damask cloth, woven in a white-on-white pattern of roses and pansies and thickly monogrammed with the entwined initials of Thessaly Chyldes Walding. Bunce took the bamboo pole and carefully measured from the floor to a certain notch while Delia smoothed each of the four corners, making sure they hung down equally all around. Next Delia brought the plates, green and gold with pierced borders and centers of roses, lilies, and pansies on a white background, and laid four places.

When Mrs. Walding had been alive, and the family was three, she had always insisted that a fourth place be laid to balance the table—and for the unexpected guest, although that water glass was never filled. And now Dr. Walding wanted it the same way: four places should still be laid, but neither the guest's nor Madam's water glass should be filled.

Master and son also continued to observe one other amenity that Madam had insisted upon. No talking about money until the evening meal was finished. Then Madam would leave the dining room to do her embroidery alone in the drawing room for half an hour while cigars and port were served to the gentlemen.

Delia fetched the heavy flat silver which had come over from England with the original Sir Percy, and folded the large linen napkins in a triangular shape so that the monograms were on top. She placed the silver salts and peppers exactly halfway between the settings, and arranged the crystal goblets for water and wine. Bunce appeared from the pantry with the filigree epergne filled with pears and grapes which had just come in from the greenhouse (flowers at luncheon but never at night, as the scent would interfere with the bouquet of the wines). He set the Georgian silver candlesticks exactly equidistant from each other and from the table's edge, and stood back to survey the effect. As always it was perfect, a gleaming white island rising from the rich garnet of the Oriental rug, dim portraits looking down from soft-green paneled walls, curtains pulled, a small log flickering on the brass andirons on the white marble hearth.

Delia put the finishing touches on the table, placed each nut dish exactly one foot outside each candle. As she bent over, Bunce noticed that her full breasts, tightly encased in black cotton under the frilly white bib of her apron, nearly brushed the rim of a glass. Swelling up she was. Full of milk no doubt. She straightened, and he appraised her full profile. It was only a guess. He couldn't really see anything.

A great light dawned in his mind. "What were you up to then, standing on the scales in Mr. Chugh's bathroom this morning? Weighin' yourself, that's what!"

He was amazed at his own cleverness. And as the girl flushed angrily, he followed up on his advantage. "Nothing under that apron, is there, girl? If there is, you must tell me. I've known about those kind of troubles before. If there is any trouble in the house, I like to know it. It's my business, you know."

"Indeed! I wouldn't know. I don't go weighin' myself like a farmyard pig on the way to market."

"Farmyard pig indeed!"

He advanced on her, expecting her to flounce at him. But she swayed a little and grasped the back of one of the Adam dining room chairs, delicately carved in a Tree-of-Life design, carefully waxed each week.

"What's under my apron is my own business, though many's the time you've tried to make it yours! If you could!"

She looked as if she was going to cry, so Bunce decided to retreat. Leaning over he moved the four Georgian silver candlesticks still more exactly equidistant from the epergne and from each other, and then he said, "Mind you don't break that chair!" And he left the room in slow majesty.

As long as there was not going to be any more sport with Delia, he started for the gentlemen's library, hoping to catch a snatch of the conversation. Mr. Chugh had spent the day in the city after two weeks of being unnaturally much alone with his father and would have much to discuss. Perhaps the subject of Madam's will. Bunce was anxious to discover if, for instance, she had remembered him. After all, it was Madam who had had all the money, so it was now or never. But Bunce didn't like to ask outright in such sad times. Sad times!

Sad times, yes. But Mrs. Bunce was very anxious to know what was to become of them. Every night in their apartment over the kitchen wing, she urged Bunce to call the lawyer. Mr. Roland Raymond, wasn't it? He was the one who had the wife who turned Democrat? Such a disgrace. The only Democrat friend the family had. She had actually voted for President Wilson. This was considered far worse than turning Catholic because the income tax the Democrats wanted was going to take away everything from the upper classes and then where would people like the Bunces be?

Lately in the kitchen there had been some discussions about this started by a young German plumber's assistant. He had scared the cook to death by talking to her about revolution. But Bunce had argued right back to him from things he had heard Mr. Chugh and Dr. Walding say at the table. Why penalize the clever people and let the shiftless and the lower classes go free?

In any case Mrs. Bunce's wages were all in the savings bank, and Bunce had done very well with some little investments he had made through Mr. Chugh. Add to this what they would surely inherit after thirty years' service in the Walding family and there should be enough to retire and buy a cottage. This dream cottage was somewhere in Van Nuys, California, where their only child, Leonard, had gone. Leonard had made a very good marriage to a nurse at the Chetford Hill Hospital and she had persuaded him to go West. Why shouldn't Leonard make a good start? Because, after all, Leonard spoke the King's English and he had been raised just as nice as Mr. Chugh, with whom he had played all day long until Mr. Chugh had gone off to Chetford Hill Academy and he had gone to the Penngwynne Public School. But Leonard's departure for California had been made bearable only by the plan to follow him out there. And so they would, especially since now Leonard was doing so well in his insurance company, and a baby girl had been born. Named Bertha after Mrs. Bunce. Mrs. Bunce dreamed only of getting little Bertha on her lap. But in the meanwhile it was their duty to stick by Dr. Walding until things were a bit more settled, and until they had their money in hand. So she kept urging Bunce to take full charge and make himself indispensable until the right moment came. Because you never know. If Madam had not left them anything, they would have to depend on the Doctor to give them a handsome severance gift. In this world you can't be too careful.

In the library the two gentlemen were sitting on either side of the fireplace, on either side of the portrait of Percy Walding, who gave Bunce an insolent stare as he entered. Bunce returned the look with pained eyes upraised and then discreetly lowered. The fire was burning brightly, and he decided not to poke it, as coming between the gentlemen might interrupt what they were saying. He checked his progress into

41

the room and turned back into the corner to inspect the whiskey tray.

One elegant thin leg crossed high over the other, Mr. Chugh was stroking his gold beard and saying, "Everybody was very kind at the office. Old Black Bullet at the front door was pulling his forelock and remembering Mother's mother. He reminded me again that he had been there since the Civil War, he wanted to know how you were, and told me how much he loved the family. It was remarkable and most touching how sad all those kind people seemed to feel. Mother always went out of her way to call them by name and shake hands. Miss Mack seemed to care particularly and wanted to know if you would like her to come out and write notes, or make out the servants' checks. Mother always attended to that herself, you know, and I guess they haven't been paid since—since—" There was a pause, as though Mr. Chugh were swallowing his pain. Bunce moved the decanter of Scotch whiskey an inch to the right. He lifted the decanter of rye as though to check its level with his eye.

Dr. Walding cleared his throat and said nothing. And Bunce, finding no excuse to remain in the room without appearing to be eavesdropping, started toward the drawing room. But no use lighting the fire there; the gentlemen no longer went in there after dinner to join Madam. So he retreated to hang around in the hall to hear what he could hear, straightening the cards in the Lowestoft bowl. There was that young lady's card right on the top, and without even the corners turned down. Miss Faith Middleton Hoagland. How the Doctor had cottoned to her! Letting her pour the tea, sitting in Madam's chair! Suddenly Mr. Chugh's voice carried out into the hall on a wave of high irritation. "Of course, it was Mother's money that paid the staff and I told Miss Mack that nothing can be used out of her checkbook until the will is probated and the estate settled. So I gave the instructions to take the wages out of your account if that's all right, sir!"

Bunce moved closer to the door and heard the Doctor say hesitantly, "Of course, of course. What difference does it make whose account it comes out of, yours or mine? It's all the same, isn't it? Robbing Peter to pay Paul, so to speak."

"I don't quite see it that way. Your account is yours, and my account is mine. And if we are to continue to live on here together as the will stipulates, we might as well start off on the right track. Who is going to pay for what?"

"Now, don't get angry, Chugh. All I mean is, we can straighten it out eventually, in a perfectly fair way. There's going to be more than enough money to go round. As a matter of fact, to change the subject a little bit, this morning after you left I was going over things in Mother's desk and I see by her checkbook that Delia gets only twenty dollars a month. Thessaly always said it was more than she was worth, being green off the boat from Ireland last year. But it occurred to me, as I was sitting out by the old pile of rotten apple wood this afternoon, watching the male wasps circling around the females and trying to alight—I mean, it was very lonely, you know—and it occurred to me that Delia has taken very good care of us these last difficult weeks. I mean old Bunce is absolutely hopeless. He sleeps all the time. And possibly Delia, who does all his work, should get a rise."

Out in the hall, Bunce gasped at the unfairness of this remark and stood as if transfixed by poisoned arrows to hear what would come next. Mr. Chugh was saying scornfully, "I wouldn't be in too much of a hurry. Mother was pretty right about household matters. She didn't believe in spoiling them and as a result she had their complete respect and loyalty."

"True. Maybe I'm getting soft in my old age. Thinking about it, though, I couldn't help saying to myself, 'The toad beneath the harrow knows, exactly where each toothpoint goes.' "

Bunce decided that this conversation had gone far enough, so he stuck his face like a pale moon into the gentlemen's library and wheezed, "Dinner is served, sir," without even checking with the cook to see if she was ready—or if Delia had lit the candles. No matter. The gentlemen wouldn't respond for at least five minutes.

Madam had been the only one ever to come punctually to the table, jumping to her feet the very instant dinner was announced. Penance to the cook for the dinner she assumed was ruined while the gentlemen asserted their masculine right to finish their drink and have a secret extra splash in pure devilment before joining her. Madam had used to sit at the table like a tiny queen, while the cook, fully aware of the probable time lapse, would only just now have moved the soup up to the front of the coal range to heat up. Then as soon as the gentlemen came in, Madam's face would crinkle in merriment as she came alive to carry on the conversation of the evening meal at a steady pace. "Well," she would have asked brightly, "what's new in the world?"

Remembering these things, Bunce reverently pulled out Madam's empty chair on his way out to the kitchen, as though she were there to sit in it and was horrified to be caught doing this by the Doctor and Mr. Chugh, who for the first time in history had come in to dinner promptly after it was announced. Candles were not lit. The cook had not been warned. Delia was nowhere. Let them see who did all the work!

Quickly Bunce got behind the Doctor's chair and pushed him in with a strong shove. Then, pulling a box of matches from his pants pocket, he lit the candles (Delia's work) and, without apology, semaphored to the kitchen to get things going. Dr. Walding and Mr. Chugh seemed not to notice at all. Things were changing here, going from bad to worse. Madam's ghost was slowly taking leave of the house.

"I came out on the train with Bellwood Hoagland," Mr. Chugh said. "I hid behind the evening paper so I wouldn't have to speak to the loathsome ass. He had a woman with him. He's not usually on the business train, you know."

"Hmmm. Quite." Dr. Walding was concentrating on finding his mouth as his head was bent further over than usual to one side, spooning up the lukewarm clear beet soup from a shallow porcelain plate. "Hurry up and finish your soup before it gets cold."

There was silence except for the scraping of a spoon as Dr. Walding tipped his plate.

Had Madam been present she would not have allowed the silence to exist for more than an imperceptible second. It meant that people weren't enjoying each other's company. She had kept up the conversation at such a steady pace throughout the meal that the gentlemen had got into the habit of not bothering to speak until she piqued them into protesting.

"Well," she would have asked brightly, "what's new in the world? Did Merion Cricket win? Did Roland Raymond play? Poor, poor Roly." And then she would have gone on to discuss Marianna's politics. Marianna Raymond, Democrat, was disappointed that President Wilson had not taken a strong stand on women's suffrage. First good thing he's done, Mr. Chugh would have said. Madam would have ignored the interruption—it was idiotic of the President to say that he had no opinion on the subject. A President ought to have an opinion.

The memory of her high-pitched well-bred voice seemed to

linger in the lengthening silence. Finally Mr. Chugh spoke again, as the last of his soup was spooned up. "I think it was an actress. I seem to have seen her somewhere before—the woman Bellwood Hoagland had with him, I mean. I suppose he's got the creature with child and has to marry her. Nice for his sister."

Silence.

"Pas devant les Sus-E-Rurs" is what Madam would have said, spelling out the first three letters of S-E-R-V-A-N-T-S in Tuttny, the secret language which she thought Bunce didn't understand. Madam had never permitted gossip about the near neighbors in front of the servants in case they might lose respect for their betters. Bunce didn't like Delia to hear it either, though for himself it was a different matter.

"Pas devant les Sus-E-Rurs," Dr. Walding said. "But I shouldn't be surprised if she is *Hash-A-Vuv-ing"*—Madam's code word for H-A-V-I-N-G a baby—"as your dear mother always referred to the sacred subject of human increase."

Both gentlemen laughed heartily before another silence set in.

Bunce brought in the warm dinner plates of gold-and-white Minton china. Delia passed the hindquarter of lamb and kidneys arranged on a silver platter with a bouquet of string beans amandine and tiny roast potatoes and carrots in cream.

"Our own lamb?" Dr. Walding inquired of Delia's bosom.

"Yes, sir," she murmured.

Bunce poured a sip of Châteauneuf-du-Pape 1905 for Dr. Walding, and waited with a haughty, distant expression as it was savored and pronounced drinkable. "A *divina potio*," he said as usual and asked to see the label. "Ah, yes. Just what I thought it was. How much more of this have we, Bunce? It's damned good."

"About ten cases, I think, sir." Mr. Chugh was apt to come down and count the wine. It was one of his special interests. But the good Doctor never bothered with such housekeeping details.

Bunce and Delia retreated into the shadows.

Silence at the table.

Dr. Walding broke it by saying, "Of course I had thought of going to town myself, but it did seem a bit soon after Thessaly's death to face the Philadelphia Club at lunch. I think maybe next week I'll go in to my Natural Sciences meeting. What does Johnny Oldthwaite think about the war?"

Here was a subject for conversation, and Mr. Chugh seized

it. "He's worried about it. He thinks we should face it in a business way and try to forestall some difficult situations in case it should drag on. For instance, there won't be chemical fertilizers coming over from Germany if the limeys decide to fight in the sea lanes. And that brings up something I was going to ask you, sir. There's a small nitrate factory starting up in Manayunk. They need cash, and Johnny wants us to buy in right now. I'm rather strapped just for the moment, as I'm finishing paying fo my seat on the Exchange, and of course my allowance from Mother on which I absolutely depend is kaput until her estate gets settled. So, I was wondering, sir, if you'd care to lend me twenty thousand. Johnny thinks chemicals are going to be an absolute sure thing."

"Humpmph," said Dr. Walding, peering through his steel rims at his son. "The only 'sure' thing is to put your money in bank stocks."

He hates to be asked for money, thought Bunce, hurrying forward to rearrange some dishes on the serving table. But I might take a bit of a flyer in that myself. Couldn't lend him the whole twenty, of course. But maybe ten. Mr. Chugh knows it. He has my account.

The Doctor asked, "Why don't you sell some of your American Tobacco? You say it's doing so well."

"Hate to do that. If it's a long war, that's going to be a good stock to keep, because there won't be any Egyptian coming over if there's a sea war. There'll be a big scarcity anyway."

Bunce made a mental note to buy some more tobacco stock with the inheritance money he hoped to get.

Dr. Walding waggled an admonitory finger at his son as he quoted, " 'Neither a borrower, nor a lender be' . . ."

Bunce thought Mr. Chugh looked a little annoyed as he swallowed with difficulty, as if an olive pit were sticking in his throat. Quickly Bunce refilled the glasses with ruby wine. Mr. Chugh took a long swig and seemed to revive. Truth of it was, it was most unnatural for the two gentlemen to be alone together night after night. Both of them had been so dependent on the heart and soul of Madam. This situation wouldn't last. It couldn't.

"Well, what about Mother's will?" the Doctor asked, the subject of Chugh's wanting to borrow now closed. "Did you find out more about it? If we don't have it probated soon, we won't have enough money to keep on running this place."

He has more than he wants to let on, Bunce thought, having seen his bank statement in the scrap basket. Tore it up he did, but not so it couldn't be pieced together.

"After lunch I went over to Roland Raymond, Raymond and Wedgewright," Chugh said. "Roland was waiting for me like a barracuda with all Mother's papers arranged in neat little piles on his great big flat-top desk, as if he expected trouble. He knows I think he wrote her will with an ulterior motive, and I think we can contest it if we want to. We can prove that he prejudiced her in favor of the Historical Society. He's president of it, you know, and this could be a big coup for him. Fellow may be smart, but he's a social climber. Anyway, he made me speechless with rage. As if he understood my dear mother's wishes and thoughts better than I did! Naturally he tried to get me to agree to probate right away, but I said you and I hadn't yet made up our minds what action to take."

"Well, did he explain to you exactly what the will meant?"

"The will hopes that you personally always remain in Finchwicke and continue to keep it up in the high state of cultivation to which her money and interest have brought it."

"Naturally I should do that!" Dr. Walding said. "Finch-wicke belongs to me anyway. And if Thessaly left me enough money, naturally I shall keep it in a high state of cultivation. What else was in the will?"

"Well, as you know, when Grandpa Chyldes sold the Three Brothers Foundry, he took back stock in the U.S. Steel Company. And you know that Uncle Knight, being the eldest and only son, inherited two-thirds and Mother divided one-third with Uncle Crispin. Her part is still all in Steel stock. Mother never changed that. Half the income to you, half to me. After you, sir, all to me."

"That seems fair."

"Well, it is, and it isn't. I never get any capital to use in my business. And after me, if I don't produce any children, the whole thing goes to the goddamn Historical Society."

"Maybe you better get married and have some children, Chugh!"

"I don't see any sign of it. But there is a further complication. The will requires that you and I live in Finchwicke together. You have to stay in it more or less all the time, and I have to spend half the year, or one hundred and eighty nights—I or a member of my immediate family. Otherwise my half goes to the Historical Society right away. As I have no immediate family to stand in for me, it does seem like a bit of a dead hand from the past—and unlike Mother. I can't help but think that Raymond put that in to get the money for the Historical Society, and Mother just didn't realize what she was signing. Of course he denies it. Says she came in with it all written out on a piece of Finchwicke notepaper and that the will is substantially as she herself wrote it. She had my best interest at heart, old Raymond said. As if he knew best! The old crook!"

"Does he have the piece of notepaper?"

"No. Naturally, he says it was torn up when the will was put in proper legal form."

Bunce stiffened and signaled to Delia to start around with the second helps so he need not miss a word. But this served only to interrupt the conversation while more food was refused and the plates, the silver filigree salts and peppers, and the butter plates were all removed, and crumbs from the table were swept onto a silver tray, and the flowered Dresden dessert plates were finally put down. On them were Valenciennes lace doilies and pale-green Venetian glass finger bowls in which floated a sprig of lemon geranium leaf. Dessert was an open apple tart with slices of orange cheese.

"Made from our own greenings?" Dr. Walding inquired of Bunce.

"Yes, sir."

There was a moment's silence as they waited for Bunce to retire into the pantry out of earshot. After giving the door a swing, he merely went behind the screen, where he stood listening. What about the Sus-E-Rurs, Bunce wanted to know.

"What's so humiliating to me is that I have to give proof to the Historical Society, whatever that means."

"Well, I do agree with you, Chugh. It is a most extraordinary will. But of course it does *me* no harm. As I said before, Finchwicke belongs to me and naturally I intend to stay here. And naturally I would enjoy your company also."

"Well, that's nice of you to say so, sir. But it is rather a forced setup. You might decide to get married again, and then you wouldn't want me hanging around."

Dr. Walding gave little grimace of pain. "That's not very amusing, Chugh. I can't think of anything more distasteful to me than getting married again, except possibly the thought of fighting my wife's will. And I sincerely hope you don't intend to."

"Well, it gripes me, having to report to the Historical Society where I spend my nights. I don't believe poor darling

Mummy understood at all for one minute how much she was insulting me. I think it's all a put-up job by Roly Raymond."

"Oh, don't be silly, Chugh. You're taking it too literally, I'm sure. Spend your nights wherever you want, and I'll not give you away. Delia will look after me."

Mr. Chugh didn't answer, and Bunce's heart sank as another long silence enveloped the two men. Not a word had they said about the provisions for the servants in Madam's will. Surely they couldn't have been completely forgotten. A foggy chill settled around his chest.

"I think I intend to fight the will."

"I hope you'll think that over." Dr. Walding was visibly upset as he pushed back his chair, unable to sit there any longer.

He repeated, "I hope you'll think that over. Think it over carefully. And as I said before, don't worry about me. Oh, my poor Thessaly." His bent shoulder humped up to hit his ear, and he blew his nose. "I'm all upset. If you'll excuse me, Chugh, I think I'll go right to bed. I'm rather tired." And then, in an effort to end the evening on a pleasant note, as the Doctor passed the bowl of calling cards he added, "It was charming of Faith Hoagland to come in. Did a lot to cheer me up. Like mother, like daughter, they say. But in this case I just don't think it's true. She reminds me so much of her father, the Judge."

"That will remain to be seen," said Chugh.

From the outside court, looking up at the roof of the kitchen wing, the dormer windows were architectural gems, the delicate mullions at the top weaving into an arch. But the maids' rooms inside, each tunneled out to one window, were little more than dark cells, stuffy and hot in summer, freezing in winter. In the center of the large square hall were piled the family trunks used to pack clothing, blankets, and silverware for the summer trips to Heron Bay. Around the edge were the doors to the servants' rooms: the cook, kitchenmaid, laundress, chambermaid, and parlormaid. At one end of the attic, without any daylight or ventilation, were two curtained stalls, one containing a toilet, the other a high-backed iron tub on claw feet.

Earlier that evening, during the servants tea hour, these facilities and the servants' rooms had been empty as Delia had stumbled up the last steep flight of stairs, hurled herself into her room and slammed the door.

After Miss Hoagland left, Delia had been carrying the heavy tea tray from the library to the pantry when a sudden cramp had seized her. Somehow she had managed to make her way through the dining room's swinging door to the sink, where the tray went down with a bang on the grooved wooden counter. Bending over, she held on until the mighty fist in her guts relaxed its grasp. It was joy like lightning—but also terror of what might be going to happen here in the pantry—floods of water coming down the insides of her legs. The pain went away, and she rushed up the back stairs not pausing to mop up the puddle.

A large basket of monogrammed linens from the dead mistress's bed and bathroom had been sitting in the second-floor back hall for a couple of days, having been left there by the laundress for Mrs. Bunce, housekeeper and lady's maid, to put away. Since the linen closets were conveniently located in the passageway connecting the Bunce apartment to the main house, it would have been perfectly easy for Mrs. Bunce to trot back and forth and put them away. But since Madam's death she had done precious little trotting. So Mrs. Bunce wouldn't notice the loss, Delia thought, as she scooped up an armful of lace-edged towels and kept on going up the stairs.

Once in her room, she had bolted the door, got out of her clothes as fast as she could and made a small nest of the fancy linens on the floor where she might lie—before another great gust of pain brought forth what appeared to be a small piece of meat, and then great clots of dark jellied blood, and then, as the cramps ceased, trickle of bright red. Delia lay there for a while in a daze of blissful relief. She was no longer carrying Mr. Chugh's child. It was over.

Delia had been going to tell Madam, because it had gotten to the stage where it was impossible to hide. But after Madam died, she was afraid to think of what would happen to her. She had no money saved. All of it (besides what the priest at the Roman Catholic Church of Our Lady of Good Counsel in Penngwynne had extracted from her in penance after her confession of guilt) was sent home to Ireland. Delia thought of the long stony lane in Connemara that led up the side of the mountain, of the thorn hedges that lined the lane, and of the thatched cottage at the end. She thought of her mother's careworn face; of the dark wiry man wrapped in a cloak, who was her father; of the one starving cow in the byre; of the empty, swinging teats of the thin old sow and the handful of hens scrabbling in the dirt near the open door. The potato crop was blighted again, her mother had written, and the fishing in the Loch was owned by a bloody English lord. All that kept her parents and her four sisters and five brothers alive was the money Delia sent to buy a few groceries.

"Holy Mother of Jesus," she cried, the tears streaming down her face, "in thankfulness for this answer to my prayers, I will sin no more."

Of course the nuns would have taken the baby away from her once it was born, but how would it have been born? Would she have had to leave her job? This was what had been worrying her that morning when she had weighed herself in Mr. Chugh's bathroom and found she had gained three more pounds.

Let Mr. Chugh keep his soft bed to himself. Her own room never looked so welcome as she lay there on the floor trying to gather strength to go down and serve the dinner. Even the large gobbet of dust hanging under the sagging iron bedspring seemed a friend, as did the hard straw mattress on top, the cheap wooden bureau, and the small mirror draped with her rosary and its crucifix. Stuck in the corner of the mirror's frame was a dried-up cross of palm and a colored card of Jesus by the Sea of Galilee, His pierced heart shining through the flimsy material of His white nightgown. On the bureau a large alarm clock with a bell was ticking loudly. It stood at five forty-five. She had been here on the splintering, bare floorboards nearly an hour.

Bunce would be wondering where she was. And she didn't want Mr. Chugh to think she wasn't well. Not yet. She had to think it over. Pulling herself up from the floor, she rolled the bloody linen into a ball and hid it under the bed, and, still naked, she hastened out to fill her pitcher with warm water from the tub.

As she washed herself, then dried with a flimsy bath towel and put on her evening uniform, Delia thought over how it had all begun. She was required to take a tray of Linden tea up to the master's room every night after he had gone to bed. Madam had always met her at the door in her nightgown and wrapper, her hair in two long, sandy-gray pigtails with pink bows on the ends, to take the tray inside. Now Delia took it in to his bedside herself. Then she was supposed to wait in the servants' sitting room until Mr. Chugh pulled the bell to signal that he too had gone up to his apartment. Then she would make the rounds, putting out all the lights.

But on one particular night Mr. Chugh had still been standing in the hall after ringing the bell, and he had asked her to bring a Scotch and soda up to his room where he planned to work late on some papers.

She had prepared a tray with a small cut-glass decanter, the siphon of soda, and a glass, and taken it to Mr. Chugh's room. Before she had had a chance to knock, he had opened the door and stood smiling down at her, baring his white teeth. He had waited while she set the tray down before advancing toward her. His eyes, she thought now, had been as blue as the fires of hell, as one by one he undid the buttons of her dress. Just for tonight, he had said, unloose your bonds. As her dress dropped to the floor he had seized her in his arms and swayed with her to the bed, where they had lain on top of the patchwork quilt, she in her corsets with her petticoats pushed up, he with his trousers pushed down. The next night Mr. Chugh had met her in his bathrobe and he had assured her that he had taken precautions that nothing could happen.

That had been four months ago.

Now buttoned into her tight black bombazine, in fresh apron and frilly white cap with black velvet streamers pinned to her topknot, Delia started down with the ball of linens to wash them out in the laundry herself, and then changed her mind. Blood was so difficult to wash out she would have to leave them soaking all night. The laundress would find them and tell Mr. Bunce, who would want to know what had happened. She kicked them back under the bed. I shall have to burn the whole lot, she thought, later, when the house is asleep.

Bunce was in a regular snit in the pantry. Delia noticed with relief that the puddle on the floor had been mopped up, although the tea tray was still on the counter. So weak she felt, and dizzy in the head, but she was determined to overcome it so that no one should guess what had happened. She went about her work, paying no attention at all to the rudeness of old Bunce, nor to the conversation the gentlemen were carrying on at dinner. In punishment for having been late, Bunce left all the dishes for her to do alone. She broke one of the pale-green finger bowls and secreted it in the garbage pail. No matter. That suited fine. Everything was now fine.

Cleaning up without any help took her such a long time that the kitchen was empty when she went in to get the boiling water for the Doctor's Linden tea. Not wanting to pass Mrs. Bunce's door, she took it up the front stairs, noting as she went through the hall that Mr. Chugh was in his mother's sitting room by himself. Let the light burn until morning. She was not going to turn it out.

The door to the master's bedroom at the end of the central part of the house stood open. A screen partially obscured the inner doorway. She gave a soft knock.

"Come in, my dear." The Doctor was propped up in his brass bed with many pillows, a knitted shawl around his shoulders and a fringed Scotch blanket draped over his feet. On his knees rested a thick dark book, a tome about the insects—his usual reading matter, perused under the light of a green-glass-shaded brass student's lamp on his beside table.

She put the tea down and said, "Is there anything more I can do for you sir?"

He looked at her with moist eyes and moist lips, "Delia," he said, reaching out to find her soft hand with his bony gnarled one. "Something I must say to you. You have been so very kind to me during these last weeks since I have lost my wife. Delia, promise that you'll never leave me! That you'll see me through to the end. And I'll promise to take care of you."

Delia felt sorry for the old man in his loneliness. And a promise of being taken care of was something she had never heard before. Without thinking she replied, "Of course, sir. I'll never leave you, sir."

She felt his hand pulling her down, as he said, "Then kiss me goodnight."

She bent, intending to kiss his translucent veined high-boned forehead, but with a quick little jerk he had transferred her lips to meet his loose, moist ones hidden under his gray mustache. His other hand patted her through her full skirts, helping to keep her bosom pressed lightly against his pajamaed chest. Then he let her go. "Ah," he said, "if age but could. However, just open the windows and pull my curtains. I'm afraid that's all you can do for me, my dear. And bring my hot lemon juice at seven-thirty. I will have breakfast late with Mr. Chugh after he comes in from hunting. The hounds are meeting in the Forty Acres."

"Yes, sir. Goodnight, sir." And then instead of proceeding back downstairs to wait in the pantry for Mr. Chugh to ring for his Scotch, Delia turned and went as softly as she could up the creaking attic stairs.

The 'tween was already exhausted in her bed and lightly snoring. The laundress had her door shut also. A crack of light showed through the kitchenmaid's door. She was probably waiting for the cook, who was on the toilet with the curtain pulled and a bath running. As no one had seen Delia, and as she was not expected upstairs this early, Delia snatched the bloody bundle of linen from under her bed and made her way back down to the ground floor, pushing shut the swinging door between the front hall and the back hall as she passed. Taking a candle from the pantry shelf, she felt her way down into the huge cobwebby caverns of the cellar, its bins filled for the winter with gleaming lumps of coal. Seizing the poker, she opened the door of the giant furnace which had been banked down for the night by the man outside who attended to it. She stuffed the fancy bloody sheets onto the hot bed of ashy coals and watched as slowly they turned to a singed yellow and then brown and then began to curl up in flames around the edges. The acrid smell of burning blood filled her nostrils. Suddenly the wind seemed to blow down the chimney with a great puff of the evil smoke so that she banged the door shut. She raised her arms in a great gesture of incantation, still holding the poker as if to exorcise the devil from the soul of the burning baby. "Hail Mary! Full of grace! Blessed be the fruit of thy womb. Jesus!"

She backed away, dropping the poker, picked up the candle, and exhausted though she was, she felt as if she were floating up the stairs. Delia ignored Mr. Chugh's tray waiting in the pantry and took the front stairs now, just to be sure that he was still sitting in his mother's room so that she could also ignore her duty of turning out the lights. He was. She thought he had turned his head to peer out at her, but she did not turn.

Passing the pilfered laundry basket in the second-floor back hall, she thought, Let Mrs. Bunce count the linen if she's not too lazy. She ll never find out now where it went. And if she asks me, I'll tell her, into the fires of hell it went!

She floated up to the attic, around the pile of shrouded trunks and into her own narrow cell. She shut the door. Hail Mary! Let Mrs. Bunce count the linen; let Mr. Chugh wait for his Scotch and soda and his roll on top of the quilt, let him wait until hell froze over. From now on she would devote herself to taking care of the Doctor, as she had promised.

Immediately after dinner Chugh stood in the hall and watched his father creep up the flying circular stairs like a crab, his head bent over, hanging onto the banisters. He was furious. Why this blatant bid for sympathy, going up to bed before the port, before the last cigar in the library? He tried to find pity in his heart for the old man but there was only disdain. Let each man bear his own loss and sorrow like a man. Chugh had felt his mother's death like losing a limb; every nerve in his body ached as though the amputated member were still there. But now it seemed that his feelings were being manipulated by his father and tainted by the conditions of his mother's will. The sorrow and sadness that he had felt was no longer pure and simple but had become a witch's brew of greed and pity. He needed his mother's money, which was rightfully his, to live on. He didn't relish the thought of scrabbling for a living without any chips to play the game. And pity—pity for his father's lonely old age—was to be the sweetener which would enable him to accept the yoke of other people's plans for his young life instead of making his own—to submit, in fact, to being immobilized at Finchwicke.

Out of pure force of habit, he started toward the drawing room, to demand an explanation from his mother, and then remembered she wasn't there. So he went back into the library to sit alone by the dying fire. But it was not comfortable for him there, the memory of the disagreeable predinner conversation about the servants' money still hanging in the air. And the eyes of Sir Percy seemed to have become accusatory, looking down at him from the wall, holding his book with the inscription, "Before him lie the fruits in their seasons, and the lovely gardens; around him float the messengers of love." How sour and ironic. He abruptly decided not to stay in this particular room but to sit instead in his mother's parlor across the hall. In her particular room he might yet be able to recapture the cheerful, acerbic spirit that he missed so much. Everything he did had been good in Mother's eyes.

One small lamp was lit on her table. The green taffeta sewing bag hung down underneath. Here she had so often sat to do her embroidery, picking the colored threads from the beak of the gold stork clamped to the table's edge. There were her tiny scissors and her magnifying sewing glasses lying exactly where she had left them. On the floor was the elaborate needlepoint rug trellised with roses which had taken her years to complete and which had been exhibited last year by the Colonial Dames. Her curly maple desk in the corner had been cleared of the neat bundles of letters and bills and checkbooks which were usually stacked on it; Chugh had been intending to do it himself, but evidently his father had already been busy there that day. And the purple glass vase on top was empty of its usual bouquet. The fire was laid with three glistening birch logs brought by his mother every year from Maine, and beneath was spread a white paper fan. There were no ashes since the fire was rarely lit, his mother never feeling cold. Since the flue from the new furnace had to occupy part of this chimney, the draft from the hearth was not very good in a damp east wind, and on the rare occasions when his mother did light the fire she made Delia take out the birch logs and the fan and replace them with regular firewood. Over the mantel, against the cream-colored paneling, hung a small oil painting of the ocean and the fir trees and the rocks in the view from her bedroom in Heron Bay, done by Chugh when he was eighteen. That had been one period of his life just before going to the university when he had thought of making painting his career. And on the mantel shelf stood Aunt Sarah's collection of Staffordshire dogs—greyhounds and spaniels and curly poodles—which had also overflowed onto the bookcase among the cookbooks and gardening books.

Chugh sat down in his regular place opposite his mother's chair, on a tufted horsehair love seat. He filled his pipe from a leather pouch which he took from the pocket of his garnet velvet jacket, tamped it carefully with a match and lit it, put his arm across the back of the couch and one foot up on the seat—the way he had always sat there. Suddenly his mother's presence was palpable in the chair opposite as though she were eagerly waiting there to hear his private news for her ears only. He began to present her with little bits of the day, with his thoughts, as though it had been in conversation.

I absolutely must have a change, Mother. This place is so redolent of you. And you were always everything. It's not good for me to settle down alone with Father, just waiting for him to die! It's unthinkable. He's completely selfish and impractical, like an elderly child. I can't tell what he'll do on the next impulse, like thumbing through your checkbooks and wanting to up the servants' wages when he never even knew what they got paid while you were running the house. And like forcing Faith Hoagland in here and making her pour tea

*when obviously she had only intended to drop a card. I mean
I'm fond of Father—but—I'm not sure he likes me or that I
can cope with him.*

*Mother, I must get away and have a complete change. And
there's a war on, and you know that Knight Chyldes has
already joined up. You always said that anything Knight could
do, I could do better. Sort of a dare situation between us.
You remember that, don't you? We talked about it, just a few
weeks ago. I know you said it was different for Knight to go,
because he's not an only. Tanta Chyldes also has a daughter,
Edith, and she's already married, and so Tanta will have
grandchildren, although personally I can't imagine Edith a
mother. She was always a tomboy. Not in the least bit maternal. And furthermore she married a goddamn foreign baron.
You did point out that I haven't gotten married to anyone.
Nevertheless, this is something I just have to do. Get out of
here, I mean. Take my chances!*

He could hear Johnny Oldthwaite's voice now: "But dammit, Chugh, Knight's a flyer, and you don't know how to fly.
You've never even been up, have you?" "I'm taking lessons!"
he had replied. They had been sitting together in the tiny
corner room that served as the office of the investment firm
of Oldthwaite, Walding & Co. on the fifth floor of the bank,
each in his own corner at his own roll-top desk, swiveled
toward each other, talking. "Of course I'd like to get away
too," Johnny had surprised him by saying, leaning away to
look out the bay window at the view of Broad Street below,
"but for me it's out of the question. Paula and the children."
They had both looked at the only photograph on Johnny's
desk, his wife in front of the baronial fireplace at Oldebrooke, the family granite castle which his grandfather had
built. Paula in a tea gown with a rose at her breast, her hair
in a loose knot at the nape of her neck, was holding a fat
baby at arm's length on her knee, Johnny the Fourth, known
as Quartus. A small Scottish terrier was being fondled by two
little girls sitting cross-legged on the floor. Chugh had often
thought that he himself might have married Paula if only
he'd been a year older—if Johnny hadn't gotten her first. She
was indeed lovely, and very amusing too. By an effort of will,
Chugh had shifted his eyes away from the picture. Paula was
forbidden fruit. Johnny was indeed a lucky man!

Chugh had said, "Well, dammit, I have no family and I'm
not about to get one." The only photograph on Chugh's desk
was one of himself and his mother, she in flowing sidesaddle

habit of her huge hunter, holding the lead line of his Shetland pony. He had put his mind back on the war. "I don't know what old Roly's going to say, but I'm on my way to his office as soon as I finish up here. Knight wants to join up with the French army. Lafayette stuff, you know."

Hearing this, Johnny Oldthwaite had relaxed. "Well, as I understand it, the French won't take anyone, the British won't take anyone, and the U.S.A. won't let anyone so. So he can forget it."

"You're probably right. But Knight thinks he has a gimmick for getting in. He's already in England. Of course, I'd leave you complete power of attorney for running the business while I'm gone—if I go!" Chugh had said. That was the moment that Johnny had asked him the pointed question, leaning back in his swivel chair and bouncing the points of his fingers together. "What is your cash situation going to be, Chugh? I've heard of a chemical factory we can buy and—"

At that moment, in the Finchwicke ladies' parlor, there was a rustle in the green-and-lavender flowered curtains as though a breath of air had moved them. Mother had forever been seeing the Finchwicke ghosts move curtains, but Chugh saw that the draft must have been caused by the opening and closing of the door from the back into the front hall as Delia went through carrying a tray with the Linden tea, on her way up the stairs to his father's bedroom.

A thought came to him. Something must be done about Delia and done damned quickly. His mother's will had left a provision that he and his father make suitable gifts to the servants of up to one hundred dollars each, depending on their length of service. Old Bunce would qualify. And Mudd the gardener. Delia could probably only get twenty. What would a doctor charge anyway? Whatever it was, it would have to come out of Chughs own pocket. But she must be gotten rid of quickly. Money would do it no doubt. Thank God there were no real feelings involved. *You never really liked her, Mother, it was only Father. And at one point I thought I was fond of her. But now she has become unbearable, so that before I leave I must see her off the place. Because if I don't, if I leave her alone here with Father, the old fool might even marry her! And though it's my baby she's carrying, maybe she could persuade him it was his! It would be my brother! My brother could inherit Finchwicke, which, after all, belongs to the old man. It was the one thing you could not give to the Historical Society, Mother, the thing you cared about most!*

"Maybe now you understand my plans, my sets of thoughts," seemed to come from the empty chair opposite.

"So that's what you meant!" Chugh startled himself by speaking out loud. "I see. I see that Father must not be left alone. The senile old man and the pretty maid ... the old fool!"

Again he remembered Roland Raymond's ice-pick voice, earlier in the day. "The will says that either you or a member of your immediate family must spend half the year at Finchwicke as long as your father is alive, or your half of the income from her estate, which I may say is considerable, goes to the Historical Society . . ."

"Thank you very much," Chugh had replied angrily, "but my private life is and will remain my own and not the property of the Historical Society. You will know very shortly what my decision is in the matter of contesting this will. In the meantime, one more question. As I am in need of immediate cash for a business deal, is there any loose money, saving accounts and so forth, which might be coming to me outright?" (*How could you have not left me any money, Mother!*)

The lawyer's dry voice had continued as though he were checking items off a laundry list rather than bits of flesh and blood. "All her savings and checking accounts, after debts and funeral expenses are paid, go to her husband. All her personal effects go to you. It appears from the bank's records that she had some jewelry in the vault there, and I assume there are some other things at Finchwicke. However, if I might suggest it, with your credit it is always possible to borrow money from the bank."

"And there are no other provisions in the will?"

"No other provisions. Except that she asks that you and your father make suitable gifts to the servants of up to one hundred dollars each, depending on their length of service."

As if by mutual consent both had stood up, and Chugh had started to leave without shaking hands.

"Remember me to your father. And if you'll permit me to offer my sympathies, I was a great friend of Thessaly's, you know. I think she trusted me. I hope that you will too."

Then, as though the lawyer sensed that he had been untactful, he added, "The date of this will is as of August twentiful, this year, 1914. Could she, by any chance, have thought that you had plans to leave Finchwicke? That might have prompted her to insert this rather unusual provision? Or perhaps she had reasons to desire that you acquire an immediate family? It seems to me that Thessaly left you rather a large loophole there."

A large family! That thought seemed to come from the chair by the sewing table. August. Just about when Knight had taken off for England, wasn't it? It was such an outrageous dead hand from the past, so like her, that Chugh laughed out loud at her. Tomorrow he must go to the vaults of the bank and see what jewelry was there. As his mother never wore anything except her wedding band and her watch, he didn't know what she possessed.

The lawyer's words came back to him again. "It seems to me that Thessaly left you rather a large loophole there."

He got up from the small sofa and desecrated the fireplace by knocking out his pipe and sprinkling ashes over the white paper fan. As he leaned over, a puff of acid smoke billowed out into his face, as if a sudden east wind had caused a down draft in the flue. He must speak to Bunce about having the furnace cleaned out. *At any rate, Mother, it blew the ashes off your precious fan.* He opened the door wider for air as the vile smell clung in his nostrils, then he sat down again on the horsehair sofa, his head on his hands.

There would have to be some sacrificial act to purify this place. It was contaminated. *But why me, Mother? Why should I be the one? Of course, if I got married, I could leave here, could go to the war.* The thought struck him with so much force of his own meanness that he intended to bury it as if it had never been. But he couldn't put it out of his mind. *In what other way could I protect Father and still do what I want? Protect Finchwicke. Protect myself, really. Who? Faith Hoagland? Now, really, Mother!*

Chugh had never considered marrying a girl like Faith Hoagland. From next door. Whom he had merely nodded to all his life. He had pictured himself with a long-stemmed girl, rather languorous and very beautiful, a girl who wouldn't be able to exist without his taking care of her. Not a short girl, filled with unattractive, boyish energy, who likes to wear bloomers and would be more than all right on her own.

He made a joke to the chair opposite. *I want somebody willowy, and she's going to be pillowy!* He waited for the ghost to appreciate him. *Now, Mother, stop pushing me around. I'm not going to marry her. As I've often told you, when I fall in love, you'll know, because as a sign I'll shave off my beard.* He gave a small smile of affection toward the empty chair. But as suddenly as the ghost had come, it had gone. He knew that he was alone in his mother's sitting room. He must speak to Bunce about having the flues cleaned. What a vile smell.

He rang the bell for Delia to come and put out the lights, intending to tell her that it was late and he was exhausted and wished to go straight to bed alone. He waited, but she did not come. He decided not to ring again and put out the lights himself.

Tomorrow they must have a talk about all this. After he came in from hunting and before he went to town . . .

3

Hunting

IN HER tower bedroom, Faith had tossed and turned most of the night. It was silly to think she had fallen in love at first sight because she had known Chugh all her life, but yesterday afternoon as they stood on the front steps of Finchwicke and she had felt the expert pressure of his fingers sending lightning up her arm, she had realized with great surprise that Chugh Walding, who had been continually laughed at by her brothers, was indeed the one person who could save her from a life of dull and worthy servitude to her mother—if *only* he found her sufficiently desirable! He had polished up her innocence with a luster of its own, which had withstood Mama's withering brilliance. His wicked touch had made her *feel* beautiful!

In the dark she slipped from her restless bed and turned on the lamp. The roses on the wallpaper jumped to life. The linen sheets were in a ball. The afghan and the rag doll were on the floor. The spaniel in his basket on the red carpet opened one disapproving eye. In her long-sleeved, ruffled white batiste nightgown, she slipped onto her knees for morning prayers. "Thy will be done," thundered through her body, as she bowed her head, "on earth as it is in heaven." No other part of the prayer made sense, but these words leaped to a new life of their own. For her to love Chugh Walding and to live with him all the rest of her life was the inexorable plan of God. Surely Bellwood and Vivi couldn't have experienced anything as overwhelming as this.

By the time Ma'selle appeared in her dressing gown and curl papers, Faith was already dressed in her hunting underwear, long tight drawers, short corset, a complicated harness to keep the bosom from bouncing. Ma'selle was carrying a breakfast tray. But to feel hungry ever again was unimaginable and Faith was not able to down the hot tea. She pulled on the tight gabardine breeches, her boots, then a pin-striped collarless silk shirt. Ma'selle fastened the crystal fox-head cuff links and wrapped her neck twice around in a white bird's-eye silk stock, jabbing in eight tiny safety pins to hold it down in back. She spread it out across Faith's bosom and pinned its snowy folds at the top with an oval crystal brooch picturing a miniature hunt scene. Next the tan gabardine sidesaddle skirt, kirtled up behind for walking; a tattersall vest with the Hunt buttons of the Silvermist Hounds; a long, flaring, wasp-waisted jacket; and finally a bowler hat set firmly down straight over her eyebrows and tied on with a veil through which poked the end of her nose. Her slippery hair was skewered into a neat doughnut and covered with a brown silk net below the derby's brim in back.

Blowing a good-bye kiss to Ma'selle and confident that her uniform was correct for cubbing, Faith picked her way down the golden oak staircase, trying to avoid the creaking steps, and went out through the conservatory and into the chill of the dawn. The sun was a rosy flush above the black woods behind the barn toward which she was heading. The stars were fading in the multicolors of the translucent sky while the world about her was still darkest green. In the barnyard the cock was crowing his head off, a cow milking in the farm barn across the road was bellowing for her calf. Birds were awake and scolding. The separate world of the dawn creatures received her into its magic as she hurried away from the shadowy wedding-cake house, down the tarmac path across the lawn and past the lily pond, into the ammoniac vapors of the stables rising like an aphrodisiac, sharp in the nostrils of the huntress.

In the tower of the coach house, the arms of the stable clock pointed to a quarter of six. Faith entered by the side door where in ghostly darkness stood the hulks of the road coach, the buckboard, the station cab, the jaunting cart, the trap, the basket phaeton, and a variety of pony carts, goat carts, and sleighs.

A long corridor of standing stalls connected this building with another, as ornately shingled and gabled as the first. Here the carriages horses—Trooper and Corporal, Fire and Smoke, and Jack—snorted and stamped at the sounds of activity not meant for them.

Lights were on in the third building, the hunter barn, where preparations for the morning ride had been going on for the last hour. Nine large box stalls of dark varnished wood formed a square court around a clay floor, the spacious quarters of the family riding horses—the pony, the brood-mare, Mayflower, and the new colt, Plymouth Rock, who was going to be made into a second hunter for Faith.

Quinn was in the stall girthing up Stormy Weather. This enormous gray gelding pulled a plough in summer and hunted in the fall, his iron mouth being immune to Quinn's savage jerks. Dressed in breeches and boots, but still in shirt sleeves, Quinn's nose was wrinkled up in a permanent sniff, exposing the white hairs in his nostrils, stiff as hog bristles. His face had set this way, so that one could never tell what mood he was in—enjoying the moment or worrying about his old age. Quinn had never worked for any other family since arriving on the boat from Ireland long before Faith could remember. He had taken the job as stable boy and risen to coachman, and the Judge had thought so much of Quinn that in his will he left it that Quinn should always have work from some member of the Hoagland family for as long as he should desire. This had been bestowed as a great privilege, more valuable than a sum of money.

But Faith knew things were beginning to bother Quinn. What would happen when he couldn't keep on working? Several times he had said he felt he was too old to take her out hunting, but he would not give in and let Paddy go with her. "She goes too far and too fast," he had complained to Mrs. Hoagland. "She should take it easy in the back with me. Someday she's going to get hurt!"

Faith had only laughed. What fun would it be hanging in the back with the grooms? None!

As she arrived, Quinn was giving one last heave to tighten his horse's girth, while Stormy with his pale eyes rolling and his ears pinned back resisted by holding up his tail and pushing out his ribs.

Quinn only managed the briefest, muttered good morning. Sensing his gloomy mood, Faith proceeded into the tack room. Warmed by a potbellied stove, two well-worn leather chairs stood by the row of men's boots. The dark, paneled walls were lined with racks of well-kept saddles and bridles with gleaming bits and buckles, and a glass case housed the bright rosettes of horse-show ribbons collected by her father and brothers and herself over the years. Faith helped herself to a lump of sugar from a glass jar and took her hunting crop with the carved ivory handle and the long braided thong from its peg on the wall.

Nimblewit stood tied near the door while Joe Monaghan, Paddy's son, the stable boy, finished picking out the last bit of straw and manure from her feet with an evil-looking hook. Then he applied a coat of varnish to shine her black hooves, stripped off the blue-and-buff checkered sheet with Faith's initials appliquéd in the corners, and with a towel wiped off an imaginary speck of dust which might have fallen from the ceiling onto the saddle beneath. He led the dainty bay mare to the mounting block, where Faith unhooked the back of her skirt to cover the pommels and eased onto the saddle. She picked up the reins and patted the silky long neck as the mare shifted, adjusting to her weight. The boy tightened the girths and the balance strap, gave a last shine to the toe of her left boot poking out below her skirt, and Faith was ready. Not to keep Nimble standing, she made small circles around in the grass, waiting for Quinn.

When he appeared in his rusty tweed coat and battered bowler, keeping a tight hold on the reins to keep from being jiggled off, they made their way together down the steep, winding, gravel drive. At the gothic gatehouse, Faith paused to discuss the alternate routes to the Finchwicke Forty. "We could take the road all the way, or jump in there." She indicated with her crop handle a log jump immediately opposite the drive. "Or do you think we would disturb any foxes along the way?"

"It's a cart tract through the field and a trail along the creek and I can't see any harm at all in jumping in here."

With a nod of her head, Faith flew over the logs and was well into the meadow on the other side before Quinn recovered himself from Stormy's tremendous jump. He had landed well back on the gelding's rump and lost both stirrups. Stormy's mouth was now open and foaming, his lower jaw pulled back from the strangle hold Quinn had on the reins.

Cheeks puffed, Quinn caught up with her. "Should have gone down the road so early in the morning," he said. "Many's the time I drove your father, the Judge, down that road. Every time they had one of them Gentleman Farmer Club dinners."

Faith applied pressure with her leg to Nimblewit's side, loping along in a comfortable, slow canter, while Quinn, pounding his saddle with all his weight, stayed right with her. At the edge of the fenced meadow, Faith urged Nimblewit on faster, kicking up little puffs of dust in the dry grass, and jumped into the woods which filled the valley of the Silvermist Creek.

Suddenly a call and the crack of a whip broke the stillness.

Out of the morning river mist ahead of them loomed the waving sterns of the hounds, jogging along around the Huntsman in his salt-sack coat and black velvet cap.

"Get on you, Warrior! Aahh, Warrior! Get in to him! Pack up you, Digby! Aahh!" With a loud crack of his whip, young Ham Birdgrove, the second whipper-in, was urging on an old hound coupled to a puppy who was attempting to pull away into the underbrush.

Faith and Quinn were automatically silent, as though they had now joined a sacred rite in Diana's temple. They reined in and joined the procession, adjusting their gait to the hounds jog of six miles an hour, keeping their distance in order not to press too close on a hound who from time to time might stop to relieve himself before again catching up with the pack. There were no greetings exchanged. The hunt servants and the hounds on their way to the meet were keeping to a world of their own.

Not far along they came to the ford where the stream widened out to level banks and the water rippled over rocky swallows. Led by the first Whip, with the Huntsman in the middle and the second Whip bringing up their rear, horses and hounds splashed in and scrambled up the beaten path on the other side; turning right they jumped a chicken coop into a grassy ride. Hounds coming from the kennels were met at this spot by the Master, old Mr. Charlton Seabreese. Sunk into his saddle, shoulders hunched, he was sitting in the shadows like a centaur, all of a piece with his big bay horse, Militiaman, who had won the Maryland four times, twice with the Master riding. The first Whip touched his cap with his crop and rode ahead to open the big red gate. The Master returned the gesture of greeting by raising his crop slightly, and with a muttered good morning, he wheeled and led his hounds out into the Finchwicke Forty.

The deep, mystical, and refreshing pure joy of the hunt! The reddening eastern sky, the dew rising from the grass in a breast-high fog, heavy with the clean ammoniac smell of the horses. Faith's foot pressed in excitement against the cold steel of the stirrup as she and her horse moved into the heart of the mystery of life, the deep visceral pull between the hunter and the hunted.

There was already a gathering of people. Some had arrived posthaste in buggies, having sent their grooms and horses on ahead to walk the distances slowly; and the vehicles were now drawn up in a neat row at the edge while riders and drivers changed places. Those already mounted were walking around in circles chatting in twos and threes, in order to keep their horses moving. A few tiny children on lead lines, surrounded by groups of older children, were paraded around by grooms who would not otherwise be privileged by Mr. Seabreese to hunt, unless, of course, like Quinn, they accompanied a lady on a sidesaddle. In the corner, a group of farmers over whose land the hunt galloped and who could not therefore be excluded, clubbed together, laughing and joking on their rough horses, nags who were used to drawing the plough when not being ridden. The country people hunted together in the back of the Field, looking for the low places in the fences, cutting corners to keep up as best they could with the fleet-footed thoroughbreds.

On arrival, Quinn immediately joined this group, fading into the fringes of the meet, while Faith rode forward to say good morning to Mr. Seabreese, who had stationed himself in the center of the Field, surrounded by the pack and flanked by the watchful Whips, thongs of their crops hanging down at the ready to dust a straying hound.

Everyone knew that Mr. Seabreese was not one to chat at the meet, and that the formality of greeting all who dared approach him would be gotten over with as rapidly as possible, with a nod, a salute of his crop, or a lift of his cap to a lady. His entire world was the breeding and feeding of horses and hounds, the habits and habitats of foxes, the special atmospheric conditions which made for good scenting. During off-hunting hours, when necessary, he would hobnob genially with the farmers on the subject of fences, crops and livestock, and vixens and their cubs. But with the exception of his brother, Welch, who worked indoors as president of the bank, taking care of the family fortunes and siring large numbers of children to carry on the family name, the Master consorted only rarely with other members of the landed gentry, and then mostly at the insistence of his brother's wife, Rhoda, who stood near him at all the meets. As Faith well knew, ladies at the dinner table dreaded him, finding that the Master had fortified himself beyond the point of intelligible conversation. His only contribution to their more formal evenings was a song, a spirited tenor rendering of "Wrap me in my old racing colors/And say a bold rider lies low, lies low ..." for which he was always called on, and after which he always sat down abruptly and lapsed back into graven stone.

Thus he only grudgingly suffered the Field for these few

moments. Faith was careful as she circled up to him, not to approach the hounds too closely, and to unobtrusively scan the gathering for Chugh Walding. Chugh had said he was coming, but where was he? She started to brace herself for the familiar feeling of high hopes dashed. "Good morning, Mr. Seabreese!" she said brightly, then turned away to permit others to file up. Out of the corner of her eye, she glimpsed Chugh arriving now, trotting along the lane from Finchwicke on Paint, the wall-eyed Appaloosa that he had had shipped East from the E Bar L Ranch two summers ago.

To hide the fact that she had noticed him, Faith called another "Good morning," to her old school friend, Gladys Whitefield, who, with red and cheerful face, now moved up beside her on her roan horse, Soup-Plates. Gladys was a girl's girl who had been popular at school but despised at dances. ("You must dance with Gladys tonight," Becca had always said to Bellwood and Rick, "because her mother is my best friend." But they had always replied, "Not even for five dollars!") In spite of having been a gooseberry, Gladys was now engaged ahead of Faith, to be married in two years to Kent Stynchman, who taught Latin and Greek at Chetford Hills Academy. She didn't see how Gee could have fallen in love with someone that prosaic. "She has to take what she can get!" Rick had commented with brotherly rudeness. "God knows she's nothing to look at. Like a bureau with the drawers pulled out!" But with every fresh insult hurled at her friend, Faith became more loyal. And at this particular moment she was especially glad of her company.

"Wouldn't you have thought Chugh Walding would have come out to the meet, because it's right here? Or do you suppose it's because he's in mourning for darling Mum?" Gladys hissed cozily. Faith was relieved that her friend had not yet spotted the approaching horseman, so she continued the subterfuge. "But he said he was coming out!" Gladys' little blue pig eyes lit up, and Faith immediately regretted the deception, for Gladys loved to pry into the things of the heart. In fact, Gee was always the first to hear all the gossip and to pass it on with embroidery, which, when it was about other people, made her company so delightful. "Where did you see *him?*" came the automatic question. Faith lied, "Yesterday at the Penngwynne Station. I was there, meeting Bellwood."

At this moment, Mr. Seabreese took out his watch and glanced at the Huntsman which was the signal for moving off. Leo sounded a short note on his horn and the Whip called "Hounds, please," to some children in his path. Gladys and Faith stood still, turning their horses' heads toward the pack as they made their way once around the large meadow which sloped up steeply to the Guard Hill woods, a big covert of twenty acres, through which ran the Finchwicke boundary near the top of the hill.

"Look," Gladys said, pointing with her crop as together they jogged along behind the Master up the hill. It was Chugh on his Appaloosa, dancing sideways, kicking up curls of dust, coming out of the lane onto the edge of the field where some of the buggies were attempting to leave. To get away from the confusion, Chugh let his horse rip up the hill until he came to a crashing, foaming halt, narrowly missing bumping into the two girls.

"How is Paint this morning?" Faith asked, getting in the first word and feeling rather superior as Nimblewit stood quietly with her dainty ears pricked forward, contrasting very well with Paint, the enormous brown splotches of hair on his thick white coat already curly and dark with sweat.

"Thought Paint wasn't fit," Chugh gasped out, "but dammit, I guess I'm the one who's not fit. Anyway, good morning." Chugh attempted to raise his velvet Master's cap, green with age, which he wore by virtue of having had one or two couple of hounds of his own, the Finchwicke Hounds, when he was a boy. His wearing it was looked on with disfavor by the old guard as an affectation, Faith knew, but it was certainly very becoming to him, as was his frayed, well-fitted tweed jacket, straight from Savile Row.

Now, as he attempted to raise the disputed headpiece in a greeting to the ladies, the Appaloosa reared up, waving both feathered white front feet, and then came crashing down on top of Soup-Plates' rear. But Gladys' horse never budged under her weight sitting there like a bag of potatoes. People with jigging horses often sought her side as a calming influence, a haven in a storm. "Mind if I ride with you, Gladys?" Chugh asked as his horse stood trembling, pressed against her tail.

"Sometimes I kick," Gladys said placidly. Faith glowed with pleasure that her love and her best friend were hitting it off. One of her worries ticked off the list.

The Master turned and glared at all the commotion.

"I don't think he's been out of the barn for a week," Chugh said. "He's feeling his oats. You didn't happen to see him turned out yesterday, did you, Miss Faith, when you came calling?" Faith turned scarlet at this indiscretion in front of Gladys.

The sun, now rising behind the trees, cast a long deep shadow along the top edge of the meadow. All was expectant within the woods as the Huntsman approached it with his hounds packed tightly around him. He took off his cap and suddenly released them with a sweep of his arm and a blood-curdling cry, casting them into the darkness. Now one Whip galloped off to the right and the other one to the left, to take up their lookout posts at the far corners of the covert so that they might detect Renard, should he try to sneak away to open fields or toward St. Jude's Cemetery. The hunters remained outside with the Master, facing the covert, listening carefully for the first hound to give tongue, Guard Hill being a huge wood, within which a wily fox could run in circles all morning. Nimble stood like a statue, Faith a part of her mare as together they listened. She was not ungrateful that Chugh had moved off to the outskirts, as Paint was still jigging, without any intention of standing still.

It was inexcusable to make conversation at such a moment; nevertheless Gladys murmured to Faith, "I hear Bellwood's engaged, and that *she* came out to pass the night at your house last night."

But now a hound spoke, sending a current of excitement passing down Faith's spine and stiffening Nimblewit, who also knew the meaning of that deep bell. Gladys' head came up, as she, too, scented the breeze. Another hound gave tongue, a little farther away. "Hoick! Hoick! Hoick to Warrior! He-hark! He-hark! Hoick!" The Huntsman was cheering on his hounds trying to gather them together on the same line. "That's old Henchman!" Mr. Seabreese said, recognizing the voice. "And Warrior!" The din grew to a crescendo in the woods as the pack took up the cry, and the Huntsman blew short, exciting blasts on the horn, mixed with piercing screams. Faith felt as if her blood would freeze in her veins as the music receded into the distance.

When it grew very faint, the Master motioned the Field to follow him—"All stay together, please. Stay together, please"—as he jumped into the woods.

As the two ladies joined the line, both clearing the logs neatly, Faith saw Paint plunging around as Chugh tried to turn him to the back in a wide circle to wait his turn. They followed in a single line along the woodland path, a Persian carpet of red and yellow leaves caught around the silver tree roots, to the center of the woods. Here the paths rayed off in haphazard labyrinthine patterns, so that one could easily get lost unless one was familiar with certain landmarks, a certain rock, a ditch, a gate out into the far country. Suddenly Mr. Seabreese called "Hold hard!" and stopped dead, as the word was passed back from one to another, "Hold hard! Hold hard!" Piling into one another, the line stopped behind him and all was silent.

The fox had, for the moment, tricked the whole outfit. The dog-pack carefully nurtured in comfortable kennels, registered in the book and bred for speed, conformation, nose and voice; the men and women whose elaborate preparations to track down the vermin had sent them all the way across the ocean to London to have the proper costumes built for this special game—breeches smooth at the knee, boots fitting the leg like the paper on the wall, the right hat, the right coat, the proper scarlet for the Hunt Ball; all the special horses, good-looking or ugly, young or old, sound or unsound, fast or slow, well-mannered or crazy, who had been bought, traded or stolen with the sole purpose of participating in the ecstatic ritual of fox hunting; the whole assemblage was, for the moment, checked by the wily red fellow who had either climbed inside a hollow log, or doubled back into his hole, or escaped into open country right under the noses of the watchful Whips. Even now, he might be sitting laughing on some gravestone in St. Jude's.

There was complete silence in the cathedral shade of the autumn woods as the Master listened.

Faith looked behind her. Gladys was there. Quinn was there. But there was no sign of Chugh.

There was a faint rustle in the underbrush, hounds at a loss, combing the covert. The Huntsman came crackling along one of the rides with the rest of the pack.

" 'Ware hounds!" went the cry down the path from rider to rider. As best they could, the Field turned tails into the woods, heads into the path to make room for hounds to pass and to prevent their horses from kicking at them, a crime which Charlton Seabreese would simply not forgive, ever. "I hope we aren't going to play ring-around-a-rosy," Gladys said. "We could spend all morning here in the woods. Is Bellwood really going to marry an actress? And what were you doing at Finchwicke yesterday? You told me you had seen Chugh at the station!'

"I was paying a condolence call for Mother, and the old

Doctor made me come in for tea. I saw Chugh at the station on my way back," she half-lied again. "And Bellwood *is* going to marry an actress, and I love her. You must too."

"Hush please, girls!" from Mrs. Welch Seabreese, who assumed special prerogatives from her close connection with the Master. She was always giving out free advice and orders to the younger people who might ride well enough to be able to get out of the way of her flashy chestnut, which she couldn't hold at all if hounds were running.

"Lady Bounciful!" Gladys hissed with a giggle.

"Hush!"

Silence again, except for the occasional questing of the Huntsmans voice, "Hoick," he hiccupped, "hoick," quietly encouraging his hounds and letting them know where he was as he cast around the covert in a wide circle.

"View halloo! View halloo!" An unearthly, thin, high cry shrilled down every nerve, as one of the Whips at his outpost spotted the fox away.

In the distance a hound spoke. "Hoick! Hoick! Hoick! Hark to Windsor! Hark to Windsor!" The Huntsman doubled on his horn to collect the pack as he turned and came crashing back down the path, cheering and blowing like mad as all of a sudden the whole pack, with noses to the ground, went screaming on ahead.

"Birdgrove has viewed him away," Mr. Seabreese said, standing and turning in his stirrups to address the riders in his great excitement. "Away from the graveyard I should think" And he galloped off, the Field jostling in behind him, horses with bits in their teeth, riders ducking low branches which rapped on their hard hats as they tore along, scrambling around corners, keeping in line. The Huntsman ahead of them, having reached the edge of the woods, blew the familiar long and short blasts on his horn, telegraphing the word "Gone away, gone away, gone away" to call the tail hounds pouring out of cover. "Forard! Forard! Fot-fot forard," he screamed.

"Gone away!" sang the Master. "Gone awaaay!" as he took a log jump out of the woods into the open country on the other side. Faith impatiently waited her turn in line to hop out into the rolling fields of Coq d'Or. The hounds had disappointingly followed along a high post-and-rail fence and into the next meadow, where they had happened on a flock of bleating, fat Southdown ewes herded together in terror. The Master had jumped in with some of the Field bunched up behind him, and some still waiting on the near side. Seeing this, Faith slowed to a walk. Where was Chugh? Would he catch up?

Suddenly, without having been given any signal from the reins, Nimblewit stopped dead, ears pricked. Then Faith saw too, a big red dog-fox coming out from behind the sheep, running down the fence toward them. The fox stopped and looked at them, then Faith was sure he had grinned before he saucily trotted off · between the woods and the straggling riders. She waited until he had a good head start and had disappeared completely in the bed of a small brook.

Then "Tallyho!" she cried, pointing with her crop, "Tallyho!"

"Where?" shouted Mr. Seabreese galloping up, having ordered the field not to move.

"There! By the swamp!"

Faith, praying for the fox to get well away, counted the slow minutes before Windsor again belled on the line.

He's gone on around again! Faith called to Gladys and Quinn, who would never be able to keep up on Soup-Plates and Stormy Weather once the pace began to sizzle. Faith galloped on without them, knowing that the stiff four-foot boundary fence of Coq d'Or was coming up, and that Nimblewit would race over it with the best of the first flight. In front of her Mrs. Welch Seabreese's horse refused and ran down the fence right across Faith's line. But darling Nimble checked, and measured her stride, clearing the bars with inches to spare. She'll never make it, Faith thought of the other woman. She'll be stuck there all day unless she goes back through the woods. Faith's excitement reached the narcotic stage of oblivion as she raced away.

Having circled back to the Finchwicke Forty, the hounds checked again. Up front, near the Master, with hot cheeks and sweating horse, Faith saw that a few buggies were still standing there, and with them, Chugh Walding and Paint. That's one way to be in at the kill, she thought. Simply by not moving. And then quickly stifling her sarcasm which she could ill afford, "You missed a lovely burst," she gasped, joining him.

"Oh? I know the Finchwicke fox well, and I knew he'd circle back. And as Paint was raising Rim I made him stand here to teach him a lesson. I had a terrific view. A big dog-fox. He's a game old boy who'll give us a chase yet," and he trotted smartly away from her and up to the Master, and pointing to the first fence they had jumped into the woods, said, "He went back in there, Charlton."

"God damn it, Chugh, you turned him! How do you expect a fox to get away with everybody spread all over the countryside? Now, kindly all stay together, please!" The Master trumpted angrily as hounds again picked up the scent and streamed back up the hill. A few out-of-breath stragglers remained at the bottom catching their breath. Quinn and Gladys were probably still on the other side, but Faith cantered off close behind the Master with Chugh Walding now following too. She heard a hard crack as Paint hit the fence into the woods, but turning in the saddle she saw that Chugh was still aboard and still coming on.

This time there was no pause as hounds flowed like cream through the woods, turning right and going toward the eastern end with St. Jude's spire in the distance. For the second time they emerged from the shadows into the bright autumn rays of the sun. Setting Nimblewit straight for the exit jump, an upstanding red farm gate this time, Faith patted her horse's neck. "Come on now, let's show him and his great clumsy jigging horse what we can do, you and I together." She touched the mare lightly with her spur.

Chugh found himself seriously annoyed by the way everything was going against him. His horse was overfed and underexercised and had not been saddled and ready to go promptly at six. That seemed to indicate that the demoralization of the household had leached down as far as the stable management. Sweeting had argued that no orders had been given, but Chugh maintained that the groom should have known that he would be hunting when the meet was on home ground. And he was livid at having been dressed down publicly by Charlton Seabreese, who thought he was God Almighty just because he was Master of Foxhounds.

Suddenly he began to wonder what Faith Hoagland's opinion of him might be. Her riding outfit certainly became her. She looked really smart, sitting with small shoulders squared on her handsome mare. He was determined to show her that he was neither a coward nor a fool, and as the fox started around on the second circle he cursed Paint, who rushed the log jump into the woods, got in too close and hit hard with his front feet, stumbling badly on the other side. Ahead of him, Nimblewit had negotiated the jump neatly.

Chugh knew the maze of the Guard Hill woods well. By

turning left a few more yards along the path, he could jump a nice low chicken coop without losing much ground. This he had determined to do rather than take a risk over the big red gate toward which Faith had put Nimblewit, the sun now full in her eyes. But the way was blocked by a wild horse charging at him—Rhoda Seabreese the helpless passenger. The horse veered off from Chugh and went crashing through the trees toward the big solid gate. Chugh stood there watching, using all his strength to hold Paint from following. Taking off sideways, Rhoda Seabreese's horse made a diagonal leap, meeting Nimblewit in midair, and knocking her into two great trees on the other side. Nimblewit did her best not to brush off her rider, but the trees were too close together and too thick with foilage. A branch, just the height of Faith's shoulder, caught her and swept her from the saddle, sending her crashing to the ground on the back of her head. Frightened, Nimblewit cantered off, the empty stirrup swinging against her flank.

Chugh immediately jumped off Paint and handed his reins to Mrs. Seabreese's groom who appeared. Then he ordered the groom to open the gate so that the rest of the riders coming along would not step on Faith where she lay motionless on the ground. Running to her, he saw that she was at least not dead but had already managed to raise herself on one elbow. Luckily for her she had landed in a springy bed of ferns.

"Please don't anybody stop!" she managed to gasp. "Please don't spoil your hunt for me. I'm quite all right." And then turning white, she sank back. Chugh motioned the hunters now clogging up in the path behind to keep on through the gate.

"She's conscious!" he waved them on. "I'll stay with her." And it being the protocol not to crowd the scene of an accident as long as help was at hand, the Field went pounding on. "Shouldn't move her," a farmer had said, gratuitously stopping. "If she's broke 'er back, we should get a barn door." But he didn't wait around either, as now Quinn appeared from the sunny meadow leading the riderless mare. "Oh my God! My God!" he was muttering, cheeks puffed out with worried exasperation. "Oh my God, Miss Faith is hurt! She's that stubborn, takin' her own line like that"—breathing hard through the thicket in his nose—"she should have stood back with me!"

Chugh took command of the situation. "She's just knocked

her wind out, I think. Dismount, Quinn, and take Paint, and let the Seabreese man go on. His mistress is going to need him. She's absolutely out of control. Keep the horses walking around in the field. But first see if you can get my flask off my saddle. It's a mixture of brandy and port. Everybody else, please go on!"

Now Gladys Whitefield had come in through the gate, all the rest of the hunt having completely disappeared, not so much as a hound or a horn to be heard.

"We saw Nimble running along without Faith. Is she hurt? Do you think a buggy is needed?" Her fat voice remained placid, even though she was obviously worried. Chugh would have liked to have asked her to get off and loosen Faith's stock, but he couldn't see how he could cope with two women on the ground. She was such a bag of meal. He would have to hold Soup-Plates. To get rid of her he said, "She was talking a minute ago, and I think she's just had her wind knocked out. But now she seems to be out again. She comes and goes. Maybe you'd better ride to Finchwicke and get help. Ask Sweeting to come out and he can drive her home." Gladys, looking scared, clumped away.

Chugh had knelt down in the ferns and taken her head in his lap, as she now appeared to have fainted dead away. He took off her hat, unbuttoned her coat and flannel vest, and one by one undid all the little pins which had been tightly done up by Ma'selle in order to unwind her stock so that she could have air.

One hand rested on her neat bosom. He pulled the stock loose and took the collar button out of her silk shirt, and gently felt her neck for the pulse, which was faint but steady. He made a little pillow of his coat, and holding her in his arms, began to fan her back and forth with her hat. Suddenly she sat up, so that he smacked her in the temple with the brim, and once again she fainted dead away into his arms. They were alone, Quinn walking around on the ground a bit away with Nimble and Paint and Stormy, Gladys having gone for help. Chugh bent over her, and as his lips were near hers, he kissed her very gently, and then as Faith opened her eyes he said to her, "Will you marry me?"

"Of course," she said.

"Don't move, darling. Gladys has gone for help."

"But I'm quite all right now. I must have had my wind knocked out. But I don't remember at all what happened."

He urged her to take a sip from his flask, which made her

splutter but brought back some color to her cheeks, and then helped her to get up and try a few steps. She seemed indeed perfectly all right. Stuffing her stock in her pocket and putting on her coat and hat, they managed to find a stump from which she remounted. Giving Quinn one rein, "You had better lead her," he said. And with Quinn holding her with the broken knotted reins, they rode back down the long lane to Finchwicke stables, where Sweeting had only just started to hitch Emmeline Pankhurst, and where Gladys had been waiting to show him the way.

Here Chugh dismounted; his offer of a carriage to take them home having been refused, he had made up his mind to ride with them no further and made his excuses that he must breakfast with his father, who had not seemed well the night before, and then he had to hurry to catch the 10:14 Express to the city, where he had a very busy day awaiting. But he stood a moment, watching the figures of Gladys Whitefield, Quinn and Faith slowly riding down the long drive on the road home to Co-Eden. As they disappeared into the flaming maples he could see that Gladys was still talking, explaining over and over again what had happened, in answer to Faith's repeated questions, and Faith still being trailed along by Quinn.

"By God, I've done it! I've actually gone and done it!" Putting back his head, his gold beard jutting out, Chugh Walding had laughed out loud, startling Sweeting, who had not heard such a sound for weeks, and giving the poor man a thwack between the shoulder blades just as he was about to throw a bucket of soapy water over Paint's rump.

"Jumping Joseph and Jesus Q!" Sweeting said. "It's good to hear you laugh again, sir. The place has been like a morgue around here."

"Sweeting, I've gone and done it! I've proposed!"

"Congratulations, sir. I'm sure. Which young lady, sir?" He looked up and Paint tromped on his foot. "Damn ye with your big foot!"

But Chugh was already walking back toward the house. He again put back his head and laughed like a crazy man. What a beautiful autumn morning it was. He gazed out over the back fields—flocks of sheep, Holstein cows, and in the distance, the farm barns and the smoke rising from the chimney of the Briar Patch, where the herdsman now lived. This was where Sir Percy had lived while he had been building Finchwicke, and his mother had always said that she intended to do it over as a dower house to move into herself should Chugh get married.

He laughed again, stroking his beard. He thought of his mother: *I told you I would shave it off, and I will.*

Finchwicke itself appeared to him entirely new this morning as though invisible bars imprisoning him had been removed: the windows were shining, the cut-stone façade was magically mellowed in the autumn sunlight. Set among studded lawns, under ancient shade trees still awaiting one great wind to shiver away their freight of gold, the house invited him to belong to it. He entered the cool hall and glanced into the empty library. "Before him lie the fruits in their seasons, and the lovely gardens; around him float the messengers of love"—Sir Percy was looking at him, holding forth the book. He laid his hat and gloves on the table, his riding crop athwart the Lowestoft bowl and went directly into the dining room.

Breakfast at Finchwicke was in the English style: food set out on the sideboard, a bowl of sliced oranges, porridge, scrambled eggs and bacon in a chafing dish, a platter of grilled tomatoes, a muffineer of toast and corn muffins. His father was sitting there comfortably at the head of the table reading the morning papers, a snowy napkin tucked into his crocheted vest, a fleck of egg on his gray mustache, exuding a sense of well-being. Delia in her delphinium-blue morning uniform with white ruffled apron and cap, stood beside his mother's empty chair, having taken over the office of presiding over the coffeepot. Looking at Delia, one would never guess that she was pregnant—these girls had a way of hiding it—but pregnant she was, Chugh knew. And it was the first problem which he had to deal with directly after breakfast. However, for the moment, Dr. Walding gave Chugh a very cheerful good morning, signifying a change in the atmosphere. The sun was streaming in through the long windows and making latticed designs on the garnet silk Oriental rug. Outside on the terrace the Guardian oak was a rusty red. It seemed that a good night's sleep had done the old boy all the good in the world, and that he was prepared to let bygones be bygones.

Seeing his father's head pulled to one side, Chugh surprised himself by bending down and kissing the upturned cheek, something he had not done since he was a small boy. Then bouncing over to the sideboard, he fixed himself a plate and proceeded to regale his father with a rather technical description of the hunt, an account of how crotchety old Charlton Seabreese had become, and how, in his opinion, unless she got a new horse, that Mrs. Welch Seabreese was not going to be long for this world. Finally, in this way, he got around to mentioning that Rhoda had caused Faith Hoagland to have a fall. "And a very good sport she was too," he said, "not, I think, like mother like daughter. She's a chip off her old man, the Judge."

The Doctor seemed pleased with this observation and said in a deepened tone of voice, "Good. I agree. I'm glad she wasn't hurt. She was so sweet yesterday. And Chugh, '*La nuit porte conseil*,' you know, my boy. I've been thinking things over, and I've decided that Mother's will is *not* really fair to you. If you want to contest it, go ahead. And if you succeed in breaking it, there'll be no hard feelings on my part. You'll be welcome to come and go as you wish. Delia had promised to stay and see me through until the end." And with that he reached out his liver-spotted hand, with the veins standing up in ridges, as if to shake.

Oh. So that was it, Chugh thought. Nevertheless he seized his father s hand from the polished tabletop and gave it a squeeze, at the same time being conscious of the musky odors of Delia as she extended her arm to place his coffee cup. Well, now might be as good a time as any for her to find out. Impulsively leaning toward his father, he let her have it. "Thanks, Pa. But that won't be necessary. I also thought things over quite far into the night and I've decided I want to get married. In fact, I've already asked her! Faith Hoagland, I mean. *Not* her mother!"

The Doctor stared at him, his eyes turning a strange milky blue behind the steel-rimmed spectacles. And then he nodded his head in approval. "Of course you'll bring her to live at Finchwicke?" he finally managed to ask.

"Of course I shall, Father. But first I suppose I have to ask the old bitch for her daughter's hand. I'll do it, this afternoon."

"It s too good to be true. It's what Mother always wanted—to carry on the name!"

Delia had carried the coffeepot over to the sideboard, where it did not belong, and placing it there carefully she stood with her back to the gentlemen.

"Never mind getting more hot coffee, Delia, we'll have champagne. Champagne breakfasts are not unheard of, and we shall crack a bottle together. Delia, tell Bunce to go down to the cellar and bring a bottle of Bollinger. And fetch champagne glasses. Delia, good news. The young master is to be married! We shall have children again at Finchwicke! We'll carry on the name!"

Without facing them Delia left the room.

"Well, well, well! How did you do it so quickly? And what does she see in you? I think I must have made a conquest of her yesterday. What do you think, Chugh, of building a new wing on the west end of the old house, stemming off toward the garden? It could be your private apartment. You could have a little privacy from the old man. Mother and I often talked of it. When is the wedding to be?"

Chugh smiled indulgently. "There has hardly been time to discuss the date! But wouldn't it be possible, even in mourning, to have a small wedding soon with just the immediate family?" And so having wolfed his food, he excused himself and said he must get to town.

"But the champagne!" the Doctor said, picking up Thessaly's silver bell, a beautiful little thing, formed like Queen Bess of England with the clapper in the skirt, and rang it vigorously.

"Let's save it, Pa, for tonight. I really must go."

Bunce had appeared in his gray linen morning jacket, looking flustered, with a napkin wrapped around a dusty bottle. "I'm afraid it's not cold, sir!"

A terrible sound of tinkling, breaking glass came from the open door to the pantry. Chugh, being on his feet, went to see what had happened. Delia was swaying atop the step ladder, surrounded by a whole shelf of Thessaly's best handblown Venetian glass which had been apparently swept to the floor, where it lay in chunks of emerald.

"I couldn't help it, Mr. Chugh," she said. "The shelf was loose, and my foot slipped."

"I would like to speak with you," Chugh turned and walked away. A very good excuse for firing her, should it be needed.

Bunce had been extremely angry, as had Mrs. Bunce, who, coming down the stairs for her morning tea, found Delia on her knees with the dustpan. She stood there directing the sweeps of the brush with little kicks of her black high-buttoned boot. And when the mess was cleaned up, Delia was ordered to scrub the pantry floor. But this being the 'tween's work and knowing her rights, Delia walked defiantly through the hall and up the winding stairs to Mr. Chugh's room. So he thought he was going to be married, did he—to that snippety girl who had been here yesterday—and he thought Delia was going to have to leave to have a child, didn't he? Another woman coming to live here? He would find out. She would make him pay. Her mind was in an angry confusion of just how. The old Doctor had been kind to her. And yet Mr. Chugh must not find out she had had a miscarriage or he could not be made to pay. She opened his door without knocking.

Surrounded by the heads of his mountain goats, trophies of his boyhood game hunting leering down at him from the stained dark walls, the young master of the house was standing, hands on hips, in full splendor of golden chest and golden loins and pointed sword, the hairs of his body like feathers in the sunlight. He had never displayed himself to her before, and she was unable to put one foot in front of the other, or speak one word. He was unbearably naked, having shaved off his beard. All that was left was a small mustache which matched the blond puffs under his arms.

He spoke to her coldly, baring his strong white teeth, as he shrugged into a sapphire-blue silk dressing gown to hide the more obvious expression of his body, as though he were arraying himself in the robes of the bloody King of England. "Delia, it's plain for anyone to see you'll have to leave here soon. We can say it's because of the broken glass. My mother's best Venetian glass!"

Instinct told her not to mention Miss Hoagland. "I promised to stay and take care of Dr. Walding to the end of his life. He's been very kind to me."

"But, Delia, you can't stay here because you are with child. Of course I don't know if it's mine or not. But will one hundred dollars be enough? To take care of you? Expenses and all that?"

Something clicked in Delia's mind. She had hit upon the right path and so she repeated, "I'll never leave Dr. Walding. I can have the baby right here in my own room and no one would be the wiser."

"And then what would you do with it? Delia, tonight I will bring you two hundred dollars which is more money than you'll ever see again all in one lump. And you'll pack up and be out of here tomorrow."

"And where would I go?"

"I don't know. That's up to you."

"I'll need more money. I have nowhere to go and I won't be able to work."

"If you find you need more than that, you can come to my office. I'll see you have everything you need. But you must leave here. Haven't you got an aunt or a cousin or something? Some place you can go? To the nuns?"

"I'll need five hundred dollars."

"Two hundred tonight, and the rest when you're out of here. But start packing!" Mr. Chugh looked very angry, the skin turning blotchy where his razor had scraped, as he wrapped the blue silk robe more tightly around his now flattened body and tied the sash with a vicious jerk. And Delia felt weak; all her accustomed courage suddenly ebbed away, she started to sob into her apron as she left his room. But she was thinking, maybe I'll pack and maybe I won't.

That morning by ten o'clock, having again inserted his brown and gold City Troop rosette in his buttonhole, in spite of his black arm-band Chugh was immaculately dressed to go to town. But first he had surreptitiously visited his mother's room darkened by half-pulled-down shades, as it was essential that he avail himself of the key to her safe deposit box and ascertain the contents which Roland Raymond had said were his. He had always thought of his mother as a supremely orderly person, in charge of every situation, so that he had been shocked at first by the dusty and disheveled condition of her top bureau drawer. Spanish combs, and lockets with hair in them, dried flowers, hanks of false hair, old gloves and faded purses, belts and pins and hairpins and rolled-up stockings and handkerchiefs were stirred around in one great stew. Had someone else been searching there before him? A knotted handkerchief contained a string of cut jet beads, and her diamond engagement ring, which she wore only on grand occasions. Inserted in the center of a pile of old letters tied in raveled violet ribbon was the long, thin, flat key marked number 93. It was where she had said it would be.

This he slipped into his pocket and shut the dresser, glancing quickly around the room before noiselessly leaving. Beeswaxed and threadbare. How narrow and lumpy the brass bed. Build a whole new apartment without ghosts? Not a bad idea of the old man's, provided it didn't take too long. In the meantime he could bring his bride into his own quarters before they would be needed again for nurseries.

In the hall Bunce appeared to be waiting to open the front door, but in actuality, with his hand on the knob, he was able to prevent Chugh from going out. He said he was sorry about the Venetian glass, but the help nowadays was just trash.

"Well, Delia must go, or we won't have any china left. Have Mrs. Bunce be sure that she is out of the house in the next few days. My father will be upset, but that can't be helped. Get somebody new immediately." Chugh was conscious of his beardlessness, but evidently Bunce was concentrating on something else.

"If you'll pardon my saying so, sir, what I was going to say was that the 'tween is a very good worker and could do the job until I have a chance to find just the right one."

Chugh wasn't sure if he had ever seen the 'tween and wondered if she was pretty. Otherwise he couldn't care less.

Bunce continued, "Congratulations, sir, on your coming marriage. Sweetin' has told them all about it in the kitchen, and everyone is very pleased, sir. And by the way, at the moment things is a bit hard on Mrs. Bunce, with her daughter-in-law expecting again in California. Mrs. Bunce and I were just wondering, you know, if anything would be coming our way from Madam's will."

Chugh did a little quick calculating. Maybe Delia's five could come out of the other servants' lump instead of his own pocket.

"Nothing outright. At my discretion, however . . ."

Bunce turned the color of cheese, and as the moment threatened to become unpleasant, and Chugh couldn't stand any more, he was glad the station trap was waiting in the driveway, with Emmeline stamping her foot against the flies. "Open the door, please. I shall miss the train."

"If you'll pardon me for saying so, sir," the man said as Chugh went out, "after thirty years of service"—he called after him, following him down the steps—"after thirty years of service, it seems very strange . . ."

Chugh paused on the steps and drew himself up, speaking in low tones so that Sweeting didn't get into the act too. "You've been here for thirty years and been paid well, with no expenses. I don't know what Mrs. Bunce has saved, but as for you, Bunce, I know that you have twenty-five thousand dollars in Oldthwaite Walding, which is enough for you and Mrs. Bunce to retire on for the rest of your lives."

"Yessir. And if you'll pardon me, sir, Mrs. Bunce and me would like to give in our notice, sir!"

Chugh jumped in the trap and smartly rattled away. Of course he intended to give them something, but he was damned if he was going to be bullied into it. What a mare's nest! Thessaly had always coped with "them," the damned Sus-E-Rurs, and it couldn't be too soon for him before Faith came over and did the same thing. He would press Mrs. Hoagland for an immediate marriage. Now that it was all decided, he was overcome with impatience at the thought of the delaying formalities to be gone through.

As they drove to the station at a fast pace, Chugh noticed Sweeting taking a side glance at his smooth chin, but the good man made no personal remark.

By the time he had arrived at the marble porticos of the bank, anticipation had replaced irritation, and he ran jauntily up the steps and scurried past Welch's door, the president's offices being just inside on the left. The less attention his visit attracted, the better. And besides, Welch's secretary was an ugly old woman with a wishbone chest, always trying to interfere and do Welch's business for him. But this morning as he glanced by she was busy blowing her nose and didn't seem to recognize him. Chugh proceeded directly to the back of the bank and down the stairs with the polished brass railing to the vault.

"Morning, Bloodgood," he said to the man in the bank uniform sitting sleepily behind the table. He was General Oldthwaite's retired butler, even now available as a caterer's butler after bank hours. Chugh wasn't certain whether or not it was legal for him to invade his mother's personal box before her will had been probated. Nonetheless, as he didn't now intend to contest, there was really no harm. So he said with authority, "I would like to get into my mother's box, number ninety-three. I have the key here."

Bloodgood looked puzzled and was about to refuse. "Name, sir?"

"Walding."

"Oh excuse me, sir. Didn't recognize you without your beard. Certainly, Mr. Walding, sir, if you'll just sign here. Just a formality, you know." Then the old fellow opened the gates, and turning the many dials on the door to their proper positions he opened the great heavy door to the vault. Together they entered, and finding the box they inserted their twin keys. Bloodgood carried the box, a large and heavy one, into one of the cubicles, placed it on the table, and shut the door, leaving Chugh alone.

Chugh sat down on the straight chair and opened the hinged lid of gray-green steel. It was going to be like one of those Russian puzzles, opening one box after another. Red leather, blue leather, ivory velvet, his grandmother's beautiful legendary jewels, which had been given to her by her husband after the Foundry had been sold to U.S. Steel, and which had been lying in the box ever since, except when his mother had taken out the pearl collar to wear each year to the Assembly. This therefore was on top, its filigree diamond clasp gleaming against the black velvet lining of the box. In the next box, a double strand of pearls bought in Paris from an impoverished nameless nobleman, lying like great pink eggs in a long purple velvet case. Next he opened a small red leather box which contained a pin in the form of a diamond crown, and another with a diamond basket of flowers, a necklace of turquoise and diamonds, a diamond watch, a choker of amethyst, a necklace of black diamonds, a box of rubies which had never been set, and many rings, a star sapphire, a black opal set in diamonds, a marquise diamond, and a beautiful dark aquamarine, the color of the Mediterranean Sea, ropes of amber beads, and a delicate diamond tiara set with emeralds, and emerald and diamond drop earrings to match. One by one he opened them until they were all displayed on the table before him, a fortune in jewels which his mother had never worn, never taken out of the bank. He was breathless with power and delight, and immediately selected the aquamarine ring for Faith—the color of her eyes exactly. Then there were a few boxes of junk; gold chains, old cuff links and stickpins of her father's masonic emblems, a small pearl-handled pistol—ah! he would like to have that for himself!—an envelope of faded photographs, and at the bottom a long brown bank envelope, marked "For Emergencies Only." In it were twenty thousand-dollar bills. He remembered asking Roland Raymond, "Is there any loose money which might be coming to me outright?" And the lawyer's dry reply, "All her savings and checking accounts go to her husband. All her personal effects go to you."

Surely, being in the box with his mother's jewelry, this money could be classified as a personal effect. Chugh remembered what his grandfather, old Theophilus Chyldes used to say—one of those family dictums that one lives by, because they prove never-failing: "Benjamin Franklin notwithstanding, a little dishonesty is sometimes the best policy, provided no one gets hurt" . . . Well, no one would be hurt by his helping himself to this money. His father didn't even know of its existence.

He slipped the envelope into his inner pocket together with the pistol and the ring, replaced everything else in the box and closed it up. Then he called Bloodgood to return it to its hole in the wall.

Upstairs on the main floor of the bank, Chugh went immediately to the cashier's window, deposited nineteen of the thousand-dollar bills into his own checking account, and changed one bill into hundreds, which he placed in his gold-edged alligator wallet. Two of them would take care of Delia, he thought and caught the elevator up. He'd put them in an envelope for her.

On the fifth floor, he paused a moment in front of the stippled glass door with its inscription in plain black letters:

OLDTHWAITE WALDING & CO.
Members of the
New York Stock Exchange
Philadelphia Stock Exchange

Perhaps Johnny Oldthwaite would be free to go to lunch at the Philadelphia Club. Old Bullitt, sitting just inside the door in his brown uniform, beamed all over with pleasure at seeing him. He stood and bowed, but was much too much of a gentleman to make any personal remarks about his beardlessness. Chugh plunged on through the desks of the salesmen—some of whom looked up and smiled—paused to tell Miss Mack, sitting just outside the inner sanctum, to make up the servants' payroll as usual, but out of his father's checkbook, which they would be using for all household expenses until the estate was settled.

"How's the market? Any messages for me? Anything special going on?" he added.

"Mr. Morris Josenthal is inside with Mr. Oldthwaite," she said in her creamy, motherly voice.

A group was gathered around Johnny's desk looking very absorbed. Chugh recognized the bald, pointed head of young Jonah Wedgewright, who worked in Roly Raymond's office and who would succeed his father as a partner of the law firm and take his place on all the various boards of directors around the city which had always had Wedgewrights on them. Jonah had been delegated to do the preliminary paper work on Johnny's deal and now held a sheaf of envelopes in his hand as he was about to rise from his chair. But he was interrupted.

"Ah, Chugh!" Johnny said exuberantly, swiveling around in his chair and looking very pleased to see him. "Just in time. I'd like you to meet Mr. Morris Josenthal. Mr. Josenthal, this is my partner, Chugh Walding."

An enormous man stood up and said, "How do you do." His clothes were well-cut and of expensive material, and except for the fact that his forked beard was kinky, one would not necessarily know that he was a Jew. His cultured British accent was a complete surprise to Chugh. Totally impossible, though, to take him to the club for lunch. Anyway, Mr. Josenthal had his accountant with him and they were just leaving.

"We've agreed on a price," Johnny said, "but Morris wants until the day after tomorrow to sign. He wants to go over it with his attorneys, and naturally he should. We want him to be completely happy."

Josenthal then suggested that he take Chugh and Johnny to the Oyster Bar for lunch, but Johnny thanked him and said they had other business to do.

"He's going to be slippery," Jonah said when Josenthal had left. "He says E. I. Du Pont is nosing around, and they've raised the ante. We've made arrangements to go out and inspect the plant day after tomorrow, and then and there the signing will take place—or not at all. We've made that plain to him. You gentlemen had better have a certified check in your pocket for the down payment. Fifty thousand."

"No problem on my part," said Chugh.

"You've arranged it then? You're in?"

"Found some of the cash, and will get up the rest in the near future."

"That's great. It's much better if we do everything together, Chugh," Johnny said.

Yes. Much better to do everything together. Except for Knight, His blood cousin, Johnny was his oldest and best friend and had been, ever since they were eight years old and had invented their own private poker game called Ticket Cricket. They were still playing it, in a way.

"Well, I'm glad you two can get together," Jonah said. "I have a feeling Mr. Josenthal isn't going to fool around with 'slow pay'!"

"Don't be nervous, Jonah. Roland will pull it off. It takes a good Quaker to catch a Spoonbill, and I think we've made it plain, it's day after tomorrow or never."

"And if you're on the way back to the office, Jonah, I've

decided to go ahead and accept the terms of my mother's will, so tell Roland. The quicker it's probated the better," Chugh added.

"I'll see that it's done this afternoon. Will you be coming over to the office with Johnny to go over the papers for the Blue Rock Words?"

"Can't this afternoon. I'll trust you and Johnny with all the details of this one. I'll go along with anything you decide." Chugh didn't want to get into any chance discussions with Roland Raymond about the found money and have the lawyer render a strict legal interpretation. Chugh had no conscience at all about pocketing it. It had been marked for an emergency, almost as though his mother had foreseen this very need.

"What happened to your famous beard?" Johnny asked, after Jonah had left.

"Delia—I mean Delilah!" Chugh felt a prickling at the back of his collar as Johnny laughed. As his fingers closed around the small box with the aquamarine ring in his pocket, he thought of telling of his engagement—but maybe better wait and get it on the girl's finger first. He had already tempted fate by talking too much. The note to Delia could wait too.

"Paula made me take mine off two years ago." Johnny stroked his own smooth chin and looked proudly at the picture on his desk of his wife, Paula, bouncing little Quartus on her knee. "Promised her I would if she had a boy. He did it to me. But you'll like it. It's really much more convenient."

"Feel like a damn servant," Chugh grumbled as they swung out into the outer office.

"Won't be back till late this afternoon. If anyone wants me I'm at 'We the People,'" Johnny said to Miss Mack, meaning at Raymond, Raymond, Raymond and Wedgewright.

"And I'll pick up the payroll in the morning," Chugh said. "I'm not available this afternoon."

"I have it already, if you care to take it now," Miss Mack answered, holding up a brown envelope. "I had it done anyway. I knew they'd be needing it. Or I can bring it out myself tomorrow. I was going out to see the Doctor. He wondered if I knew where Mrs. Walding kept the key to her safe deposit box, and I think I can find it, as she showed it to me once."

Chugh took the envelope quickly. One more thing to stuff in his wallet. "I'll talk to the old man. Maybe Mr. Oldthwaite will be needing you tomorrow, and a day next week might be better for your visit to Finchwicke." The last thing he wanted was Miss Mack and his father rifling the bureau drawers together.

They rode down in the dim elevator without speaking because of the other passengers, and placing their derbies on their heads, one black and one pearl-gray, they exited onto the street through the side door. At the corner of Broad they both glanced up to be sure that William Penn was still atop City Hall, silhouetted against the blue sky. All was well. Chugh then began to detail Faith's accident, Rhoda Seabreese's part in it, and how it had caused him to miss the morning's burst. Shoulder to shoulder they marched down the street through the crowd of noonday shoppers, canes swinging, gloves in hand, not in the least concerned about the clanging of the trolleys, nor the smoke from the soft coal blackening the marble stoops along the way. They, after all, had moved to the country and no longer lived here. Turning up Walnut Street, they arrived at the white fanlit front door of the eighteenth-century mansion which was their club. It was only through the discreet opening and closing of this aperture that the air of the outside vulgar world entered.

They gave their hats and canes to old William, who looked as if he had been born and would die under these very stones, serving the gentlemen of Philadelphia who were now filling the club—drinking in the bar with its cozy prints of cricket teams and four-in-hands, playing sniff, eating lunch. Gentlemen from the Troop, the Fish House, the Contributionship, the Green Tree, bankers, doctors, lawyers, collectors of art and books, country squires, fox hunters, yachtsmen, architects, publishers, businessmen, gourmets, gardeners, and golfers; gentlemen who were comfortable with one another, having arrived at a certain level of comradeship—whose word was as good as their bond in business, from whom one knew exactly what to expect socially, to whom this lunch hour, shut in among their own kind, was a nurturing, fostering, and re-creative experience.

But today there was a particular hush and air of sanctity in the dining room, and there were long faces at the members' table where the two regularly sat. George McCusker was complaining to Stewart Farrington that this damn Presbyterian in the White House was going to bankrupt them all with the damn graduated income tax, which was most unfair and would penalize not only the people who worked harder, but the people with any brains and "git-up-and-go." It'll kill

89

the goose, Farrington," he was orating, "and the real culprit, of course, is Roosevelt. If he hadn't split the party, Wilson would have never got in!"

Chugh pulled out the chair next to Dr. Marshall Hoagland, who delivered babies for such enormous prices, he was told, that he, too, would probably worry about the new tax. The doctor was a very handsome man, with whom all his patients were reputed to fall in love. Chugh welcomed the opportunity to get to know him better, his future brother-in-law, and he described to Marshall in detail how Faith had had her wind knocked out and how he had revived her with a stiff swig of port and brandy.

"It probably would have been better if you hadn't given her alcohol,' Marshall said, "but she's strong and she'll survive."

Roland Raymond came in and took the chair next to Johnny. Since it was against the rules to talk about business in the club, the conversation turned to the morning's dreadful accident as Birdgrove Jaspar and Jaspar Birdgrove, the twin first cousins, both baby-faced, small, hard-riding men, leaned across the table.

"I was right behind you, Chugh!" said Bird, "and I saw Faith Hoagland get knocked over. I would have stopped, but you were already on the ground, and my horse is only a four-year-old green—his first season—anyway, thought I better keep going. How is Faith?"

"She seemed all right. Rode home with Gladys and Quinn."

"Dreadful, isn't it, about Rhoda Seabreese," Jap said.

"What about her?"

"She's dead," the twins said together.

"Dead!" Chugh, who had just ordered whitebait and oyster crabs, let the menu fall on the table. The obsequious, liveried James, older than God, noiselessly shuffled away, his pale translucent face never changing. Members of the Philadelphia Club died quite regularly, and the ranks immediately closed with other distinguished, indistinguishable men. Chugh could see that it meant nothing to James. But a woman, killed hunting! "God!" What happened?"

"Every horse she rode she drove crazy," Jap said.

"The going was like cement," Bird said, "but just the same, the hounds took that old Finchwicke fox down the backside of Guard Hill and through the hollow and straight for Church Hill and then down at the cemetery fence. Charlton checked the Field there because last year, ya know, the Vestry called him down for galloping over the graves." Bird giggled. "Says his ancestors wouldn't mind—but, ya know—so he sent my cousin Ham in to lift the pack. The field was just standing around when down the hill from the other direction comes Rhoda Seebreese—but I mean she was really tincanning! That horse had taken her all around the back of Coq d'Or. There was no way she could stop him. He was just motoring on with his head up and his teeth showing and the foam flying. Jap tried to grab the bridle as she went by, but everyone thought she'd be able to stop when her horse saw the other animals standing there. But he was really running away. He took her over the highest part of the cemetery fence, just a passenger, ya know? And there was an open grave on the other side. We could all see the mound, and Ham, ya know, he had jumped in at a lower place further down. Landed right in the grave, she did. Of course Rhoda was pitched over his head, and she broke her neck."

"It's horrible. Poor Welch."

There was an unnatural silence in that naturally silent room. Everyone had heard the news and felt the shock, whether or not they knew the lady.

"Old Charlton always wanted to bring her to bed and at last he succeeded. Glad it didn't happen on my place!" George McCusker said. There was a ripple of relief at the lewd remark. George was incorrigible.

Meanwhile Chugh's lunch was served and he ordered some white wine. After more discussion about what the new young parson must have thought, and some deep-dish apple pie and cheese for dessert and coffee, Johnny went off with Roland Raymond; and Chugh, his fingers clenched around the ring in his pocket, feeling deeply shaken and glad that it had not been Faith who had been killed, excused himself and sought the privacy of a writing table in the small library.

As usual, the library was empty except for old Strawbridge Simpson, totally deaf, in his leather armchair by the worn spot on the carpet, the ashes from his cigar dribbling down the cascades of his enormous vest, the silky white hairs carefully drawn over his pink bald spot, reading his *Bulletin*. He made no move of recognition as Chugh entered.

Overhead, the curlicue chandelier hanging on its heavy brass chain, its six gas globes shining up onto the ceiling and six shining down diffused an unflattering greenish glow of truth over the room. A delicate mantel carved with a basket of fruit attested to the fact that this had once been the parlor of a private mansion. Now sporting prints hung on long wires over dark mahogany shelves full of leather volumes, properly masculinizing the room. Chugh pulled out a nail-studded leather chair and sat down at the large writing table in the center of the room. Tall, black tole lamps cast a brighter pool of light onto the fresh blotter in leather brackets and onto the matching desk set, leather calendar and neatly filled notepaper holder. Feeling like a criminal, Chugh selected a folded sheet of cream-colored stationery, thickly embossed with THE PHILADELPHIA CLUB in square black letters, dipped the sharp new nib of the pen into the glass inkwell, and began to scratch in his precise, forward hand.

My dear Delia,

As you are leaving, this should take care of the immediate future. Be sure and let me know if you ever need anything more.

C.W.

He sullied the new blotter with fresh ink on the letter. But the hen-tracks he had made could be easily read so he carefully blotted the envelope on top of it to obliterate his words. Taking two of the hundred-dollar bills out of his wallet, Chugh tucked them into the envelope and sealed it. Outside, the muted clanging of a trolley. Within, no air moved.

As he sat there hesitantly holding the envelope, Chugh caught sight of himself in the mirror, tipped down because it was too big for the space over the fireplace. Its ornate gold frame curled right up over the dusty egg-and-dart design in the cornice. His face was the color of Roquefort cheese, and his hand looked distorted in the wavy glass: exactly how he felt, because he now had another note to write for which all his courage was going to be needed. This was it. In black and white he was about to sign away his manhood. There were no alternative pathways of escape. He had to bind himself to free himself. Never in his life had he said the words, "I love you," except to his mother, and he knew now it must be gotten over very quickly. As a man who has taken the decision to disembowel himself falls upon his own sword, he seized the pen again and wrote in a rapid squiggle,

To the dearest girl in the world—these flowers and this ring are messengers of love.

C.W.

There. That should do the trick. He blotted the note on top of the other message, and its envelope addressed to Miss Faith Hoagland now effectively scrambled all the writing on the blotter. He took the ring out of his pocket and out of its black-velvet satin-lined box, enclosed it in the note, and licked it shut, sealing his doom.

However, once out in the nice autumn afternoon, Chugh felt himself decompressing as if rising from the depths of the sea. In H. H. Battles flower shop, he selected two dozen velvety dark-red American Beauty roses, tucked the envelope with the ring into the waxed paper inside the box, which was then tightly tied up with green tape. Tucking this under his arm and consulting his watch on the thin gold chain draped across the front of his vest, he saw that he had minutes to spare, so he stopped at the Oyster Bar on the way to the station and had two dozen Chincoteagues on the half shell to restore his strength and pass the time before catching the 2:33. This train was a poor one, stopping at every lamppost, and there were never as many friends and acquaintances on board as would be on the Express. Just to protect himself from any possible conversation even with lady shoppers, Chugh ensconced himself on the prickly red plush of the rear seat and hunched into the corner with his *Bulletin* held up in front of his face. With a toot and a lurch the nearly empty train began its slow, smoky, bumpy journey through the hinterland of the railroad yards, past the dingy factories and tenements, the streets of row houses, on its way out to God's green countryside.

Sweeting, as ordered, was waiting for him at Penngwynne Station, not in the station trap as usual but in the big buckboard, with one of the three seats removed from the back, pulled by the chestnut team of Fire-Away and Wildfire. The stable boy was on the box as groom, dressed like the coachman in gray whipcord and brown felt high hat.

Chugh directed them to take him to Co-Eden to inquire for Miss Hoagland, and then asked, "Why this wagon?"

"The Bunces, sir. They packed up and left, and we needed this vehicle to bring their trunks along. Mrs. Bunce said such things about Delia to the master. We 'ad quite a time gettin'

93

them out of the house in a 'urry. And we didn't 'ave time to go back and get the trap for you, sir. So we just waited in the shade. Thought you wouldn't mind, sir."

Chugh made it a practice never to discuss one servant with another, and as there had never been any love lost between the coachman and the butler, he simply said, "Quite all right. Drive on." Mrs. Bunce's parting words would make more domestic complications, he supposed, but he filed it away in his head for future worry. Sweeting, turning around, wanted to discuss the pools of blood which had reddened the earth of the cemetery where the wild horse had bled to death in the open grave, but Chugh sat in icy silence, concentrating on the ordeal immediately before him.

Wildfire and Fire-Away lowered their heads and pulled the heavy wagon up the steep drive to the comfortable sprawling house which Chugh had not entered since he was a small, sailor-suited boy going to Bellwood's summer birthday parties. The place looked very well kept up, Chugh observed. One man raked the wheel tracks out of the gravel, another chopped and sharpened the clean edges of the pear-shaped turnaround, and still another, with a horse and a blue farm cart, was removing last summer's red geraniums from their lead planting boxes in the niches of the porte-cochere and replacing them with clipped yews for the winter. Rick's Pierce Arrow touring car was also parked under there, filling Chugh with a determination to look into getting one for himself to replace his mother's old electric. There also, tied to the painted jockey hitching post, stood Dr. Merritt's gig.

Sweeting maneuvered the buckboard to the front steps, and the groom jumped from the box to take the horses' heads. Chugh was relieved to see Dr. Merritt, whom he knew well, as he attended the Walding family also, coming out the door. He was a small, busy man who still had time for everyone, and he paused a moment, with one foot on the step of his gig, to talk to Chugh. It was merciful, he said, that Rhoda Seabreese had died instantly. If she had lived, she would have been a helpless baby. But what a terrible thing it was!

"And how is Faith?" Chugh ventured.

"Fine. Just a slight concussion. Nothing to worry about at all. Heart and pulse fine. And no broken bones. In fact, nothing that a little rest won't put right. Of course, she doesn't remember anything that happened after her bump on the head, but that's perfectly normal."

"I was with her, and I gave her a sip of brandy. I hope it didn't do her any harm."

"None at all, although it wasn't such a good idea. She'll be all right. But no visitors, I'm afraid. I must be off. A woman in labor in the village. Nice to see you, Chugh. Remember me to your father."

"Thanks, Doc."

With a flick of his whip, the doctor started his nag away. The maid was still standing at the open front door, and so Chugh handed her the box of flowers for Miss Faith and inquired if Mrs. Hoagland was at home and would receive him.

"I'll be back for them," the maid muttered, dropping the box on the golden oak credenza.

And so Chugh Walding was left in the lower vestibule of Co-Eden while Mary Quinn clumped away with one of his cards on a small brass Indian tray. She had offered him a seat in an ornately carved Chinese walnut chair with dragons for arms, but he preferred to stand, tapping his toe in icy elegance, staring at the suit of armor, sniffing with distaste the odors of stale soap and damp coats that came from the open door of the gray marble coatroom.

And if Mrs. Hoagland wouldn't see him? To hell with the old witch. How his mother hated her! How he hated being here! He and Faith should elope. He wasn't going to take any nonsense. He would get the interview over with, and either the old woman would consent to his wishes, or else.

Becca had been sitting in her usual gold chair in the bay window of the drawing room wrapped up in a cozy tea hour alone with her beloved Rick. It was the vantage point from which she had received the little doctor, making a beeline toward her over the Aubusson through the forest of chairs and tables. From his air of hurried determination she had judged correctly that he had not been about to sit down and take tea, and therefore had no bad news to break to her gently.

"Is she going to be a lunatic old maid living at home forever?" Becca had asked. No, Faith was not going to be funny in the head. A light diet. A good rest. No emotional upsets if possible. She would be quite all right in a day or two.

"We must count our blessings. When I think of poor Rhoda Seabreese . . ." Becca said to Rick after the little man bounded away.

"It makes us very relieved and thankful for Twinkle," Rick finished in an emotional tone unusual for him.

They hadn't sat there long after the doctor left when Mary Quinn knocked and entered with a rapid rolling gait. She just missed knocking the edge of the birdcage table with the fragile collection of ivory elephants as she made her way and finally presented the tilted tray so that Becca could read the card without picking it up.

"Chugh Walding! Show him in at once!"

Mother and son looked at each other with horrified amusement.

"Carrie? Good God! How can I escape?" Rick said, almost to himself.

"Don't you dare leave me alone with him! It's very polite of him to call. His father might have come with him, after yesterday."

"Mr. Waldin'," Mary announced in her broad Irish voice.

Becca pealed her best guest laugh. "How too delicious!"

Chugh came carefully, dodging the furniture by swiveling his hips, on his toes, and when he reached the throne, bowed deeply over Becca's hand and gave a brief, hard shake to Rick's.

"Hello, Chugh. Understand they had quite a hunt over at your place this morning," Rick said, by way of a greeting.

"Indeed we did!" And after inquiring after Faith and accepting a cup of tea, the young man rubbed his newly shaven chin with a silk handkerchief and didn't seem to know what to say next.

If only Rick wasn't here, Becca thought, I could win him with compliments. He would be quite a catch for me. Young, but wouldn't it make his mother revolve in her grave if he started coming to me for tea?

"I really don't understand how anyone can enjoy such dangerous sport," Becca said, retreating into her chair and flashing her rings. "Do describe to me how you saved my daughter's life this morning. How can I ever thank . . ."

"Mrs. Hoagland, you don't have to thank me. I have come to ask for your daughter's hand in marriage."

"What?" She laughed tentatively. He must be joking. Didn't he know that his mother had been her archenemy? That her sons thought he was a namby-pamby? This was so cruel, to hear the words spoken that she had been hearing in her dreams by a young man who couldn't possibly be serious. She had had her daughter on the marriage market for two years now without a sign of a taker. All the boys' friends seem to prefer me, she had thought often. This young man was rich, handsome, and lived next door. But Chugh Walding! It was ludicrous. Ludicrous. And yet Faith is already on the shelf. Beggars can't be choosers. We could do a lot worse.

"I've known Miss Faith all my life, but of course not well," Chugh went on, despite the awkward silence that had suddenly come between them. "I've always admired and respected her. And then yesterday ... she came, as you know, to call on my father, and I fell in love with her ... head over heels ... so now I am presenting myself to you, ma'am, to make a full and frank statement of my affairs if you wish it. However, I can assure you they are adequate to support your daughter in comfort at Finchwicke."

At Finchwicke! A cold hand gripped her heart. Her daughter to become the mistress of a house in which she had never been accepted? Becca gave a helpless little laugh and said, "How too delicious! But it's very, very sudden, Mr. Walding."

"Please call me Chugh."

"What does my sister think about it? Have you bothered to ask her?" Rick interrupted rudely. Becca saw Chugh's face harden in a determination she didn't like.

"To be quite honest with you, I have asked your sister and her answer was 'Of course.' Possibly, according to etiquette, I should have asked her mother's consent first, but in any case, we intend to get married."

"You understand my sister doesn't remember anything? She's had a blow in the temple?"

"I must request permission to see her."

The two young men were like angry terriers. Becca thought she must grab them by the scruff of the neck and separate them before Rick ruined it all. Faith had to be gotten rid of somehow. It wasn't complimentary to a mother to have an unmarried daughter hanging around the house with nothing to do but good works.

"Good heavens, Chugh. You have quite taken my breath away. I do wish the Judge were here. He would know what to say and how to question you. But, as he is not here, and I am an old lady, I must have time to get accustomed to the idea."

Hallowell had left her so much to decide. But why hadn't he left her all the money? If Faith were to leave Co-Eden, she would take her portion with her. In the meantime there were some things to recommend the new development. She would ask the trustees for a good lump sum out of Faith's capital, to buy the trousseau and give a large appropriate wedding—a formal wedding with all of Hal's old friends from the city, a wedding to give people something to talk about other than the secret marriage of Bellwood and Vivi, and the obvious imminence of an addition to their family. And a large wedding would inform the world that Becca Hoagland was coming out of mourning, and that her head was still held high.

"Do let me refill your tea cup, and we'll think about it. Let's not rush into anything. Take your time, Hallowell would say if he were here." Becca paused to give Chugh time to melt away that determination around his jaw, to show appreciation for her magnanimity. "After all, she is my only daughter, you know!" But his face was set so hard his cheeks were twitching.

"Ma'am, about the wedding. I was thinking of something very small, since my father and I are in mourning."

"But naturally you'll want to wait at least a year, maybe two. Marshall and Hebe waited three, until Marshall got out of medical school. And I'm sure your father would agree there's much to be said for a long engagement. One looks back on those years of joyous anticipation, of getting to know one another, as the best years of all." She stared at him with a straight face as she said these words. Both of her own weddings had been quiet and quick, but Chugh need not know that.

"On the contrary, ma'am. I know it's very sudden, but as long as we've both made up our minds there's really no point in waiting. I was hoping maybe in two or three weeks?"

"Two or three weeks? I never heard of such a thing! It will take me at least two months to write notes to all my friends—to announce the engagement. What would my friends think?"

"Your friends would think it was a shotgun wedding, and so would everyone else," Rick said angrily. "And *I* don't think we should discuss any of these things without Faith here. She comes into it too, you know. You say it's all decided, Carrie, but my sister doesn't remember a single thing that happened this morning."

"She will remember this very clearly, that I guarantee. And I'll thank you to stop calling me Carrie, or I believe I shall strike you!"

"Now, now, now." Becca was terrified. How pig-headed Rick was being. But it was very difficult to stop him, he was just like Hallowell at times. "Now, now. As it's my only daughter, naturally I will want to give a nice wedding. There will be plenty of time to talk things over calmly. It will take at least a year just to get the linens marked."

"Linens, ma'am? We don't need linen. I mean, we have our own linen at Finchwicke. My mother's. It's perfectly good still!"

His mother's linen! Becca was shocked by the impropriety of this remark. Chugh Walding didn't understand anything, and it boded very ill for their future relationship. He had finished his tea and was setting down his cup in a very stubborn way, without having delivered himself up as dough to be kneaded by her jeweled hands. The migraine stabbed at the back of her head. This ridiculous interview must be terminated forthwith.

"Do ask your father to call on me tomorrow. He and I will settle what's best!" She would be able to charm the old doctor if she could get him alone. And she had a momentary vision of herself invading and possessing Finchwicke. That would really settle old scores with Thessaly Walding. Turn her over in her grave. All at once the proper strategy became clear to Becca. She would appear to insist that Chugh and Faith come to live with her! And she would give up on this point only in return for a nice long engagement. At last, all the stains of being a newcomer would be washed from her escutcheon.

Chugh bowed stiffly. "Let me assure you that this matter doesn't concern my father at all. Nevertheless I'll deliver the message and I'm sure he'll be delighted to come." And having said good-bye, he bounced from the room as if he had rubber in the balls of his feet. He had an air of stiff self-assurance that Becca had never before confronted.

She and Rick stared at each other. "The cad," he said. "The slinking cad. Why can't she marry somebody decent like—like Bird Jaspar.

"Thessaly's dirty linen! What an impudent young man!"

"It has to be stopped."

These words scared Becca again. Why did men have to be so difficult? Faith had to get married even if it meant sacrificing the use of her money. Maybe Rick would help out with part of his? Maybe he would live here with her forever? My beloved! She looked at him with adoration. "We mustn't be selfish, darling. We must think of what's best for Faith. The only question is this: Is he better than no one, or not?"

Early the next afternoon, the inevitable dull gray day after a brilliant one, the Reverend Guy Fitzjoy was sitting in his linenfold golden oak study in the rectory of St. Jude's-under-Buttonwood, gazing out the narrow diamond-leaded window at the view of the well-kept cemetery, where the gravediggers were at work. He was trying to write next Sunday's sermon, but there were problems. The opulent atmosphere here didn't seem religious compared to the large, light plain-glass churches in South Forkville in the western part of the state, where he had worshiped as a child and with which he had come to associate God. It wasn't that he had never seen beautiful churches with stained-glass windows and ornately carved rood screens and even the solid silver altar of St. Marks in Philadelphia. But St. Jude's-under-Buttonwood had started off as a plain Colonial chapel. Then it had been enlarged, refurbished, and decorated to the point where it didn't seem compatible with an American version of the Holy Spirit or with the historical landscape of the American Revolution surrounding it.

The Reverend looked around his study. All this beautiful linenfold paneling, the beams in the ceiling, and every piece of old glass in the windows had been brought piece by piece from a country rectory in Buckinghamshire, England, and reconstructed on this spot at heaven knows what expense by Judge Hoagland, with money that could have been better spent on the poor.

But he had other questions on his mind as well. Did he really belong in parish work? Or did he belong in a more contemplative order? And should he or should he not go through with his marriage to Lettice Wishabaugh from South Forkville to whom he had become engaged last summer? Was it really better to marry than to burn, as St. Paul said? He had not worried about such things last summer when he had gone back home on his vacation and sat on the swing of the front porch of the Wishabaughs' yellow frame house, exactly like the one next to it, with its pretty yard, and asked the pretty child to marry him next June when she graduated from high school. But now he felt himself much older and wiser. This parish was very, very different from his first one at Heron Bay. What was going to happen to Wee Mouse, as she was known in South Forkville, when she was forced to dine out regularly at such places as Coq d'Or? Dawesfield? Deepdene? Where the conversation was of horses and hounds, styles, pictures and books and gossip about people she didn't know? Was he being selfish in bringing this un-spoiled small-town girl here, to this place? He was.

But he was so tired of the dreary meals the char slapped down for him. He constantly suffered from hunger pangs. And while these might have served to help mortify his flesh, in actuality they only made him dream of Wee Mouse cooking delicious meals in the kitchen, sitting opposite him at the table while he told her all about the day's doings. And his empty stomach had even caused him to arrange his after-noons so that he called upon one sick, one poor, and one rich parishioner, leaving the last for the tea hour. Today, the last call was planned for Co-Eden.

As to next Sunday's sermon, he wished it to split the atom of truth all the way down the center of the hair. So it was necessary to find the text which would exactly illustrate his theme. Last week his message had been that this present world is nothing, and the next world is everything. But it ap-peared he had offended some of the largest Christian contrib-utors in the county . . .

Christian! They were pagans, all—no matter how faithfully they attended services on Sunday. Senator McCusker, un-snapping his large gold watch in the front pew and waving it at him when twenty minutes had gone by . . . But when the power of the Lord came upon him he was unable to stop. He had asked the congregation to visualize themselves in the Holy Land—some of them had been there he knew, and, oh, how he himself longed to make the Holy Pilgrimage—he asked them to visualize themselves kneeling outside the tomb of Jesus, as Mary Magdalene had done, her hands out-stretched in supplication. The woman, he had said, typified human frailty before Almighty God. Thus (he had said this looking directly at Senator McCusker) we are all as women in the sight of the Lord, as we grovel at His feet in our mani-fold sins, asking for forgiveness, asking to be made as slaves, as women.

The Senator had glowered and waved his watch again, but he had kept right on, the Holy Spirit speaking through him, as he quoted from the rule of St. Benedict. Thou shalt be a stranger to the world's doings. Thou shalt not love much talk. Thou shalt be oft on thy knees in prayer. Thou shalt hate thine own self-will (looking directly at the Senator). "Who," he had thundered, banging on the lectern with his clenched fist, "amongst this congregation would leave their comfortable home, their business, their sport, their very family, and go out to meditate in the Syrian desert like the apostles of old? Were they not tied to Broad Street? Fifth Avenue? Piccadilly? The Ziegfeld Follies? The Philadelphia Club? Wanamaker's store" And then dropping his voice to a whisper, he had concluded by saying "Oh God, let us have" and quoted the old familiar hymn:

> *"A simple trust like theirs who heard*
> *Beside the Syrian Sea*
> *The gracious calling of the Lord*
> *Let us like them without a word*
> *Rise up, and follow Thee. Amen."*

It had been one of the more emotional of his renderings, which he was beginning to notice always brought on a more or less severe attack of the doubts. Was he wrong? Was this perhaps the only, the real world? And was he a priest simply because his mother had wanted him to be one? So that when he was asked what he was going to be, instead of saying a Pennsylvania Railroad man like my Dad, he had automatically said, "I'm going to be a minister." And his mother would always add, "An Episcopalian minister. And maybe a bishop, who knows?" It had been such an accepted fact of his boyhood that his nickname in high school had been Deacon. And pitching for the town baseball team, the Deke.

Yesterday he had thought of giving a hunting sermon, and he had been considering using a text from St. Macedoine, who had said to a hunter he met in the mountains, "You run after beasts, but I run after God." Hunting in the mountains was something Guy Fitzjoy understood. In the fall one went gunning for deer and bear in the forest, those predators who destroyed the farmers' crops, a natural part of life back in South Forkville. But here in Penngwynne, hunting meant fox hunting, an exclusive way of life with enough rituals so that it was almost a religion in itself.

Yesterday, in the middle of his meditation about St. Macedoine, he had heard the sounds of hounds baying right under his window, the Silvermist hounds, who had been led into the cemetery by their quarry. There had come a knock on the door, and men in heavy boots and spurs had carried in the broken body of a woman, laid her down on his kitchen floor, and then borrowed his cloak to wrap her in. She was dead, and they used his telephone to call the undertaker. They had sprawled in his chairs as if they owned the place—

which they did—knocked out their pipes wherever they pleased. And they had not even asked him to say a prayer when Springbeer's hearse arrived to take the body away. Like a swarm of bees following their queen, they had clumped out the door, remounted and ridden away, the only trace of them being the small piles of manure their waiting horses had left in his yard.

Later that morning a farm wagon had come with seven men, who had pulled the dead horse out of the open grave with ropes just in time for him to conduct the Christian burial service scheduled in that hole for a young boy that afternoon.

And tomorrow Mrs. Seabreese would be brought back and buried in a new grave that was right now being dug.

Because of all this, he no longer felt able to use the text from St. Macedoine, and was now searching for a new one. Of course, he couldn't forget that dreadful moment after the service last Sunday when Senator McCusker had reprimanded him right on the front steps of the church, saying in a loud, angry voice that the vestry had stipulated that sermons were not to be more than half an hour long, and that he had run on for one hour and a half. And that the topic had been ridiculous. "Why not say something about the autumn season, the beauty of the earth," the Senator had suggested. "Something cheerful for a change. Let's stop all this nonsense about this world is nothing. We're here, aren't we? And we damn well better face it!"

So the Reverend Guy Fitzjoy was thumbing through his Concordance to the Bible, looking up references to the fact that the earth is the Lord's. That was the atom of truth—in His hand are all the corners of the earth ... Ah! Here was one that was a little different. Deuteronomy 10:14. "Behold the heaven and the heaven of heavens is the Lord's, thy God, the earth also and all that therein is." His eye wandered to the next verse. And on to the next. "Circumcise therefore the foreskin of your heart, and be ye no more stiff-necked."

Guy Fitzjoy sat back and ran his fingers ruminatively through the soft tan curls that covered his cheeks and chin. What a sermon he could make out of that text! Aimed right at the Senator's foreskin! He felt a small bonus of cheer. God moves in a mysterious way, His wonders to perform!

He could see out the window that the livery boy had now arrived with his horse and buggy and the time was at hand for him to go out on his routine afternoon calls—one poor, one sick, and one rich around teatime. And perhaps since Miss Hoagland had a fall from her horse he could combine the sick and rich call and arrive at Co-Eden for the buttered scones? And would he be admitted to her bedroom? The thought filled him with such pleasurable trepidation that he sternly resolved to punish himself by staying away. He would take rich tea somewhere else, at the McCuskers' for instance, to punish himself for his desire.

> *Tenthredinae Waldingianae. The Sawflies connect the Hymenoptera with the Lepidoptera. In the perfect state they conform to the hymenopterous type but as larvae they would often be mistaken for lepidopterous larvae, and in their habits closely resemble many caterpillars.*

Thus wrote Dr. Walding in his notebook, sitting at the secretary-desk in the gentlemen's library at Finchwicke trying to calm himself and keep himself occupied until Chugh got back from the city. Chugh had requested that he go to Co-Eden to seek an early date for the wedding. "But why?" Dr. Walding had wanted to know. Chugh had said simply, "Because I wish to join Knight in France. War is coming."

From time to time Dr. Walding looked out through the window at the courtyard, or up at the green marble bust of Benjamin Franklin in his bookcase niche as if seeking some sensory beam of sophistication with which he might have coped with Becca Hoagland. Dr. Walding seldom went about socially, and he felt she had played ducks and drakes with him. "All cats are gray in the dark," honest Ben Franklin had said about the unimportance of the age of the woman with whom one might find oneself in bed. Maybe so. But by God, he wouldn't bet on it after the way he had been clawed by the tabby up on the hill. In the dark she would still be ginger! "The cat in gloves catches no mice." But as Faith had already caught Chugh, why should Becca wish to scratch him with her long fingernails and diamond rings? As far as the Doctor was concerned, his son Chugh was the catch of the year, a giant in the land, a prince among men. Why didn't Becca keep her gloves on as her daughter Faith had insisted on doing at tea? Why not be polite? Why not indeed hasten to snap the trap before Chugh might get away?

Sir Percy in his yellow coat looked down from the wall

with his lower lip hanging out disdainfully. The Doctor stuck out his, and returned to his notebook with a restless sigh.

> *During the last summer, we observed a locust tree which had had some of its branches completely defoliated by a genus of this species which we may call the "Depressaria Waldingianae." The head, palpi and forewings are light brick red, spotted irregularly with yellow, and the antennae are slate brown . . .*

He made himself keep at it until at last Chugh came in and he could lay the pen down, pour himself a whiskey, and unburden himself about his dreadful experience. Becca had begun by being very pleasant. She had made great apologies for sending for him, instead of coming herself to Finchwicke. "And when I said we hoped to see her here very often in the near future, she said in the future yes, but not in the near future. She seemed to think I should take her part against you, Chugh! But in such a faint, weak voice that I could hardly hear her, as I am a little deaf, you know. She said of course she understood that I, being in mourning, wouldn't wish to be in any hurry; that she, having only one daughter, would naturally want to have a decent-sized wedding. On the other hand, she said that *you* wished to be married immediately, and that I was to persuade you that as long as Faith was living under her roof, Faith would do as *she* said, 'It's completely my province,' she said, 'and has nothing to do with what anyone else wants.' By Jupiter, I told her that if she wasn't careful you might change your mind! I tell you, Chugh, I know I had no business to say that, but I was very provoked!"

Chugh sat gazing into the fire, and his father could see his fury rising as the flood of details continued on.

"Then she took another tack, As a fool thinks, so the bell clinks! She said the wedding could be sooner if you would both live with her at Co-Eden! Live with her, mind you! But I told her that there were plenty of rooms at Finchwicke, and that I myself would even move out into the guest room so that the young couple could have the master apartment, my room and my wife's rooms. You won't believe what the old bitch said to that! Thessaly's rooms would be depressing to a young bride! As if I were planning to put her in a pigsty! I tell you, Chugh, I found her most unreasonable and I told her so. And of course I was not allowed to see Faith or know her desires!"

"Well done!" Chugh had a feeling of great warmth for his father, who had joined him so wholeheartedly. Sooner married, sooner to the wars with Knight. And he took a sip of whiskey, which also trickled heat all the way down his gullet.

"So nothing was settled, and I was in a fury, by Jupiter. I got up and stalked out! Oh God, Chugh, I hope I haven't ruined everything. That minister fellow was coming in, and I hope he said his prayers because I could hear her laughing! Laughing at me!"

They each had another whiskey which they carried in to dinner. They were served most efficiently by Delia and the 'tween (who was not at all pretty), and Dr. Walding, feeling suddenly very lively, began to fabricate plans by which he and his son, like two young pranksters, would abduct the young lady from her tower on the hill and foil the red-headed dragoness.

"It shouldn't be hard to hook a ladder onto one of the hidden balconies," Dr. Walding said, "and have her climb down on a ladder of twisted sheets in the dead of night. You could be waiting to catch her if she falls, and I would be holding the steeds in the shadows:

"One touch to her hand and one word to her ear,
When they reached the hall door and the charger stood near;
So light to the croupe the fair lady he swung,
So light to the saddle before her he sprung!
She is won! We are gone, over bank bush and scaur:
They'll have fleet steeds that follow, quouth
young Lochinvar."

Dr. Walding laughed.

Delia served more wine, a Château Haut-Brion 1907.

"Well quoted, Father!" Chugh raised his glass and squinted at the ruby liquid, made to dance by the candle shining through it. "Co-Eden's such a jumble of roads and paths, we should never be caught."

"Ah yes. A jumble. Hallowell used to say the house was built in a style imitating nature. I hadn't been inside since the Judge died and I found it just a clutter of too many objects. Becca seems to have moved all the furniture from the parlor in the townhouse and combined it with what was already there, discarding nothing! One seems to be breathing invisible cobwebs, as one does in an old attic. Which clogs one's brain. Whereas Finchwicke is designed to celebrate *reason*. Everything is in balance. Take this room, for example. There is a demilune console with a crystal girandole in front of a tall Chippendale mirror. And there at the other end of the room is the same console, girandole and mirror, reflecting and balancing each other. There is a corner cupboard filled with Thessaly's Lowestoft, and there is the other corner cupboard filled with Aunt Sarah's Crown Derby. The sideboard on this wall balances the mantel on the other wall, and the windows are the same height as the doors. It is all in beautiful balance. In this house, one can think!"

Delia and the 'tween appeared to roll back the tablecloth in preparation for serving the port, but Dr. Walding decreed all that was too much trouble, that from now on it should be served in the library before the fire. And father and son rose to go.

Settling himself in his wing chair in the library, Dr. Walding took a new look at his son. "Of course, I've never really believed all this business about joining Knight. But I must say, it is a very good lever for getting married as soon as possible. On the other hand, if you're serious about leaving for France, you better make damn sure you get her with child before you go! Otherwise I might have to do it myself!"

Chugh looked at his father as though he had been stabbed. "I don't think you need have any worries about my doing my duty on that score!" And the rest of the evening wore on as usual, until they both went to bed.

Johnny Oldthwaite's Hudson sedan was exactly like a station cab without horses. Brass carriage lamps lit the doors, and in front was a small engine and headlights. Riding cozily inside with Johnny, Chugh felt exhilarated and relieved as they tooled down the Peppertown Pike away from the Seabreese funeral. It had been pathetic, they agreed: all the children, Welch, and old Charlton. The young minister seemed like a good chap, though McCusker was down on him, wanting him thrown out because his sermons were too long. But there was absolutely no way to get any preacher out once he was in, unless some other parish calls him, which wasn't likely in this case.

They stopped at the Coaching Change Inn for a beer and lunch, and Johnny pulled out a large yellow envelope which contained the financial statements and reports as analyzed by Raymond, Raymond, Raymond and Wedgewright, the partnership agreement to be signed by himself and Chugh; and the copy of the bill of sale, which, if possible, they were to get Morris Josenthal to sign today.

"Of course, it's a little different than originally represented. These things always are," Johnny explained. "In the beginning, old Morris Josenthal, who invented this special cooling process we're getting, wanted to sell out, retire, and go back to England. But he saw the war clouds massing, and he got his son Walter and Walter's family to come over here for a summer's visit. Of course they've never gone back! So now old Morris wants Walter to stay in with us for a third of the ownership. I think old Morris wants to watch over us as a sort of guardian angel until we're able to learn the business."

"Sounds fishy to me. Why didn't he come out and say all this in the beginning?"

"Well, the fact is he didn't. I don't want you to feel pushed, but on the other hand, if the war really takes off and we want to expand the place, the Josenthals might be able to help."

"I don't feel pushed, Johnny. Anything Oldthwaite Walding does, we do together. Count me in."

"Well, I'm glad you feel that way, Chugh, because I really do think it's a great deal. Jonah emphasized to me again yesterday that the Du Pont Company has been nosing around trying to pick up odd competitors ever since the Gunpowder Trade Association was declared unconstitutional under the Sherman Antitrust Act. The price of these little factories is going up day by day. Anyway, Jonah will be meeting us at the works, with the down payment, a certified check of fifty thousand, and Raymond has arranged with the bank to take over their mortgage of five hundred thousand. The agreement calls for the final settlement of one million dollars to be spaced out over the next three years. Very good terms really. I don't think we could have got them without taking on young Walter too."

Chugh nodded. "As I told you, Johnny, I'm planning to join Knight in France as soon as I can; and in business matters I've decided to defer completely to your judgment. Just as long as I can raise the money. And I certainly need to make some independent money. When I think that my Grandfather Chyldes sold out his foundry to U. S. Steel for fifteen million! Unfortunately for me, he believed in the law of primogeniture, so Uncle Knight got twelve million of it and Mother only got two."

"And you can't touch one cent of it! Don't worry, Chugh. We'll make a pile. All on our own."

It was with a high sense of excitement that they raced through Chetford Hills, blowing the brass horn with its large bulb at people in their way. They sped down the Park Drive, and then turned off onto a twisting dirt track which descended dangerously fast into the valley where the Blue Rock Creek emptied into the Schuylkill. At the bottom stood a wooden stockade, with a painted sign hung on a cross bar high above the ramshackle gate.

BLUE ROCK WORKS INC.
All persons
are warned to keep away
from these works

DANGEROUS

Inside, beyond the fence, they could see a collection of wooden, tin-roofed buildings with smokestacks lined up from the top of the hill all the way down to the muddy stream and the railroad siding.

"The damn place looks like it might blow up at any moment. Hope you know what you're doing, Johnny. Are you sure we really want it? Why don't we just let him sell it to Alfred Du Pont?" Chugh was nervous. This wasn't what he expected.

"I admit it doesn't look like much," Johnny said as they bumped along, looking for what might be the main office, "but they have a good little business going in ammonia liquor and ammonia sulphates. It all fits in with the coking of coal, you know. By-products. I think we'll do well to snag it off."

The Hoaglands own mines, Chugh thought. Maybe I can talk to Rick Hoagland about the coking of coal, if not about his sister.

Johnny was still talking away about their luck in finding the place. Then he suddenly said, "I think Josenthal would *like* to be associated with us, Chugh." He glanced at his friend.

"You mean," said Chugh, "you think he wants to belong to the club?"

"He might. Or he just might want to be invited to your house for dinner. Jonah had him to the Book Collection dinner."

"I know," said Chugh. "But for me, of course, that is impossible."

Jonah's tin lizzie touring car was parked in front of a small wooden building marked "Office," straight ahead. They jerked to a stop. Mr. Josenthal met them just inside the door. "Come in, gentlemen. I believe we've already met each other." He led them into a neatly varnished wooden room, where several clerks sat in front. Behind a small picket fence was the doorway to Mr. Josenthal's personal quarters. A large calendar hung on the wall showing a picture of a hunter aiming at a heavy-antlered moose, courtesy of the Blue Rock Works Inc. Chugh was struck by the immaculate orderliness of the place and again by Mr. Josenthal's worldly dress and manners as he introduced them in a faultless English accent to the two other men in his office—his attorneys, Mr. Solomon and Mr. Andrews. "Johnny tells me you're a fox hunter," Josenthal said to Chugh. "Which pack do you hunt?"

"The Silvermist. A private pack."

"Ah, yes. I've heard of it. My son used to hunt regularly. With a small pack in England. He really enjoyed that. But come now, why don't I show you the plant now and we can talk later."

As they went through the long sheds, Josenthal showed them the nitrating pitchers and the long cooling troughs. He explained the special process he had invented and patented which greatly reduced the danger of explosion in foundries. It involved agitating the coal with compressed, cool air as well as washing it carefully. Chugh and Johnny understood nothing about the business, but since they planned to retain Josenthal's manager and his complete staff of employees, they hoped to learn in time.

"These inventions are my life's work." Josenthal explained. And he went on to describe how chance had worked in his favor. He had been a very sickly youth, ordered to take a long sea voyage for his health. He had landed in California and worked his way East. Coal was something he knew about, and although he had started small, in time he had managed to make quite a fortune.

"Why do you want to sell?" Chugh asked. "Why not just pass it on to your son?"

"Several reasons. My son has other ideas. He wants only a small portion of the works. Because of this European war, Mr. Walding, I believe someone is going to make a very good thing out of this. In fact, I almost decided not to retire. But I've been working hard for a very long time, and so, having said I'll sell, I'm not going to change my mind now. It's only a question of who's going to buy. I sincerely hope it'll be you, gentlemen. But of course the Du Ponts are interested too."

Having completely toured the works, they ended up at a small row of company houses on stilts along the stream bank. As they were all alike, Mr. Josenthal suggested that they inspect just one to get an idea. The dirty children playing in the dust under the high porch made Chugh feel that even one might be too many, and he longed to be back in Johnny's car and on the way out of here. But Josenthal was holding open the unpainted door. "They're mostly German families here. Immaculate people. Do come in."

Chugh hung back, letting the others go first into the small kitchen, its window darkened with green plants in cans. An old woman was cooking on the polished iron stove. Rocking in a chair in the corner, a young woman with her blouse unbottoned looked down at the large blond baby peacefully suckling at her white breast. Chugh couldn't help staring. The young woman stared back and then smiled, totally unconcerned with this male invasion. To his total horror and inconvenience, Chugh felt the tugging of the child's lips in his own body as it flared up in response.

On the way back to the office, Johnny walked ahead with Josenthal and his lawyer. Following, Jonah said to Chugh, "We must get him to sign today before we leave." His keen eyes narrowed as he spoke under his breath. Chugh nodded and took Jonah's arm as they increased their pace to catch up with the others, now hurrying with the office in sight.

After each page of the agreement had been gone over in detail, Morris Josenthal sat with his pen poised, about to sign. But then he laid it down. Chugh's heart sank. He was physically very uncomfortable and had been all day. Secretly he made up his mind that much as he disliked visiting a common sporting house, a trip to Molly's would be an absolute necessity before taking the train home. Josenthal interrupted his thoughts. "Of course, you know I have been approached by the representatives of E. I. Du Pont de Nemours, but I would rather sell to gentlemen like yourselves."

"These gentlemen would like to buy it," Jonah Wedgewright said, "but they don't wish to get into an auction with the Du Ponts. There are other things they can buy. So this is it, Mr. Josenthal." Jonah Wedgewright clenched his pipe, showing his shark teeth, and lit a match, cupping it in his hands and emitting clouds of smoke. Gentleman Jonah, a lawyer's lawyer.

"My son is here now," Josenthal said, still looking down at the document. "He would so much appreciate an invitation to hunt with the Silvermist."

Chugh laughed inside at the baldness of this. He could imagine the look on Charlton Seabreese's face if he, Chugh, should appear in the hunting field with a Jew. "Never!" Old Charlton had once said, "never will they hunt here as long as I'm Master. Mark me! I have no prejudice against them. Simply don't believe in mixed bloodlines. Believe in the thoroughbred book." Rhoda, who was supposed to have a little touch of it on her grandmother's side had agreed, "If they hunt we'll have to have them in to the hunt breakfasts, and next thing you know, they'll be wanting to marry our daughters." Chugh remembered the conversation clearly. He rose to his feet and started walking toward the door.

"It could be easily arranged," Jonah Wedgewright intervened quickly. Jonah had originally heard of the Blue Rock business and had brought it to Johnny's attention, and, of course, he didn't want to see it fail now after having invested so much time and thought and tact into getting the parties together. He knew Morris Josenthal through their mutual interest in collecting Renaissance incunabula and had already invited him to one of the Book Collector's dinners. Josenthal had a page or two of the Gutenberg Bible which Jonah wanted for the Free Library. The Book dinners were intellectual gatherings, purely male, easily controlled, quite different from the gregarious and dangerous sport of the fox hunt. Yet here was old Jonah jumping in to save the deal. "I would be glad to mount your son next time they meet at my place. I have a very safe old horse."

"That would be very nice. I think you'll find Walter an excellent equestrian."

Chugh was nearly out the door when Josenthal picked up his pen and signed.

The whole visit had taken barely three quarters of an hour, and in the Hudson going back to town together the two young business partners were jubilant. "It was you, getting up and pretending to leave like that, Chugh. That's what clinched it!"

"I knew he wouldn't sell without a social quid pro quo."

"One hunt won't hurt."

"Maybe we should have him out for dinner. And Mrs. Josenthal, too."

"I never mix business and family. Paula simply refuses."

"Well, then, let's invite just him. I could have a men's dinner at Finchwicke."

"Perfect! No ladies involved. What harm?"

"No ladies involved at the moment. But there are about to be . . ." Thus Chugh informed Johnny of his engagement to Faith Hoagland.

Later, having cleared up his desk at the office and approaching Molly's, Chugh thought that he saw Josenthal arriving from the other way. Since he didn't want to meet him again quite so soon and under such circumstances, Chugh changed direction and headed for Reading Station.

* * *

Confusion.

Faith could remember having started out on Nimblewit in the beautiful dawn. She remembered the meet, and that Chugh Walding had gotten in everybody's way, jigging around on his horse, Paint. He had looked like a stick and shouldn't have been hunting at all. Then what had happened? There was a blank spot in her memory, and again she would ask Ma'selle, "What happened? I thought I was on Nimblewit, but here I am in my bed."

Ma'selle would make clucking noises and wave the bottle of spirits of ammonia under Faith's nose. Tiddy-Boom came and lay down on the checkerboard afghan on the end of her bed. The fat yellow roses on the wallpaper winked and jumped around, changing places with each other. Custards were brought on a tray. And hot tea. And milk toast.

Faith could remember plainly and shamefully having thought she was in love with Chugh Walding last evening and on the way to the hunt. Now she no longer was. She felt like a fool—to think she could have loved a man who rode so badly as Chugh had done this morning! Her head ached. Waves of nausea rose up in her throat. Ma'selle brought a china bowl and she retched up the tea and custard.

Ricky came and stuck his head around the corner. She didn't want to say it but she was unable to stop herself: "Carrie was so awful this morning. He couldn't paint—I mean he couldn't hold Paint." And then she had to lie back as she felt like fainting again.

"She comes and goes," Ma'selle said.

"Maybe a little whiskey," Rick suggested.

"Ah, *non, non, non. Pas de whiskey. Ça va mieux* if you leave the room and she can go to sleep. Very, very bad for her to talk."

Thus Ma'selle tried to keep everybody out of her room— even Mama, who came nevertheless and sat by Faith's bedside, patting the covers with her jeweled hand, wearing her white lace-edged coat with the purple taffeta sash, which she affected for mornings, with her amethyst lorgnette chain.

"Mama," Faith heard herself saying in a strained voice, as if it came from somewhere else, perhaps a ventriloquist in the bookcase. "You were right. I never should have gone inside at Finchwicke. Mama, I will never disobey you again." And then she burst into tears. Ma'selle interceded with "*Calmes-toi, cherie*" as Mama, who hated tears, rose and moved about the room, opening the window a crack, adjusting the collection of little china animals on the mantelpiece. Ma'selle, like an old terrier, followed behind her until finally she edged Mama out of the room.

"I'll send in something," Mama said. "Maybe she'd like some flowers."

Faith slid into another faint. The wallpaper came and went. She heard Dr. Merritt saying, "Of course, she mustn't hear about the dreadful accident. No visitors for a couple of days. She must stay very quiet. Not even get out of bed."

Ma'selle had just gone for a cup of broth when a faint knock came at the door.

Mary Quinn, looking frightened, had come in on tiptoe with a long white florist's box, tied in green tape.

"Are ye feelin' any better?"

"Much, much better! Put the box down here," Faith said, pointing to the heart-shaped chair. "Ma'selle will open it."

Mary backed out of the room, and pushing the door without looking, knocked into Ma'selle who spilled the soup. Ma'selle looked daggers at her and withdrew out into the corridor. "*Merde,*" she scolded loudly. And then the voices grew fainter as Mary slipped away and Ma'selle retreated down to the kitchen for more hot soup, leaving Faith in peace. But she wished that Ma'selle could have opened the box of flowers. Whom were they from? Faith tried to reach the box herself. She plucked at the tight knots in the tape, but they were too well tied, and she fell back dizzily onto the pillow.

She was still faint when Ma'selle came with the soup, and too excited to sip it until the darning scissors were brought and the flower box slit open. Such beautiful red roses! All damp and dewy and lying in a bed of waxed paper. Their tight red buds were arranged like peas in a pod at one end of the box, and their long stems and leaves, dark green, stretched all the way to the other end.

"I'll get a vase to put them. And *violà billet doux!*"

Ma'selle left the room, and Faith opened the lumpy envelope tucked in beside the roses. Onto one of the red blocks of the crocheted afghan fell the sparkling ring.

An aquamarine in a circle of diamonds! How beautiful! Now who . . . ?

She examined it carefully, held it up to the light. It was the blue-green of the summer ocean on a flat day. The diamonds were like a circlet of sunlight, the gold like bright sands. Much too beautiful for me, Faith thought. It can't be from Mama. It's not hers. Heart racing, she tried it on. It fit only the fourth finger of her left hand. Bad luck to put a ring on your engagement finger, she remembered, but I'll never get married now. Chugh Walding was so unattractive. She pressed the ring to her lips, so that it cut into them hard, knowing, fearing. Picking up the note with trembling fingers, she saw the black bold letters THE PHILADELPHIA CLUB dancing before her eyes. She wasn't supposed to read. With difficulty she focused on the scratchy forward slanting hentracks.

To the dearest girl in the world—these flowers and this ring are messengers of love.

C.W.

She shut her eyes as the flowers on the wallpaper bent down sickeningly toward her. Then she lay very still, feeling cold, and she suddenly remembered galloping through the woods trying to get away from Chugh Walding. Ahead of her was a huge red farm gate. If she could get over that, he would not be able to catch her. His horse was behaving so terribly.

She opened her eyes again. There were the yellow roses on the wallpaper, and standing in front of them, a tall cut-crystal vase filled with crimson roses. Ma'selle was standing at the foot of her bed, hunched into her black wool shawl, her whole face sparkling with pleasure, her tongue circling her thin lips.

"*Les fleurs viennent de Monsieur Walding,*" Ma'selle explained. "*Il est ici, et il les apporte. Maintenant il parle avec Mama au salon.*"

"I think I'm going to faint again." Faith held up her hand and showed Ma'selle the ring.

"Promise to take me with you, *ma bébé,*" Ma'selle said.

The next morning it was arranged that Gladys Whitefield would come to see her. Faith hoped that she might be able to clear up exactly what had happened. "Did you see it happen, Gee?" But Gladys had said no, the only person who had seen it happen was Chugh.

"When I got there, you were on the ground with your head in his lap. Honest. Cross my heart and hope to die. He was fanning you with your derby." Gladys giggled. And that was all. Gee was allowed to stay for only a few minutes before Ma'selle hustled her out.

Chugh had sent the ring. None of the girls on Miss Applegate's hockey team, looking down at her from the wall, would accept a gift like that. Neither could she. The time will come when I shall have to send it back, Faith thought. I hate him! I hope I never see him again! But the aquamarine and diamond ring was still on the fourth finger of her left hand. If Dr. Merritt says I can get up tomorrow, then tomorrow I will take it off, she promised herself.

When Dr. Merritt came later in the morning, Faith kept her left hand hidden and gave him her right to take her pulse. Ma'selle sat there, looking on like a Cheshire cat. And after the doctor left, Ma'selle said once again, "When you go, I will go with you."

And then they both giggled. "But Ma'selle, I'm not going! Tomorrow I shall take it off and give it back!"

Oh why couldn't Chugh ride like Robert E. Lee on Traveller? Faith wondered, looking at the painting of The Mount.

By that afternoon Faith felt considerably better. Her hair was combed out in a black fan on the pillow. Dr. Merritt had made his second visit of the day, and she was looking at herself in the silver hand mirror, supposedly to test her improving vision. Her blue-green eyes were enormous in her white face. Mary knocked on the door and again there was a slight scuffle as Ma'selle tried to keep it closed. In her mirror, Faith caught sight of Guy Fitzjoy out in the hall, very tall and thin, peering in over Ma'selle's head. How kind of him to come! She had so much she wanted to tell him. And she wanted him to pray with her.

"We pray for the departed soul of Rhoda Seabreese ..." he had begun.

So this was the terrible accident that everyone was whispering about! Could it have been my fault? Faith was determined to know. I'm well enough to be told, she thought, and as soon as the minister had gone she said, "Please, Ma'selle, send in my brother Rick if you can find him."

Rick came in his tweeds, covered with burs, red-faced, an air of the outdoors trailing him. Faith kept her hand carefully under the covers. "Ricky, tell me what happened. Everything. Please."

"Everybody's been telling you for the last few days, and you haven't remembered a thing. How did that minister get in here anyway?"

"Please tell me. I have to know. Did I kill her? Was it my fault?"

"Good God no, Faith. Her horse ran away, took her on a tour of the countryside over all the biggest fences and then back to the cemetery, where the hounds had checked. It was ten minutes after your fall."

"Then what?"

"Her horse jumped the cemetery fence into an open grave, and she broke her neck instantly. Nothing to do with you, Faith."

"Poor Mr. Welch Seabreese. And her children! It's dreadful!" And then, after a pause, she added, "I'm glad it wasn't my fault."

"Of course it's dreadful," Rick said in a matter-of-fact voice, "but I never really liked the woman."

"Nor me!" Oh lovely intimacy with Ricky. One could say the most shocking things.

Then she said, "I hope I never see Chugh Walding's face again," knowing that Rick would understand. She pressed the prongs of the ring into her side, under the covers. "*Carrie,*" she giggled.

But Rick suddenly looked angry, his normally brick-red face turned white, so that each red hair stood out individually on his cheeks. His voice was much too loud for a sickroom. "That cad! He came to call on Becca yesterday. He seemed to think he had become engaged to you while you were out hunting yesterday morning! Probably while you were unconscious on the ground!"

"Really?" So it had not been a dream! His face coming toward her among the ferns. His lips on hers coming out from his beard. "He said that to Mama? What did she say?"

"Well, naturally, Mama was quite pleased. I mean she wouldn't pick Carrie for a son-in-law, but on the other hand she doesn't want an old maid on her hands all her life. The only objection she made was that there would have to be some kind of decent interval for all this wedding folderol. But by God, I objected!"

"Whatever Mama wants, I want." She giggled again, hoping to change Rick's mood and the subject.

"The thought of that effeminate ass with his scraped chin touching my sister!"

"What scraped chin?"

"Jesus Christ, Faith. Thank God you think he's an ass too. You should see how weak he looks with his beard off."

"Don't swear in here!" she said, suddenly angry. "What right have you got to interfere? I'll make up my own mind about Chugh Walding." Her clenched fist came out from under the cover and lay on the folded-back monogrammed sheet.

"Where did you get that ring?"

"Chugh Walding sent it to me. It came with these flowers."

"Well, here. Take it off and give it to me, for God's sake. I'll return it to Carrie in a hurry. The goddamn, lecherous ass! How do you know what he did to you while you were unconscious!"

"Don't be silly. And I like Chugh Walding."

"You just said you hope you never see his face again."

"I take it back. I love him."

"You give me that ring!"

"I'll never take it off."

"You don't know what you're doing! You're out of your head! Jesus, why can't you marry one of my friends? Somebody decent, like Bird Pardue, for instance."

"Bird Pardue?" She managed to emit a high note, a thin hysterical laugh that trickled off insanely. "You're the one who's out of your head. Not me. Bird Pardue is my best friend's younger brother."

"You'll make yourself sick again," Rick warned, standing up. "Here. Give me that ring!"

Defiantly, she slid her hand back under the covers. "I

swear I'll never take it off." In all their lives, they had never had such a bitter disagreement.

"I'll expect Ma'selle to bring me that ring before I go back to Princeton tomorrow. You fool!" Defeated, Rick had stamped angrily out of her bedroom.

Confusion. He had made her say it. I love him. I hate him. I need him. I never want to see him again. This ring . . . She was weeping and Ma'selle was standing there with a bottle and a spoon. "Now, now. Take a little of your calming potion . . ." The heavy scent from the red roses was overpowering, and at the end of that second day they had started to turn purple and curl around the edges.

Faith slept fitfully that night, waking from nightmares and having to have the linen changed on her bed, which was soaked all the way through. Finally, near dawn, she fell into a deep sleep.

In the morning, Ma'selle spotted the Finchwicke mail phaeton coming up the drive. She ran down to the door to intercept a note from Chugh. She didn't want Mary Quinn coming up again and disturbing Faith, who needed rest more than anything. As the flap of the envelope was barely stuck together, Ma'selle opened it and read:

My dear Faith—

As soon as you're feeling well and allowed to have visitors, I beg to be the first. Do send for me at the earliest possible moment.

Most impatiently,
C.W.

Then she tucked it inside her sweater, determined that before reading it to Faith she would show it to Dr. Merritt when he came.

That afternoon, when Faith opened her eyes from a drugged sleep, there was Dr. Merritt coming in the door, and Chugh Walding following behind him without his beard. The thin line of his pointed mustache, waxed at the ends, made him look excitingly like Mephistopheles. Not weak at all, but devilish and much nicer.

"Here's Chugh," the doctor said, taking her pulse. "He's come to explain everything, in the hope of clearing up your mind so that you can rest more comfortably. You must be quiet, you know. So don't let him stay long." Dropping her wrist, and sweeping Ma'selle in front of him, Dr. Merritt bounced out of the room.

Chugh sat down on the low, velvet heart-shaped chair beside the bed. They were alone.

"I very nearly had an accident myself just now." Chugh was smiling. "Coming up your driveway in my mother's old electric, I met your brother, Rick, booming down in his great Pierce Arrow. Going back to Princeton, I guess. He would have pushed me right over the rock edge into the Japanese dell if it hadn't been for Doc. As luck would have it, he was coming right behind me in his gig."

"Oh," she whispered weakly, overwhelmed by his startling presence in her tower room.

He picked up her limp hand with the ring on it lying on top of the sheet, and turning it palm up, kissed it expertly. Faith closed her eyes, falling down into the boiling center of the earth. The Fall, Adam and Eve before the Fall. Pride cometh before a fall. Falling in love. The heat in the palm of her hand was nearly more that she could bear.

"I had a fall. Please tell me exactly what happened."

"Yes. You had a fall, and I stopped to pick you up. I was holding your head in my lap, and had taken off your hat, trying to keep you from being stamped on by the passing horses. You had fainted too, so I had loosened your stock. It wasn't easy, you know. It was pinned here and here and here." And with that he touched her neck very gently, but with fingers afire. "There was no one there to help me, so I unbottoned your vest to help you breathe. Here." His hand touched her breast under the covers, but he quickly took it away. "I was fanning you with your hat. I bent to kiss you." Leaning his elbow on the edge of the mattress, he bent over and brushed her forehead. "Like that, just like that. I asked you to marry me and you said, 'Of course,' and then you sat up so suddenly that I hit you with your hard hat. And you fainted again. Oh my love, there is something I must know. Do you remember saying, 'Of course'? You will marry me, my love? I need you so much."

"Of course," she said very softly, her whole mind and judgment melting into the flames of her fingers which she now disentwined from his, unable to bear the thundering decibels of sensation coursing through her body, painfully splitting her veins.

Quickly he sat back, baring his teeth in a smile as if he, too, were in pain.

"You shaved off your beard!"

"I wanted to do something different for you."

"Oh, Chugh. This ring! Thank you."

Submerging and swirling in the magnetic power of his presence in her innermost bower, she was glad when a knock came at the door and Ma'selle returned.

Chugh rose. "I must leave. Don't worry. Don't worry about anything . . ."

Forced by Mama, Dr. Merritt and Ma'selle to remain for two weeks in her secluded bedroom, where it would be totally improper for Chugh to call on her again, Faith now made a rapid and bouncing recovery.

She didn't see Chugh again until Mama gave permission for him to come to tea. Faith waylaid him in the red-leather smoking room, hoping for a few moments alone. As he entered, slim and elegant in a pale-gray gabardine suit with the black armband of mourning, all the prepared words flew out of her head. He opened his arms and she rushed into them, fluttering there like a small, plump bird. A very pleasurable situation. He bent down and buried his nose in her silky black puffed-out hair and told her it smelled like violets in the rain. Then he found her lips: a stolen kiss in front of the hooded stone fireplace emblazoned with the Hoagland crest. It was only an instant's lightning, sealing them, before they went in together to the gray drawing room. Faith led the way across the expanse of Aubusson to where Becca sat smiling graciously in her usual chair in front of the bay window. Her hair was curled and flaming, and her tiny feet crossed neatly before her on the footstool. Chugh bowed and kissed her fingertips, and then shook hands formally with Rick, thus marking the accomplished fact of the Hoagland–Walding engagement, the exact date in June to be settled in consultation with the minister.

4

Accepting

Guy Fitzjoy, sitting at his desk in the rectory, pushed back his papers and raised his head. Wearing his stiff high collar backwards in clerical style was truly a mortification of the flesh as it cut into his Adam's apple when he bent to write a sermon.

He was indignant about what had happened yesterday. He had gone to town to a financial meeting of the vestry where he had discovered that there were several properties owned by his parishioners that had been rented out for questionable purposes, and that revenue from some of these was finding its way into the coffers of the church. The wages of sin were washing up against the white stones of the cemetery which surrounded St. Jude's-under-Buttonwood, sitting atop its green country hill.

The list of investments had been ticked off in the comfortable inner offices of Welch Seabreese, president of the bank, along with a pompous joke: that our Lord's talents had not been buried in the earth, but put out to the exchangers so that He might receive his own with unsury, as the Bible commands. The meeting then had been adjourned for lunch at the Philadelphia Club. After that, Guy had made his way down a block or two to the grimy slums, to where the once stately townhouses had been turned into cheap hotels and rooming houses and hole-in-the-wall shops. To Guy's great surprise he had seen Chugh Walding in his pearl-gray derby, and swinging his cane, coming out of one of the more pretentious edifices, a large square house still intact and with clean white steps. Checking his list of addresses, this was indeed the location of the building known to the vestrymen as Molly's and was one of the properties in the Hoagland estate whose rent, by the Judge's will, came to the church.

After much thought of what to do about it, Guy had decided that he would first give a sermon aimed at the bankers and trustees of the community who permitted these things to go on, and that next he would have to go and point out the situation to Mrs. Hoagland. Through the diamond-paned windows of the rectory study he could see the dominating red stone on the top of the hill under which lay the remains of the late Judge, "Mark the perfect man, and behold the upright: for the end of that man is peace." He drew his eyes back into the dimness of the study, picked up his pen, and scratched on yellow foolscap his text for next Sunday.

The wages of sin is death ... He had just finished the words when the telephone hanging on the wall gave three rings. On the other end was the tinkling voice of Mrs. Hoagland herself, calling to tell him that her daughter, Faith, was engaged to be married to Chugh Walding—a cause for great happiness in spite of the bad relations which had existed between herself and the late Mrs. Walding; bygones were going to be bygones in a case like this—which, of course, the rector knew all about, but he was to put it out of his mind forever. Nothing was to cloud the happiness of the young couple. And she would appreciate it if he would be so kind as to come to her for tea, bringing his engagement pad, so that a date could be set for a June wedding.

Every hair on the Reverend's body stood up in revulsion. Chugh Walding! A man who was not pure and spotless in himself should not carry off such a prize. Still holding the phone, he resolved to do everything in his power to stop the wedding. "I have something of utmost importance to discuss with you alone, Mrs. Hoagland. I would appreciate it if you could receive me a little early. Say at half past three."

"It is the hour when I am usually lying down. Could you come a half-hour later?"

"As long as I can speak to you alone—privately—without Faith. There is something I must tell you. He is a dreadful man ... The marriage must not be ..."

"Indeed?" Her voice was like ice. "I think I know the family very well. Nevertheless I shall hear what you have to say. Be here at three-thirty if you wish."

Mary Quinn opened the door to the minister at exactly three-thirty. Guy Fitzjoy was upset to find Faith in the vicinity, dancing circles around the suit of armor in the vestibule, gaily demanding to know what secrets there were about Chugh which should be hid from her. Furthermore, she announced, she was allowing him only twenty minutes alone with Mama. Then she would be coming in to plan the wedding service.

Immediately upon entering the drawing room, Guy realized that his mission was hopeless. Faith was buzzing around in the hall, and Mrs. Hoagland was waiting for him in her usual bay window, but not alone as he had requested. Her daughter-in-law, Hebe, the social secretary, sat beside her in a straight chair. Hebe's mouth was set in a grim gash, her bulldog chin stuck out at him under her toque of pheasant feathers. Her full tweed skirt fell in folds of iron to the floor, where her little Pekingese dog, Ogden, sat yapping and snapping at her feet. Hebe was ready for him, pad and pencil in hand, the arbiter of the lists, the keeper of the social citadel.

Guy knew what he was in for, as he had tangled with Hebe over weddings before. She plunged into the welter of details with the authority of a general directing a battle from the top of a hill. She always knew exactly when to feint, or fall back, or press on for the final victory: to deliver the little bride to the altar drilled and overworked to a frazzle, with every hair on her head in place, her maids following like a cloud of butterflies. The theatrical effect was always dazzling, but Guy sometimes felt that his sacred precincts had been overrun with florists and dressmakers. And the spiritual atmosphere symbolizing the marriage of Christ and His church seemed to get completely lost in the dotting of i's and the crossing of t's.

It was plain he wasn't going to get a sympathetic hearing in his effort to get this wedding completely called off. Nevertheless, there was no turning back. The trip across the Aubusson carpet had never seemed so long and so fraught with peril. How could he have planned to say, "Mrs. Hoagland, this wedding must be stopped because your son-in-law-to-be visits the whorehouse"? The gauche words would stick in his throat like old, burnt-out clinkers. One didn't mention whorehouses to ladies.

Mrs. Hoagland was jabbing her needle in and out of her tapestry, her rings sparkling, her eyes glittering, her tiny feet crossed on the footstool, looking like a huge china doll. Hebe sat waiting as he approached—like a female pit-bull ready to spring. Guy Fitzjoy shivered with revulsion and wished himself far away from all ladies' parlors—himself in a monastery praising the Lord, and Faith in a nunnery, safe and inviolate forever.

"Good afternoon, Mr. Fitzjoy. It was good of you to come. I hope you have brought your calendar for June. I've asked my daughter-in-law, Hebe, Mrs. Marshall Hoagland, whom

I'm sure you know, to be here also, to help select a suitable time." Becca spoke to him in gracious tones—rather as though she were making an appointment with her chiropodist—preserving the class distance by her meticulous politeness, warning him not to step over any bounds.

But Guy Fitzjoy, feeling a rush of inner power, refused to be treated like a tradesman. It was an insult to our Lord Jesus Christ. So in order to remind them whose emissary he was, he said in a deep voice, "Blessing of the Lord on you two ladies. And my holiest good wishes for the happiness of Miss Faith Hoagland. However, I feel it my duty to raise an objection to this particular marriage."

"Now, now, Mr. Fitzjoy," Hebe interrupted, "don't begin with any 'howevers' . . ."

"However," he continued desperately, "there are no afternoons left in June."

"We *must* have a date in June. And as it is to be a very small wedding, it doesn't matter what time we take. We can take the morning and have a luncheon wedding. I assume that's why you wanted to see us alone, in order that the bride would not be too disappointed not to get an afternoon . . ."

"Not at all. I wished to see Mrs. Hoagland alone on quite a different matter. However, as long as you are here," he said to Hebe, "I will carry on. It won't do any harm for you to know, too." Feeling like a plucked rooster in a hostile hen coop, he puffed out his chest and plunged in. "Do you know," he said to Becca, "that there is a certain house of ill repute, Molly Franklynne's, in your husband's residuary estate? Do you know that you are living off the wages of sin?"

"Oh heavens, am I?" Becca looked up, as one who receives a piece of juicy gossip from a servant and betrays no personal interest. "Am I really? How too, too delicious. Molly Franklynne's, did you say? I have never heard of it."

"I believe it is near your son Bellwood's theater, not far from where you used to live."

At these words, Mrs. Hoagland stiffened her beautiful fingers around her embroidery ring so that the knobs of the knuckles showed white through the fine pink skin. She stared at him as though he had struck her.

But it was the minister's job to scrape the whitewash from the sepulcher. He was, after all, on his way to being a bishop. He must stir things up, not be stuck here forever in the green pastures of the rich.

"What did you say was the exact address, Mr. Fitzjoy? I

should very much like to know! Naturally, I like to think that the precincts where I used to live are still well tended—"

But Hebe broke in indignantly: "I don't understand what the family financial matters have to do with you, Mr. Fitzjoy, or why you should bother Mrs. Hoagland with them at a time like this. We have more pertinent things to discuss. We want to set the date for Faith's wedding so that we can get on with the plans."

But Guy refused to be put off.

"What really concerns me," he addressed the senior Mrs. Hoagland, "is that I don't want that kind of tainted money coming in to the church collection plate. After all, part of it goes to pay my salary, and I personally do not wish to live off the wages of sin."

"Well, how do you expect me to separate it out? The Hoagland family has many other sources of income, too, you know. We own coal mines as well as fancy houses—if what you say is true. Besides, I don't come to church often enough to taint your plate."

"I come from South Forkville, which is in the mining district. The poor, overworked miners there are my friends, so I know about the profits from your coal mines, too! They also taint my plate. But that's beside the point I wish to make to-day—"

"Really!" Hebe interrupted angrily, and after a suitable pause, she said, "Kindly let us look at your date book, Mr. Fitzjoy. I think it best that we stick to the business at hand."

He felt himself flushing with earnestness, trying to make them understand. But he was only annoying them more and more. "I'm thinking about Faith, too. She *does* come to church, and the inside of her purse too is being soiled by the rent money from Molly's."

"I'll tell her, then, not to put any money in the plate. Is that what you want?" Becca smiled at him venomously.

He floundered on. "I don't want to marry her to Chugh Walding. He is not a proper person. The wedding must be stopped. I saw him coming out of . . ." Mrs. Hoagland blotted out his words with her tinkling laugh. She laughed at him! She was making a fool of him. He trailed off into speechlessness as the heavy-footed maid plodded into the room to set up the tea table, which she covered with an elaborate lace cloth. A second maid followed with a silver tray. The first maid struck a match to light the alcohol flame under the kettle.

"You're accusing him behind his back, you know," Mrs. Hoagland said as the servants started from the room.

"Please understand, ma'am. It's a very embarrassing subject for me to discuss with you ladies. I'm not accusing the man of anything. It's his choice to do as his own conscience dictates. I'm only trying to protect your daughter, to warn you that sin is taking place in the Hoagland estate."

"I should like you to prove it by telling me the street and the number." Mrs. Hoagland's voice became soft and Southern, somehow accenting her obstinate insistence, as though she herself were going to investigate.

But it was too indelicate for him to tell her. "I'm afraid you'll have to find that out from Mr. Welch Seabreese. He is in charge of collecting rents there."

Like a breath of crisp autumn air, eyes and cheeks sparkling with health, Faith now appeared in the double doorway carrying the tiered stand with the muffins, cinnamon toast, and chocolate-iced cupcakes. "You look starving. We need to feed you by now, I'm sure. I couldn't wait any longer to find out. Have you found me a lovely Saturday in June?"

There was nothing left to do but to pull out his engagement book. "No. We haven't talked about that at all. I've been telling your mother about some serious problems I have in the slums of Philadelphia with some buildings in the Judge Hoagland estate."

"It's about a home for motherless girls," Hebe said quickly. "Nothing that concerns you, Faith."

"But it does!" Faith's pale eyes deepened. She twisted the ring on her engagement finger. "Particularly if it belongs to us. Why couldn't we take them in some Thanksgiving baskets. Where is it? Everyone in Penngwynne is well taken care of. I've often thought we should go back into the city, where people are so poor."

"Without taking on motherless girls, we have enough on our hands. More than we can do properly, between now and June. A scant eight months. Kindly let us have a date, Mr. Fitzjoy." Hebe leaned toward him, pointing her sharp pencil at his heart.

He opened the pages of his little black book. Indeed all the Saturday afternoons were already taken, but if they wished a weekday ... Or they could take noon on Saturday, June fourteenth. Then there would be time to remove their decorations and install the ones for the next ceremony, which wouldn't be until five.

"Very good," said Hebe, "June fourteenth it is. Just as long as we come first. We must start writing notes immediately to all family and friends before we put the notice in the paper. It will give people something to talk about—blur the fact that it was only two weeks ago that we announced that Bellwood and Viv had been secretly married for over a year ... Because, of course, we had to do that ..."

Guy knew that Bellwood had turned up with a wife and a three-and-a-half-pound daughter very suddenly. Faith had wanted him to baptize her, but the little thing, being so premature, had to be kept in her basket with hot water bottles around her and couldn't be brought to the church. And the parents were nonbelievers. Of course there had been gossip about whether Bellwood had really married the girl, but then she was an actress. Too bad to have such a thing happen in the Hoagland family.

Hebe was continuing: "Announcing such a nice engagement will hush up poor Bellwood's affair. Nothing could be more correct or above reproach than Mr. Chugh Walding and Miss Faith Hoagland."

"Hebe! Don't be such a wet blanket," Faith blurted out. She looked so distressed that Guy suddenly felt guilty about the gloom he himself had tried to cast. The poor little thing. How he longed to rescue her, sweep her up with him into heaven, or to do the good works of the parish together. But there was obviously no use his trying to get through his message about Chugh Walding. None of these people wanted to hear it.

Faith followed him to the door. "There's something I want to say privately."

He paused on the porch steps. The flower boxes in the niches of the porte-cochere were blazing with late fall chrysanthemums. The crickets made a pleasant thrum deep in the grasses and bushes. He felt the precious warmth of the end of the year. The late autumn sunlight scarfed around the two of them, as though they were alone in the heart of nature. Blood rang in his ears as he stood there, smiling at her.

"Heavens!" she said, "when I get with Hebe and Mama I do feel pushed. I don't know how to explain it, but my own feelings don't seem to belong to me any more. They're everybody's property. Oh, Guy! I do love Chugh so much. Just the way you love Lettice, I'm sure!" (The husband of one wife, he thought. That is what is required of a bishop. That is all I'll ever get to be. Even if Chugh should die, I'll be stuck with Lettice.)

"I love you, too, you know." His words came out wistfully. It seemed the nearest he would ever come to declaring himself.

"Oh, and I love you, too. Like a brother. Like a friend."

"Then like a brother, I must tell you I'm worried that you don't know your true mind about Chugh Walding. Are you sure you are sufficiently recovered from the fall on your head? What kind of a man would propose to a girl who is unconscious out in the woods? Only one, I should think, who hasn't the courage and honesty to do it any other way. Are you sure you know him well enough?"

Her pale eyes shone up at him, filled with a happy light. The sunlight struck the same pale light from the huge ring that shackled her finger as she placed her hand on the arm of his black sleeve. He set his jaw hard, so that his cheeks twitched and one eyebrow worked up and down as he fought back the desire which overpowered him, the current running high in his body under the black cloth. He saw the curve of her breasts pushed up under her white blouse swelling out like lilies from a slender vase. How delicious to sink his teeth into the white fruit of her neck. "Chugh Walding is a cad!"

She quickly removed her hand and stepped back. "You do sound like my brother Rick. He's already said all that! I don't wish to hear any more!"

It was hopeless. Guy stepped down to his shabby gig. But Faith called out after him. He paused to listen.

"I expect I would prefer to have my uncle, the Bishop, perform at my marriage ceremony," she was saying. "But, of course, as it is your church, we cannot help but invite you to assist. That is, if you wish!"

It was a perfectly ordinary request—one made all the time by families that had relatives wearing the cloth—but he hadn't expected it. And he felt stung by her phraseology, *We cannot help but invite you to assist*. And the words had been delivered in a high-pitched tone he had not known this girl possessed—an imperious tone, often accompanied in other females by a tap of the foot.

As though his soul had been stung by a nest of hornets, he felt a sudden intolerable itching under his scratchy high white collar and at the stiff cuffs around his wrists. Looking down at his hands he could see great red welts rising and running together. He was going to break out all over in hives, the way he had sometimes in South Forkville during the ragweed season. The only help was a warm bath with baking soda. He must get home to the rectory's tin tub.

"Of course. Anything you wish." He turned and ran to his carriage, unhitched it from the post, and with a slap of the reins sent the old spavined mare galumphing off down the drive.

Driving back to the rectory he remembered again the words of St. Paul: Better to marry than to burn! He wondered how he could possibly wait until June. There was no doubt now that he should marry, but was he marrying the right girl? In agony, he had ardently desired Faith as she had stood there on the porch. He had had a hint of what a cruel crucifixion he was to be called on to endure.

A young gray squirrel with a nut in his mouth leaped from an oak tree and ran across the Stone Mill Road. A sudden cold wind sprang up and whirled up the leaves lying along the road. Winter was on the way. The nag quickened her step as Guy Fitzjoy slapped the reins on her bony rump. Rounding the corner, he met the Silvermist Hunt coming toward him. Old Charlton Seabreese in his pink coat, his velvet cap green with age and weather pulled low over his craggy face, was roading his hounds home. Ham Birdgrove who brought up the rear cracked his whip at a young hound who started to investiage the minister's buggy wheel. "Woodbelle! Pack in! Yeah!"

Just ahead of him an old man with his fishing pole over his shoulder was trudging along, with the peculiar jerk of a man with a wooden leg. It was George, Minnie Washington's husband, who had been down to the creek to catch a carp for dinner. Even though it would be out of Guy's way to carry him to the colored section back of Penngwynne Station, the minister called "Whoa!" and pulled up beside him. The old fellow's coat was patched over the tatters, his torn straw hat pulled down over his face. "Would you like a ride, George?"

The old fellow looked up at him. "I thanks you very much sir. Reverend, sir. But my shoes are muddy. And my bucket of fish would soil your buggy."

"Not at all." The puffing mare was glad to stand still for a moment as Guy seized the pail of fish and hauled the old man in beside him. "You live near Penngwynne Station?"

"Yassir. Just a small piece down the road. I guess you know Minnie's place. God bless you, kind Reverend, sir. The bucket was getting powerful heavy." The old fellow smiled with great gentle sweetness, exhibiting a set of broken teeth. One eye was covered with a milky rheum.

Just before the station, Guy pulled in to the lane that led to the colony of slum shacks which had taken over a once beautiful farm when the railroad tracks were laid right by the bedroom windows. The Washington house was distinguished by the expanse of flapping sheets and towels hung out to dry on the clotheslines strung throughout the yard. A group of shy little black children playing in the dirt under a tree scuttled up onto the broken porch at the appearance of the horse and buggy.

Guy vividly remembered the scene he had witnessed here on his first Christmas. Mrs. Hoagland had just moved out from the city to make her permanent residence in Penngwynne, and she had asked Guy whether or not there were any needy families to whom she could give Christmas. He had told her of the colored family living very near her behind the Penngwynne station. It appeared there were a great many children, a crippled father, a mother who took in washing.

"Probably shiftless. Most darkies are. I understand them very well. Being an invalid, I don't go about very much any more, but if you will be kind enough to ride along with me in my carriage, I will make it my duty to go."

It had been a bitter cold day, but she had donned her fur hat and coat and carried a basket filled with jars of jellies and vegetables and covered with a white linen napkin. Quinn had driven her and Guy to the slum house, in order to take down the names and sizes of all the children so that they could be sent the proper useful clothing for Christmas. But, on arrival, there had been another phaeton standing outside the hovel, with the coachman from Finchwicke holding the horse's head. And out the door had come Mrs. Walding, her merry face withered like a raisin.

"Why, hello," she had said, with an icy edge to her voice. "What are you doing here, Becca? These are the Washingtons. My people. I've been taking care of them for years." And then she had turned to Guy. "You can be forgiven this once, because you haven't been here long enough to know that the Washingtons are *my* poor family."

On the drive back to Co-Eden that day, Mrs. Hoagland had declared she had been made a fool of. All the little black children's grinning faces pressed to the window. The basket of jellies and vegetables was still on the seat next to Quinn.

"Please take this to someone who will be grateful," Becca said to the minister. "Get Faith to go with you. Never again will I set foot on an errand of mercy. That woman was insufferable."

Now here he was once again in front of the shack. Old George was inviting him to come in and bellowing at the children to come and hold the horse for the kind Reverend. And suddenly Guy felt that they didn't matter at all—Mrs. Hoagland and Mrs. Walding—his ministry was here, among the humble, the gentle, the poor, the courteous. He would go in.

Minnie was singing in the laundry. Singing to sweet Jesus in a voice of high quavering sweetness, a voice like water that trilled as it slid up to a top note, rippled down again to a low note of prayer. A voice that pierced the minister's heart with pain as he stood for a moment on the broken back porch, surrounded by hampers loaded with heavy ironed linen, each carefully covered with a clean cloth.

Inside, the laundry was very dark. The old beams and the chipped plaster walls were stained with age and damp with the constant steam. In one corner was a large coal stove and above it the hot-water tank which it heated. On top of the stove were irons of various sizes for Minnie to use. Minnie stood at a large white table, her sleeves rolled up, a gingham turban on her head. Her capable black arms took swift, sure strokes as she pressed and folded a white sheet. Two little children sat playing with an old paper box under the row of soapstone washbasins. Another lay in a wash basket in a pile of old soft blankets, happily curling and uncurling his tiny black toes waving in the air.

"Gracious, Mr. Fitzjoy, you only sent over the choir dresses *yesterday*. I haven't even begun . . ." Minnie looked at him in soft reproach.

"Oh no, Minnie, no hurry about them. No weddings this week. Don't need them until Sunday. I just came in because . . . because . . . well, I picked your husband up down the road, and he invited me in. And because my hands seem to have got the itch. I thought maybe you would have some soda in a bowl of water that I could dip them in." And he held out his hands, now swollen to twice their size.

"Corn starch is better, Mr. Fitz. My mother always use cornstarch on us when we got the 'blains." And seating him in a broken rocker, she found a chipped enamel bowl, filled it with warm water and shook in the powder from the yellow box.

As he sat there in Minnie's laundry soaking his hands, she kept right on working. "I done all Mr. Chugh Walding's shirts. Except his boiled fronts. He sends them to London, twelve at a time. Seems no one in the United States can suit him when it comes to boiled shirts." Minnie laughed heartily.

Guy picked one hand out of the water and looked at it. It had shriveled from soaking, but the welts were fading away. He felt his neck and face. The itching had stopped all over. It was a miracle. " 'Inasmuch as you do it unto the least of these, you do it unto Me.' Thank you, Minnie. You have ministered unto me, and I am quite healed."

"No miracle, Mr. Fitz. Just common sense. But it did work powerful fast!"

Feeling light-hearted and happy, Guy Fitzjoy drove away from the shack, past the smoking dump, past the stinking sty where pigs were fed with garbage scrounged from rich houses, past the little brook that carried away the excrement from the row of outhouses on its banks—past the slums of Penngwynne.

The minister's call and his mention of the house of ill repute had awakened old thoughts in the mind of Becca Hoagland. In her bedroom, against a wallpaper chinoiserie background of tropical birds spreading their wings through a tropical jungle of palm trees and passion vines, she watched her reflection in the black-and-gold bamboo pier glass, spotlit under a pink beaded light shade. Old Ma'selle's fumbling fingers had at last undone the row of tiny buttons, and her black taffeta dress had slipped from her white shoulders and fallen in a silken heap on the thick gold rug. Next dropped the pieces of black silk underwear. Two petticoats, lace-trimmed drawers. Now she stood in nothing but her black high-heeled slippers, her embroidered black stockings showing an inch of soft white flesh bulging over their tops, and the lacy garters hanging from the bottom ruffle of her black satin stays. These were unhooked, the red marks from the tight whalebones were gently rubbed away, and her white bosom was released from the ribboned black corset cover. Finally, Becca stood and looked at herself, turning slowly in front of the glass.

How beautiful I am! she thought. A full-blown rose blooming alone in the desert of widowhood. No one to appreciate me.

Ma'selle stood patiently by, holding out the thin black nightie, the black lace dressing gown. Then she brushed out Becca's red hair and was dismissed without helping her into the black-and-gold lacquer bed, with the yellow Chinese silk hangings minareted over it.

Sleep was still far away in spite of the large dose of her regular pills—Luminal—which Dr. Merritt had prescribed as a calming tonic for nervous headaches. "They'll make you sleep well at night too, so the good effects will carry over into the next day and the next! Can't possibly do you any harm except maybe a little constipation now and then," the doctor had said. "And as the nurse comes to give your high colonic once a week, that shouldn't bother us too much! We can have her come twice if necessary." And in truth, swallowed down with a little gin and water which Becca kept in the pitcher by her bed, one pill had at first produced an excellent free-floating feeling. But as time went on and the wedding approached, she would begin to require two, then three, and high colonics every other day.

But today, the pills had no effect at all on the horrid nail of a headache which had pierced her skull during the minister's visit and was now stabbing at her thoughts. If only she could straighten out her thoughts!

She pushed the black bamboo armchair, loaded with little lace pillows, up to the plate-glass window near the sleeping porch. The autumn moon was rising like a great red balloon through the trees, casting sufficient light in the darkened room to enable her to move around in the forest of furniture. Shaking out her mane of silky hair so that it spread in a perfumed cloud around her shoulders, she settled herself comfortably in the chair and placed her small white feet up on the wooden sill, where she could contemplate their shapely perfection and forget for a few moments the dreadful boredom of the plans for her daughter's wedding.

The full moon had kept her awake for a week, drawing through her mind a boiling tide of memories. As a flame-haired girl, she had seen herself through Granny Huger's eyes. She had been the darling of the house. Granny had praised the rose Becca had embroidered, the English composition she had written, the way she had learned to drive her matched black ponies in tandem down Tradd Street.

Then, as a young lady, Becca had seen herself as a romantic heroine of the Old South reflected in the eyes of eighteen-year-old Beauchamps Marshall, who had shared with her a passion for amateur theatricals, portraying the older days of Charleston, before the War Between the States. She and Beech had been rummaging around in the attic for some costumes for a play they had organized for Christmastime. Playing lovers, they had imagined they had fallen in love with each other forever and had laid down to kiss on a bed of shawls thrown from an old trunk. Of course more than that had happened, and a hasty wedding in the azalea garden under the live oaks had to follow in the early spring. Becca had hated Beech Marshall for giving her a baby at the age of sixteen so that she hadn't been able to go to her first St. Cecilia Ball. And Beech had been furious that the birth of his son had prevented him from going off with his friends to the University of Virginia and, instead, had forced him to take a job as a ticket agent with the Railroad.

Drunk every night, he had boasted of his exploits at the fancy house of Flossie Lee Jones, until he took to his bed with a painful disease. And that fall, polishing up his guns for the duck-hunting season, Beech Marshall had shot himself. As if by accident, of course.

This was all long ago and Becca could only remember the unpleasant facts of the romance. All the love memories were dead. Even with the moon shining into the back of her mind, she could recall no feelings of fondness for Marshall's father.

Becca had moved back to the big white townhouse on Tradd Street after her husband's death and seen herself in the eyes of her budding young maiden friends as a tragic heroine who would live out her life in seclusion. Unable to take an interest in her child, she had handed him over to Mammy's black bosom. But then, the young lawyer, Hal Hoagland, had come down from the North on behalf of someone's estate. He had been well received at the bank. Her brothers had invited him out to spend the night. Becca had first met him at the front door, dressed in her stylish black, and for once she had just happened to have the adorable baby in her arms. She had been immediately able to see how beguiling she was in his eyes.

That night she had dressed her hair with a high Spanish comb, and at Granny Huger's request, after dinner, she played the harp, her white arms moving gracefully like the necks of swans as she plucked the strings and sang in her pure, high soprano. All the while she was able to watch her performance in the long mirror, reflected back in Hal Hoagland's love-struck eyes.

Next morning she had appeared before dawn, when only the men were supposed to be up and about—dressed in her many-pocketed canvas shooting suit, long full skirt, jacket nipped in at the waist, tweed boater hat. She had led her black retriever down to the edge of the marshy river with Hal Hoagland at her side and stood pressed close behind him as the long lines of ducks began flying toward them out of the night sky into the dawn before settling down into the rice fields to feed.

She had happily watched him fall in love with her, even though she had been raised to think that everything about the North was odious, and he was a damn Yankee. Nevertheless the vista of escaping from her existence of widowed virginity in the closed circle of Charleston society had been too tempting to resist. Hal, in a great tide of energy, swept her into marriage and up to Philadelphia to make a life with him. He adopted her son and made him Marshall Hoagland, and by this stroke of the pen had wiped out her past.

Becca had been immediately popular in the new city, even though she had felt superior, knowing far more about life and about men than these Northern women and their tradesmen husbands. Coming from the South, she already knew that all men are drunks, or effeminate, or unfaithful. But she had resolved to give Hal Hoagland everything that a woman can give a man, so that he would never need anyone else. She kept house impeccably, entertained elaborately for her husband's family, friends, and clients, and established a salon of her own on Spruce Street. Then, almost immediately she had borne him a son of his own, and then a daughter, and then another son.

But after Rick's birth, a terrible flow of blood which the doctors had been unable to stop had kept her out of the Judge's bed much of the time. Even so, he had appeared to be completely devoted to her, a contented family man. But Hal had died! And in such a way!

It was as if the mirror of love which he had held up to light her beautiful face with sunlight had been dashed from his hand. He had left her alone, and now she saw only the shadows of what had been. She had gone into widow's weeds again—this time from the skin out and forever. When she discovered that Hal had not even left her all of his money, but had doled out some to the children too, it was the crowning blow. She had taken to her bed and sent for Dr. Merritt.

Gradually, because of the courtship and attention of her sons, she had come to see herself through their eyes as a precious invalid. A brave, inspiring lady, too delicate to move, attracting all to come to her.

To Bellwood she had come to seem a fascinating elder sister. Only today, Bellwood had come clicking his heels to tell her that he had decided to sell the Mews, because the district had become too shoddy for a successful small theater, and that he and Vivi and the baby would like to stay in Co-Eden's guest rooms until they could find new quarters in the city further uptown. That silly little Vivi. Becca would be able to handle her. Just a little actress who counted for nothing. She could be made to dance attendance, brush hair, run dull errands now that Faith would be moving away.

And then there was beloved Rick, in whose eyes she saw herself as the most intimate and sainted of mothers. When he graduated from Princeton, she planned to have him come home and live with her forever.

And lately she had seen herself in Dr. Walding's eyes as being much easier to get along with than his wife, Thessaly, had led him to believe. Even Chugh was beginning to pay court to her, though she was very careful to maintain a cool position with her future son-in-law. Time enough, later on, when Faith would be great with child and it would be fun to get Chugh away. Of course, right now he was being taken care of by some fancy woman. How ridiculous and unpleasant of Mr. Fitzjoy to try to bring it to her attention. Right now—yes, oh yes—the wedding must go forward.

In fact, the namby-pamby minister was the only man who entered her drawing room through whose eyes she couldn't see herself as utterly charming. Looking at him was like trying to see oneself reflected in a flinty, gray-shingle wall: dark, dreary. He absorbed all her light, giving her nothing back. But then he had eyes for Faith!

Becca laughed out loud. A trip to a fancy house would do the minister no harm. Settle him down a bit. Keep him from interfering with everybody else's business. The man was a busybody, with his fanatic, glittering, rugged face. Talking of the wages of sin, and his home for motherless girls. Still, the words he had spoken had kept reverberating in her head all week, "Do you know that there is a certain house of ill repute in your husband's residuary estate?"

She was sure that the minister had stumbled on the knowledge she had craved all these years, the place where Hal had died. It was as though a scar had been peeled off her heart, leaving it naked and bleeding again.

He had made her remember how it had been between them, Hal strong as the branch of an oak, herself as the wild goddess of the moon. Summer nights on the sleeping porch out there. She gave a little moan as her thoughts walked over his grave. All her desires reawakened. The agonized longing, after all these years, was again fresh and sharp, a knife turning in her heart. Coming alive again.

The moon, shining through her bedroom window, and now turned from harvest red to a cold silver coin. Too much of the moon could make the bugs crawl under the nerves of her skin. She got up from her chair, and trailing clouds of perfumed black lace, crossed the room to the dressing table. Out of the clutter of silver brushes, mirrors and fancy bottles she picked up a small enameled box and extracted a much larger white pill—bitter-tasting cocaine made from the leaves of the cocoa tree. Perfectly harmless, Ike Merritt said, made from the same plant as the hot chocolate she served on her Sunday-nights-at-home. Most comforting. The newest drug for unbearable headaches when the Luminal no longer did any good. He had warned her not to take too many, lest their effect also wear off in time. "But I can no longer live without them! Please give me a few more!" she had pleaded. And he had complied, thinking of laudanum as a last resort. Sitting here night after night looking at the moon, she had decided it was not only the migraine she could not survive without the vivid lift the pills gave her, but all the dull events connected with Faith's wedding.

If only she could be healed of her terrible wound that sapped all her strength. Oh Hal! Hal! If only I could make you pay! She had tried to imagine, day after day, night after night, what it was like inside that house. She was consumed to know in what bed, in whose arms, Hal had died. Who had supplanted her? What was she like? If she could rub this salty knowledge across her raw heart, she might cauterize her wound. She must see the woman. And see that bed. Even play that role herself! This last desire had come to her in a flash of hate for Hal as the minister had been speaking.

She would get into town and find the house. But how was she, an invalid, to accomplish such a feat? Not only was it a dangerous undertaking, she must do it secretly, by herself, without even old Quinn taking her. There could be no gossip about such a visit at such a delicate time as her daughter's marriage into the Walding family.

If she could learn to drive a motorcar! Though it would involve giving up her role of invalid, getting up and getting around, this was indeed a normal point for a woman to throw off mourning, to celebrate a joyous family event—getting rid of a daughter who had threatened to remain an old maid and a bad reflection on her mother.

Becca had already sought out the one person, besides the Reverend, who knew the address she wanted. On the headache-making trip to town, she had paid a call on Welch Seabreese, on the pretense of needing extra money. It was very unpleasant having to discuss finances with Welch. She could discern a note of coolness toward the whole Hoagland family in the man's voice. As though his wife Rhoda's hunting accident had been in any way Faith's fault! Nevertheless she had pressed on. "It's hard on me, Welch, to have to scrounge!"

He flicked over the thick blue report on his desk which covered Hal's estate listings. "I see that last year you received over one hundred and fifty thousand dollars. That's not exactly having to scrounge!"

How much Welch knew about everybody's finances! Everything. But he had said again that Faith could pay for the wedding expenses. Pay! Pay! Oh Hal, I will make you pay!

But when she asked him about the house the minister had mentioned, he had become the icy embodiment of gentlemanly discretion. He had muttered a comment about how the old neighborhoods were changing, and how did anyone know where anything was any more?

But she had pressed her point home. "I insist on knowing exactly where this place is."

"I really don't know, Becca. And if I did, I wouldn't tell you."

They had sat facing each other in the library of his office, with the secretary straining in the anteroom to hear every word they said. But no secrets could have been prized out of him with a chisel. Probably because he went to Molly Franklynne's himself. The old goat!

In her moonlit room Becca laughed out loud at her own joke. Now she felt a delicious warmth in her toes and fingertips. The pill was working. She flexed her tapered hands to be sure they were still hers and let them flutter to her lap, catching the moonbeams in her diamond rings. One foot fell from the window sill, parting the folds of her diaphanous wrapper, exposing for her pleasure her marble leg. How lovely I am! she thought, stroking her breasts, her thighs, her bare knee.

These moments alone in her bedroom when she could revel in her own beauty were the only solace she had from the great bore of going into the details of the wedding with Hebe. Hebe had made her write notes to all her relatives and friends apprising them of the coming event. Hebe had sent for Mme. Makalapoof to bring samples of sheets and table-cloths to be embroidered in France. Thirteen dozen of everything. The announcement to appear in the newspaper tomorrow had been composed by Hebe. Chugh and Dr. Walding had been invited up to Co-Eden tomorrow night to dinner to celebrate. And after that? Yes, indeed, let Hebe take over.

Becca wiggled her slender white toes in the moonlight. "Of course I never could learn to drive a car. I'm much too delicate. But on the other hand, if I could get darling Rick to teach me—"

The moon was waning into dawn and one foot, long abandoned on the window sill was numb and cold. There was a faint cheeping of the birds in the trees. She had not been to sleep at all. Down in the paddocks she could hear the thundering hooves of the young stallion, Plymouth Rock. She could imagine him running free, mane and tail streaming in the tired night, calling to the mares snug in their stalls. And down by the lily pond, through flashes of lightning in her head, she seemed to see moving lights and the mirage of a wedding tent.

Clinging to the backs of chairs, jerking every nerve and muscle in her disused body, Becca again groped her way back to the box of pills. Picking out one of the chased-glass bottles—the one with the amber liquid—she removed the silver stopper and sniffed it, just to be sure. It was Wine of Laudanum which she had carefully decanted, and which Dr. Ike had warned her was made from opium and should be saved for only the most unbearable migraines. Pouring a few drops into a half glass of water, she washed down another white pill from the little enameled box. The spirits burned comfortingly in her gullet. Nothing that did so much good could possibly do any harm.

Now the swaying tent, its tall thick posts finialed in flames, appeared to her in the corner of her own room. Within its curtains lay a turbanded desert sheik, waiting to assuage her with his jeweled sword. With a moan of weakness she fell to her knees and made her way, crawling, toward the bed.

Coming up the Co-Eden driveway on this chilly night in early December, Dr. Walding and Chugh were thrown violently against each other in the back seat of their station cab as Wildfire nearly shied off the road and then bolted around the hairpin curve on the bridge over the Japanese dell. A loud neighing call rent the air from the paddocks behind the stable, and the sound of pounding hooves running up and down the fence line. "Christamighty!" said young Sweeting on the box. "That's Plymouth Rock! Why don't they keep their bleedin' stallion in when they're havin' guests!"

"Hell's bells," the Doctor snarled, recovering himself into his corner and touching his aching back.

"Goddamn if I wouldn't rather fly a plane than come up this drive at night with horses. It's safer. Did you hurt your neck?" Chugh inquired.

"No indeed. Quite all right."

Sweeting had managed to get the little mare straightened to rights, and they arrived under the porte-cochere only slightly shaken up, Dr. Walding's head bent down to his shoulder a little more than usual.

This was the first ceremonial meal he had been invited to at Co-Eden, and Horace Walding had made up his mind to put his best foot forward as Thessaly surely would have done had she still been alive. He had not been inside these doors since his argument with Becca over the timing of the marriage, but now that all was arranged and the announcement had come out in the paper that day, there was no other course of action to take than to follow the line set out by Becca and her daughter-in-law, Hebe, until the wedding was over and he and Chugh had gotten Faith down to Finchwicke forever. Being a lovely girl—not at all like mother like daughter, but in truth a chip off the old Judge's block, they would have no trouble handling her. They would train her easily to do exactly as Thessaly had done—devote her full time to taking care of him and, of course, Chugh.

But tonight was probably going to be a difficult evening. Dr. Walding knew that Chugh did not get on well with the Hoagland boys. In fact, none of them liked each other at all, and he felt there was nothing more unnatural or unpleasant

141

than forced intimacy with a set of new relations one doesn't like. They had nothing in common with the Hoaglands other than the fact that a commingling of blood was about to take place to form the next generation. Nevertheless he had determined to do everything in his power to make the evening pass smoothly.

Therefore, arriving at the threshold of the drawing room, he wreathed himself in smiles, and, his hand outstretched in greeting, made his way to the family grouped around the fireplace. Like a diplomat arriving at a foreign court, he took Becca's jeweled hand and bending low, brushed the back of it with the tips of his mustache. "My dear, what a very, very happy occasion. 'Oh East is East, and West is West, and never the twain shall meet!' But tonight we have met!"

He then turned and kissed Faith on the cheek. "Fair maiden of the mist!" He noted that the child was trembling, probably because Chugh followed close behind, and the young couple were to be permitted one of their rare opportunities to kiss. And rightly too, thought Dr. Walding, for a female does not understand that a kiss fuels an immediate reaction in the man's body, a drive toward the consummation. Best then, to remain on formal terms until he can take her. Very wise. Dr. Walding smacked his lips.

And here was the sister-in-law Hebe, who Chugh said had been hired to spy on him day and night. The pearl collar around her neck served only to make her look more than ever like a Boston terrier. Her evening gown bared the shoulders of a football player. "Good evening." Dr. Walding bowed.

He even condescended to speak politely to that little actress who had married Bellwood. He appraised her. Not a bad little thing. "Good evening," he said, and then he silently shook hands with the three Hoagland men.

When he turned back to the group he saw Becca patting the tapestry seat beside her on the sofa. Bowing slightly, he sat down beside her and took from his inside pocket a newspaper clipping he had brought with him.

"Hear ye! Hear ye! Hear ye!" He waved the little piece of paper.

"The town crier!" intoned Bellwood, who loved any kind of performance.

"Hear ye! Mrs. Richard Hallowell Hoagland, of Co-Eden, announces the engagement of her daughter—"

"We've all heard it, Horace," Becca's voice tinkled above

his. But Dr. Walding, having begun, was determined to finish. While his hostess fumbled in her reticule for a little pill box, and signaled Faith to bring her a glass of water, he raised his voice another decibel and began reading again. "Announces the engagement of her daughter, Miss Faith Middleton Hoagland . . ." Through his reading he could hear angry words behind him. Chugh was scolding the youngest, red-faced Hoagland boy, who appeared already to have had too many Scotch and sodas. "Your damn stallion was running loose, and almost tipped us over." How stupid of Chugh to mention it. Dr. Walding now spoke up very loud in order that no one in the room could hear anything but his insistent voice: "Mrs. Richard Hallowell Hoagland, of Co-Eden, announces the engagement of her daughter, Miss Faith Middleton Hoagland to Mr. Chugh Flickwyr Walding of Finchwicke. No date for the wedding has yet been fixed. It will probably take place in June."

Hebe and Vivi clapped when he had finished, but otherwise there was dead silence in the room. Dr. Walding longed for the maid to offer him a whiskey and soda, as he could think of nothing else to say.

Hebe broke the silence. "I hope it suits everybody. I wrote it, of course." She looked as pleased as a Cheshire cat. "Do you like it, Chugh?"

"It's all right," Chugh said disparagingly.

Dr. Walding felt he had to keep on talking bravely. "Hebe, my dear. One question. Why did you say the marriage will *probably* take place in June? I thought it was all set, *mutatis mutandis*, the the fourteenth!" He permitted himself a fatherly wink at the bride-to-be, who was nervously twisting a loose lock of her hair.

"Not in the least necessary for the hoi polloi to know the exact date!" Hebe answered very crossly, looking hurt that her efforts had been criticized.

"Forgive me, my dear. Of course not." Dr. Walding felt that things were going very badly. Becca had not spoken at all. Her small foot, crossed over one knee, was kicking up and down beneath her taffeta skirt.

"Whether the stallion is in or out is none of my business." Rick Hoagland, addressing Chugh, slurred his words. "He belongs to Faith. Speak to her! She plans to take him down with her to Finchwicke—that I know. But, of course, we haven't been able to get him gelded yet. One of his testicles hasn't come down." He underlined his words by picking up a silver letter opener in the form of a dagger from a table of bibelots, and flicking it threateningly at Chugh's crotch.

Dr. Walding was embarrassed and ashamed at this barnyard discussion in front of the ladies, even though they were not supposed to understand. Quickly he decided to switch the subject to world affairs, even though he had been planning to save that topic until he and Chugh were faced with the Hoagland men alone after dinner.

"Not all the news in the paper was good." His voice again filled the silence in the room as he turned to his hostess, who was staring at him with a fixed look in her strange pale eyes. "Wasn't it dreadful about the *Hawke*?"

"The what?"

"The British ship. Sunk by an absolutely unheard-of device. A torpedo from a German submarine. Very, very serious implications for international shipping, don't you think, Doctor?" Dr. Walding found himself addressing the handsome Dr. Marshall Hoagland, looking deathly bored, standing in front of the fireplace, hands in his pockets, rising up and down on the balls of his feet. "I mean, if there's going to be a war, one would assume the place to be would be in the British Navy. But who wants to be shot at from underwater?"

"If there's a war," said Rick Hoagland belligerently, "the place to be is in the cavalry, in the First City Troop. I'm sure Chugh would agree, great goddamn fox hunter that he is. Wouldn't you, Chugh, old man?"

"I intent to join my cousin Knight Chyldes in the Air Force."

"Oh, fat chance. You'll be a foot soldier, you know."

"Do stop talking about the war!" Becca said, "I can't bear it. And Faith! Do stop twisting your hair like that."

Dinner was announced at that moment and Dr. Walding jumped quickly to his feet and offered his arm to his hostess. There didn't seem to be any easy subjects for conversation, and he was famished for food and drink. It was the first time he had been out to dinner with ladies since Thessaly had died, and he felt slightly disloyal to her as he paced through the big hall with another woman.

In the darkened dining room the stained-glass shade of the electric chandelier had been lowered down over the center of the table, shining on the mounds of purple and green hothouse grapes dripping from a gold and crystal epergne, and leaving the faces of the people most becomingly in the outer dimnesses of the golden oak paneled room. Dr. Walding was seated on Becca's right, with the little actress next to him. Chugh was across the table on Becca's left, with the terrier next to him. At the other end of the table, surrounded by her brothers, sat Faith, so that the Hoagland family presented a united front.

Dr. Walding had planned to make a speech to the engaged couple composed from the clipping from the paper, but he had already used that up. Couldn't talk about the war. Couldn't talk about the hunt, nor Thessaly.

"Chugh really is learning to fly," he suddenly volunteered. "He's found some man at the old Taylor farm who has a Curtiss-Jenny."

"Perfectly safe! I love the feeling of it and can't wait to go up alone. I'll fly over and buzz your chimney tops, Mrs. Hoagland."

Hebe threw up her hands like a statue of horrification. "Fly? You'll be killed before the wedding!"

The little actress leaned forward. "I do hope you'll take me up for a ride, Chugh." She had been sitting there like a cameo with her heart-shaped face, her slanted eyes. The remark seemed strangely out of place, and a horrible, wide silence followed.

Why didn't the others talk? Dr. Walding wondered desperately as he drained his sherry glass. Becca was sitting there, not hearing. Possibly she was having one of the migraine headaches for which she was famous. Dr. Walding had tucked the expanse of white napkin into his vest and prepared to spoon up the plate of steaming terrapin soup when suddenly Becca shook the long diamond drops in her ears and leaned toward him from her corseted waist.

"You can all have your horses and your flying machines. I—you won't be able to guess what I am going to do. I am going to learn to drive a motor of my own!"

Ah! At last a subject *she* would be interested in. She had made it sound as though it should be an amazing subject. Herself. A motor.

Dr. Walding looked suitably amazed. "*You?* Driving a motorcar?"

"Why not? I think it's a delicious idea. It just suddenly popped into my mind this minute."

"I suppose next you'll be telling us, Mama dear, that you're going up in one of those crazy flying machines with Chugh. Skipping about among the moon and the stars," Bellwood said in light, dinner-table banter from the other end of the table, helping to pass an awkward evening.

"I'm serious. I'm determined to learn to drive."

"Why not get a little electric? Thessaly had one," said Dr. Walding, wiping the terrapin from his mustache.

"Not at all! Chugh has been crawling over here in that several times. It can scarcely get up our steep drive. It's much too slow. I want something to go into the city, to concerts and plays. You see, Doctor, you're stealing my only daughter and it's going to very dull here for me without her. I've determined to start a whole new life. I've settled my mind on a Cadillac coupe." And in order to include the whole table in her topic, she called down to the other end to where Rick was seated between Vivi and Faith. All their faces were turned toward her, spoons poised over the steaming soup. "Rick, I commission *you* to buy it. You're the one who really knows about automibiles."

Dr. Walding saw a gleam of pleasure shoot from the son's eyes toward his mother, a nod of total understanding, as though they two were alone in a wasteland of strangers around the laden table.

"I will start searching tomorrow, for my beautiful, beautiful Mama."

And after that the conversation was all about how brave and wonderful she was and always had been. And Dr. Walding said that if she was really getting a car, she would be expected every day at Finchwicke. Which was, after all, very close, and she mustn't feel that she was losing a daughter, but rather gaining a son, and in himself a new, well, a new compatriot.

In the middle of dinner, he noticed the maid had come in and whispered something in Dr. Marshall Hoagland's ear, who immediately, without a word, got up and left the dinner table. A woman in labor, of course, but not a subject that could be mentioned.

"My dog and I will spend the night here," Hebe said, "to be ready for the influx tomorrow." But nobody listened to Hebe. Becca, at the head of the table, her white skin shining like moonlight, was delighting Dr. Walding with tales of herself as a child, all designed to prove that of course she could learn to drive a fast car.

"No one could drive a skittish horse like my Grandmother Huger! One day on Tradd Street she gave a sharp tug of the reins and swerved the wheel of her carriage into Miss Flossie

Lee Jones, who was crossing. It was made to look as if the horse had shied, you know. But no one was hurt except Flossie Lee, and she limped for the rest of her life. I shouldn't have known about it, of course, except Granny used to boast a little. Ah! Flossie was an octoroon. Quite beautiful, of course, but diseased. She ruined the lives of many young men, but Granny took care of her, and made it look like an accident too. She was a superior driver. And I see absolutely no reason why I couldn't be the same in my Cadillac."

"I do hope you have no plans to run anyone down!"

"At the moment, I have no cause to do that!"

All around the table laughed at the sprightly talk. But when the men rejoined the ladies in the gray and gold salon, having had their coffee and cigars in the red-leather smoking room, Dr. Walding was not surprised to find that the hostess had already excused herself and gone upstairs with a headache. She overdid, the poor, brave darling. Dr. Walding pinched Faith's cheek, and said that she hadn't said a word all evening, and the cat must have got at her tongue. Then he said goodnight all around and bore Chugh away with him.

"We must get them down to Finchwicke to dinner," he said to Chugh on the way home. "Really a damned attractive woman, Becca Hoagland. I shouldn't be surprised if the excitement and joy of this wedding restore her health completely. The brothers drink too much. Faith a quiet mouse. We'll be able to handle her!"

"I'm grateful you think so, Father. She hasn't given any trouble yet."

5

Presenting

HEBE AND FAITH grew to be very close friends in the course of the long, closely chaperoned winter. Faith was hardly permitted to be alone with Chugh except for an occasional luncheon in town at a restaurant, a Saturday jog to the meet, or a Sunday walk in the woods. Instead she spent most of her time with Hebe working out the details of what was to happen on that particular day, after which Faith would spend *all* her time with Chugh.

The work of organizing the wedding had begun in the small office which Hebe had set up in the back of her own house in Rittenhouse Square. But now that spring was coming—all the gutters unfreezing and gushing, all the hens scratching around in the coop anxious to begin laying their eggs and hatching out their chicks—Hebe transferred her headquarters to the Present Room at Co-Eden.

Leaving the house at just about the same time Marshall left for his office, Hebe caught the nine-thirty train out from town every morning, carrying her brief case and her little Pekingese dog, Ogden, under her arm. She proceeded directly to the Present Room, which had become the center of activity of the house.

The creation of the Present Room and the transfer of activity from Becca's own salon to that room had taken place in accordance with her wishes that Hebe take over the performance of the rites necessary to ensure a happy earthly union—such as Faith remembered Mama had had with Papa. The large storeroom next to the laundry, formerly the children's playroom had been swept clear and designated as the Present Room. It was in a perfect location on the ground floor, with a door to the outside through which the presents could be brought from the station express office and deposited in a pile in one corner, without the men's muddy boots dirtying up the house, and from which could easily be carted out the piles of wrapping paper, excelsior, and other mess which packages always make. It was also a strategic spot for the wedding guests, on their way from the reception tent in the rose garden into the house for luncheon, to conveniently come in and find their own particular donations displayed.

Long planks had been set up on wooden horses and covered with white sheets to make sturdy display tables. These were arranged around the edges of the walls, and in the middle of the room was a flat-topped desk where Faith and Hebe sat with their lists and their writing materials. A round-topped table was kept for the display of everything new that had come that day to show to Chugh on his late afternoon visits, when he would come straight from the station, bringing red roses or chocolate Algaras for the girls. Gee Whitefield might be there. Or darling Viv and her little daughter, Becca Bee. "Look, Chugh, isn't she sweet?" Faith would seize the beribboned baby girl and hold her up close for Chugh's inspection. But Chugh always made a funny face and turned away. "I like them when they get a bit older. Get doing things. Stop drooling."

Hebe's sister, Mariette, dropped by often to share in the fun. Oh such fun, opening things. Darling Mariette had given the first party for Faith, sending out cards of invitation to their whole class at Springbank. "A cup-and-saucer shower for Miss Hoagland at four-thirty."

These most precious mementos stood on a special little tea table of their own on an embroidered cloth. Thirty-four teacups to be remembered by, each one different. "Look at this one in the Blue Onion pattern. Isn't it exactly like Gee? These teacups are my favorite things. I'll never forget my friends."

The first long table had been left empty for the rest of the presents which would start arriving after the invitations were mailed in a day or two. On the next table, samples of the linens that had been ordered from Mme. Makalapoof for the trousseau. Tea cloths, luncheon cloths, tablecloths for dinner with their embroidered matching damask napkins, linen sheets and embroidered pillowcases, finger towels, hand towels in damask linen from Ireland. Huck towels, bath towels and bath sheets. Lace doilies, and bureau scarves, and everything for the kitchen. On another table, examples of the flat silver, three dozen of everything all marked with Faith's initials and being given by her brothers. A set of marked crystal—two dozen water, burgundy, claret, white wine, sherry, and champagne glasses—from Tanta Chyldes in

Boston. A Limoges dinner service from Knight in Paris. Dessert plates in Royal Worcester. Breakfast sets. Silver ornaments. Candlesticks. Lamps. Vases. Bowls. Tea sets. Ten sets of demi-tasse cups.

Hebe presided over the putting of gifts into their correct places, moving an object an inch to the left or just a bit forward. "There now, that looks much better. Don't touch it again. Doesn't this ginger jar look exactly like Leonora?" Hebe liked to see the women as beautiful things, like porcelain jars. It seemed the essence of morality. Hebe was happiest in the Present Room, among the "things."

Hebe took it upon herself to open most of the presents. "You don't mind, do you, darling? Marshall had to go away in the middle of the night last night. Again. I don't know what I'd do if I couldn't come out here and open packages." And Hebe would place the object on "the new arrival table." After Chugh's inspection it would be placed on the long table, in a strategic place among the other children, as Hebe called the presents.

Each present had to be personally acknowledged by a prompt note from Faith. No excuse for delegating this chore! And sometimes Hebe kept Faith slaving in the Present Room most of the day until her neck ached and her fingers were numb. Every present was registered and numbered as Hebe opened it, in a red-leather ledger: the sender, the present, the date, from which shop, to be kept or returned. Then Faith began writing to each person down the page, each note a little different

Dear Mrs. Smyth,

Thank you for the marvelous crystal goblets. They will look beautiful among my own things when I move to Finchwicke. Chugh and I are most appreciative of your thoughts and good wishes.

With thanks again,
Faith M. Hoagland

This afternoon Faith and Hebe sat together at Hebe's large flat-topped desk going over the lists of the people who had been invited to parties already given for Chugh and Faith and who, therefore, must be invited to the wedding. The Birds had given a dinner dance at Birdgrove during Christmas holidays. Here was the list of Jonah Wedgewright's New Year's party for them at The Rabbit. And, of course, the

Oldthwaites! Johnny and Paula had given a formal dinner at Oldebrooke. Faith had wanted to appear at her best that night because these were Chugh's closest friends and now would be hers also. But she had come away with a little hollow feeling. Johnny had been scrupulously polite, but she had found it heavy sledding with Paula who was so much more sophisticated than she, and who had been surprisingly intimate with Chugh. Faith hadn't realized they knew each other that well.

But never mind, here was the list of people that the dear McCuskers had invited last night.

"It's such a beautiful day, Hebe. And my head is positively spinning from the McCuskers' party. Can't we stop and gossip a little?" Faith asked hopefully.

The party had been such fun. With ladies in the coxswain's seat, rowing out on the river from the University Barge Club. Supper and shuffleboard, music and country dance afterwards at The Lilacs. The dear McCuskers, they had gone to so much trouble because they weren't going to be able to come to the wedding. They had booked passage on the *Lusitania* on the seventh of May and were off to Europe to investigate the war for President Wilson. Senator McCusker was on the Munitions Committee and was enraged that the territorial waters around Great Britain had been pronounced by Germany to lie within the region of hostilities. He was determined to defy them.

Faith mimicked the Senator's booming voice. "I consider it a gross provocation. It was received in the Philadelphia Club with disdain and mockery! The insolence of the Imperial German Embassy in Washington issuing a warning in American papers to *Americans*."

But then the Senator had risen and displayed quite another side of himself, being most courtly and charming as he had proposed a toast to the happiness of the daughter of his dearest old friend, Hal Hoagland. And he had brought down the house with his retelling of the midnight race of the station cabs between Co-Eden and Coq d'Or and of how he had been dumped out at the gates of his own driveway.

"Wasn't he screaming, Hebe?" Hebe, of course, had accompanied Faith to this party as well as all the others.

"Screaming. And I thought the fireworks quite the most beautiful I ever saw!"

"Yes. But they made Chugh and Johnny so nervous. The way the glow lit up the whole night sky so that you could see the leaves on the trees in the gorge of the Schuylkill. At first they had thought it was an explosion at the Blue Rock. All the labor there is German, you know. And there have been so many explosions Chugh thinks that maybe there's some plot!"

"Back to work," Hebe ordered. "We *must* get this list in order to show Chugh when he comes in. He'll be here from the station any minute now. If we don't stick to it, we'll never get these things addressed and mailed. And they *have* to go out exactly twenty-one days before the wedding. That's the correct thing."

Hebe was in charge, and Faith submitted to her willingly. Hebe was the high priestess of the household gods who had to be propitiated to pull off the great miracle of this wedding. Hebe pointed to the shiny white boxes from Bailey, Banks and Biddle stocked up in piles on the end of her writing table. "When I think of what difficulty we had getting these done. I never thought they'd come in time with all the fuss your mother made about the crest. So odd of her, don't you think, when she'd kept 'out of things' so much? But they're very nice, after all."

Inside the boxes were double sheets of fine white dull paper, exactly seven and one half inches high and six and one half inches wide, engraved in shaded Old English print, with the Hoagland shield embossed on the top. Hebe had told her mother-in-law that the shield was not correct except for a man, and had ordered the design reworked in the form of a lozenge, for a lady's use. But Becca had reverted to her soft Southern accent, as she always did when annoyed. "I always have, and always will continya to act as if the Judge were still alive. Therefore at his daughter's wedding we will use the male form of the Hoagland crest, which my husband had traced back in his family to Charlemagne."

"Chugh says it's not correct to use a coat of arms in America, Mama!" Faith had dared to intervene.

"There's nothing not American about it. We've never severed our relationships with our royal ancestors. At least not we who come from Charleston. It would have been better for us if we had remained under the Crown."

And so the invitations had been re-engraved, and here at last they were, with the crest, a crown within a shield, over a stag courant, pierced by an arrow, the pennant bearing the Hoagland motto, SEMPER SUPERBUS ET FASTIDIOSUS.

And having made that show of authority, Becca had retired from the scene and given herself over completely to her fascination with her new car.

"Anyway, while we're waiting for Chugh to come and join us, here are the lists . . ." chanted Hebe, picking up a pile of papers. Faith doodled with a pencil on the back of an envelope. Make a list of the lists. And don't forget to add love. Love. Love. They were lists of all their close friends and the Walding family and all the Hoagland relations. But the list for the wedding invitations had to be boiled down. Because Chugh was in mourning, it had been decided that all those on the calling-card lists of both families would be invited to the church, plus all the current servants and retired family retainers. Absolutely no business associates would be invited. These people would get announcements mailed on the day after. And only those who could be seated at small tables in the great hall and in the dining room would be invited to the wedding lunch by a small card enclosed with the invitation.

Chalk, of course, was to do the catering, and he had said that one hundred and fifty was the maximum he could set up for, provided there was also an outside reception tent.

"But Chugh has submitted a hundred and fifty, and you, Faith, have submitted a hundred and twenty, only a hundred of which are the same. And as there are seventy in family, the fat of a hundred names now has to be boiled from the list. As soon as he arrives, we must get right down to it. Here's the list of things to tell the caterer. The menus for the wedding breakfast. Transportation to and from the church. As Dr. Walding is having that special train come out from town, we will need carriages and automobiles at the station. Here are the ushers. And—oh yes—here it is, the list of the bridesmaids . . ."

Faith drew a valentine heart around the scrolled letters LOVE and plunged ahead with something else she had been meaning to say. After all, she and Hebe had grown so close. Surely Hebe would understand. "I've decided to have darling Viv as matron of honor. Not that I don't long to have you, too, Hebe. But you'll be too busy pushing me in the door." She could see that Hebe was hurt to the quick. One sister-in-law in the procession, the other a menial at the door with a list. But one couldn't imagine Hebe with her matronly figure even considering . . .

"Of course I wouldn't consider it. But I would like to have been asked."

"But darling, you must understand. I *want* you. It's just

153

that Viv doesn't know anybody, and I thought it might help to get her *in*."

"Don't you think she might be a little conspicuous? I mean, the baby and everything? Only three months after the marriage was announced! It does take nine, you know."

"But, you see, I've already invited her. She's gone in to Miss Meeley's to be measured for her dress."

The bridesmaids were to wear yellow taffeta, with the fashionable wing hips and hobble skirts, the fichu necklines to be filled in with high-boned net collars, their hats to be toques of lavender velvet. They would each wear an amethyst pendant, the gift of the bride to her maids. And Hebe had already ordered the bridesmaids' bouquets of violets with a yellow rose in the center from Battles—the bill, of course, to be sent to Chugh.

"Of course if you've asked her without consulting me, there isn't much I can do."

"But I don't think, darling Hebe, you'd *want* to be."

"You're quite right. I don't." Darling Hebe was stung, suddenly unable to move her right hand.

A figure darkened the glass in the door. It was Chugh, coming in by the back way, swinging his cane and carrying a bunch of daffodils done up in green waxed paper. "I bought them from a little man in the Reading Station. The first I've seen."

Hebe jumped up. "Look, Faith. Here's Chugh! We'll arrange them in one of the wedding vases!"

Faith had to admire the way Hebe greeted him as though nothing had happened. But then, whenever Chugh came into a room the whole atmosphere changed, and whatever had been unpleasant was cleared away by his electricity.

Chugh put down his hat and stick on the empty present table and Hebe leaped to pick them up again. "We have to keep it spotlessly clean," she said, placing the contaminated objects on a folding chair.

Faith was glad for the diversionary flurry and happy beyond words when at last he got around to speaking to her. How she longed for just one stolen kiss. Her lips and the palms of her hands ached.

"Good afternoon, my sweet!" Chugh surveyed the tabletops, as he always did. "Whew!" he said, "I don't know what we're going to do with all this loot. There's not going to be any place to put it away. We already have everything we need at Finchwicke."

"Now, Chugh, you know very well that Faith needs her own things."

"What! Nothing new in the delivery room?" Chugh taunted Hebe, pointing at the empty table for new arrivals.

"Yes, there is a box. A huge box over there in the regular corner," Faith interceded "But I told Hebe this once we'd have to wait for you to open it, as you were coming early. Sort of a prize, you know, for getting through this dreadful list."

"From J. E. Caldwell's again," said Chugh, inspecting the box in all its white ribbons.

"Never mind that. Sit right down here opposite us, and we'll discuss these names one by one and get the job done. This is the first time I've really gotten you in my grasp, Chugh. You've been as elusive as a fish. Now you must concentrate. As I've explained to you before, it's entirely the prerogative of the bride's family to set the number of guests, and you've exceeded your share, Chugh!"

Circling around like a terrier reluctant to kennel up, Chugh sniffed among the tables, pointing with his cigar—dropping an ash—fingerprinting this and picking up that while Hebe held her breath, until he finally settled down in the chair placed for him on the opposite side of the flat-topped desk.

"Now we'll just begin, going right down the list from name to name until we get it all done." Hebe pulled her pince-nez on a chain from where they had been tucked in the bosom of her purple serge and placed them on the end of her fat nose, authoritatively pinching the nostrils together as though it were not necessary for her to breathe.

Suddenly Faith felt her feet bracketed by his. Warmth flooded her. How dare he? With Hebe sitting right beside her! Surely Hebe, too, would feel the heat beneath the desk. But she was being sensible and businesslike.

"I have collated all these lists. A list of the lists of the lists. Who, for instance, are the Leonard Bunces?"

"Our old butler. He's made a fortune and moved to California. Leave him on because he won't come."

"An announcement, I think will do."

"Just as you say." Chugh was very affable to Hebe but not very sensible, hacking away indiscriminately at the older relations of his own list as long as he could, prolonging the delicious footsy-wootsy. "Why do I have to have Uncle Monkey and Aunt Lara? Let's chop them off."

But all Chugh's cousins and uncles and aunts had come to

call on Faith and her mother during the winter. Many had brought engagement presents. Faith protested, "Oh, but Chugh! They came to call and they were so sweet! And he's your father's brother! Of course we have to have *them*."

"She'll wear her ratty ermine cape and the whole church will smell of mothballs."

Faith giggled.

It was decided that Rosalie Chyldes, adorable and blond and Chugh's second cousin, would be the flower girl. "That will be all right, won't it, Hebe? Even if she is on the *other* side?" And then Chugh said how much he would like to have Faith invite his cousin Edith, Knight's sister, Baroness Bellanowski, from the North Shore of Boston to be a bridesmaid. And Hebe had said that would be quite all right because even though Edith was married, she was, after all, married to an Estonian baron, and what could be more romantic? And, of course, the Baron would be an usher?

To that, Chugh said no. He couldn't stomach the Baron.

That would be all right too, Hebe said, as long as Chugh included Bellwood and Rick in his list of ushers. "Of course Marshall will give the bride away," Hebe had decreed. "He's the eldest brother. At least I'll know where he is *that* afternoon."

Faith looked up from the list, interrupting the roll call. She looked at Chugh adoringly. "And oh, Chugh! I've decided to have *Viv* for matron of honor. I'd just been telling Hebe when you appeared."

Chugh's face darkened and set in a stubborn way. His feet ceased to caress hers and retreated under his chair. "Not in my wedding. I'll refuse to pay for her bouquet!"

The worst part was that Hebe looked triumphant, as though Chugh were serious. But Faith couldn't believe that he was. "Chugh, you must be teasing. She doesn't really know anybody and she's lonely out here. It would be such a good opportunity for her to meet our friends and . . ."

Chugh remained severe. "She knows more of my friends than you realize. She's just a common actress. Not a proper person to go down the aisle with you, my sweet."

"If you mean she hasn't been baptized and isn't a member of our church . . ."

"That's not what I mean at all. There are some things you have to take my word for."

"But after all, she is my brother's wife!"

"But after all, so is Hebe your brother's wife!"

Faith subsided in deep embarrassment. In *front* of Hebe.

"Thank you, Chugh." Hebe took over in syrupy tones of gratitude for his consideration. "Thank you. Faith was kind enough to include me, but I've explained to her, I'll be much too busy. But now you listen to me, Chugh. Fair is fair. You invite exactly who you want for your ushers, that's your prerogative. Faith has nothing, nothing, nothing in the world to say about it. *But,* she has a right to her bridesmaids."

Faith was grateful to Hebe for backing her up, under the circumstances. No one understood how much she did love Viv in the way of wanting to save her.

"Oh, all right then, Hebe. You're the boss." Chugh's indifference solidified. "Let's not have any tempests in the Present Room. Too many damn teapots in here."

"That's settled. Now let's go on with the list. We *have* to finish . . ."

But Chugh had pushed it aside. "Hebe, you do it. I don't give a damn at all, who's invited and who isn't. Let's have some fun and open that box."

Faith knew enough about men to agree. If he were forced any further, Chugh might simply go away. Then she and Hebe would be left with a wedding on their hands and no groom. As smoothly as possible she reached for the enormous pair of desk scissors kept for the purpose of opening presents and handed them to Chugh before Hebe could pick them up from force of habit. Then she established herself to make the entry in her red-leather book.

"It's from Caldwell. Put that in before we forget." Hebe's sage advice.

Chugh cut the white ribbon rather than untying the complicated bow, and removed the lid from the glossy white box.

Hebe dived in.

"I do wish they'd leave the card on top so we could know right away who it's from. But they haven't, so we'll have to be careful not to throw it out." Hebe started burrowing through the mountains of excelsior and came out with an object in a purple flannel bag. "Silver! I do hope they haven't gone and had it marked in case I don't like it."

"It's *my* present, Hebe," said Faith, smiling, sitting behind the desk, pen poised.

"Well, of course. It's for you and Chugh both. It's only that I get so excited being in the thick of things. Here, you undo it." Hebe handed the heavy object, still in the flannel bag to

Chugh. He removed a silver coffeepot, embossed with raised roses and lilies and intricately chased with curlicues around the fat bellying bottom which curved up in a swan's neck to the cover, tipped with an ivory pineapple. "It's marked, all right, but the initials are so fancy I can't see what the monogram is." Hebe seized it.

"Well, there's a large running W in the center, and C and F intricately twined together. Chugh and Faith Walding. It's brand-new. And of the very best and heaviest quality. I think it's perfectly beautiful!"

"I'm not sure I care for it." Chugh set the pot down with a thump on the table for new arrivals. "We already have so much beautiful old silver at Finchwicke. We don't need anything more."

Hebe dove down and pulled out the rest of the objects, which she handed to Chugh to uncover. "A sugar bowl. A creamer. A pair of matching tongs. And *here* at last is the precious card." Hebe started to open it, but Chugh took it out of her hand.

"Let me see it, please." He was silent, studying it for a moment. And then he read, "From Walter and Erlene. By cracky, that was nice of them. They're invited, of course, to the luncheon, aren't they?"

"Who are Walter and Erlene? I never heard of them."

"Well, maybe you haven't heard of everybody, Hebe. They're the Josenthals, my partner, and his wife. I can't imagine how we forgot them. Put them on the list right away, Hebe. They're the most important to me."

"It's impossible, Chugh. Your quota is full. The list is closed. We can't add one more person."

"Damn you, Hebe! You seem to forget this is my wedding, I invite whom I want. A lot of my mother's relations from Boston won't come, even though Tanta Chyldes is lending her yacht for our honeymoon. My aunt is practically in a wheelchair, so my side of the church is going to be empty. It seems to me we could take that into account and fill their places with my friends, dammit all!"

"Don't swear at me like that!"

"I'm sorry, Hebe. But I insist on having them. They mean a lot to me in business."

"But we aren't having any business people, Chugh. They can have an announcement."

"We're having the Josenthals, I tell you." Chugh's tongue clicked behind his teeth, baring the row of even white lowers.

"But they're Jews! Charlton wouldn't even let them hunt! They arrived one day and he told them to pack their saddles back into their buggy and be gone." Hebe spoke the words as though the Josenthals had tried to sully everything that was most precious and private. She was drumming on the table with her knuckles. Her chin extended pugnaciously toward Chugh. "We are going to have such a lovely wedding. Day after day we've slaved. We were going to have just the people we know best, and now you want to spoil it all by having outsiders. Cheap!" Hebe spat the last word.

"If that's the way Faith is going to feel about my friends, I think we better call the whole thing off."

"Indeed you're right. We're not having a wedding that I'm running if we're having Jews from your back office."

"Oh please! Please! I haven't said . . ." Faith's heart sank at the way she was being misconstrued. Things were suddenly going in the wrong direction. "I haven't said a word. Please stop it, both of you. You think you know everyone in society, but actually you don't, Hebe. And you yourself said that Chugh's list was sacred to him."

"And Chugh said he didn't give a damn who was invited and who wasn't!"

Chugh advanced on Hebe as if he were going to strike her. "I suppose you're not inviting my ushers either, you smug prig!"

"After everything I've done! To be spoken to in this way. To have you turn against me too, Faith!"

In a sudden gust of temper, Hebe gave an involuntary twitch to the white sheet covering the table where the Josenthal's silver stood, sending it crashing in a heap on the floor. In the shocked silence that followed, the ivory pineapple could be heard rolling across the floor into a corner of the hearth.

"Now see what you've done!" Chugh was cold and angry.

Hebe turned away from him with a rough gesture of furious disdain, tripping as she did so over the tablecloth under the most precious teacups, the fragile mementos that had been presented at Mariette's school-chum shower. In a sickening avalanche, slowly tipping at first, gathering momentum and speed, everything on the table crashed to the floor. Each teacup different, each one irreplaceable, now a bright heap of broken chips, the remains of her girlish happiness in shards on the floor, lying with the Josenthals' dented silver service.

Faith felt the tears standing in her eyes. She was too paralyzed by the dreadful scene to speak to Chugh when, picking up his hat and cane and exhibiting the superior self-control of the male, he turned and walked out through the nearest door without a word. The only sign of him was the vase of station daffodils, already perceptibly wilting in the warm dead air of the Present Room.

Hebe was sitting at her desk, her head down on her arms. Faith stood with her eyes tight shut, praying for help. After a moment, she felt herself swaying and opening her eyes to face the mess. One by one, Faith bent to pick up the pieces of the Josenthal silver. A little dented here and there, but they could be repaired. She inspected each massive piece before placing it back on the new-arrivals table.

Next she faced the teacups. It was as if the friends themselves were a broken thing of the past, a delicate remnant of a handle here, a jagged piece of saucer there. Automatically she went to the corner and got a dustpan and brush to sweep up the bits of bright brittle rubble which she poured into the empty silver box. The lightning disaster had numbed her feelings, but there was the certainty of pain to follow.

The new sound of broken bits breaking into smaller bits was accompanied by breath-catching sobs from Hebe, hiding her face at her desk.

Ignoring her, Faith extracted an invitation from the stacked boxes, and sitting at her own table, went about the task of addressing an invitation to the Josenthals, trying her best to form her hen-tracks into a reasonable copy of Hebe's perfect script.

Mr. & Mrs. Walter Josenthal
Deepdene
Germantown, Penna.

Deliberatly she creased the invitation, inserted the small card which invited the favored ones to luncheon, and stuffed the two into the thick white envelope. Carefully she pasted the stamp with the profile of George Washington exactly straight with the edge. She left the envelope unsealed. This evening, she would have it hand-delivered down to Finch-wicke for Chugh to see, and with it she would include a little personal note of loving apology. Quinn could stop by Finchwicke when he took Hebe to the train. It wasn't far out of the way.

And now the question about what to say to Hebe. Poor Hebe. It was as though she had undressed herself in an obscene way in front of Chugh by losing her self-control. She must be made to regain it, to take charge again; too many people were estranged already. Without Hebe, who would help her put on the wedding? Papa was dead. Mama was unapproachable. Rick was alienated. And when Guy Fitzjoy, her strength and buckler and Christ's vicar on earth who preached that God is love, had also tried to stop her marriage, the link between them had been severed. Guy had been a soul-brother, but he had acted in a most unchristian manner.

After that, she had begun to judge those around her by a new standard. Those who liked Chugh. Those who did not. Old friends were dropped. New friends were made. And now Hebe, who had seemed to understand the importance of Chugh, had fought with him.

Poor Hebe. So many of her friends were H-A-V-I-N-G this spring. It was all very hard on her. Faith put her arms around the shaking shoulders. How solid they were. How broad for a woman. How terrible that they were shaking!

At the touch, Hebe raised her streaming face and sobbed that she had come to the end of her rope. "I try to do the best I can, and now I've spoiled everything. But it's so hard. Marshall is giving up his general practice and opening a new office, *just* for people we know having babies. Two blocks from the Walnut Club! And he's hired that pretty Mrs. Proudfoot for his office nurse. She's a wonderful good, sweet woman, and Marshall is selfless in his career. I know all that. But it's very hard on me. She spends more time with him than I do. They're over there alone together, and when he comes home there's only me and the dog. So I try to keep busy too, to have something to talk about. Oh, Faith! I have tried so hard. And now I've gone and ruined the happy times we were having in the Present Room! I've made Chugh angry! And worst of all, I've broken your tea-tea-teacups." Stuttering over the words, she started to sob again.

Faith gave her a good shake from behind. "Oh please, Hebe! It was just an accident! Stop it at once. Don't you understand I *need* you? It doesn't matter about the teacups. Stop it at once and behave yourself!"

Faith was amazed at the sound of her own voice. She ap-

161

peared to have changed places with Hebe or to be like Miss Applegate, encouraging the hockey team to win the game. She wasn't sure she liked being Miss Applegate. One of the reasons for getting married was to prevent turning into Miss Applegate. Miss Applegate could be forgiven her bossiness—she had no husband. Hebe could be forgiven—she had no children of her own. But why, wondered Faith, am I turning into people like them? Why? When I would rather be like Vivi?

At the authoritarian words, Hebe sat up straight, fished her hankie out of her purple serge pocket, blew her nose, and straightened her spine. As the sobs abruptly ceased, Faith had a vision of Hebe's future, managing the social life of the young people all over the city, punishing any wild impulse with the strictures which an unkind Fate had imposed on her. "Off the list with them!"

Suddenly Faith was famished for Vivi, and only able to survive the ordeal of the rest of the afternoon because of the knowledge that Quinn would be taking Hebe to the train, delivering the note to Chugh, and returning with the Bellwood Hoaglands for the night.

Vivi had a sophistication, a secret knowledge, a worldliness—as did Chugh—which fascinated Faith. Vivi never gave orders, never seemed to put herself forward, and yet she always managed to be the focal point. Still, when one tried to remember Vivi's face, one could only remember the impression of a faunlike mask. Whereas with Gladys Whitefield one could remember her faintly perspiring, heavy cheeks bouncing as she tried to keep up with the rest of the hunt on Soup-Plates. One could recall the faces of any of the girls at Springbank, as well as the evil, glittering, beautiful, selfish face of Becca. But Vivi was like water. And yet, she would be a friend, because Faith was parched for a friend from whom she could learn the ways of the world. And whose soul, in return, could be saved for Christ.

"Everybody needs you, Hebe. How would anyone have parties without you? How would anything get done? Come on now, put the Josenthals on the list, squeeze them in to the lunch!"

"But who will they sit beside?"

"They can sit with Guy Fitzjoy."

Chugh Walding, having left the Present Room by the inner door, found himself in a dark warren of laundries, storerooms, and kitchens of Co-Eden. Enraged, he fought his way up the back stairs, only to be trapped in the pantries. Opening one wrong swinging door after another, he finally came to the dining room and then the front hall.

To question his business friends! Indeed that was a poisoned prick to the very heart of his way of life. What would be the point in his sacrificing his maverick's freedom to satisfy his mother's will and inherit the money to run Finchwicke if he had to be dictated to by Hebe? Perhaps he should begin by making a fortune on his own, be free to make his own acquaintances who could help him on the way to success. And after that, maybe he would seek a wife—a long-stemmed girl, more sophisticated, who could tell a whore from a bridesmaid. Someone like Paula Oldthwaite, who would be a help to a man.

He ran down the last few steps into the vestibule and slapped his gray derby on his head. "God damn you forever! That's the last you'll see of me!" In clipped, icy tones, he cursed the suit of armor standing in the corner. The visor hanging from the empty helmet grinned stupidly back at him. He stomped out of the house, slammed the door, and set the design of vaseline glass in the mullions of the front door shaking and shivering in his wake.

Mrs. Hoagland was standing on the steps under the portecochere about to enter the front seat of her tiny new car. It was a black gleaming jewel, the spokes of the wheels painted plum, two fine lines of plum around the black enamel body, Becca's crest and initial on the door, the interior upholstered in a fine plum wool. Mrs. Hoagland was like a demon in the little bullet, practicing by herself hour after hour on the driveway, her eyes like pinpoints, her diamond rings standing up from the fingers clenched on the ivory wheel, fresh roses jiggling the crystal bud vase in a pure gold holder on the doorjamb.

Feeling more annoyed than ever, he brushed past her without a word and strode over to his mother's electric, parked in the circle. He would have liked to have gone off with a spurt of gravel, but the old lady's buggy could only move sedately down the hill, no threat to creatures on the road—a skunk, a squirrel, a dog, a cat, a pheasant on the windshield. The engagement was broken, as far as he was concerned. No Josenthals, no wedding. He would go to France immediately and join Knight Chyldes and kill Huns. Possibly get himself killed. Die a hero's death. What was the point of sitting around in these fenced fields, pastured in, made to galumph around on a bucking horse to please the women? Maybe the Historical Society would put up a plaque to him at Finchwicke. Birthplace of Chugh Walding, famous ace who gave his life flying for France in repayment of the debt of his own country to Lafayette.

And right now he had a place he could go. Up in the air—solo.

He couldn't wait to get up in the sky. And what difference would it make if he were killed? That would serve them right. He had visions of Hebe and Faith waiting for him on the church steps, with Vivi in her bridesmaid's dress. Every man in Philadelphia, including Bellwood Hoagland, knew who Vivi was. Molly Franklynne's daughter. Supposedly fathered in England by a Coldstream Guardsman, a cousin of a cousin of Hal Hoagland's. When Molly arrived in Philadelphia with a letter of introduction from him and a little hush money in her pocket, Hal had helped set her up in one of his properties.

Molly's was a very special, high-class place. And everybody knew that most of the money Molly made went to pay the expenses at the convent where Vivi had been brought up. After that, the money went to get Vivi started on the stage in New York, acting bit parts with the Barrymores. Molly adored her daughter with every breath in her body ("She had royal blood, you know"), and only infrequently would she allow Vivi to sing and play at private parties for a select group of gentlemen in the front of the house, and would never allow her daughter to go upstairs with anyone but Judge Hoagland—and after his death, with no one. Nevertheless, on one very fancy occasion, New Year's dinner a couple of years ago, Chugh had toyed with the idea of getting Vivi for himself, but Bellwood Hoagland had wanted his father's young mistress for himself and had offered her the lead part in his stock company as well as marriage.

Vivi annoyed Chugh very much. "I do hope you'll take me up for a ride, Chugh." The nerve of her, putting on airs, bringing her brat out to Co-Eden to spend the afternoon in the Present Room. She had sat there, with the whore's grandchild on her lap disguised as an aristocrat baby in her long lace petticoats. Ah, Viv was a good actress, all right, taking on the genteel coloring of Mrs. Hoagland's gray and gold salon like a chameleon. Naming her baby, Rebecca, thinking that Mrs. Hoagland would leave her all her diamond rings!

And Faith had cried, "Isn't she sweet?" and hugged and kissed the baby in her arms, a pure girlish happiness streaming from her face. Faith was so innocent there was no way he could explain to her about Vivi. Nor did he wish her to know anything about that side of his life. He cursed as he crept along toward the old Taylor Farm, dipping down under the dark trestle, coming out again into the spring sun on the other side.

The very existence of Molly's had been threatened by this busybody little girl he had been thinking of making his wife. If only the damn minister had kept his mouth shut and minded his own business. Wages of sin indeed! He ought to take what money he could get for his church and be thankful. Instead, he got Faith all stirred up by what he had called a home for motherless girls being in the Hoagland estate. It had been a very near thing—Faith wanting to go in there with her Thanksgiving baskets! Thank God Welch had stopped her when she had asked him for the address. He had explained it was not a good time to visit, as they were in the process of moving the location of the Home to a better district uptown. Faith had told Chugh that it was a great comfort to her that a man like Mr. Welch Seabreese was looking into things, and that she had asked him to have the matron send measurements of all the girls so that she could send each of them a new blouse for Christmas.

Damn all Lady Bountifuls, anyway! Why couldn't Faith be just for him?

Besides all the fuss about the wedding, it had been a tight eight months financially. As he himself had no working capital, Chugh had borrowed heavily against his future income from the Josenthals to expand the Blue Rock Works. The war promised quick and easy profits for the works, and young Walter Josenthal, who knew the business, had been taken back as a third owner. All this was in their favor. But there were worries. Around the country, there had been a rash of explosions, many of them set off by the German workers in the plants. Chugh remembered the girl in the workman's shack at Blue Rock with the fat German baby at her bare breast and wondered if she, too, was connected to the international plot which had resulted in the recall of the German and Austrain ambassadors. If Blue Rock went up, Chugh's finances would go with it . . .

Thank God for the relaxation of his flying lessons. He loved taking the Curtiss-Jenny further and further afield, wondering if he would get back alive to land in the cow pasture of the old Taylor Farm. And he loved sharing his experience with Knight Chyldes, to whom he had written regularly:

> *I am to be married on June 14th, and how I wish that you could be my best man! Up to now, Knight, we have always been together in everything we have done. Is there any chance that you might have leave?*

And Knight had written back:

> *I won't be able to come to your wedding, as every leave I get, I go to Paris to confer with our friend Myron Herrick, the American Ambassador, who is working out the details with both our government and the French that will allow Americans to serve with the French Army as a unit without giving up their citizenship or joining the Foreign Legion. As Lafayette came to aid George Washington, so now we may repay them and join them in their desperate fight for freedom . . . But . . . I wish to make my presence felt at your nuptials, Cousin, and have suggested to Edith and Mother that you pass a night with them at Whippen Point and then honeymoon on the yacht. Take the* Viatrix II *to Heron Bay, as that is where you tell me you are going. Where else, indeed, could be so beautiful? But a proper honeymoon must begin with a sea voyage, and I trust a pleasure yacht will not be torpedoed in the Gulf of Main. Nonetheless, keep a weather eye out for periscopes, not discounting your own, good cousin! May you be happily submerged in the warm waters of marital bliss for many years! My best to your bride, whom I remember in the hunting field when I came down to visit with you at Finchwicke as being a bold sort of Diana . . .*

To which Chugh in turn had replied:

> *I grow increasingly angry at the continued aggressiveness of the Boche. I feel more and more tied to my mother country, England, and incensed that she should be threatened by the barbarians. I long to join you in France. I need the adventure, Knight. I really do. But the situation south of the border here is very bad. The Germans are stirring it up down there too, encouraging Pancho Villa. And, of course, if the City Troop should be ordered into Mexico, I would have to go with them, unless I resign now. And there is a lot of agitation in our newspapers, most of it German-inspired, I'm sure, that our aviators should return from France to defend the United States in her southern borders . . .*

Chugh continued to go, with most of the younger members of the Silvermist Hunt, to the weekly evening meetings of the First City Troop, Philadelphia City Cavalry. The troop had been organized in 1774 and had followed George Washington across the Delaware to win the Battle of Princeton against the British. And now with the rumblings of war, the activities of the troop had assumed a new and romantic importance as they galloped their black horses round and round the riding ring of the Armory. In Washington, D.C., the debate was rising daily in the Congress about whether or not sending arms and munitions to France and England constituted hostilities on the part of the United States against Germany. "It's academic," Welch Seabreese had contended at the Philadelphia Club. "The U.S. is in no way prepared militarily to fight a war. Except for the troop, of course."

For sociable reasons, Chugh hated to resign from the troop. It was a genial group, and last month he had enjoyed taking part in the Washington's Birthday parade which had escorted the governor from the Philadelphia Club to the Armory for the troop's annual dinner. Clattering along on his black horse in full-dress uniform of hip boots, epauleted jacket, and silver-mounted, bear-tailed Greek helmet, he had spotted from under his visor the figures of Faith and Hebe shivering together on the corner of Broad and Walnut to watch him ride by.

Nevertheless, everyone knew that this war was not being fought with swords and cavalry charges, but with tanks and machine guns and from the trenches. The thought of coming over the top of a trench and grappling breast to breast with a German was repugnant to Chugh. Far better to take the dizzying plunge from the air than to lie dying underneath a man with the sweaty breath of a Hun in one's nostrils, eyeball to eyeball, meaty fingers clenched around one's throat.

Water filled the furrows of last year's corn field; Chugh turned into the long lane leading to the Taylor Farm. A huge stone barn stood at the edge of a flat field, and a wooden shed extended from it. Slim, who tinkered all day long with the two planes in the barn, *his* mistresses, would help him get started. He was there in his greasy overalls, shading his eyes with his hand, watching the approach of the car.

"Hullo, Slim. Just thought I'd take her up, if she's in shape. Think it's too windy? Too soft to land?"

"Not too soft to land out on the turf, Chugh. It is a bit

breezy and she's liable to buck a bit. But I'm sure you can handle her if you're feeling strong."

Chugh had already taken his leather fur-lined jacket, his helmet, and his gloves from the hook, and he had located the little pistol he always flew with in one of the jacket's capacious pockets.

"Plenty of gas?"

"Full."

Slim was removing the chocks from in front of the open-cockpit biplane. Like a huge double-winged bug it stood, its silken wings as delicate as any dragonfly's, struts as slender as the ribs of a moth. But the biplane was as unwieldy as a box kite, a boy's toy. Together they wheeled it out to the strip, and Chugh climbed up into the front cockpit.

"Oil and gas!" Slim called.

"Oil, gas," Chugh called back after switching them on, poking his head out at the same time to scream into the wind. "Contact!" He turned the ignition switch. Slim was standing out there, slowly spinning the propeller. Chugh watched him over the edge, waiting to see him jump away when the motor coughed and then caught in a great roar. He was off, bumping down the rutty field. Faster and faster, forty miles an hour. Would she lift off? This was always the moment when a hand of excitement clenched at Chugh's stomach. Two feet off the ground. Now ten feet. Struggling up into the gusty wind that suddenly took him up and let him drop again with a thud. Chugh wrestled with the stick as though it were a weather helm in a tiny sailboat in a storm. Up over the wires. Up over the trees. He felt his thoughts clear as he rose. He was free!

"Free!" he screamd. But he could hear nothing, not even the sound of his own voice above the roar of the engine. The wind clawed at his head, as though to lift his helmet off as he peered out over the side. The wind tore the words from his throat and blew his own breath back into his lungs. Bucking and kicking on the wind like an Appaloosa. There was Finchwicke below him. Chugh swooped down. How small the house looked, set among the trees and gardens like a jigsaw puzzle. The cows in the fields were black dots. A buggy going along the lane to the Briar Patch looked like a child's toy. The brook winding through like a thin black snake.

Chugh spun down over the Finchwicke Forty until he seemed about to crash in the wheel of fields coming up to meet him. Then giving her the gun and feeling her nose pull out of it, he was off and up again. He dived at the brownstone spire of St. Jude's with the speckling of gravestones under the buttonwoods. There lay his mother, Judge Hoagland, Rhoda Seabreese. There lived the minister with his deadening conscience. Let the dead bury the dead. With a roar of the motor, Chugh flew off to the Guard Hill Woods, looking for prey.

Just below him was a fleet of turkey buzzards circling around near their rookery in the Guard Hill Woods. Ugly birds, like filthy Huns in their Fokkers, waiting to finish off the carrion left by the foxes. They seemed to be hanging in the air below him—nearly stationary—with their great wings spread. Chugh had never managed to hit one yet, but he now turned off his engine and quietly coasted down among them. He took his mother's little pearl pistol out of his pocket and took aim, straight-armed, over the edge of the plane. To hit a moving target with one bullet would be a shot in a million.

Knight had written about his *mitrailleuse,* the machine gun mounted on the roof of his Nieuport, which sprayed a broad pattern of death. Knight swiveled it around with one hand, flying with the other hand and with his feet. But Knight had also described close-up dogfights with the goddamn Boche when they sometimes fought with pistols, firing point-blank into each other's faces. The Boche flew tandem, so if you could get the pilot in the front seat, the rear gunner, unable to reach the controls, would be whirled helplessly down to certain death.

Chugh pulled the trigger. His hand flew up from the recoil and one great clumsy bird plummeted out of the sky. Down, down, to crash on the Chruch Hill Road.

A hit! One slug! And out of a moving plane! But she was beginning now to wobble. Chugh turned on the switch, opened the throttle, pulled back on the stick, was off and up.

He passed through a cloud with a lot of wind in it that buffeted him from side to side. He flew until he was short of breath and managed a few barrel rolls over the Chetford Hill Academy to show the boys down there who were already out playing baseball on the green handkerchief south of the buildings. Then he turned off the motor again. No sound but the wind washing over the wings. Blessed quiet. The long leisurely glide back to earth. A little back pressure on the stick flaring out at about ten feet above the earth, landing softly in Taylor's pasture.

On the way home, feeling exhilarated and refreshed,

Chugh's heart softened. He remembered the time this winter, when, on one of their woodland walks, he had explained to Faith his concern to be in France with Knight. "Oh my darling, you know that I can't contemplate being separated from you for an instant, but you must understand how I feel about this bloody, dastardly war. It is a war of good against evil, Christ against anti-Christ. I'm sure our country must get into it sooner or later, and that sooner or later I must join Knight—and probably in the not too distant future." And Faith had understood. "I wouldn't want you to feel any other way," she had said. "I remember when Knight came out with the Silvermist once. So handsome! But, of course, not as handsome as you, my love!"

He remembered vividly now that she had moved him deeply that day, both by her sympathy and by her clean freshness. He had been gratified by his choice of her. "I must be able to tell you everything, darling Faith. Nothing must be held back between us—ever. Promise?" Her green eyes had darkened with ardor. "I promise," she had whispered. And pushing up the veil that covered Faith's face, holding on her winter hat against the wind, he had stolen a kiss. Her lips had been chilly and her breath sweet. He had crushed her to him, all his hot blood rushing up his legs as if to melt the ankle-deep snow around them.

Now he sensed his passion for her rising again in unbearable desire for fruition. He must get away before it tricked him. He could leave immediately for France! A broken engagement. A broken heart. What could be a better excuse?

He could visualize himself arriving in France. Knight had led the way and described all the steps to be taken. There would be pages of complicated applications forms to fill out on arrival. So Chugh would first seek out Rita Sinclair, a friend of Knight's from Boston who had lived in Paris for many years. She knew all the ropes and had made her apartment a center of hospitality and information for all the American aviators who had come over. She would know exactly where Knight was. With her help and the assistance of his old family friend Ambassador Herrick, Chugh's papers would be quickly expedited through the War Ministry, and, as Knight had been, he would be assigned to the flying school at Pau. Since he had already had experience at home, he would rise quickly from *pilote élève* to *pilote chasseur*. Then back to Paris for assignment to the *Service Aeronautique*. A few strings would be pulled to get into the same escadrille with Knight. That's when it would really pay off to know the right people!

He could picture himself lunching with Knight in the Ritz bar in Paris, wearing the dress uniform of the French Army. Strolling around the boulevardes, they would be besieged by the little midinettes. They would dine at Maxim's. And after that, Knight, the *bon vivant*, would surely know of some highclass place to take him, where they could sate themselves with exquisite pleasures of the flesh such as had never been dreamed of at good old Molly's.

After a week or so of that, he and Knight would leave Paris together to join their escadrille on the Swiss border in a countryside of pine trees and waterfalls.

Knight had written of evenings in a country inn, the Pomme d'Or, among genial friends. *We are most amply fed with fat chickens and ducks, terrines of hot and cold foie. The wine from the local vineyards has to be tasted here to be believed. Too delicate to travel well. And each morning we're pleasantly awakened at dawn by the farmer's daughters coming in to pull the curtains. And we're then ready to fly again. Alas for you, dear Cousin, on that dreadful jigging nag of yours. Hunting around Penngwynne was never like this. We're not out for pheasants and foxes—we're out gunning for the Boche!*

Chugh turned in at the Finchwicke gates, cheerful at the prospect of at last getting away. No matter that the evening was cold and windy for spring, the trees like cast iron, not yet leafed out. But arriving in the familiar courtyard at the end of the long driveway, he saw the new wing he had forgotten about while mentally changing his plans. There it stood, stark and complete and ready to receive the new mistress of Finchwicke.

Dr. Walding had talked of nothing else all winter. Over the port wine, he had worried endlessly about how to hurry along the construction, how to utilize all the old materials that Chugh's mother had collected. It had been her hobby to buy up whole rooms out of decaying buildings, and then, not knowing what to do with them, store them away in a shed. Now in the new wing, the pieces had been fitted together. Dr. Walding had supervised everything, so everything was perfect. Where necessary, new wood had been stained and waxed to look like old. The large bedroom had been set with woodwork from Massachusetts, a carved mantel with baskets of fruit and swags of drapery. The dressing room had been paneled entirely in walnut from an old house in Baltimore, its secret doors cleverly opening to deep closets for riding clothes, winter clothes, summer clothes. The large bathroom had a fireplace and cupboards taken from an old Pennsylvania kitchen. The walls were painted a soft blue, which Dr. Walding had had mixed at the museum. Downstairs was a sunny glass porch with an antique brick floor and arched windows copied from the Orangerie at Tulip Hall built by Sir Charles Walding in 1684 on the Eastern Shore. Tubs of orange and lemon trees were being grown in the greenhouse especially to set among the comfortable wicker chairs and sofas.

Who would use the new wing now? Chugh shivered as he thought of having to explain the situation to his father. The engagement is broken. The bride will not be moving here.

It appeared Dr. Walding was not at home; no lights were on in the old part of the house. The windows looked cold and deserted. Chugh had to push open the door himself, as there was no servant waiting to let him in. Switching on the hurricane lamps, he looked on the road table for mail and messages, as he always did. There was a large manila envelope addressed to him in Faith's handwriting in the Lowestoft bowl on top of the calling cards.

As he picked them up, the library door opened and Delia stepped out, carrying the tea tray. Why was the house dark? What had she been doing in there with his father, under the gaze of Sir Percy?

Chugh stared at her without speaking. Well, he knew whatever it was, she was up to no good. Ye gods and goddamn little fishes! He thought he had got rid of the woman last fall but Finchwicke had just not run well without a mistress and with new help. Dr. Walding had complained that he couldn't find any of his things, and so in February he had sent for Delia to come out on the train and spend a day straightening things out. Then Dr. Walding had met her in the hall and had persuaded her to take up her old position. She agreed after demanding that her wages be raised to the astronomical sum of fifty dollars a month. And that had meant that all the others wanted a raise too! Chugh admitted that Delia was a very efficient servant, so he had permitted the arrangement— but only until Faith moved in and took charge.

Chugh rarely spoke to Delia any more. He didn't want to think about the baby that he presumed had been safely born and seen to. He only prayed that it was a girl. If it was a boy, his son, he certainly never wanted to know it—so that when Delia blackmailed him for regular contributions to the nuns who haunted the kitchen, Chugh gave them and asked no questions.

Seeing her now, smirking at him across the hall, all Finchwicke's ghosts and devils came crowding around him. He turned from her and stepped to the other side, seeking the safety of his mother's sitting room, where nothing had changed: the birch logs in the fireplace; his sketch of Heron Bay above the mantel; and on the shelves, Aunt Sarah's china dogs. By the light of the cut-glass lamps on top of her maple desk, Chugh opened the manila envelope and extracted a wedding invitation addressed to the Josenthals. Clipped to it was a note in Hebe's handwriting.

> *My dear Chugh,*
>
> *I thought you might like to see this, although we will not be mailing them out just yet.*
>
> > Sincerely,
> > Hebe Pardue Hoagland

And there was another piece of paper: a valentine heart with LOVE doodled all over it, from Faith.

Ah! So there it was. They had capitulated on the Josenthals! And they simply assumed he was going to get married anyway, in spite of their behavior. To his surprise he felt relieved that he had not lost his girl by having walked away in a huff.

All right. But, by God, he would drive a hard bargain for this, would demand and obtain absolute obedience. There would be no Vivienne Curle in his wife's circle of intimate firends at Finchwicke. Chugh's future wife must be completely cut off from anything in his past that was unsavory. She must be set up on her pedestal and respected for her chastity and worshiped for her purity. As yet untouched by any other man, she would remain untouchable except by him.

He wouldn't want to take her on Vivi's or Delia's terms. He wished to keep her like his mother's pink pearls, beyond price in the vaults of the bank. She was to be *his* wife. Viewed that way, his marriage began to appear sacred indeed!

Still, for the present, he would have to continue to make his displeasure known by rigid politeness, a distance kept until she came begging for mercy. Then he would repeat again that he did not want her to have Vivienne Curle in her train of maids.

Therefore, tomorrow, no apologies, no further tributes of candy and flowers to the Present Room. Until Faith had subjected herself to his wishes, he would not address her directly, but only through a third person. "Hebe, be so kind as to ask Faith who sent this present? A friend of mine or a friend of hers?"

Chugh was confident that the silent treatment would be effective quickly. Many times he had observed his father using it on his mother. At the table: "Bunce, be so kind as to ask Mrs. Walding to ring the bell for the next course." Or, "Chugh, ask Mother where she's going tomorrow." Other than these interchanges they would sit together in total silence for three or four evenings until his mother was reduced to a purging flood of tears and self-accusation. After this, Dr. Walding would hand down Olympian forgiveness and return to their lives a pleasant flow of chat.

Thus, Chugh, too, would simply wait for Faith to give in.

Having decided on this plan of action, the next thing he had to do was to calm himself sufficiently to greet his father. The sudden freshet of desire for his own wife to come and live with him in Finchwicke made immediate light conversation distasteful. His feelings must be kept private. And so he sat down on his mother's sofa until the uncomfortable and familiar prickles of the horsehair covering helped him to collect his emotions. He rose and crossed the hall.

The Doctor was sitting there by the fire, under the eye of Sir Percy, his head on one side, looking as though he had almost ceased to breathe—the very picture of dozing innocence within these book-lined walls. As though he had not been feeling up the maid in the dark for the last half-hour!

"Good evening, Father."

The old man jumped. "Why, Chugh! I didn't hear you come in. I don't know how long I've been sitting here, waiting for you. Where is Delia? Why aren't the lights turned on. Ring for her immediately!"

Chugh gave a vicious jerk on the needlepoint bellpull, accepting without comment the prevarications of the old man. After all, the physical desires of one's parents are repellent and accepted only reluctantly in the back of the mind. Chugh went to the whiskey tray and poured himself a stiff Scotch and soda. "By God, I'll be glad when this wedding is over!

Been spending the afternoon in the Present Room finishing off the damned list. What hornets women can be! And if I'm to be preserved, goddamn it, a specimen of a husband like something in one of your jars, old boy, you can bet I intend to be pickled in good grain alcohol." Chugh took a long swig. "And another thing. As soon as the wedding is over, Delia is leaving this place."

"I don't understand why, Chugh. She's the only one who knows where my winter underdrawers are, and how many handerkerchiefs I need. She mends my socks. She runs the house."

"She thinks she does. But my wife will be running this house."

Answering the bell, Delia had entered silently, and heard these last words. Good! As long as she was eavesdropping in the room, poking up the fire, turning on the lights, drawing the garnet curtains, let her hear!

The bride's dress was a total secret, a tiny-waisted white satin gown with a satin train and Great-Granny Huger's point d'esprit lace veil, which, pinned to the peak of Faith's puffed hair, would fall just-so around the lace set into the neck and shoulders. She was to wear short white gloves, with the fourth finger of the left hand split so that it could be rolled back to receive the wedding band. Hebe said the sapphire-and-diamond engagement ring would have to come off so that the fourth finger would be all naked and bare, but on this one point Faith took a firm stand. "I'll never take it off! It's a vow I made." And so Hebe let her have her way.

In addition to the gown, there were exhausting fittings for each item in the trousseau. Faith spent many afternoons at Miss Meeley's second-floor dressmaking establishment, standing for hours being pinched and pinned. One particular afternoon, she and Hebe came out from a fitting and were met by the cries of hawking newsboys: "Extry! Extry! *Lusitania* sinks! Extry!"

They stopped to buy a paper, and there it was, in huge black letters. Below the headlines was a report from the British Admiralty. Hebe read it aloud:

"As the Captain was altering course another message was passed to him, saying that submarines had been seen that morning south of Cape Clear, which was not thirty miles astern. Accordingly, feeling himself well clear of that danger,

he held on till, at one-forty, the Old Head of Kinsale came in sight to port. He then returned to his original course, which would take him past the headland at a distance of about ten miles. The weather was now quite clear and the sea calm.

"Shortly after, as the passengers were coming on deck at two-fifteen from luncheon, the great liner was torpedoed amidship on the starboard side. The Lusitania soon began to take a heavy list. The engines stopped, and in twenty minutes she plunged down head foremost and was gone. Her crew and passengers numbered within two score of two thousand souls, and of these, there perished of men, women and children no less than one thousand one hundred and ninety-eight (one hundred American men, women and children)."

Faith pressed her fingers into Hebe's plump arm as the two of them continued to walk automatically down Walnut Street among the shocked pedestrians. "Oh dear, Hebe! The McCuskers probably drowned. It brings the war right into the heart of Penngwynne. I can't believe they'll never be coming back to Coq d'Or. Oh Hebe, I'm so worried about Chugh. Probably now that this has happened he will rush right off to France to join Knight Chyldes! Why does he refuse to speak to me? He hasn't been by the Present Room for a week! Maybe we should just have a small family wedding after all, with no bridesmaids and no Josenthals."

Hebe stared primly ahead, plowing along to where Quinn stood waiting with the horses. "There are many different kinds of bad luck. Think of Marshall and me, no children. But I have to keep on living. I think it's best, Faith, to stick to things the way they have been planned."

By the next morning, there he was again, beloved Chugh, standing in the doorway of the Present Room, bringing in a breath of outside life to the dark basement room where the tables were loaded with linens and china, silver and crystal. And voicing Faith's sentiments exactly!

"Why don't we just forget all this?" Chugh said, addressing Hebe only. "It's getting to be too much. I see that the Birds are inviting us to an enormous Sunday luncheon at Birdgrove with all the wedding party. And as I've told you, there's one member of the wedding party I don't approve of, why don't we cancel out the wedding party? This thing about the *Lusitania*—it makes the war pretty certain."

But Hebe said it would be bad luck to change now. The fruit cake had been ordered, a special plummy loaf from

Charleston, packed in one hundred and fifty white boxes with Chugh's and Faith's initials entwined in gold.

Chugh shrugged and walked away. "I'll take tea, I think, with Mrs. Hoagland."

"Why does he have to take tea with Mama when I haven't seen him at all? And oh, Hebe, he didn't even speak to me. I can't bear the silence, and yet I refuse to hurt darling Viv! Oh Hebe, I think I'm going to have to break the engagement myself. I can't imagine anything worse than a whole lifetime of silence! Nothing could be worse, except possibly a whole life spent with Mama!"

She looked down at the ring on her finger, a bit of frozen ocean imprisoned forever in a cold stone. She pressed it to her cheek until it cut.

"Nonsense. The ceremonial can't possibly be reversed now."

Faith saw that it was like a juggernaut—the plans had become sacrosanct and had acquired a momentum of their own which would carry them on through life. Dr. Walding was donating a special train to bring guests out from town and had arranged for carriages to be at the railroad station to meet the guests. How could they be disinvited? What would they do with all the presents that had been sent?

Faith went upstairs and found Chugh getting on famously with Mama, who was shaking her curls and amusing him and Mr. Welch Seabreese. Amusing herself too, judging from the sounds of her tinkling laughter and the roars of the men.

Faith passed on by and went upstairs to find Ma'selle. But when she arrived at Ma'selle's door and found the old woman threading the ribbons through her underdrawers with an ivory bodkin, she saw on her face the same look of suppressed excitement that purpled Hebe's cheeks. She couldn't talk to Ma'selle either.

Faith went into her own room, and taking the dog onto the narrow bed she wept into her fur. Life was a hopeless stretch of girlhood, made worse by the fact of being in love with Chugh Walding, who now appeared to prefer the fascinations of Mama. She wept until it was time for dinner, when she arose to dress with very swollen red eyes and a dull headache.

6

The House

THERE WAS magic in Vivi's soothing fingers as she massaged the scalp. And unlike Faith, who used to pause uncertainly at every snarl, Vivi pulled the silver hairbrush through the red curls with vigorous, sure sweeps. Becca, watching her in the dressing-table mirror, complimented her, and told her that she would expect the Bellwood Hoagland family to spend at least two years with her, now that Faith was leaving. They must stay at least until Rick came home from Princeton and until their new theater was ready in town. Becca-Bee, as the darling baby was affectionately called, and her nursemaid could have the old playroom and be kept out of everybody's way, once Faith's presents had been moved away. "And you, Viv, can brush my hair every night. You do it so well," Becca added.

"That would be very nice, and I thank you," Vivi replied, "but of course, the minute the new apartments are ready, I'm afraid we must go to town. I expect to be acting again, you know. And Bellwood is opening in the spring with *The Importance of Being Earnest.*"

"Oh really? I hadn't heard that before. I thought you were giving up the stage. I'm not sure I approve at all. But no matter. By that time you'll probably be having another baby. You had the first one easily enough. And my goodness! I do hope next time it'll be a boy."

Her acid tones might have dissolved Faith, so that the hairbrush in her hand would have begun to shake, but Faith would have had to apologize for something—or everything. But this girl was different. She neither shook, nor turned to stubborn stone. Rather she turned to water. One could make no impression on her at all. Of course, she was an actress and was only acting the part of daughter-in-law.

Becca added for good measure, "Yes, Vivi, you must expect to be expecting for the next twenty years." Then: "To change the subject, however, let me ask you this. Have you ever heard of a place called Molly's? It is, I believe, what's called a 'sporting house.' "

Vivi had an annoying way of pausing. Her face seemed to melt back into the soft white curtains. Becca, watching her in the mirror, saw her hand arrested in midair, holding the hairbrush.

"Yes, of course. It's only a few blocks from Bellwood's theater." She had emerged from the background briskly playing the part of the matter-of-fact housewife. "Their marble steps are the cleanest in the neighborhood. Gleaming. The maids wash the coal dust off twice, or sometimes three times a day."

"How do you know that's the place?"

"Everyone knows, Becca."

"I lived there for more than twenty years, and I didn't know. Not until too late . . ."

"The neighborhood has changed since you lived there. We have an influx of immigrants. Small shops. Boarding houses. Noisy trolleys. All this you know yourself, of course, It wouldn't do at all to live there any more. Naturally, that's why we're moving away."

"Naturally. But the House was there when I lived there. Molly's, I mean. It's always been there, hasn't it?"

"I don't know, Mrs. Hoagland. I've only lived there since being married to Bellwood." The girl's voice had taken on a careful English accent, learned in elocution school, as though she were speaking softly but distinctly to the back row in a dark theater. "I don't know what it was like when you lived there." Vivi gave a particularly vigorous tug to the hair in her hand.

"Please call me Becca. You know I prefer it." She had turned and grasped the girl by the arm. "Where is it exactly?"

"Molly Franklynne's? It's down on Spruce Street. Below Second, I think. I'm not sure of the number. Why are you asking me?"

"Because, for reasons of my own, I wish to see the inside of it, without anyone knowing who I am. I need your help. I want you to disguise me as a woman of the street. That shouldn't be hard. You have all that grease paint at the theater. You are an actress. You can come along with me."

"Oh, I don't think that would be possible. I'm sure we couldn't get in that way."

"Then how do you get in?"

"I suppose you have to meet him first. The manager."

"The pimp, you mean? You seem to know a lot about it."

"Actresses hear these things."

"Exactly my point. That's why I told you I want you to come along with me." Becca's tone was wheedling now. Two women in the boudoir. Vistas of confidences opening up. But the girl had taken a step backwards, a bird huddling in the corner of a cage staring at an extended crooked finger. This frightened shyness was all a pose, hiding a stubborn streak. "Well, if they wouldn't let us in as two streetwalkers, we'll have to think of something else. It'll be a lark you know."

"You could go alone, Becca." The girl attempted a smile and a joke. "Pretend you're another madam coming to call. But why do you care?"

"Because I've discovered I own it."

"You! Own it?" With a twist of her arm, the girl managed to leave the hairbrush in Becca's empty hand. She had turned to air, faded from the room. Very well. So she had been shocked. An actress has no business being shocked. Becca had found out what she needed to know. The address.

On the pretext of learning to drive her new car, under the tutelage of young Monaghan, one of the gamekeeper's sons, who was proving to be a handsome and able chauffeur, Becca began taking frequent trips into the city. At first she had avoided the old part of Philadelphia where she had lived the happy years of her married life, but now she took a spurt of interest in Bellwood's project. He was packing up the old Mews, having found another stable uptown on De Lancey Street which could be remodeled into a theater. Becca spent many afternoons there presiding over the moving of props and costumes.

One day, she borrowed back a large flowered hat and a feather boa which had once been her own. They were among the clothes she had given Bellwood for his theater when she went into mourning. Becca seemed to remember the flowered hat with particular fondness and could not bear to see Viv pack it into a box with all the other dresses and shawls and coats in the costume closet. The hat would be perfect for her plan, Becca thought to herself.

Often she had young Monaghan circle the block in which Molly's stood. Then, the week before the wedding, just before her brother the Bishop and his wife were due in at Co-Eden from Charleston, she decided it was time for her to put her plan into action. This fine hot June day, she directed young

Monaghan to wait at the Mews while she took a little stroll around the old neighborhood by herself. She was wearing the flowered hat to keep off the broiling sun and a black dress which she had had taken in to make it very tight, showing off the double outline of her magnificent prow. Turning the corner, she fished a small box of theatrical rouge out of her bag. Since Vivi had refused to make her up and join in the escapade, she had to do it herself. She stopped for a moment as though she had something in her eye and rubbed a round réd circle on each cheekbone. Then she popped a white pill into her mouth to ward off the horrid headache she felt coming on. Catching sight of herself in a tobacco-shop mirror, she looked transformed, unrecognizable. No one would guess her identity. No one would expect Becca Hoagland to have left her invalid's chair in the cool of her own veranda and be walking the streets in the slums of the city on a June day.

The House, with its geranium flower boxes, stood out on the decaying block like a landmark of shabby gentility. It could have been taken for a private red-brick residence, except for the fact that the windows were always shuttered on the inside and the sidelights of the front door had been boarded over. With her heart beating against her corsets, Becca surged up the white marble steps. A knobby man who had been sweeping the sidewalk leaned on his broom as she rang the bell. Someone flicked the louver of a shutter and peeked out. The door opened as far as a chain on the inside would permit. A black face under a bandanna-turban peered through the crack. "Yas, miss? Who?"

"Ah'd like to see Miz Franklynne." She laid on her Southern accent like thick butter.

"Who is you, miss?"

"Tell her Flossie Lee."

"Jessa minute."

The door remained barely open, held by the chain, and Becca was left standing, her back to the street, prey to any man who might approach. To keep up her courage, she invoked the spirit of old Granny Huger who had stood off a whole regiment of Union Cavalry at The Mount.

Finally a woman's loud voice sounded on the other side of the door. "I don't know any Flossie and I don't need any Flossie. Don't let anyone in here we don't know. The place is torn apart. Don't know how we're going to get ready for business toinght, let alone the lunch hour. We've had enough trouble around here."

The black face appeared again through the crack. "Miz Franklynne say she busy. She don' need no mo' hoes."

"Tell her it's Mrs. Hallowell Hoagland, the owner of this property. Tell her to let me in immediately."

The door shut in her face with a snap. Becca rang the bell again, keeping her finger on it until the door was opened wide. "Come in, I'm sorry to keep you waiting. We're busy straightening up this morning. I try to keep everything in good repair, but we had a bunch of young studs from Oklahoma in here last night. Soldiers, you know—they went wild."

Becca instantly realized the woman was Molly Franklynne herself. There was something familiar about her expression which Becca couldn't place. She had obviously been a great beauty at one time, but now her face was like a theatrical mask of a faun. The slanted eyes were deepened with grease paint, her hair was twisted into hard black ringlets, her mouth a painted wound. "Come in, Mrs. Hoagland. I'm sorry you've been kept waiting." Her voice was soft and ingratiating. Almost as though she'd been expecting Becca.

Becca put her pointed, buttoned boot in the door. "No doubt you're surprised to see me here!"

"I'm never surprised at anyone who rings my bell. I've been in this business too long. Anyway, do come in and sit down."

The woman in a bright-blue cotton housedress with a neat white collar pinned with a cameo brooch motioned Becca into the main parlor. A ladder stood in front of one of the shuttered windows, where the yellow satin drapes had been pulled loose from the brocade wall. "I was up there on top with the hammer and tacks when you rang. We're just setting the place to rights."

Becca blinked to accuston her eyes to the dimness of the long, furniture-filled room. It stretched from the front to the back of the building and reminded her of her own townhouse. She felt perfectly at home here. There was an open grand piano, draped with a fringed shawl, and a plump, circular red-velvet sofa in the center of a multicolored Oriental rug. From the ceiling, directly over the sofa, hung a chandelier, strings of a waterfall of prisms, sparkling crystal, that split the sensuous colors of the room into rainbows. Palm trees in brass tubs disguised ashtrays and spittoons. But despite the contrived air of luxury, the smell of dead cigar smoke and stale liquor hit Becca like a wall. This place could never be aired out. The windows had been nailed shut for too long.

"Please sit down." The woman indicated two ruby-velvet chairs in a niche, conveniently placed for a tête-à-tête. Opposite them was a large oil painting of a nymph, thinly veiled, bathing in a rocky brook, and from a nearby corner a brilliant green parrot in a brass cage cocked his yellow eye at Becca and said, "Hello. Wanna fuck?"

Molly hurried to cover the cage with a piece of yellow satin and said, "There, you foul-mouthed old bird. Be quiet and go to sleep. He doesn't know if it's night or day, unless I cover the cage. Can I offer you a glass of wine, Mrs. Hoagland?" She pointed to an array of cut-crystal decanters on a side table.

Becca remembered hearing something about drugged wine being served in these places. "No thank you. I'm very warm. But could I trouble you for a glass of ice water?" Her throat was suddenly parched.

"Certainly. Excuse me for a few moments." The woman was gone, although her voice could be heard giving orders. There was a quick scurrying of feet overhead. The front door opened again, and the man who had been sweeping the sidewalk came in followed by a colored maid with the ice water on a tray. She was not a pretty girl, but her dress of starched gingham, with ruffled white fichu matching her apron, and her head tightly bound in a scarlet turban, made a charming costume. The woman, Molly, evidently had a flair. Molly waved the man and the maid away and sat down in the chair next to Becca, displaying an ankle in an embroidered black stocking. "You must forgive the appearance of things. We had a very big party with musicians here last night. It's the war, you know. The U-boats. People who had confidence in President Wilson think now he's going to get us into the fight. Makes the men nervous. We've started to get a lot of strangers coming by for entertainment. All our girls are lovely, and I'm sure you'll understand how worried I am about taking care of our regular clients. So, ma'am, I ask your pardon for leaving you standing on the steps. I've given strict orders not to let strangers in. And we did not expect your visit this morning. To what do we owe the unexpected pleasure?" The woman's voice was throaty and as deep as a man's, her accent slightly foreign.

"I've come on business," Becca said.

"This is no place for you, Mrs. Hoagland. If you have come on business, it would be far better if we met someplace else. For instance, at the bank."

"Why?"

"Many of my customers are people you know. They come in for a little lunchtime—well—nooky. I wouldn't want to embarrass them by having them find you here. Nor would I wish to embarrass you either, madam, by having one of them invite you to go upstairs."

Becca laughed. The parrot laughed. And the chandelier tinkled as a trolley clanged by outside. "That is exactly what I wish to do, Miss Franklynne. Go upstairs. You knew my husband, the Judge? I'm quite sure."

The woman never hesitated. She was a cool customer. "Why yes, I do believe I remember Judge Hoagland. He came here occasionally."

"And he died here?"

'Yes."

For a long moment the two women sat staring at each other. A curious sympathy in Molly's expression forced Becca to be the first to drop her eyes. "I wish to see the room in which he died."

"I'm afraid that won't be possible, Mrs. Hoagland. Let me just assure you it was our very best room. It hasn't yet been put to rights. As I told you, we had a very big night here last night. We're getting ready to close for the summer and go on vacation. As I explained to you, the war and everything."

"Vacation? Where do you find to go?"

"Cape May, madam. It's cool there, and a very comfortable hotel. We all need a good rest."

The two women sat there talking as though they were equal. Molly was not at all afraid of the great Mrs. Hoagland. Becca liked her for that. Somewhere along the line, they could have been real friends. But Becca got back to the subject. She had come here to see the bed in which Hal had died, and in some way to find Hal here, find some way to ease her deep malaise. "Cape May sounds very pleasant. I shouldn't mind coming along with you."

"I'm afraid, madam, that wouldn't be possible either."

Becca could see she was getting nowhere as friend to friend, and that she must apply force. "There are complaints from the Church about this house being in my husband's estate. If you wish to remain here, then you must recognize that I have the power to have you removed."

"The neighborhood is changing here, and I am thinking of moving anyway. You see, Mrs. Hoagland. I only like to cater to the very best people. I used to stay open Sundays, as a special service to the members of the Philadelphia Club, but now all the best people have their places in the country. Sundays are dead in the city."

Still using her intimate and wheedling voice to disguise her absolute dire necessity, Becca said, "I have the power to expose you and send you to jail!"

"I'm afraid you'd have to send the whole police department and the judiciary with me, ma'am. I have very high friends."

"Nevertheless, I own this house. I have the right to inspect it. That is why I have come here."

"And I pay you a very good rent, which you won't receive from the run-down flea-house it'll turn into. Nevertheless, if you'll give me a few minutes, I'll just see——"

"We'll go right up now! No matter who's in there." Becca rose, leaving the feather boa on the back of her chair.

"Very well. As you say."

The summer heat of the entire baking city seemed to be trapped at the top of the stairs. A knobby man was standing at the top, at the end of the dark hall, with a leather thong drooping from his hand. And beside him, a girl in a wrapper, in bare feet, hair down her neck, whimpered, "Just a little walk in the park, please, Jack!"

The man raised his hand. The girl scurried down the thick carpet of the hall. A door slammed. A maid was gathering up piles of dirty linens outside the doors. The housekeeper, a stone-faced white woman in a black silk uniform, a bunch of keys hooked into her belt, was counting towels on the shelves of a capacious lined closet. The man twisted the leather thong. Becca looked back down the stairs, but a huge dog, a white pit-bull with one black eye, had followed halfway up. The place was suffocating with the musky drench of desire, which communicated itself to Becca. She felt she would like to stay here. It was different from her dull life in Penngwynne. To be ordered to her room by a man with a whip would not be unpleasurable.

"In here."

Becca stepped behind the woman into a square white room, with bright red curtains and waxed floors. Sunlight filtered in between the shutters, a breath of hot air came in through a cracked window. A gentleman's room, Becca thought. A cheval glass had been hung on the wall opposite the foot of the large comfortable bed to reflect it. There were two comfortable chairs, a washstand with a fine Spode china pitcher and bowl, and a generous pile of clean towels. Yes, unmistakably this was the place where Hal would have come after deciding a particulary difficult court case. She walked to the opposite side of the bed, turned down a corner of the clean white quilt, touched the fine white linen sheets, cool and silky to a man's fevered skin. From here he would have come home to her like a whipped dog begging forgiveness with liquid eyes—going into details of his legal decision, bringing a new jewel from Bailey, Banks and Biddle. Taking his daughter on his knee to read to her—A *Tale of Two Cities*: "My little girl. My darling Twinkle. Now get down and run along. We're making Mama jealous of us." Jealous!

Becca was disconcerted by a blank expression in the woman's face. She seemed to be able to defend herself, as Viv could, by going blank. "In this very bed?"

"Yes. We still call this room the Judge's chambers. It's a little house joke we have."

"Yes, this would be the room. And the woman? You?"

"I never go upstairs with the gentlemen." Miss Molly Franklynne spole icily, as though she had been insulted, her rank questioned. "I'm always too busy seeing to the entertainment of the clients who are waiting."

"I see. But I still insist on meeting the woman in whose arms he died. That is my price."

"Someone else came here asking that same question a few years back. The young lady never was one of our regular girls, and she has long since left here. She only took care of the Judge."

"Someone else inquired about the girl? Who else could have possible cared? Who, I ask you." Becca was shaken.

"I suggest Mrs. Hoagland, that you drop this whole investigation, or you'll regret it." The woman was like water. It was impossible to pin her down.

Why, pray, should I drop it?"

"It can only cause more scandal in your own family."

The way the woman had melted out of her grasp reminded Becca of Vivi.

"VIVI!"

The smell of all the chamber pots festering in the cupboards assailed Becca's aristocratic carved nostrils. She

186

grabbed on to the bedpost for support. AND BELLWOOD! She was harboring Hal's woman in her own house at Co-Eden! She swayed, knocking her flowered hat off.

Like a cat, Molly had sprung to open the door and called down the hall. "Quick! Quick! Bring snow." The broiling heat was billowing up from the furnaces of hell. The thought of snow . . . Molly had pushed her into one of the chairs. The housekeeper was there in an instant with a saucer. "Here. Sniff this. I knowed you was a hophead when I seen you coming in here all tricked out like a whore." There was some white powder in the pink palm of the woman's hand. Becca didn't have the least idea of what she was talking about. "Here, have a sniff. You'll feel better. It won't hurt you. Our doctor gives it to us for some of the girls who need it. Sniff!"

Immediately the room sorted itself back into place. That was the bed where Hal had slept with Vivienne and died in her arms. Becca laughed like breaking glass, the finest, thinnest champagne glass. She had come here to cauterize her wound with pain. "I think I would like to lie in that bed. You can send up the first man who comes in. That will be my price for not having you thrown into the gutter."

"Mrs. Hoagland, you can never throw me into the gutter. I'm already there. Only yourself. Your son. Our granddaughter. Besides, I can retire any time I wish. I have stocks and bonds. Good ones. The U.G.I. and the Pennsylvania Railroad. Now here's cold water. Wash the rouge off your face. Comb your hair. Have one more little sniff, and get out of here. Go to your home in the country and stay there. Forget Molly's."

For answer, Becca Hoagland lay down on the bed. "Send me Hal!"

On this June day, Mr. Welch Seabreese was sweltering under the portraits of past bank presidents in his paneled office. He had almost finished signing the letters he had dictated that day. Through the open door, he could see Miss Emma Fox, his hollow-chested secretary, inherited from his father, sitting sidewise at her desk, her good ear always alert to catch his most faintly imagined wish.

Today he was feeling particularly in the pink, having returned from a good lunch at the Philadelphia Club, his spectacles gleaming, his high white collar sparkling in the sunshine. He was definitely in the mood for a visit to Molly's, an afternoon of rolling on the Judge Hoagland bed, a bit of tit-pulling and a final relief from his asceticism.

Ever since his wife, Rhoda, had been killed in the hunting field, Mr. Welch Seabreese had prided himself on being a model of propriety. With the help of an ancient housekeeper he had conscientiously performed the duties of a father to his large brood. He was frequently invited out to dinner, the perfect extra man, the hostess's delight. He often accepted, but by never showing any interest in any one particular lady, he had preserved his independence. He felt he could forgive himself a secret pleasure now and then.

He was on the verge of telling Miss Fox that he was leaving early—it was such a fine day, and he had promised the boys a trip to the Cricket Club to play tennis. A lie, of course, "Emma," he began, "why don't we both—" But the telephone rang on his desk. "Who is it, Emma?"

"She didn't care to give her name. But it's Miss Franklynne, sir," Emma said with a disapproving sniff.

How did she know, anyway? It was horrible having no privacy. One had to have the hide of a crocodile. Welch picked up the receiver and managed a cold, businesslike tone. "Hello?" He had told Molly never to call him at the bank.

"My God, Mr. Breesey! You better get down here as soon as you can!" She had one of those telephone voices that could be heard across a room. "Mrs. Hoagland is here, dressed up like a madam herself. She's up in the Judge's room! I don't know what'll happen if I can't get her out. I don't know what to do with her. For the love of God, get down here and give her one of your regular Friday afternoon symphony concerts. And then maybe we can get her out of here. Otherwise I hate to think what might happen to her."

"I beg your pardon," said Mr. Seabreese. "I'm not sure who you think you're talking to."

"Not only will she ruin a whole afternoon of business by being here, but the whole town's wife will know where the house is, because of her. This neighborhood is going to hell anyway. I'm giving my notice about the lease. Maybe you can find me something down in Atlantic City, near the boardwalk."

"I don't think this is business we can discuss over the telephone." Welch hung up abruptly. Clapping on his strawhat down over his brows, he marched past his guardian secretary with a muttered goodnight, even though it was only two in the afternoon, and down the street in the general direction of the club. He was in a fine rage at the entire Hoagland family. He had always thought that girl, Faith, had caused his wife's hunting accident. And Becca had made it difficult for him about needing more money for the girl's wedding. Good advice he had given the girl not to use her own money. Small thanks he had gotten for it. "Your father put your money in trust until you reach the age of twenty-one—that's this year—to protect you from unscrupulous people. So that in the future, when people try to borrow from you, be sure you consult your father's memory." Thinking about old Hal Hoagland, holier than thou, Welch Seabreese was angrier than ever.

He arrived at Molly's marble steps with a delicate dew of perspiration on his high white brow. Molly herself, still in her apron, was waiting to open the door.

"My God! I'm glad to see you. She's upstairs. We've kept her sniffin' all afternoon to keep her quiet. This is the most terrible situation. Every madam's nightmare. She demands to sleep in that bed and I can't get her out without pulling her out. And I'm afraid she'd sue me if I touch her. So for God's sake, do something. Drop your teeth! Drop your pants! But get her out of here!"

Mr. Welch Seabreese shuddered at the situation, but stepping gingerly, followed Molly upstairs into the Judge's chamber, where customarily he would have been awaited by two tiny kittens naked under their thin kimonos. Now there was Becca Hoagland, legs spread upon the bed, skirts pushed up around her waist, pink flesh showing around the tops of her black stockings tightly gartered to her black stays. Her beautiful face on the pillow was framed in a fan of red hair, her fixed green eyes staring up at nothing.

"This is what I have for you today, Breesey. Do something."

For the first time while at Molly's he was ashamed at the rush of desire.

"But I can't . . . she looks like a tarantula . . ."

"Do it. Even if it takes all afternoon."

Molly drew the red curtains and went out, shutting the door with a firm click.

She dreamed.

A beautiful cello which had lain forgotten for years in the corner of the dusty attic—in perfect condition, wrapped in a

Spanish shawl in its shaped box—needed only tuning with expert fingers testing the plucked notes, tautened into an arch over the frail wooden bridge whose notches held up the deep-toned gut and the high wire. Slowly and sweetly, the concert begins as the maestro draws out the high thin notes. Now the masked dancer invites her to the carefully controlled minuet, step by step, alone on the ballroom floor, under lights twinkling in the chandeliers like shooting stars. Ah! Suddenly the music changes. They are like leaves caught up in the whirlwind by the stormy lake, rising in a wild crescendo. Oh Hal! Hal! Let me see your face! But in answer, the cellist stops her lips with his and draws from his instrument one wild, high, sweet tone that tremoloes higher and higher until the vibration fades beyond the human ear.

When she came out of her blackness the knobby man was on one side of her and the housekeeper on the other, and they were floating her down the stairs while Molly continued her soothing, deep croon. "Don't worry, Mrs. Hoagland. We're moving out of your house. Business isn't what it used to be since the quality like yourselves moved out to the country. Here, Mrs. Hoagland, set your hat to rights. Good-bye. This is the direction you came from. The theater. This way." Becca found herself propelled onto the street, walking on a cushion of hot air. Her feet were down there, but a very long distance away, disconnected from her legs. How brilliant the sky was, pressing down on all the red-brick buildings glowing like rubies. And there was Monaghan standing by the little car under the shade of the tree. What a good-looking young man he was. Her legs were heavy with desire for Monaghan. "I'll drive," she said.

They went along very slowly, sticking to the edge of the river. The heat of the road rose up in waves of nausea to hit her in the face. She asked Monaghan to guide the wheel while she fished in her bag and took the last pill out of the blue enamel box. The small nail withdrew itself from the back of her head.

Fifteen miles to the Stone Mill Road!

Very slowly now, around the corner into the drive. Don't hit the gatehouse. Push down hard on the throttle. Get up speed for the winding hill. Speed around the monkey tree. Speed around the Japanese table pine. Ah, there was Viv standing by the bosky dell. Damn chameleon Vivi, melting into the trees in her green and gray dress, her dappled strawhat. Ah! She knew how to handle Vivi all right! Just as Granny Huger had handled Flossie Lee. Aim at her with the wheel of her carriage, chop off her hip.

Becca's knuckles whitened on the ivory wheel as she aimed the car straight for the girl with the white face in the summer dress, clinging to the tree trunk. Monaghan was fighting her for the wheel, but with uncontrollable joy she pressed her foot down to the floor and aimed.

A sudden jolt threw Becca forward so that the wide brim of her hat hit the windshield and the steering wheel jammed into her corsets. The car had come to a crashing stop. Monoghan was on top of her, with one hand on the wheel, the other reaching to flip off the switch. "Be careful, Monaghan, you're hurting my shoulder. Please. You're right on top of me."

"Holy Mother! I thought we was all dead for sure! What happened to ye, ma'am? Ye must have thought the exhilarator was the brakes." The man had opened the door and jumped out. "It's lucky this granite wall was here, with the chips of the dragon teeth on top, or we would have had a drop of twenty feet down."

What a fuss they all make. Low, common people, Becca thought, angry at them all. Angry at Hallowell for having built that wall. Angry at having scraped her beautiful car against it. There was surely a dent in the door on her side, which now wouldn't open at all. She put her head out the window. Vivi? There wasn't a sign of Vivi. Only a tree. And where her face had been, the large white blossom of *Magnolia grandiflora*.

Bellwood called a family conference a few nights later when Rick had unexpectedly appeared from Princeton.

"There's no question about it, Rick. Mama was drunk tonight, last night and the night before." The shocking words hung inside the leafy porch like a miasma. Now that they had been said out loud, they would never be quite out of mind. "It hurts me to say these words about lady Mama, just as much as it hurts you to hear them. Uncle Bishop and Aunt Claire are arriving tomorrow, the wedding is in one week— something has to be done."

"I don't see any sign of what you're talking about." Looking as though he had just slain the dragon and had shed his knightly suit of armor in the hall, Rick was standing on the lawn with one foot up on the porch steps, indignantly disputing Bellwood and defending the honor and purity of fair Mama. Dressed in a fresh white linen suit, his carrot curls burnt to a crisp by the sun, his face florid from anger and from too much to drink at dinner, he was a flamboyant figure. "She had a sprained shoulder tonight, poor darling. I thought she was a very good sport to come down to dinner at all. And as for being drunk, I, myself, mixed her usual julep. Mostly ice. She barely touched it. She wasn't drunk. She was in pain! Anyone could tell the difference."

"You're not around here much, and so you're not a very good judge. She has this fantastic ability to pull out of it and be herself in front of certain people. But believe me, I'm not making this up for fun." Bellwood looked hard at his younger brother's face, purple in the twilight. There was no way he could tell him everything he knew (Viv was our father's woman and now she's mine), so he simply said, "A few days ago Viv was helping Becca down the stairs because she was unsteady and about to trip. Trying to save her, Viv fell to the bottom. It was just a miracle she wasn't hurt. Viv is expecting again, you know, though be so kind as not to mention it. She might have lost her baby. It might be my son."

No one seemed embarrassed at the mention of Viv's expectancy. Of course, if she'd been a "good woman" one couldn't have mentioned it. But it was precisely because she wasn't that Bellwood loved her—being an actress, being Viv, being deliciously loose. Bellwood moistened his lips and continued, "Doc Merritt says something has to be done about Becca. Her behavior has been extermely odd since the engagement. He thinks maybe a nurse—someone to watch her. He thinks it's because she's terrified of losing Faith, who's always done so much for her. Viv's tried to make up for it, brushing her hair every night, but things are worse. You have to face it with us, Rick."

"Face it how?"

"You're the one who got her the car. You're the one who has to take it away from her. It's dangerous for her to be driving. She's going to kill someone. Maybe herself. You have to tell her the car is ruined and can't be fixed."

"Much ado about nothing, in my opinion! Mama had a flat tire, that's all, and veered into the teeth of Dad's Japanese wall. Blame it on the damn wall. Young Monaghan told me it was just an accident when I went down to see the dogs. No reason at all to take the car away from her, when she knows it can be fixed."

But Bellwood would not give in. The porch hammock, hanging from chains in the ceiling, squeaked raspingly as he moved it slowly back and forth, one elegant knee crossed over the other, a pointed white shoe with freshly lacquered black sole swinging in the air to punctuate his words. "And tonight she hit Vivi in the cheek with her handbag as she tripped out here on this porch. On purpose, too, I thought."

"And very hard. I didn't appreciate that!" Viv spoke very softly with her crisp enunciation. She raised a thin white hand to her cheek and nervously got up from her wicker chair in the shadows of the *Clematis Jackmanii* vine. In her light summer dress, she seemed to be part of the screen of purple passion flowers around her. The pleasure dagger twisted in Bellwood's guts as he looked at her, at the visible swelling of her dress under the wrapped satin sash, her breasts already starting to fill again, so early in the game too. He hadn't expected a whore to be so prolific. It must be due to his own virile powers. But he brought his mind back to the subject in hand. "We all have to face it. Becca is nipping up in her room. Viv took a sip out of a glass of water on the dressing table when she was brushing Becca's hair. It wasn't water. It was gin."

"Straight!" said Viv.

Silence on the porch between the three of them. Except for the loud concert of the summer night insects, fiddling and croaking in mad crescendo.

"Doc Merritt says if this keeps up, she might have to be committed to an institution. He thinks she's going crazy."

Rick pounded his fist against the porch post. "You make me feel like a damn conspirator against my own mother. It's that goddamn Carrie, swiping Faith when she should stay home and look after Mama. It disgusts me even to think about it. Let Faith stay here and straighten out this bloody mess. Now I'm going up to tell Mama goodnight and find out if what you say is true."

He stamped into the house, banging the screen door behind him. Viv trembled in the vines.

7

Rehearsing

LIFE CONTINUED as usual in the Present Room except that the atmosphere had changed from girlish pleasure to business-like tension. Chugh came by much less often on the excuse of being very busy with his affairs, and when he did come, he was polite and distant, giving the New Arrivals only a cursory glance, not caring whom they were from, carefully answering Faith only through Hebe. "It's perfectly all right with me if she'd like to return these goblets for credit. We already have too much glass at Finchwicke."

But in spite of the blowup over the Josenthals and Viv, now that the big day was inevitably approaching, Hebe still seemed unable to restrain herself from chivvying Chugh.

"Have you got the twenty-five-dollar gold piece for Guy Fitzjoy? And the fifty-dollar gold piece for the Bishop? Of course he expects it! What a silly question. Simply press it in his palm after the ceremony. And the sexton has to be tipped ahead of time for opening the doors for the rehearsal. What about the carriages for getting the ushers to church? They're sure to be late—after the night before."

"Never you mind about the night before. I'll have my ushers' dinner in my own way in my own house. Don't you try to arrange that too, Hebe!"

Ogden smirked. Chugh gave the dog a little kick. Hebe was furious.

"Please be sure the ushers haven't had too much to drink when they come to the rehearsal. They won't listen to directions."

"Watch Faith's brothers for me. Especially Rick!" Chugh shot back.

Faith flared. "Don't you ever say anything against my brother Rick!"

Immediately she wanted to apologize for speaking in that rude manner, but she couldn't go back on Rick, no matter how much he had hurt her. Life seemed to be laying traps to turn her into a virago she didn't want to be, forcing her to drive Chugh upstairs to Mama.

She debated in her bedroom whether or not to ask Chugh why he was so cold, and if she could see him alone. Maybe if she rode down to Finchwicke she could find him. But once she had changed into her riding clothes and gotten aboard Nimblewit, she felt shy at the thought of searching out Chugh and galloped off in the other direction, toward Chetford Hill. And anyway, she knew what the trouble was. For some reason he was displeased about Viv. And there was no use discussing it until she could devise a way to make him see how sweet Viv was.

The strenuous exercise restored her equilibrium as it always did, so that the next time she saw Chugh, nothing was said except to make the appointment for him to come to Co-Eden and meet with Uncle Bishop, who had written to say that he wished to give religious instruction to Chugh and Faith together before he would consent to marry them.

With some hesitation Chugh had told Hebe that he would do his best to be present at the hour specified but he couldn't promise. The Baron and Baroness were arriving that morning from Boston in the Chyldes' private railroad car, and Faith must understand that he would be very busy, as they were Finchwicke's house guests and wanted to sight-see: the Liberty Bell, the Blue Rock Works, everything. Chugh was very cool and correct in what he said.

Faith was more anxious to please. "Of course I'll understand if you can't—but do please try. There's something very important I have to say." She had a plan. If Uncle Bishop were to baptize Vivi, surely Chugh would have no objections to her being a bridesmaid!

Then Mama promised her a midnight visit, the traditional heart-to-heart between mother and daughter about the facts of life. Faith was pleased and touched when Mama said, "Before my brother Gault gets ahold of you and fills you full of illusions, you might as well know the truth."

Being a country girl, Faith was aware of the natural process of copulation. She had watched the geese and ducks on the pond, the cattle and sheep in the meadow hop upon each other's back and she knew this was the way it was done. Having presided over the whelping of Tiddy-Boom's litters in a basket in her very own bedroom, she knew this was the way the young were born. But what she he was not sure about was exactly what happened between a man and a woman which would make her have a baby. She and Mama had never discussed these questions, and now the moment was about to arrive when they would speak together as woman to woman. Faith was not sure that she wanted to hear the physical details from Mama. That was to be something infinitely precious and private between herself and Chugh. What she wanted from Mama was to be loved as a daughter who was turning into a woman and a friend. She wanted to ask Mama as a friend why Chugh was so cold and distant just now. Was it normal? What was the secret of the happy marriage that Mama had had with Papa? Faith at last wanted to be admitted into it with them.

Propped up on the pillows of the sleigh bed in which she had spent her childhood, Faith waited for midnight. One lamp on the dressing table had been left on, sending its beam of light to pick out the fat roses on the wallpaper and illuminate the painting of The Mount, the photograph of the Judge in front of the townhouse and of the school picnic group in their hockey bloomers. Tidy-Boom nervously thumped her tail in her dog basket. And then the clock on the stairs finally chimed midnight.

The door opened, and Mama appeared in a frothy peignoir of wool lace and satin bows, an illusion of black cobwebs floating out from her creamy, ample body, her glorious red hair flaming down her back in a cascade of perfume.

Faith, as always, felt diminished by her mother's stunning good looks, which tonight seemed to glow with a kind of phosphorescence. It was a strange new quality Becca had which made her even more attractive to men—Mr. Merritt, Bellwood, even Mr. Welch Seabreeze, who had been added to the list of admirers. It was a cold, snakelike beauty and it made Faith more shy than ever.

Her mother circled around the room, rearranging the china bits on the mantel before alighting like a moth on the chintz window seat. "It's going to be a very great sacrifice for me to lose my only daughter. I hope the Waldings realize that!"

Here was the dreamed-of opening. Faith felt deeply touched with excitement. Her mother was going to say she cared for her. "Oh thank you, Mama. You have always been the best of mamas. And I know the last years haven't been easy for you. You and Papa were so understanding and so close. I hope that Chugh and I can be the same."

"Certain economies will have to be made after you leave

because I no longer will get the share of your trust fund to keep Co-Eden going. Your father left it in his will that Quinn should always have a job here, but as there won't be any more fox hunting with you gone, I don't really see how I can keep him on. Monaghan can do all the driving which I will require in the automobile. I think, therefore, Faith, that as your part, possibly you might consider taking on Quinn. I mean giving him a monthly wage."

Faith was stunned by the harsh inappropriateness of these words. But if this was the price of satisfying her intensely deep longing for one real conversation about her own self instead of always about Mama's problems, Faith was glad to pay it. She tried. "Of course. I'll speak to Chugh. Maybe he can even find a cottage at Finchwicke."

"I don't know how I shall manage at all." Her mother stood in the bay window, her ruffled sleeve falling back to display one alabaster arm raised to pull back the wisp of curtain. She looked out at the stars; she seemed to be speaking only to the summer night. "The tent. Down by the pond." Her speech was thick and hard to understand. "It's appeared again. Where my lover lives."

"That's the reception tent, Mama. Chalk was here and started to put it up while you were napping."

"The bed is hung with Persian tapestries. Maybe tonight he will come and take me." She shook with silent laughter at the amusing horror of her own thoughts. "It will be far more romantic than the Judge—the great Judge Hoagland and Bellwood's wife."

Faith, not understanding her mother's private joke, and beginning to fear that her mother had gone crazy as Bellwood had intimated, giggled dutifully, hoping that amusement would allow communication if sentiment would not. Her mother now moved over to perch on the edge of the bed as she used to do when hearing Faith's childhood prayers. Her mother's amplitude tipped the edge of the mattress. They had both grown larger, the bed was still small and narrow. Tiddy-Boom growled at her approach and stirred around uneasily in her basket. Becca fastened her eyes on Faith's eyes. "Really, Faith. That awful old rag doll!"

"Ma'selle has sewed a whole new face on him." She had not realized until then that she had been lying there with Woggy clutched in her arms. "He's going to be packed into the honeymoon suitcase." Faith made her own attempt at a joke, but Becca was deadly serious now.

"Is there anything you would like to ask me?" Her skin was like thick white writing paper. Her eyes had a pale, inward glint.

Faith was suddenly oppressed by the power of the other woman, as though the intimacy which she had craved was deathly. She seemed to breathe in a decayed odor as she struggled to regain the memory of her fascinating mother as she had been in the past. But there was something rotting behind Becca's white flesh. In sudden fear she realized that her mother's intent was to contaminate what was most precious.

"No. Nothing I need to know. Unless you could tell me what was the secret of your own happy marriage? Of course, I know that you were more beautiful than I, and that Papa was the dearest and kindest of men, but somehow, beyond that, you and Papa seemed to be so much more romantic than, say, good Mr. and Mrs. Pardue or solid old Dr. and Mrs. Walding. Is there some sort of password that you can give me? What did you do to make Papa worship you."

Having exposed her most sensitive feeling, Faith waited for Mama to say something about the nature of love. Her eyes were fixed on the blue of the ring flashing on her finger, her thoughts on the saving fire which flashed deep in Chugh's eyes sometimes when they were alone.

Mama put out her hand and closed it over Faith's—her touch was grasping. "There are three kinds of men: worthy bores, drunken fools, or the fascinating lovers who are always unfaithful. So my motherly password to you tonight is that marriage is harsh. Have no illusions about that, no matter how much pap about heavenly love you will be fed tomorrow by my brother Gault. Gault is a saint. But you will notice that Aunt Claire spends her time trying to beat herself at solitaire. And if she wins, there is great jubiliation in the front parlor." Becca laughed. "Maybe that is the best answer I can give you. That is the secret of a happy marriage. Get plenty of money, and win at solitaire."

Faith tried to withdraw her hand, but Mama's claw tightened.

"So when you get down there to Finchwicke," Mama continued, "remember that it is yours—that everything Chugh has is also yours. And be careful that he makes a proper will in your favor. State your rights before it is too late. And give him nothing that belongs to you."

"Oh, Mama! I don't know how I'd be able to do that. And

surely Chugh and Dr. Walding will be the soul of kindness. And you will visit us often."

"Things will be different. You will have only gone a mile away, but you will have gone from your girlhood forever. And if you think of me, think of me in this way. I come from a long line of people who have stubbornly refused to drop their eyes to the rude stare of any common devil. So this then, my daughter, is my advice to you on your wedding night. Stare back! Stare them down!"

She rose, planted a perfumed peck on Faith's forehead, and turned out the lights. "And another thing that every mother should tell her daughter is about the bad house. All men use it. That motherless home the Reverend Fitzjoy was prating about—that it is the place where men go to see dancing girls with no clothes on and to get into bed with them. Even your minister must have been there, for he was the one who told us that the Hoagland estate owns it. And though I don't want to spoil your illusions about your father, I have investigated and discovered that you darling Papa did not die in his courtroom after a particularly arduous morning's work as you have been led to believe. He died after a morning's hard work in the bad house which put a strain on his heart."

Feeling as though stung and utterly poisoned to death by a whole nest of hornets, Faith sprang to her feet and stood facing her mother. She was vile, wicked, evil. And yet, Faith thought, she is my mother. I am a part of her. I can never really get away from her. "Kindly get out of my room, Mama. Get out this very minute. Get out now. And never come back."

"I only want you to know what every mother should tell her daughter as a matter of duty. I only want you to know that marriage is harsh."

Faith stood there in her thin embroidered nightgown, clutching her hands together until the ring on her finger cut into the flesh. She managed to stare at her mother until finally even Becca turned away.

Faith spoke icily, making a last effort to have an understanding. "I doubt your words about Papa. I remember the presents he brought you. The teas, the balls, the dinner parties, the drives out into the park on top of the road coach. Have you forgotten all these things, Mama? How can you say these wicked, cruel words?" But she sensed that there was no use talking, that whether there was truth or not in what Mama had said, her crazy words could never be forgotten.

Faith couldn't bear the sight of her mother for one more second.

"Get out!"

Lurching across the floor with a faint laugh, Becca left the room. The floorboards creaked heavily as she went down the hall. Faith snapped the door shut and leaned against the fat roses on the wall in a welter of horrible feelings, terrified at having screamed at Mama. Revolted at what Mama had said about Papa, and yet suddenly remembering the mysterious words spoken in the front parlor of the townhouse by the men who had come to tell Mama that Papa had died, but not in his court.

But what does any of that matter? It was *me* that he loved. Me. His own Twinkle, Faith thought in desperation.

She made her way to her bed and knelt down and buried her face in Ma'selle's crocheted coverlet. There was no one left but Ma'selle and beloved Uncle Bishop, who would cleanse and wash away all the cruelties and unkindnesses spoken here tonight—and Chugh, who seemed more golden and godlike than ever in his distant coldness.

The retired missionary bishop of Chile and Mrs. P. Manigault Lee, Becca's brother and his wife, arrived with their Indian lady's maid two evenings before the wedding and injected a saving note of pomp and ceremony into the fevered prewedding turmoil.

Next morning, coming into the smoking room at Co-Eden, Faith felt things falling back into place as she found little Uncle Bishop pale as wax, as though carved from Ivory soap, sitting in the Judge's comfortable old leather chair. Here her father had always sat, huge feet up on the fender, whiskey glass in hand. And if, after a day's shooting with his boys, he had caught sight of her peeking around the corner in her little white dress, ready for tea, he would have boomed out her name and summoned her also into the male sanctuary, picked her up on his knee, and laughed when she took the pipe out of his mouth to kiss his fresh cheek, feel the prickles of his mustache, nestle down into his shoulder. How she longed to ask him what he thought of Chugh!

But the Judge was dead, and dearest Uncle Bishop was waiting in that chair dressed in his exquisite black broadcloth clericals, trimmed with grosgrain lapels, his golden chain and cross around his neck, his starched white backwards collar holding up the soft wattles of his neck. The Bishop was clean-shaven. His sandy hair was parted in the middle and plastered neatly down. He raised a well-tended hand, whose only toil had been to pass the translucent wafer, wipe the rim of the silver chalice with a fine linen napkin.

Now her uncle motioned her into one of the two straight chairs which had been pulled up to make an intimate circle around him. He was patiently waiting to have a little talk with Chugh and herself on the religious significance of their marriage, and Faith had come to tell him that Chugh hadn't arrived yet and to apologize for his lateness. "He's busy, you know—sight-seeing with the Baroness, his cousin, and her husband."

"A Baroness!" The Bishop's pale cat's eyes protruded with humor. He seemed pleased, and his long nostrils quivered happily, but his mouth remained thin and pursed with the effort to keep from smiling on this serious occasion. "Come in, anyway, Niece. There are some private things I always like to say, just for the ears of the woman!"

Outside, the June sun was shining brightly on the clipped lawns sloping down to the rose garden. Here the striped tent was being pitched to the shouts of workmen and gardeners. Inside the house, too, there was an atmosphere of humming excitement as preparations went forward for the bridesmaids' dinner tonight and the wedding reception tomorrow. All the heavy mahogany furniture had been removed from the dining room and stored in the coach house overnight, and everywhere the caterer's men were setting up small round tables. Hebe was giving the orders; Ma'selle was running around like a chicken without a head, jabbering in French.

But Uncle Bishop was able to give a hush to the air immediately surrounding his body, so that the smoking room remained calm, sanctified like the anteroom to church. The mantel, hooding the garnished fireplace and rising to the ceiling in slanting stonework and emblazoned with the family motto, appeared like an altar. The Bishop continued talking in his cultured Southern voice in that certain monotone of authority which came from many years of making himself heard all the way from the pulpit to the back corner of the cathedral. His voice fell upon the ears of his niece, seated with head bent and hands folded, with the true ring of authority. "Now, I wouldn't want Chugh to hear me say this, but it is up to the woman to preserve the illusions of the marriage, to veil all the ugly things which may and will come up, with her love. Lying, cheating, unfaithfulness—none of these are excuses for undoing the knot of a Christian marriage. For in a truly Christian marriage there will be self-sacrifice, and illusions must be supported at great price. Otherwise illusions can only be supported by great economic selfishness, and then they lose their magic, degenerate, lose the sheen of love, and become false trumpery. The utter belief in the veiling of ugliness with love is what makes a lady of the upper class. It is truly a royal calling. And how is she able to do it without losing, at times, her self-respect? She is able to do it because she is able to rise above the foibles of her mate and identify herself with Our Lord Jesus Christ."

The Bishop paused, and Faith broke in. "It won't be difficult, Uncle, because Chugh has none of the foibles you mention. He is the soul of honor. And his manners are most considerate. There is only one thing, he doesn't understand about Viv . . ."

This evidently was not what Uncle Bishop had wished to hear, and without being deflected he continued with his train of thought, becoming more solemn and admonitory. "The most solemn, the most holy, the most sacred and unbreakable bond is that formed between a man and a woman on their entering together into marriage. As God sent His Son, Jesus Christ, to be the Bridegroom of the Church, so will your husband come upon you and enter . . . your heart." And as he said these words, his hands rose and fluttered down like white doves to rest again on his black lap.

Faith trembled under his spell and did not speak; the moment was too intimate and solemn.

"As I was saying, the success of the marriage will depend entirely upon the woman, on how well she serves her lord and master. Comforting and keeping him. Doing his will. Strengthening his manhood so that he is able to go out into the world and do his job—making her proud to be his wife; happy to bear his children; run his household; and stand in his reflected glory, making it her own as she binds herself unto him, asking nothing more for herself."

"Yes, Uncle, I will. I truly want to," Faith murmured, as the Bishop had paused, expecting her to answer.

"And one more thing." His voice took on a playful tone as he leaned forward and tweaked her ear, signifying that the serious part of the deeply communicative moment between them was ended. "If there is anger—which there will be from time to time, as, after all, we are but human—never let the sun set without the connubial kiss which signifies forgiveness, one to the other. Your Aunt Claire and I, you know, we still sleep in the same bed, even though she accuses me of snoring! None of these newfangled twin beds for me! After all, we are not twins! We are male and female, Husband and wife. And I recommend that you kneel and pray together each night. These three thoughts then I leave with you: preserve all the illusions; go to church regularly; and pray nightly to God that He will bless your every act, as you cherish your husband. Pray that He will bless you with children."

Faith was so moved that this time she could not speak. One did not speak of having babies.

There was a knock on the door and Mary announced Mr. Chugh. Without pause, he wafted in with profuse apologies for being late. But he had done an exhaustive tour of the Blue Rock Works with his cousin, the Baron Birge Bellanowski, who surprisingly had known quite a lot about the subject and had wanted to see everything from the nitrating pitchers to the finished product, fertilizer and coke. And it was the first opportunity Chugh himself had had to inspect a new railroad siding. He stood before the Bishop explaining all this in his urbane accent, and even though the words were apologetic, the tone was not. In his pearl-gray suit and polished brown boots, Faith thought him as elegant in every way as Uncle Bishop, far more attractive and worldly.

Immediately the atmosphere changed and became one of jovial good wishes and good will, as the Bishop congratulated Chugh and motioned him into the other chair. The Bishop even cracked his prenuptial joke. "Let me introduce myself as the man who will marry your wife!" And when Chugh looked puzzled, he added, "To you, of course!" and laughed heartily. Then the Bishop tried to reiterate for Chugh some of the advice he had given Faith. But since the two men had never met before, the words were more stern, more frightening, not at all intimate. "You must honor her above all women, esteeming her divine as the goddess of your household where she will reign and keep order whilst you wend your way out into the world—to win fame and fortune, I hope, and not forgetting at all times to serve the Lord. And then I would say a word about the difference in the vows which you will take. Chugh will say to Faith, 'With all my worldly goods I thee endow.' Now this is part of a contract and in English common law no contract is valid unless something is given in return. In return Faith will promise not only to love and honor you, but to obey. And that is the security which will hold you together in the worldly sense. For marriage is not only of this world, but beyond this world, symbolizing the marriage betwixt Christ and His Church."

The Bishop paused, and Chugh broke in. "Yes, sir. I agree to that most wholeheartedly."

But the Bishop wasn't listening. He rose from his chair to terminate the interview. He leaned forward to shake Chugh's hand, trying to stand as tall as Chugh, bouncing on the balls of his feet in their shiny black buttoned boots. In his most Southern voice, he said, "And should it ever come to my attention, suh, that you have treated her cruelly, or dishonored her in any way, you will answer personally to me, suh! I will challenge you, not with swords or with pistols, but by this cross, suh!" He held out toward Chugh the elaborate gold cross which had been made for him by the Indians, which he wore on a heavy chain across the front of his buttonless backwards black vest.

At this point, Faith gathered up her courage and said, "Chugh and I have had a disagreement, Uncle, which I feel is separating us. He doesn't want me to have Viv, my sister-in-law, in the wedding party, even though Hebe says it's none of his business. However, I thought if you could manage to baptize Viv tomorrow morning before the rehearsal, it might remove Chugh's objection to her being an actress."

"Me? A Bishop? Baptize an actress?" He laughed in disbelief. "Whatever for?"

"For the same reason anyone gets baptized. To make her one of us, by giving her a real Christian name."

"Actresses don't have real names, my child. They play first one role and then another. They are chameleons, not Christian soldiers. They are only *actresses*. Don't you see?"

Chugh intervened. "It doesn't really matter to me at all whether or not she is a member of the Church, though Faith seems to think Viv would gain friends that way. It's simply that I feel strongly that if she comes up the aisle, it will cause comment, that's all. Therefore I've asked Faith not to include her."

"But she is Mrs. Bellwood Hoagland, my brother's wife! And she's my dear friend! And if she's done anything wrong, I feel she should be forgiven, as Christ forgave Rebecca at the well."

"Phaugh!" the Bishop said. "Nobody said she was a harlot. That would be something real to forgive. It's as I said, my child—actresses are not real, and they are certainly not ladies."

"But I had already asked her before Chugh objected, and to change it now would raise so many questions." She summoned all the persuasive earnestness of which she was capable. "In the future I promise to do everything you ask. I'm going to be a very inadequate wife, I know"—she looked up at him adoringly—"but I want to say this in front of Uncle Bishop. Please don't command me to turn my back on a dear friend."

She threw her arms around Chugh's neck and felt his warmth and a faint smell of bay rum as she kissed him on the cheek and begged him to speak to her. But, in answer, he looked down upon her with a disapproving godlike stare, untwined her arms and disengaged himself by taking two steps backwards.

She then threw herself upon Uncle Bishop, hugging him until he truned pink and he, too, shook her off. "What? What is all this?"

Chugh answered the Bishop in a lordly way, over Faith's head. "I am confident she will give in. I ask you, sir, does it not seem a small matter?"

"A very small matter," agreed the Bishop.

"A friend is never a small matter with me," Faith said. "I mean, it isn't as though she were a Hottentot or an Aztec. You have baptized them, Uncle."

"Of course! It was my mission to convert the heathen."

"Then you will baptize Viv?"

"Not at all. It might be held against me in the House of Bishops. But to please you, I'll speak to your regular man about it. He might be able to get away with it. Whatshisname?"

"Guy. Guy Fitzjoy."

"Yes, yes, of course." The Bishop was heading for the door. "I'll leave you two alone for just a few moments to talk things over." Looking like a glossy black mynah bird, he fingered his cross as he disappeared into the hall, where he gave a most unpriestly whistle and exclaimed, "Women! Women! Whew!"

For the first time in weeks they were alone. Faith was aching for just one touch of Chugh's hand, but he made no move toward her. The male atmosphere of the red-leather smoking room and the faint odor of cigar and pipe smoke that lingered in the upholstery and in the dark curtains was suddenly stifling. Faith went to the window. Workmen carrying tent poles were struggling down to the rose garden. The arrangements for the wedding were proceeding according to schedule. It was unbearable. She turned back to Chugh and faced the angry blue glare of his eyes. "How can we talk things over if you won't speak?"

His mouth was set in stubborn silence.

"What is the point of getting married if you hate me?"

Chugh took a step to the Judge's red-leather-topped desk. He took the quill pen whose nib was buried in a round glass of buckshot, dipped it in the inkpot and helped himself to a piece of the best Co-Eden notepaper, a thick gray containing multicolored minute hairs like dollars and embossed in high red with the name Co-Eden. Without sitting down in the Judge's chair, Chugh scratched out a message and handed it to Faith.

It read, "Have it your own way."

A big tear dropped onto the wet ink. How terribly embarrassing. The last thing she wanted was to cry in front of Chugh—she who hand never cried as a child, now constantly giving in to the weeps. She could feel her resolve eroding away like the sand running out of a stuffed doll. She did not trust herself to speak the words: Very well then, I will never see you again. For surely her voice would break. There was only one thing to do.

Flee.

Mary sounded the musical notes of the lunch gong. The Judge's desk clock sounded the Westminster chimes for the half-hour. It was already one-thirty. Mama's tinkling laugh was heard leading Aunt Claire in from the Chinese pagoda, where she had been sitting all morning, doing her needlepoint. Aunt Claire was always starving for lunch.

There was no time to lose if she were to give Chugh an ultimatum. The escape up the stairs and to her bedroom was quickly becoming blocked by hostile troops. Faith tore the note up into little pieces. Sunlight flashed off the pale blue of her aquamarine ring, circled with diamonds. It was there on her finger, still hard and clear. She concentrated her will on it, a trick she had learned in dealing with Mama.

"I will not go back on Viv, who is a friend. But if you haven't spoken kindly to me, Chugh, before the reception is finished, I will kill myself rather than go away with you." Her voice was measured and cool. What a relief! The words sounded quite reasonable.

"Don't be so silly." He had actually spoken to her! The words rang in her head like bells of hope. Now the handle turned and the heavy mahogany door opened and there was the whole family in the hall: Uncle Bishop fingering his cross, Aunt Claire's long nose quivering to meet dear Chugh, Becca trying to bear him in to luncheon with her.

Chugh turned and escaped with a polite bow and a perfect excuse. "My cousins, the Baron and Baroness are awaiting me at Finchwicke . . . " And he was gone down the few steps to the vestibule and was out the door, leaving a momentary vacuum in the air where he had stood. It seemed to Faith that there was simply no one in the world as attractive as Chugh Walding . . .

Quinn drove the Hoagland carriage with young Monaghan on the box behind the horses Fire and Smoke. Faith, Mama, Bellwood, and Viv were a bit late to rehearsal and arrived at St. Jude's to find bridesmaids and ushers already gathered on the lawn bordering the cemetery. Becca, in a swirl of veils to ward off the afternoon sun, lowered her parasol and proceeded directly in to the cool of the church. With an imperious wave of her hand, she summoned Viv to follow her.

But Viv hesitated and melted in between Faith and Bellwood. She moved with them toward the circle of grass under the trees where gossip about the arrival of Baron and Baroness Birge Bellanowski was creating a hubbub. Gladys Whitefield was holding forth to Mariette Pardue and Hebe who were gathered in tightly around her. But she was talking loudly enough to be heard by Perry Markoo and Johnny Oldthwaite, Bird Jaspar, and Jap Birdgrove who lounged just outside her circle. That morning, Gee had accompanied Edith, the Baroness, to the city to Miss Meeley's for a final fitting on her bridesmaid's dress while the Baron had gone off to see some factory with Chugh.

Every word that Edith had spoken had been stored for repetition in Gee's empty mind. "Edith has never seen the estates in Estonia. Can you imagine being married to somebody with a castle that you couldn't visit on account of the horrid old boring war? A castle! Of course they had planned to live there eventually. But Edith said the place was frozen up tight for long winters, and the only way to get around was by sleigh over the fields of snow. It was very, very primitive, Edith said. Nothing has changed there since the Middle Ages. And the peasants on the place virtually belonged to the Bellanowskis . . . No running water! Can you imagine it? All the dirty linen was thrown into a tower—a whole year's supply—and when the tower unfroze, the women washed all that linen, beating it out on the rocks in the streams, drying it in the sun, folding it and putting it back in the castle.

"Wait until you see Edith. She's like a princess in a fairy tale—and she smokes cigars too! Bigs came over from Oxford last year to play polo on the North Shore and visited the Chyldes. And that's how she met a baron."

"I don't think you should call him Bigs," said Hebe, "even behind his back."

Gee kept right on, including Faith in the range of her voice. "She married Bigs because she thought it would be jolly to live in an old castle in Europe and try the shooting and fishing over there. But in the meantime, with Knight gone, they have to stay on in Whippen Point with old Mrs. Chyldes."

"I think he probably sleeps out in the barn with his polo ponies," Faith heard Johnny remark to Perry and Bellwood. "Met the fellow this morning. Little better than a groom, I thought."

Even though Viv was standing there in the circle, Faith felt that her sister-in-law was being assiduously left out, as though she didn't exist. As if to confirm this, Gee turned and spoke only to Faith.

"And would you believe it? Edith has crowns embroidered with her monogram all over her underwear. Miss Meeley noticed it once! Crowns, my dear! Meeley said only princesses and queens should have crowns on their drawers."

Faith was annoyed at this bad taste, to speak of drawers within the hearing of gentlemen. Besides, she thought that for once *she* should be the featured star of the occasion. But the arrival in Penngwynne of semiroyalty, even though the Baroness was only a Chyldes from Boston, seemed to have shaken up everybody from Pop Winkler at the station, who complained about the weight of her trunk, to Hebe, who thought *she* should sit beside the Baron at the wedding lunch, to Becca, who had flashed her diamond earrings and announced that he would sit on *her* right, where Dr. Walding belonged. Faith longed to escape from Gee's giggling recital. She looked at her fat perspiring girlfriend in distaste and wondered what she had ever seen in her.

Only Guy Fitzjoy seemed unimpressed by the talk of Bellanowskis. Standing apart, his prayer book in hand, he looked out into the haze of the distant summer hills. A breeze ruffled his hair, which was getting a little thin on top. He was waiting, outcast from the group too, and Faith noticed that Viv had moved closer and closer to him until they stood together. All God's children were the same to Guy Fitzjoy because that's what God's love is—be it a baroness or be it Viv. Faith could almost forgive him his remarks against Chugh, for standing there with Viv.

Faith moved over and joined them. In the distance were the green Guard Hill woods, where George Washington had bivouacked with his troops on his weary winter retreat to Valley Forge. Just below in the cemetery, there was Rhoda Seabreese's grave. In a sudden wave of shame Faith remembered how she had said yes to Chugh Walding without even knowing him, responding only to the thrill of his fingers unbuttoning her vest as she had lain half-fainting and out of wind on a bed of oak leaves. She had given into the desires of her own flesh.

She spoke to Guy Fitzjoy, a good and pure man. "It is my dream that Viv will be baptized and confirmed in our Church."

Guy looked startled and turned to Viv. "Do you believe?"

A half-smile curved her lips as she gently shook her head. The enormous pouf of her tulle hat shadowed her eyes from view. "I would like to, to please Faith. She almost persuades me with her special friendship. You see, I believe that all the love in this world comes from the people in it."

Guy smiled and shook his head. "God is love," he said with finality.

Now at last the Finchwicke victoria was arriving, drawn by the high-steppers Wildfire and Fire-Away. Chugh handed out the Baroness, a stunning girl in a white linen suit with a man's collar and tie, a mountainous pompadour of bright curly hair, and the same sapphire eyes as Chugh. "This is my cousin Edith." He spoke to the group, and then he turned to the Baron and Baroness. "And may I present Faith, my fiancée." Edith took a long stride forward and squeezed Faith's hand so that the knuckles cracked.

Chugh went on, "And may I present Baron Bellanowski— this is Miss Hoagland, my fiancée." The Baron was an older man with thick hair. Faith started to shake hands with him but he caught up her fingertips, and bending over, dropped a mock kiss there, which surprised her—she had forgotten the European custom. His smile was crooked from the dueling scar across one cheek. "Enchanté," he murmured in a guttural accent. A stranger from a strange world, a relation of Chugh's, a part of Chugh's world which she was entering without knowing where she was going.

The wedding party was now gathered together and everyone was introduced around. Conversation stopped when Hebe mounted the front steps of St. Jude's and clapped her hands for attention. Behind her the late afternoon sun shone on the lacy brown stone fretwork of the arched doorway. Viv stood behind Hebe, listening from within the shadows of the church.

"Don't wait for Uncle Bishop," Bellwood shouted up to Hebe for all to hear, "He didn't feel up to a rehearsal after his long trip. Says he knows what to do and tomorrow he'll do it."

"Very well." Hebe clapped her hands again and waited for the laughter to die down. "Very well. Have the ushers all got matching black frock coats from Deger and Berg? White piqué double-breasted waistcoats? White linen shirts? Dark folded neckties? And gray gloves which they mut be sure to keep on while serving! Gray toppers? And you, John Oldthwaite, you're the best man. Have you and Chugh got matching light silk ties?"

"Great God, Hebe! Let's get on with the rehearsal and get it over with," Chugh said angrily.

Tears stood in Faith's eyes. She, too, found Hebe very difficult, and now she was being embarrassing in front of the Baron and Baroness. Turning toward her father's grave, lying under the large red-granite stone in the plot at the top of the hill, she caught Quinn walking Hebe's Peke in the cemetery nearest the church. The little dog was lifting his leg on Hebe's unborn baby's tiny grave, a granite tasseled pillow, marked "Baby Hoagland, 1911." No spot was sacred, it appeared.

Hebe's voice continued, "And as I've said before and feel I have to say again, I hope the ushers will have a good sleep tonight and be here on time in the morning!" Hebe paused, looked around, and then continued, "As a matter of fact, where's Rick right now?"

Bellwood answered, "Rick said not to wait for him. It's Princeton graduation on Monday, and he had some things he had to do." But then Bellwood added, "And where's Marshall? I thought he was supposed to give the bride away?"

"Don't you worry about Marshall, he will get here tomorrow one way or the other," said Hebe. (No one ever asked where Marshall was. He was, of course, with some lady who was H-A-V-I-N-G. It was too embarrassing.) I'm sure the Baron won't mind rehearsing *in loco parentis.*"

The Baron take the place of her dead father? Faith wouldn't have it. She said, in protest, "Oh please, Hebe, I'd much rather not!"

"All right," Hebe replied, "Then I'll take the part of the bride. It would be bad luck for you to rehearse anyway."

The group was herded inside the church. The Baron and Baroness were introduced to Becca, who sat waiting in a pew, and then Faith quickly took a seat beside her mother on the hard red-velvet cushion. She took off her gloves and stared at her ring to make herself cloudless and blue, if she could.

The organist played the wedding march softly. Hebe started the ushers up the aisle, slowly pacing, two by two. After a space of ten feet had opened up, they were followed by Mariette Pardue and the Baroness. But Edith's stride was so long they easily caught up to the men. Hebe clapped her hands and made them start all over again. "The bottoms of the skirts will be tight tomorrow and short steps will have to be taken." Then came Viv, small and dainty, and Gladys Whitefield, quite huge and purple in the face—the matron and the maid of honor; and Chugh's little cousin Rosalie, strewing wild flowers to the right and left. Then walking slowly and alone, Hebe and the Baron, as the bride and father. Behind them came the Peke, Ogden, his pink tongue hanging out, his bloodshot bug eyes rolled up in an expression of permanent disapproval.

The minister was waiting at the foot of the chancel steps with the bridegroom and the best man.

"My God," said Johnny Oldthwaite as the organ died away with the arrival of the bride, "did you ever see a pug dog look more like his mistress? They're *exactly* alike. Be careful which one you marry, Chugh!"

Ogden yapped. The procession was swept by a wave of giggles, which Hebe ignored and at once ordered the group to break ranks, pushing half to the left and half to the right until they were spaced just so, the two bridesmaids moving on higher up into the chancel, forming an arc in which the bride and groom would stand.

When the rehearsal was over and Gee Whitefield had pretended to turn the bride's train and lift the veil from her face, Hebe paired off the ushers and the bridesmaids according to height and started them off down the aisle. "Don't gawk at people in the pews, Gee!" she commanded. "Just keep looking straight ahead. And Edith, don't run."

On the steps of the church, Hebe took a final stand, calling out loudly as the group dispersed toward their cars and carriages. "Everybody, please be sure to be here on time. Eleven o'clock. *Please!*"

Chugh was shepherding out the Bellanowskis without a word to Faith. Bigs was to attend the ushers' dinner while Edith was to be driven over to Co-Eden.

In a rush of panic, Faith seized Hebe's arm. "Call them all back, Hebe. I don't want to get married. I won't show up. I don't know Chugh and his friends. You'll have to make an announcement now, before they get away!"

"Nonsense. All brides get cold feet, I assure you. It's too late now." And with Ogden pressed tightly against her bosom under one arm, Hebe firmly propelled Edith and Becca over to the buckboard, where Quinn was standing at his horses' heads.

* * *

Rick Hoagland, careening up the drive to Co-Eden in his Pierce Arrow, too late for the rehearsal, too early to get dressed to go to the ushers' dinner, had dropped by the kennels to see how his dog, Major, was doing on this hot day.

It seemed the poor old boy was being driven crazy by a fox caged in a box just outside the dog's run and smelling to high heaven. A burlap bag underneath the wild animal was just the kind used to drag along the ground to simulate a fox's trail. Rick went looking for Monaghan and Paddy to ask what was the big idea. Why was anyone planning to lay a drag in June? Was this some kind of a wedding trick?

But he discovered that Monaghan and Paddy had gone over to the stables to aid the vet, who had unexpectedly arrived to castrate Plymouth Rock. Quinn, who had driven the ladies over to the church, had not been forewarned. Monaghan and William the gardener had managed to get a line on the chestnut colt that had been running free in the paddock, his mane and tail streaming in the breeze. They had led him, neighing and prancing into the largest stall, where a good bed of clean straw had just been laid down. Here Rick found the group.

"Help us, Mr. Rick, will ya? Quinn wants the job done before the weddin'. He has enough on his hands without the stallion. We need to get this twitch around his nose before he goes up on his hind legs again. Watch it there! He'll strike out with his front feet!"

The vet managed to get the hobbles on, and passing a chain through them, slowly pulled the horse's feet together until he went inexorably crashing onto the straw while Paddy pulled on a rope to keep him from breaking his neck as he fell.

"Kneel, Mr. Rick! Stick one knee right there in his neck and hold his head up to forty-five degrees. Pull back on it hard!"

Rick knelt.

The vet tied one front leg to the hock of the hind leg on the same side, and the gorgeous creature could no longer struggle.

"Now, my fine fellow, we'll just have your nuts with this here crusher. We'll serve them up for dinner tonight, and you'll never know the difference."

The horse's eyes were rolling wildly, and Rick could feel the sweet, hot, pasture breath fluming into his face. Paddy's boy was given a large sponge which the vet had saturated with chloroform to pass in front of the colt's nose.

"Watch that! Keep it away from me! I wouldn't trust you fellas . . . "

The colt appeared to relax, and then the vet, squeezing the scrotum in his left hand and drawing it over one testicle to see the dividing line appear, took a sharp knife in his right hand and carefully slit through the inner coverings one by one, until at last, the testicle popped out clean. He put steel clamps on the cord and bit it off.

"Now the other one! More chloroform, boy!" The colt bled profusely and rolled up the whites of his eyes as his testicles, like silver golf balls, were extricated from their velvet envelope and passed from hand to hand in wonder, ending up in one of the many horse-show cups from the tack room. His empty scrotum was now rinsed out with cold water, and Plymouth Rock was let up.

Rick was rather surprised that he felt no empathetic pain. Instead he shared an extraordinary sense of power and well-being with the men who stood about wiping their hands in gesture of a job well done. The horse leaned up against the corner of the stall.

"He'll fergit all about it by day after tomorrow," the vet said, putting his instruments back in his bag.

Now, back at Co-Eden, Rick saw the carriages, back from the rehearsal at the church, crunching to a halt at the porte-cochere, so he decided to slip in through the back door with his trophy. He offered the contents of the silver cup to the cook to mince up for the Bishop's breakfast, but she screamed and threw up her apron at him and threatened to give notice that night if he didn't take them out of the kitchen at once. Rick took the trophy, laughing all the way, up the back stairs and offered them instead to Ma'selle, who was pressing out the wedding petticoats in her room. "Pack these in Carrie's getaway suitcase tomorrow!" She kissed him on both cheeks. "*Zut alors!* Take zem wiz you to ze dinner, if you desire, but take zem out of here zis minute! Aaaach! What a terrible day it has been, packing and unpacking!"

At Co-Eden, dinner was to be served at small tables on the piazza. The bridesmaids and the bride would sit at one, the Bishop and Mrs. Lee and Becca, who had not yet come out, at another. The girls were out there singing gentle songs and exchanging gifts when Rick bustled out among them on his way to dinner, interrupting them for the sheer fun of seeing them all fly around. The girls had given Faith a lovely silver tray for her bureau, and each had received a small jeweler's box containing an amethyst pendant to wear the next day. Edith Bellanowski had been smoking a thin black cigar down in the rose bushes. "Oh, but she's absolutely splendid, Rick! She was hockey captain at Winsor School and waltzing champion at the Boston Skating Club."

The girls all giggled at the thought, and Rick swaggered away, fingering the stallion's nuts in the pocket of his tuxedo.

Dr. Walding had not attended the rehearsal at the church. He had remained at Finchwicke to supervise the final arrangements for the dinner. Ordinarily he would have left this for Delia, but she had been giving him a very bad time, and it got worse that afternoon.

He had been sitting on the terrace, trying to escape the bustle going on in the house in preparation for the ushers' dinner, even though the menu had been carefully planned weeks ago, with the proper wines selected and extra servants rounded up. There was nothing more he could do now. It would either go well, or it wouldn't. Dr. Walding had been looking out across his lawns at his Holstein herd on the hill across the brook and trying to enjoy a moment of solitude when Delia had appeared before him.

"Have you got something on your mind, Delia?"

"Yessir, I'd like to give in my notice. I know I promised I'd stick with you to the end, but with the new mistress comin', I don't think I'll be needed here."

"But, Delia, this isn't really the moment to talk about it."

It had been quite a day. Hebe Hoagland had decreed that more space was needed to display the presents at Co-Eden and that the linens had to be gotten out of the way. Today of all days, trunks of stuff had arrived in wagons from Co-Eden, linens and china and a lot of old furniture that Faith was bringing with her. Their Mademoiselle had ridden along, to supervise putting it away. A bonnet-top highboy and a chaise longue had been carried up the stairs by the younger gardeners and stable men. A truly beautiful Charleston double bed, a present from Becca, had been set up by young Sweeting and young Monaghan in the middle of the bedroom.

Apparently, Mademoiselle had antagonized Delia, and that had prompted Delia's sudden decision to give notice just when he needed her most. Dr. Walding recalled the fuss he had overheard while working in the new Orangerie.

Ma'selle had sent for young Sweeting to come and open up the crates of china and glass which had been deposited by young Monaghan on the pantry floor. But Sweeting had taken his good old time about appearing. When Delia had come down the back stairs, the old Mademoiselle was up on the ladder, taking down all the cracked and stained dishes and cups that had been hidden for years at the back of the shelves. She was complaining in a volatile mix of English and French that there wasn't a decent dozen of anything, eleven of this and nine of that. "We'll put ze wedding present on ze shelves. We won't use all zis dirty china. Zese cracked glasses. Put Zem in the boxes. Up to ze attic wiz zem."

"That's the Doctor's favorite jug you're puttin' away," Delia had objected. "He has his linden tea in it every night. That's his favorite cup. These is the gold and white soup dishes we use every night."

"We won't be using zem any more."

"We're usin' them tonight. We're havin' Mr. Chugh's bachelors' dinner here tonight and we're very busy gettin' ready."

"We're very busy at Co-Eden too, and zese sings have to

215

be out of ze way of ze caterer's men. So put zis someplace else!"

"I'm not takin' any orders from you. Old French crow! Buckin'am Palace wouldn't be big enough to hold you and me. I'm leavin'. Right now!"

Interrupting this horrid scene, Dr. Walding had managed to send Mademoiselle home and calm Delia down—or so he had thought.

"This isn't really the time to talk about it, Delia." He had to summon all his charms this time. "Let's just get through the dinner tonight and everything will be all right. You know I can't do without you. Why should you worry about the new mistress? 'For the Colonel's lady and Judy O'Grady are sisters under their skins!' You know that."

"But is it true that she's bringin' that French housekeeper with her? And who will be in charge? Will it be you, Doctor? Mr. Chugh? Mrs. Chugh? Or the new housekeeper? Because if we're havin' a new housekeeper and she's anything like Mrs. Bunce, sir, I don't think it's quite right, sir."

"Mrs. Chugh will be in charge, of course." (That's one reason we're getting her, he thought.) "She will be the lady of the house, the new mistress of Finchwicke. The French woman will act only as lady's maid to Mrs. Chugh."

"But Mr. Chugh left word to have the Bunces' apartment made ready for this Mademoiselle. And I've been thinkin' maybe Rachel and I should have it. After all the work we've been doin' since last October."

"I don't know where else we'd put Ma'selle then."

"Why can't she go up in the attic with the other girls?"

Dr. Walding thought a long time. He couldn't say because she's not a servant, Delia, because she's not really a maid. "You see the little cottage over there, the Briar Patch? Someday maybe you and Rachel and I will move over there."

"Ye won't. I heard Mr. Chugh tellin' her. They won't let it happen, sir."

Dr. Walding laughed in surprise. "Maybe they'll change their mind when the babies start coming. You have no idea, Delia, what having a baby can do to a woman. They want to get everyone else out of the way. That's the way it was with Thessaly when Mr. Chugh was born."

"I'm sorry, Dr. Walding, but I don't care to stay here with a new madam and new babies and a new housekeeper. I'm very partial to you, sir, but I've found another position. It pays a lot more, and I need the money for me mother in Ireland. Times is very hard for them over there just now."

"When will you be going?"

"Tonight, sir."

"Tonight?" Dr. Walding was shocked and angry. "Why, you she-devil, Delia! You couldn't do that to Mr. Chugh, who has been so kind to you. How could you leave him in the lurch on the evening of his big dinner?"

Delia seemed unmoved. "Well, sir, I was wonderin', sir, would there be anything more comin' my way from Madam's will?"

"I'm not sure, I'm not sure at all. If it's money that's bothering you, I'll have to talk it over with Mr. Chugh. We'll see what can be done."

"I need a hundred dollars tonight, sir. Me nerves is shattered."

They're all she-devils, he thought. What a time to hold him up for money. There was no use bargaining her down. The dinner simply wouldn't go off without Delia. He opened his wallet and pulled out the green bills intended for tomorrow's tips for the waiters and porters on the special train. "Here, take this. And you can leave first thing in the morning."

"Thank you, sir. Tomorrow then."

His evening meditation ruined, Dr. Walding had gone inside to help himself from the whiskey tray and was glad to see Chugh and the Baron and some of the boys arriving in the hall, ready to join him. They were all complaining bitterly about that bitch Hebe Hoagland.

"Sufficient unto the day is the evil thereof ... It's been pretty bad around here, too. Friday the thirteenth, you know. But I'm determined everything will go well from here on in. Sometimes I wonder how any of us managed to get married at all," the Doctor had said to the men.

"It is better to go before the Justice of the Peace in a neighboring town," said Baron Bellanowski. "Just do it quickly before anyone can get you to make elaborate plans. Elope, I say. Elope!"

Rick Hoagland squeezed the bulb of the Pierce Arrow's French horn and gave a defiant blast as he turned in the historic white gates of Finchwicke on this beautiful summer evening. "All dogs have fleas," it blared, startling the mares and foals peacefully grazing in the meadows. He drew up with a disrespectful spurt of gravel in front of the dignified house and parked his car directly in front of the path to the front door, effectively blocking it for anyone else who might arrive. Late on purpose, he assumed he was the last one. And for anyone else, he didn't give a Continental goddamn!

He had not been to Finchwicke since the old days of Chetford Hill School baseball picnics when he had been on the sidelines cheering for big brother Bellwood playing for the Green team, battling the Old Blues in the final game of the series. He could still remember the home run Carrie had knocked out, right there on that stretch of lawn. It had sailed over that high brick wall and disappeared into the garden. Carrie, of course, had been wearing his clean white suit, playing for the Old Blues. And he had defeated the Hoagland boys, traditional members of the Greens.

Tonight Rick was determined to toss down the gauntlet and erase old scores, and send Carrie to the altar with a mouse in his eye.

Rick passed through the hall and out the Dutch door onto the terrace, where he could see groups of men standing about in the twilight. Candles flickered on little tables. The lush land stretched away to the edge of the woods, and the lower sky was pink, but stars were beginning to glitter in the dark-blue cup of the heavens above. All of the ushers were gathered out here, clinking glasses and laughing loudly, washing away their sour memories of Hebe Pardue Hoagland and her scolding with plenty of Scotch and soda.

"Better watch your step or she'll have you roped and tied too. Good God, I've never seen such a bossy officious bitch," Bird Jaspar was saying to his twin cousin, Jap Birdgrove. In imitation of Hebe he added, " 'I do hope the ushers will have a good night's sleep and be here on time in the morning.' By God, Richardson, you were lucky to miss the damn rehearsal. Enough to make you think twice about letting any young filly get you on the lead line."

Rick accepted the hardy slap on the back, happy to join the cocktail party. Ordering a glass of whiskey neat from the white-coated servant, he poured the amber liquid down as though his throat were a cast-iron pipe, without seeming to swallow.

Dr. Walding, detaching himself from the group of older men, including the Seabreese brothers, Welch and Charlton, came over with his hand outstretched. "Good evening, young man. I'm your host here tonight."

"Good evening, sir. As you were sitting way over there in

the shadows, I didn't see you, sir." Dr. Walding and the older men had been sitting in a circle under the Guardian oak. "Only these chaps here by the rum were here to greet me as I came in." Rick knew this would seem rude, but he was unable to hide his mood.

"You're very late," Dr. Walding responded gruffly. "We're about to sit down at the table."

Rick's anger boiled up, and he took it out on Chugh by bowing in mock deference when he introduced Baron Bellanowski. What was a goddamn German doing here? The fellow had a nasty dueling scar across his cheek.

"Bigs is a polo player," Chugh said. "He came over from Oxford last year to play Myopia and couldn't get home to Estonia without going through Germany, you know."

Rick couldn't bear to be polite to anyone, so he started to move away to join his brother Bellwood and Peregrine Markoo, who were talking together off on the edge of the terrace. But the Baron blocked his way. Surprisingly, when he spoke, he turned out to be a perfectly common, ordinary chap. "Your brother tells me you know people who play polo on the North Shore. I'd been staying there when I met my wife for the first time. Great People. Who do you know?"

Of course Rick knew people, having been to St. Paul's and being in the Ivy Club at Princeton. So this fellow thought he could move in on Rick's friends, did he? One had to watch out for foreign dukes. Rick rolled the stallion's balls in his pocket—slippery, hard chunks of gristle. He took another drink. He felt an urge to provoke this fellow and punch him in the nose. And he was just about to call Bigs Bellanowski with his crooked smile a goddamn foreigner when Dr. Walding noticed Rick's anger rising and seized his elbow. "Come on now, young Hoagland, don't get too red-headed around here tonight. Dinner is served."

Jap and Bird closed ranks behind Rick as he lurched off to follow the host. The stallion's balls were still in his pocket; he rubbed one against the other, saving them for the moment when Chugh would be unfrocked, sent to the altar with his parts painted red. Damn his sister, Faith—fickle, untrue. Damn all women. The whole thing was nauseating. How could she allow the lily of the field to touch her with his white clammy fingers?

In the candlelight of the dining room, the portraits of the men of Finchwicke looked down with the glassy-eyed innocence of the dead on the sumptuous table, set with all the

Walding silver, crystal, and porcelain, on the best Belgian lace cloth, in honor of the present young master's last night as a maverick. Bert Bloodgood, who had come out from the vaults of the bank to take charge, immediately moved out from the shadows with his two young nephews to pull out the chairs for the gentlemen now filing in.

Delia and her sister Rachel were behind the screen of the pantry door, ready to serve the cream of clam bisque and sherry. Then, after the Kennebec salmon hollandaise with sliced cucumber and thin brown-bread sandwiches had been served and the goblets filled with a white Rhone wine, Dr. Walding rose to his feet. "I wish to propose the first brief toast, as is customary at Finchwicke. And it will be the only toast to which we will drink standing." Solemnly the Doctor intoned: "To absent friends."

There was an awkward, sobering silence. It was a portentous moment, casting each man into the somber recesses of his mind to reflect on those nearest him who had trod the path into the next world, on which his feet also were inevitably set. As they all sat down again, scraping the Tree of Life chairs against the bare summer floors, conversation had also died.

The silence was broken by the ultracivilized voice of Bigs Bellanowski. "May I ask, does the *droit du seigneur* exist in Penngwynne as it still does in some parts of Estonia? It's a quaint custom whereby the lord of the manor has not only his son's wife first on her wedding night but also her serving maid, should he so desire."

Chugh laughed. "He can have Ma'selle, but I am taking Faith far away from the old beast! That's what honeymoons are for. As you know, Knight wrote and offered the *Viatrix*, and we'll be turning up at Whippen Point to embark for Maine in a day or so, after all danger is passed about my not being served first!"

"Ah yes, I see," the Baron reflected solemnly. "The yacht is in first-class condition, and I'm sure you'll find it to your liking."

A revived hum of conversation now washed over the group as Bloodgood and his minions served the saddle of lamb with mint sauce, the garden asparagus, the escalloped mushrooms, and the new potatoes, along with a claret, Château Mouton-Rothschild. Rick Hoagland, glowering at his end of the table, allowed himself to be served the wine but refused all food, and sat, flicking his table knife in Chugh's direction, turning it over and over to catch the candlelight. Dr. Walding rose again.

With his head pulled over toward one shoulder, his glass held out in front of him, he set off on another speech. "It is my privilege on this happy occasion to welcome you all to Finchwicke. My remarks will be brief and will concern the pleasure, the responsibility, and the positive duty of families such as our own to produce sons. There are but a handful of families, such as the Waldings, who still live on the lands which their forefathers wrested from the wilderness. We have remained here since the days of the thirteen colonies for one main reason. We have reproduced ourselves well. In fact, to reproduce is the primary duty of all living things, and a very pleasant one it is too." A general titter ran around the table. "Indeed you may laugh, gentlemen, but Mother Nature had decreed that the reproductive act shall rank as the most pleasurable in all the world. And it has always been my belief that out of the memory of this pleasure is generated a deep pool of strength. This is my thesis, allow me to elaborate. I have deduced the secret of founding and continuing a dynastic family. It is quite simple: pleasure in reproduction. Great families make love with ardor and vigor. They like themselves and want more of themselves around. They like their offspring and see to it that they are properly trained to compete in the sporting and intellectual fields in order to maintain their position above the hoi polloi: which is their birthright—"

"Ah! Very good indeed," interrupted the Baron.

"Not true at all," Jonah Wedgewright objected in his lawyer's tone. "No such thing as class birthright in these United States of America. Haven't you ever heard of the Revolution?"

Charlton Seabreese spoke so seldom, his voice was unfamiliar to most except when calling hounds. "You're a damned Democrat, Jonah, bringing the damned Jews out hunting."

"The damned Josenthals had ancestors who were officers in Washington's army!"

"Please, gentlemen!" Johnny Oldthwaite rang his knife on his glass for order. "Our host was speaking."

"Now, as for Chugh, he is the exception that proves the rule. He is an only child. Not, I assure you, from any abstinence on my part or dislike of performing the necessary act. Not from any shrinking, I say, but because of one of those freaks of nature, when, having produced a perfect specimen, one chooses to go no further!"

"Rot!" said Rick, under his breath. "Filthy, bloody rot!"

"However," the Doctor continued, "up to now, Chugh has not chosen to pay serious court to any member of the fair sex. He has seemed singularly unaware of what most common garden insects are instinctively aware. And, if you will pardon me, I will quote very briefly from my own writings, which describe how the male Cerceris has in fact only *one* duty in life. Not for him, going to the office. Nor bringing home the bacon, nor building the hive. This is all left to slaves and drones. Now hear me please, gentlemen, with patience, please.

> *"The male wasps hang about the hatching female, who has spent a snug winter within her ancestral portals eating freshly preserved spiders and beetles. One of them is chosen to go off and copulate with her, almost as soon as she emerges. Then the male's life is fulfilled. He does not work in the wasp community, but flies about with his friends, sipping nectar from flowers.*

"So, gentlemen, such is the lot of insects. However, such is not the lot of men. We have other stern duties: to manage our estates and our families, to preserve the institutions of our great city, and at all times to serve our country—in peace, gentlemen, and also in war." Here Dr. Walding's voice dropped to its lowest, most solemn register. "And, as we all know, Chugh has made it plain that he intends to serve in France. But he has also made it plain that he does not intend to leave without performing his basic duty of founding a family to carry on here at Finchwicke. And by the greatest good luck has also fallen head over heels in love with the most charming young lady.

"May I say that Chugh has made me very happy by choosing as a bride the daughter of my good and old friend and nearest neighbor, Judge Hallowell Hoagland, the finest and most honorable gentleman of his age. This happy event was facilitated by me after the young lady had been here to drop a calling card for her mother and herself, but by the *droit du seigneur* had been trapped inside for a cup of tea by the old lord of the manor, namely, myself. Then, on the next morning, there was a certain fox hunt ... " Mr. Welch Seabreese let his eyes drop to his plate in respect for his dead wife. "There was a certain fox hunt, I say, at which my son

222

popped the question while the young lady lay unconscious on the ground." Cheers went around the table! Well done, Chugh! Very bold! "And the young lady must have given some fluttering sign of assent, for the successful conclusion of the hunt was signaled to me by Chugh calling attention to himself by shaving off his beard, giving himself up to her in all his strength as Samson gave himself to Delilah. Permit me, therefore, a little poem to Chugh's erstwhile beard.

> ''Tis merry in the hall
> When beards wag all
> Then was the minstrel's harp with rapture heard
> The song of ancient days gave huge delight
> With pleasure too did wag the minstrel's beard.'

"So before I sit down, which I promise to do very shortly, let me urge you to enjoy our meager hospitality and to drink all toasts sitting down, as is our custom here. So, gentlemen! I give you Chugh's long lost beard—even though no longer able to wag it, he has other blandishments to please his bride. Here's to Chugh! And to his sons! Long may they wag!"

Rick Hoagland, called upon by Dr. Walding to drink to Carrie's offspring, rolled the stallions's nuts at the bottom of his pockets between his thumb and forefinger and silently drank to them instead. And he bided his own good time to punch somebody in the nose.

"Cock-a-doodle-doooo!" Bird Jaspar mimicked a whole barnyard and bottoms-upped his wine. "To his cock!"

Now Johnny Oldthwaite, the best man, rose to his feet and assumed the role of toastmaster, calling next on Mr. Charlton Seabreese to render "Wrap Me Up."

The distinguished white-haired gentleman—thin and hard as a rake handle—evoking the sporting spirit of all outdoors, his quavering voice part of the familiar charm of the song as verse followed verse, inspired the whole table to join in the final thunderous chorus:

> "Wrap me up in my old racing colors
> And say a bold rider lies low
> Lies low
> And say a bold rider lies low."

"I call next on Mr. Bellwood Hoagland, brother of the bride." Rick turned sideways in his chair and slouched over, one elbow on the table. It would be Shakespeare, of course.

Too good a moment for Bellwood to pass up the opportunity to show off.

Bellwood got to his feet. With both hands in his trouser pockets, his long tails pushed back, a gleam in his eye, he began, "Dr. Walding, sir, a wedding is indeed a momentous event, where not only two persons come to be joined together, but two families join their blood to flow through the veins of the next generation. There is no other way to have a next generation. Now I myself am of the opinion that blue blood needs at times to be strengthened and refreshed, and I have chosen to add just a touch of red to my children's blood. Happy to say, the first throw of the dice has brought forth a beautiful girl-child. I could wish Chugh nothing less than a bevy of daughters to wait on him in his old age, though I do confess that I have high hopes that my next one will be a boy. Let me then propose a toast to the ladies of the family which tomorrow Chugh will join. To my beautiful infant daughter. To my mother, whom we esteem as a queen. And to my sister, who has been well trained by her brothers to serve her prince."

Bellwood is a pompous ass, thought Rick. But as he is my brother I cannot call attention to it here, on enemy territory.

Bellwood sat down to a light smattering of applause. The toastmaster called on Welch Seabreese for a song, which was "Jolly Boating Weather," since Welch had gone to Eton. All joined in the chorus—"And we'll pull, pull together"—as the next course—garden lettuce, assorted cheeses, and English biscuits, and a rich Beaujolais 1905—were served.

When the Baron Birge Bellanowski was called upon for a song or a few words, he amazed everyone with his agility as he whirled his short and stocky body into a wild peasant dance, circling the table with snatches of song and weird shouts. Whirling and stamping, he ended up doing twenty-five kickouts from a squatting position to the rhythmic clapping of the group. Then he jumped to his feet and resumed his seat, not at all out of breath.

Jap Birdgrove pinched Rachel's luscious buttocks as she leaned over to change plates, causing Rachel to jump and drop a spoon with a loud clatter against a glass. Dr. Walding glared down the table in disapproval of her clumsiness, and Bird Jaspar laughed more than the episode was worth.

Peregrine Markoo reminded everyone that he was a Yale man by giving a serious rendition of "We are poor little lambs who have gone astray." All around the table, they bleated the chorus, "Baa, baa, baa." And then Johnny Old-thwaite called on Rick. "We will now hear from the bride's baby brother."

Rick rose unsteadily, his hand jerking from his pocket as he did so, casting the stallion's balls like dice upon the table. "Snake-eyes! Who would like to have a game of craps with Carrie's balls?" Quickly he swept them up again and back into his pocket. "Carrie Pots," he called out, pointing his glass at Chugh. "He's going to marry my sister, and I suppose you could say that I would never think anyone good enough for her." And he then muttered under a belch, "Except my-self." Loud laughter rippled around the table. "Twenty years a chambermaid and never dropped a pot—that's Carrie, my future brother-in-law, the goddamn lily-livered lily of the field who's going to marry my sister. Gentlemen, I propose a bot-toms-up rising toast to the groom, damn his eyeballs."

He drained his glass, and then, reeling around, smashed it to smithereens on the green marble hearth. The old Doctor looked horrified. "The last of Thessaly's best crystal!" he cried. Chugh gripped the arms of his chair, and his cheeks worked in anger. There was an uncertain moment of silence, but then old Dr. Walding rose to the occasion and to his feet, drained his glass, and in a fine gesture, also let fly. Then each man followed suit, goblet after goblet, splintering in the fire-place.

The frightened maids appeared around the pantry screen at the sound of breaking glass and heard the shouts.

"To the groom! Damn his balls!"

The dining room was in a shambles, the dessert had not even been served. Glass was all over the floor, and the gentle-men were milling about. Rick decided it was the moment for him to leave, but Johnny Oldthwaite pushed him back into his chair and announced that he himself was going to sing.

Johnny's familiar voice rang out around the Finchwicke dining room, in a great reassuring shout:

> *"It was Christmas in the harem*
> *And the eunuchs all were there . . ."*

A welcoming murmur of anticipation followed as the men took their seats again around the table. This favorite song would lift the rather somber atmosphere which had lurked at the ushers' dinner in spite of the amount of wine which had been drunk.

"The lovely girls were in their rooms
Curling their golden hair
The sultan donned his turban
And shouted down the halls
What will you have for Christmas, boys?
And the eunuchs answered. 'Balls . . .'"

As the rich cream-rum sponge with flaming cherry sauce was served as dessert, Crispin Chyldes called out, "Forty-second verse!" to remind everyone that he had gone to Harvard and had belonged to the Porcellian Club. And so Johnny began again, and they all joined in, hanging on the table, shivering the Lowestoft in the corner cupboards, vibrating the enormous chandelier with the off-key volume.

"It was Christmas in the haremmmm . . ." Then Johnny's voice boomed out, "What will you have for Christmas, boys?"

"Balls! Balls!" The gentlemen shouted. Bellanowski thumped Rick on the back. Chugh got to his feet. The Lily is going to make a goddamn speech, Rick thought. Before the evening was over, he was going to make him swallow the goddamn balls in his pocket.

The table had been cleared. Fingerbowls with sprigs of floating verbena had been brought. And now Bloodgood appeared, carefully carrying a heavy silver tankard.

"Thank you, Johnny," Chugh began, "I could not possibly face tomorrow without Johnny standing by me as best man. Nor could I have gotten through this dinner with all the Hoagland men at Finchwicke without their killing me. And now my friends, I'd like to call your attention to this historic treasure bearing the coat of arms of Sir Charles Walding, which came over with him from England in the sailing ship *Blue Quail* in 1684, and which was then given by him to his son Percy who built this house." Bloodgood set the tankard down in front of Chugh. "It is filled with champagne. Gentlemen, it is my personal privilege, according to the custom here at Finchwicke, to propose a toast to my bride. But first I'd like to say a few words of farewell to my bachelor days. They've been great days, and I've enjoyed them and they're over forever. Finchwicke needs a mistress—and I've combed the countryside with a fine-tooth comb—and found the girl next door to be very sweet indeed. Even if she does have a mind of her own, she has promised to do everything my way, and so I've chosen her to be the mother of my sons, and I look forward to having her for my life's companion because she is, to put it simply, the very best! And so, gentlemen, I ask you all to rise and drink a toast from a loving cup to my bride!"

"To the bride!" each one called out before passing it on. And when it got to Rick Hoagland, there was scarcely a pause as, unnoticed, he dropped the two gleaming balls into the communal cup. Carrie, by God, would swallow them as he bottoms-upped. But when the cup got around to Chugh again, holding it high above his head, he called for Bloodgood, who, as a matter of fact, was standing in the shadow directly behind his chair.

"According to the custom of Finchwicke, the cup will now go the rounds of the pantry and the kitchen, in order that everyone in the household will drink to the health of the bride. Bloodgood! Go first."

"Thank you, sir. To the bride!"

"For he's a jolly good fellow, he's a jolly good fellow!" Once more the room rang out with song as the trusted butler took a decorous sip, managing a sly wink at the same time, and then bore away the bowl to be bottoms-upped in the back regions. Seeing the stallion's balls disappearing with it, Rick Hoagland felt ill and rose to his feet. Gripping the table edge unsteadily, he felt his face burning to a purple. "I have a desire to pullulate—whatever that means—on top of the tallest box bush I can find. I desire to pullulate—or else punch someone in the nose."

"Shut up, Carrot-top. Sit down." It was Chugh.

"Puuululate. I said. Urinate. On your goddamn lawn. By your leave, Carrie. And if you'll come outside with me, I'll punch you in the nose. Or knock your teeth down your goddamn throat." Not knowing exactly where he was going, he lurched from the room, feeling the walls and bumping into chairs and tables until, miraculously, he found himself outside, in the cool night air. Standing alone outside, he heard the songs coming faintly through the halls: "Which nobody can deny . . . nobody can deny . . . And the sultan donned his turban . . . and the eunuchs answered 'Balls' . . . " He felt himself sobering up in the fresh summer night. Light was streaming out of all the tall windows, amid snatches of song and laughter. It was nicer out here. Quiet all around, and meadows stretched away to the Guard Hill woods in the peaceful moonlight. But the moment didn't last. There was a figure darkening the doorway. Good old Chugh was coming out. And he was followed by the Baron.

They stood for a minute on the top step, in front of the formal entrance. Chugh's voice was clear. "I don't want him coming back in and causing any more trouble tonight. I just wish he wouldn't always get so damned drunk. He's rude enough when he's sober. Anyway, I'd hoped he'd gone on home, but he hasn't. There's his gorgeous car. So he must have passed out somewhere. We'd better scout around and see if we can find him."

The two men started across the courtyard. Rick could see them plainly in the moonlight striking off on the cobblestones. He stepped out from behind the bush. "I'm right here, and I'll take you on one by one or both together, goddamn it."

Now Carrie was coming toward him. "For God's sake, Rick, come to your senses. I'm not going to fight you, my girl's brother, in my own house. Now, why don't you just calm down, old fellow, and go on home peaceably."

Chugh was bouncing on his feet as he moved toward Rick. His evening costume was completely unruffled. His white tie and vest shone like pearls in the moonlight.

"Just this once, Carrie, I'm going to muss you up." Rick struggled out of his jacket and stood in his shirt sleeves, fists raised. "Come on, you son of a bitch, take off your coat and fight."

"Watch out!"

Rick heard the footsteps behind him and whirled to face the Baron, slowly advancing, head down, long arms swinging. Rick was disappointed that he wasn't going to be able to get them both. Oh, how he wanted to kill them! He chose Carrie, and taking a chance he turned his back on the Baron. He swung. At the same moment, a stinging blow behind his ear hit him. No pain, really, just a helpless feeling of his knees buckling as he fell down into blackness.

He had no idea how long he had lain there as he fought his way to consciousness through a sharp headache. Someone had folded his jacket into a neat pillow under his head and placed a lily in his hands folded across his chest. The smell of it was overpowering. Rick sneezed. A sharp pain passed through the back of his neck. It was very important to remember why it was so important to remember something. Who was he supposed to get? Meanwhile it was dangerous lying out here. He must pull himself together. The lights of a car were coming up the drive.

Edith Bellanowski got out, wearing a floating blue dress and a crown, and went into the house. Everything came into focus. It was the goddamn Baron who had gotten him by sneaking up from behind. Slowly Rick got up, testing his legs. The back of his head was a little sore but he was sober. The dinner here was over. From where he stood behind his bush, he could see the figures in the lighted hall as Bloodgood held the door open. Edith was going upstairs. Bellwood, wearing his long purple evening cape, was riffling through the cards in the bowl on the table. Evidently he was getting a ride home with the Seabreese brothers and was waiting while they said goodnight. It was important now to reenter the house casually, as if nothing had happened.

Rick waited until the Seabreeses and Bellwood were packed into their car, and the car gone. Then he stole into the house. He blinked his eyes for a moment in the lighted hall. There was no one around. He reconnoitered the empty dining room. The table had been cleared and the only light was coming from the open pantry door. A noise like a pistol shot made him jump, but it was only Bloodgood, popping the cork on another magnum of Veuve Clicquot for the help, who were at last getting around to the merry business of the loving cup.

Bloodgood poured, took a deep draft, and passed the cup to the ancient cook who was there in her white apron. As the cup made the rounds Bloodgood lit up one of Dr. Walding's best Havana Belevederes. "A woman is only a woman, as the Doctor always says, but a good cigar is a smoke! Here, Delia dear. Have a puff!"

"Thank you kindly, sir, but I'd rather have another taste of the wine, Mr. Bloodgood."

"Then bottoms it up, Delia dear. Dreen the cup to the dregs!"

The buxom woman drank for a moment, and then put the cup away from her, peering into the bottom with a puzzled look on her face. "What nuts is these? Mr. Chugh's?"

Luxuriant laughter broke out in the pantry and rippled out into the dining room, where Rick stood watching.

"Swill, I calls them? Swill!" Delia exclaimed as she tossed them into the overflowing garbage pail. "Swill and bad cess to them?"

Rick started to laugh himself, and afraid he would be caught he went out to the terrace through the dining room, nearly tripping over the body of Jap Birdgrove lying quietly under the table, wrapped in the fold of the lace tablecloth. Rick bent to be sure he was breathing. He was.

"And say a bold rider lies low," Rick intoned over the body of his friend, "and so, for that matter do I."

In the cold predawn, when the tide of courage drains from the human heart, Rick had to face up to the facts. He had come here with the express intention of blacking the eye of his future brother-in-law so that he would have to wear that mark of disapproval to the altar on the following day.

He had failed. There had never been any way that he, the younger brother, the brash pup, could have defeated Chugh on his own territory. The bacchanalian rites held in honor of Chugh had affirmed the ancient male prerogative to profane that which was most pure—in this case the virginity of Rick's sister—and the sacred vows to be taken tomorrow would only change that prerogative into a duty.

"And I am the one who got K.O.'d," he muttered. As he stumbled over the body of his stuporous friend he accepted defeat—at least for tonight. The last ounce of fight had gone out of him and he knew that he should get into his Pierce and go home. But he also knew he had to find Chugh and say goodnight, at least claim the dignity of being a good loser.

Outside, the terrace was deserted. The moon was setting low in the distant woods, and the fields around had grown black. Only the light spilling out from the windows of the house made patches on the stones and on the empty tables and chairs. Rick picked up a half-filled cold cup of coffee and gulped it down. Low voices were coming from the darkness in the circle of chairs under the Guardian oak. Even though it might entail eating crow in front of the Baron, Rick knew that he must walk over there. Then a sudden shadow, moving across one of the panes of light on the flagstones, caused him to look up just in time to catch a glimpse of the Baron, naked and hairy, passing from one room into the next. So the beast was safely upstairs, no doubt ready to entertain his lovely wife.

It was Chugh under the oak with Johnny Oldthwaite and Peregrine Markoo. The conversation stopped as Rick approached. Nobody made a move.

"Mind if I sit down?"

Nobody spoke.

"Well, never mind then, Carrie. Don't feel much like witty conversation myself. Just would like to say a couple of things. First, I think the Baron is a goddamn German spy."

230

Nobody spoke.

"That's all right, Carrie. But if he burns down your damned Blue Rock Works, don't say I didn't warn you. The other thing I want, Carrie, is to wish you and my sister all the happiness in the world. I love her, and no one else will ever be to her as I have been, or she to me. But I hope you'll be a very happy married couple, Carrie, because I think you're a damned good fellow. I really do."

The words were not spoken easily. Rick's voice was choked and broken and resounded with a conscious sense of hypocrisy in the name of good manners. But once spoken and with the Lily rising to his feet with hand outstretched, Rick felt immediate relief. He had done the manly thing. And he had learned a lesson: from now on his battles would be fought in a more sophisticated way.

"Thank you very much, brother Rick. And may I ask you just one favor? Will you quit calling me Carrie, just to prove you really meant what you said?"

"All right, Chugh. Thank you for the dinner." And he turned and walked quickly away to where his beautiful car gleamed in the dark of the courtyard. The padded leather seat was smooth to his touch, and the feel of the wheel was a beautiful thing. He started her up and listened to the lovely hum of her motor. He punched the horn in a fit of ebullience and let a good loud "All Dogs Have Fleas" float through the night.

At cockcrow!

It was as though a whole symphony orchestra was tuning up outside her tower window in the pitch dark of the early hours of Saturday, June fourteenth, in the year nineteen hundred and fifteen—her wedding day. All the birds of Penngwynne were testing their trills, tightening their throats, and Miss Faith Middleton Hoagland awoke to the din in her narrow sleigh bed, for the last time.

The ginger-and-white spaniel, sensing her mistress awake, rose from her basket and stretched, shook herself all over, came and tugged at the bedclothes with her plumed paws, insisting she needed to be taken outside.

"Oh my poor darling Tiddy-Boom, what is to become of you? There have never been any dogs or cats at Finchwicke. Chugh's mother wouldn't have them. Cats eat the baby birds, and dogs ruin the ancient box bushes and dig up the flowers in the garden. No dogs! It's a rule, Chugh said." Faith

231

stroked the intelligent bump of the forehead, drawing back the skin from the loving eyes, turning back the ears to show the pink velvet insides. "Darling Tiddle! Love, honor, and obey, but if I go to live at Finchwicke, then you are coming too. Of yes, darling Tiddy. I have told them all how well you lie in your basket and take your walks at my heels and never, never dig for bones. How well you obey!"

To obey Chugh! It would be a deeply passionate pleasure, which, if attainable, she felt would raise her life onto a plane where no sorrow or disagreement could touch it. But he had asked of her the one and only thing in which she could not submit to his will: to turn her back upon a friend. There seemed to be no way out of it.

The dawn wind puffed out the ruffled cretonne curtains, showing that the sky was fading from midnight-blue to faint gray, breathing a faint scent of new-mown hay from the barns. Was it going to be a nice day? Faith put on her old pink-and-white flannel wrapper for the last time, flipped her long black pigtails tied with pink bows, and padded barefooted down the prickly red carpet of the golden-oak staircase and out through the conservatory, filled with wedding lilies. Dickie-bird, the canary, was still sleeping in his curtained gold cage.

Each blade of grass bowed over with the weight of a diamond. The cool wet dew bathed her small feet. A low mist at the bottom of the lawn lay over the pond, veiling the tent and the rose garden below.

Now the sky was flushed with pink and saffron in the east. The birds were suddenly hushed, poised in the trees as if waiting to strike the opening note of the great concert of this day. Now in harmony, they began to sing their individual melodies, each one sweet and clear.

Faith sat down on a Chinese stone-garden bench and watched as the sun rose and lit the blue sky, turned the passion vine covering the pillars of the piazza to a brilliant purple and the geraniums in the Italian pottery jars to pink. Today of all days was to be her day. Never before and never again would she be the central figure in such an elaborate ritual. It had been difficult, all these long winter months, to bear with good humor the bossiness of Hebe, the hostility of Rick, the coldness of Chugh who seemed to prefer Mama's tea table to her own company, and the bitter cynicism of Mama, doing her best to spoil the happiness of marriage. But today was the day which would change all that, in one final way or the other. Nothing would ever be the same again. For she, Faith Hoagland, was leaving Co-Eden and her childhood, to be married.

Tomorrow morning would find her in a strange room in the Plaza Hotel in New York City with a husband who was also a stranger. They would take the ten o'clock train from Grand Central to Boston; drive to Whippen Point to meet Tata Chyldes, mother of Edith and Knight, and also a stranger; embark on the yacht *Viatrix* for a strange place in Maine called Heron Bay for two whole weeks alone with Chugh Walding, with whom she had never been alone for two whole hours.

Or, this afternoon would find her lying dead on her bed upstairs. For as she had told Chugh, if he did not give her some sign of her worth—some hint that he desired her as desperately as she desired him—if he had not shown some understanding that her kindness to Vivi was more valuable than his rigid pride, if he would not speak kindly and directly to her rather than always through Hebe, then she had decided exactly what she had to do. She would excuse herself from the wedding luncheon, run up the stairs to her own bathroom and remove from the medicine chest a secreted vial of Mama's Wine of Laudanum, which Dr. Merritt had cautioned could be lethal if more than a drop or two were taken at a time. After removing her aquamarine-and-diamond engagement ring and her new wedding band, and throwing them out the window into the deep bushes, she would drink the poison, still wearing her wedding dress and veil. After a while, someone would come to look for her and find her lying cold and dead as marble.

She would envision them all standing around. Hebe wringing her hands, Chugh on his knees begging forgiveness. But all too late. Guy Fitzjoy would say a little prayer: "The Lord gave. The Lord hath taken away. Blessed be the name of the Lord."

"Don't be so silly!" Chugh had said.

Now the sun, quite high in the east, was beginning to strike out with its warm rays. The birds had finished their morning chirping and were flying off to breakfast on cherries and fat worms.

Breakfast! Faith was suddenly starving. She gave a low whistle for Tiddy-Boom who was sniffing at the tunnel of a mole, preparing to dig him out and leave a scar on the greensward. (Oh, what would they say at Finchwicke about the lawns there? It would be just too bad.)

The ice chests of the pantry, where the milk and fruits and filled with dark, gold-tipped bottles of champagne. Faith were usually stored, had been emptied by the caterer's men made her way through the swinging doors into the kitchen pantries. Only Rick, the cook's favorite, was allowed to forage freely in this territory. Poor old Ma'selle was not tolerated. Faith could wander in only when the cook was not busy. However, none of the servants appeared to be up yet. She took courage and proceeded into the large kitchen, where the clock was ticking at six forty-five, and George the white cat dozed on the high window sill among the herbs. Copper pots and pans hung in a wheel over the great soapstone kitchen table, and a gentle warmth came from under the hood of the deep coal range, which would soon be shaken up and stoked by one of the gardener's boys. My, but it was going to be hot in here later!

"Hello, Sir Richard! Whence whitherest thou?"

The sight of her brother, sneaking in the back door and looking like a small bad boy—still in his tuxedo, his bow tie hanging loose—had triggered her into using the old familiar language of the nursery when they had acted out plays and ballads under Bellwood's Shakespearean influence. The foolishness came gushing out, even though she and Rick had not spoken in any but the most polite and distant terms since he had castigated Chugh.

"The Princess Fidelia?" he answered in the same parlor-drama vein, bowing. "I am whencing from your next husband's ushers' dinner, and a damned fine guy, the Lily, a helluva guy."

Rick stood with his bandy legs far apart as though to keep his balance on the slanting deck of a ship. A foolish smile flittered across his scarlet face and rippled upward through his orange hair, as though he had been naughty and was proud of it. She could hear Hebe's admonitions! But maybe with a bite to eat and a few hours' sleep he could make it to the church in sober condition.

"Just getting back from dinner now?"

"And a damned fine dinner it was. And right now, I'm whithering to the icebox for a glass of milk, and no questions asked. And hoping to get Cook to make me some bacon and eggs. Whitherest thou, fair maid?"

"I also to the ice chest for a glass of milk. Cook isn't

around. Nobody else seems to be up. Wouldn't you think that on this day of days there'd be a bustle? But soft! Sir Richard! Hark! Here she comes!" Faith took a step behind Rick to avoid the ire of Cook.

"It's not Cook. It's Mama!"

Faith was shocked to see her mother here. She didn't think Mama even knew where the kitchen was. Cook always came upstairs with her pad and pencil and menu while Mama was having her breakfast in bed, propped up on a small mountain of white linen and lace pillows. The yellowed and stained old walls of the back passage were an incongruous background for the elegant figure in the floating black wrapper. Faith stood aside, knowing that look on her mother's face—the crazy, set expression she used for raking Faith over the coals when whatever Faith said would be taken wrong and add fuel to her mother's irrational ire. That look had taught Faith to keep still.

But as her mother passed, Faith noticed something different about her eyes. The dilation of the pupils gave them a strange effect of looking in on some single-minded goal while her feet clicking along in her satin mules carried her forward automatically. Faith felt the familiar sick fear of an unavoidable debilitating scene which Mama, of course, would automatically stage to ruin her wedding morning. And having done that, Mama would show up at the wedding exuding personal charm as though nothing at all had taken place. Thank God, beloved Rick was there with her.

Mama had entered the larder and was fumbling with the catch on the double doors of the oak ice chest which occupied one whole wall of the room from floor to ceiling.

"Do you want a glass of milk, Mama? Can I help you?" Faith was relieved that Rick had spoken. That same suggestion from her would have brought forth a tirade against milk. But Rick could do no wrong, and his voice did seem to penetrate her trance. "No, darling, not milk. Ice."

Mama's soft white fingers explored inside the zinc-lined cabinet, among the picked chickens and the garden lettuces and the jugs of milk.

"That's the wrong place, Ma. Ice is in here." Rick opened another heavy door, a section filled with two-foot blocks of ice, scored and cut from the pond and hauled by horse and sledge to the ice house in the woods, where it was stored all summer and fall in layers of sawdust and brought into the main-house kitchens with huge tongs.

"Oh, yes, my dear. My head. So Viv can chip some ice."

"Mama, let me!" Rick said earnestly.

"No! Mama is busy, little boy. Run and find Ma'selle in the nursery."

With that, Faith realized that either Mama's mind was wandering or she was drunk, as Viv and Bellwood had been claiming and Rick had refused to believe.

"Have you ever seen her like this before?" Rick looked stricken. "Come on, Ma, dear. Let Faith help you back to bed."

Mama's red head was inside the ice cabinet and she had her hand on the big ice pick, which she extracted with a jerk. She turned to leave without bothering to shut the door, oblivious of the existence of other human beings. To Faith's horror, she was smiling, her frightening single-mindedness as sharp as the mean weapon she held in her hands.

"Follow quietly. It might be dangerous to wake her. She's walking in her sleep." That was what Rick chose to believe.

Becca paused for a moment in the dining room, and as though unaware of being watched, concealed the ice pick in her wrapper. Then she glided out toward the corridor leading to the downstairs guest wing. The Manigault Lees were asleep in the yellow room, the Bellwood Hoaglands in the blue room, which they always occupied. Faith and Rick stepped into the large bathroom across the corridor.

Mama knocked on the door of the blue room and called in a soft voice, "Vivi? Vivi?"

There were padding footsteps and Bellwood came to the door and stuck his long nose around the corner. His thin hair was tousled from sleep, the fly of his crimson silk pajamas hanging slightly open. "Are you all right, Becca?"

"I have a splitting headache, Bellwood dear. I came to beg Viv to come to my room and brush my hair to relieve it. And my ice cap needs to be refilled. Could she come up to my bedroom and get it? I hope I'm not disturbing you too much, dear."

"Viv will be right with you. Go on back to bed."

Because it was what they always did whenever things blew up day or night, Faith whispered to Rick as they crept past the telephone closet following Mama through the den, "Call Dr. Merritt and tell him to come right away. I'll try and get Mama back into bed."

Feeling her way up the banisters, her red hair floating out behind her, Mama mounted the staircase and entered her black lacquered bedroom at the top. As though she knew she was being followed, she firmly shut the door behind her.

Faith was suddenly fearful of forcing her way into that room alone, and she paused on the landing to wait for Rick. She could hear him still turning the bell crank on the telephone, trying to rouse the Penngwynne operator to action. When Vivi arrived on the scene, she was barefoot and wearing a low-necked nightgown that only an actress would dare, showing her creamy neck and arms, the slight swelling of her newest pregnancy, smelling warm and sweet from Bellwood's bed.

They met on the landing, under the stained-glass window, the delicious actress and the pigtailed hockey player, the bride. Joining in a crisis, they were two against one, opposites forged together for a lifetime friendship. Faith felt that, and took heart. "I'm worried about Mama! I think she's walking in her sleep. We must be careful not to wake her suddenly."

"I saw her looking like La Somnambulista outside our door. That's why I hurried. Let's try and get her back to bed."

"You go first," Faith whispered. "She's expecting you!"

Viv knocked softly on the door and opened it. "You sent for me, Mrs. Hoagland?"

Becca, who had been waiting just inside, swept out into the hall. Her hand closed on Vivi's shoulder as she pushed her back toward the top of the stairs. In the other hand she held the ice pick. "Yes, I sent for you—to go down and fetch some ice. That is the only way my headache will be cured. Here is the pick. Go now, and be careful not to fall!"

Mama's voice rose. Her nostrils were black as death as she lurched at Viv and gave her a shove toward the stairs, raising the ice pick high as though to save her own balance. She forced Viv backwards down one step, and with the other hand she raised the ice pick higher.

Faith knew then that Mama wanted to kill Viv. But Viv stood there like a rabbit waiting to be struck by the talons of a circling hawk, holding her breath, eyes unblinking, as though she had no right to fight for her life against Mama.

But this was Faith's wedding day. No one must die! And it was up to her to take action. She took a quick step toward Mama and grabbed her raised arm from behind. Mama had the advantage of being taller than Faith, but Faith had the strength and she managed to hold her mother's right hand up. Mama's left hand was still clutching Viv's shoulder. Viv, still entranced by fear on the step below, pushed up against the banister to receive the blow.

Faith prayed she could hold Mama's hand up until help came while she repeatedly tried to pump it down. She borrowed breath to speak softly into her mother's ear. "Let her go, Mama. In Papa's name who prized *you* above everyone—even I know that, even more than me—let her go, Mama! Let go!"

Mama obeyed suddenly, releasing her daughter-in-law with a little push away from her. Whirling out of Faith's grasp, Becca Hoagland brought the ice pick down with both hands, burying it with great force into the hard wood of the golden-oak newel post. "There now! She's dead. And may all her female children go with her!"

Glancing down to the landing, Faith saw that Viv, clutching at the banister as she went, had fallen on her back and was going to slide all the way down to the landing, the long nightgown above her head showing the vulnerable white belly, the dainty, pale-brown bush.

For a moment Faith thought she should rush to Vivi's aid, but suddenly Mama herself appeared to be toppling forward, about to fall with all her weight. Using everything Miss Applegate had taught her in her bloomered days of vaulting the wooden horse in the school gym, Faith gave a spring forward and caught her mother around the waist and pulled her back. With all her dead weight, they went down hard together, but safely away from the stairs.

Faith lay breathless in her mother's embrace for a long minute, as though drowning in that stream of their common life so dimly remembered, since they had not touched for a long time. She had longed for it, but love had become poisoned at the source, and she quickly sat up and gathered her mother's head into her lap. Mama had cut her eyelid, and blood was trickling back into her hair. Mama's face crinkled up like a child's as she started to cry. Faith pressed her mother to her "Now, hush, Mama. Hush. Don't cry."

Rick was running up the stairs, two at a time. "You let her get hurt, the poor darling! I warned you she was walking in her sleep!"

Behind him came Bellwood, supporting a shaking Viv. Her face was set in a cold determination that, to Faith, seemed so unlike her. "You just don't want to face it, Rick!" Viv was saying. "You are never around when it actually happens. Your mother tried to murder me! She will have to be put away as Dr. Merritt well knows. She is insane! It's not safe around here with her loose."

Faith could not help agreeing with her. Cold and practical, then, this was the way Viv would vanquish Becca, the young putting away the tyranny of the old.

Rick pulled off his evening tie with an angry flip. "Mama is not insane. She is very ill."

"There is something that everyone needs to understand!" Viv shouted back, pointing to the newel post. "That is very hard wood. Whoever had the strength to chip it away, had the strength to crack my skull. Mrs. Hoagland was trying to kill me, and she *has* gone insane."

Viv's words angered Rick beyond endurance. He turned on her, standing there, appealingly dishabille. "What have you done to Mrs. Hoagland to make her hate you so much, then? Is it because you have come between this mother and her eldest son? If so, you must try to be more patient and understanding."

"Indeed, I think I understand very well. Mrs. Hoagland, I repeat, is insane, and she is obsessed by the idea that it was I who was found with the Judge, her husband, on his deathbed."

To Faith the words were catastrophic, dropping a curtain forever on the sentimental view of the past, galvanizing the present into something hard and ugly.

"I never heard such utter rot." Rick spoke with scorn. "You're all making up these crazy things. Papa didn't have a deathbed! He died in his courtroom, I've always been told."

"Of course it's a preposterous idea," Bellwood said quickly and confidently. "And therefore I think Viv is right. Tomorrow some plans must be made to get Mama to a hospital. It's not safe to have her wandering around here by herself after Faith is gone. There's no telling what she might hallucinate and try to do."

The way Bellwood spoke made Faith realize he knew *all* about Mama's idea that Papa had died in a bad house. But Faith had heard only half of it. At least Mama had spared her the details about Viv. Poor darling Mama! No one had understood how the collar of pain which she had borne all these years had been drawn in like a wire noose by Bellwood's marriage. Sitting there on the floor, holding her mother in her arms, Faith felt a surge of strength passing into her own body as though she and Mama had exchanged roles. She had become the protective mother, Mama the weak and helpless child. Never would Faith fear her again, but would care for her as best she could—Finchwicke was only a mile away. Bending over her, Faith made small crooning sounds to soothe her while the trickle of blood from Mama's cut and the salt tears squeezed from the closed eyes drenched her lap.

They all heard the front door bang. Dr. Merritt had arrived, dark circles under his tired eyes, running up the stairs with the doctor's satchel. "Did she trip and fall?" The good doctor's voice was full of concern. He loved Mama, and was completely under her spell.

"She pushed me, and I fell," said Viv, "and I am the one who is expecting a child. She has nothing more than a scratched eye."

But the doctor knelt down and took Becca's pulse, took out his stethoscope and pressed it to her ribs. "Can we get her into bed? Mrs. Hoagland, can you hear me?" The doctor spoke very close to her ear.

"Quite well, thank you, I can hear quite well." Becca managed to sit up, and then she was helped to her feet and guided by the doctor and Rick into her room. "I also heard who said I was insane."

She stopped by the dressing table and would not move. "That little silver box, Faith. Let me have it." It was full of small white tablets.

Faith looked at Dr. Merritt, who nodded his permission.

"And a glass of water."

Mama stood there swaying while Faith filled the glass from the pitcher on the bedside table. It was gin. But no arguing about it now. No one was going to wrestle Mama into bed. She swallowed three of the pills before consenting to resume her slow progress to the yellow curtained bed. With great deliberation she sat down on the edge while Rick and the doctor picked up her feet and swung her in. Faith covered her.

Becca immediately fell asleep.

"The best thing that could happen. Have Ma'selle come in to watch her. We must let her sleep until the last possible moment. Then we'll attempt to wake her. I'll have someone come up from the hospital and wash her out with a high colonic. And then we'll attempt to wake her with cups of coffee. This is just a superficial scratch over her eye. I think we can cover it up with some powder." Dr. Merritt smoothed back Becca's red hair. "Somehow we'll have to get her through the day in creditable shape."

"But what have you done to her, Doctor? What are those pills she takes?" Faith asked.

"They're cocaine cantharidate for her nasal catarrh and her headaches. I can't understand why they seem to have this adverse affect. I thought them harmless painkillers. Oh there is some evidence now that people become dependent on them and become crazy if deprived of them." A look of anguish came over the good doctor's face. "I should know, for I have been taking them myself in moments of extreme exhaustion when it is necessary to make yet one more and one more house call. They seem to give me strength to go on." Faith had never seen him look so tired and strained, as if he too were near a breaking point.

Ma'selle appeared, fully dressed, her old gray sweater pulled around her. She took the chair by the bed, her lips moving as she said her rosary, slipping the comforting beads through her gnarled fingers. Mama by now was snoring lightly. The others tiptoed from the room, leaving Ma'selle to watch.

Viv and Bellwood were still waiting in the hall. "Will she be ready to leave the house at eleven, Doc?"

"I'm not sure. Mrs. H. must have had a very bad headache and taken too many pills, but I intend to try and bring her around. And you, Mrs. Bellwood, are you quite all right? Perhaps you should stay in bed today after such a fall."

"Thank you, Doctor. Except for some bruises, I'm feeling fine."

The Doctor wasn't going to argue. He took himself off as quickly as he had come.

"Are you sure?" asked Bellwood of his wife. "It might be my son, you know!"

Suddenly Faith saw a way out. "If you don't feel well, Viv, I don't want you to feel you must come to the church."

"Because you want me, dear Faith, I will be there." Vivienne faded off on the arm of her husband. "I will be there."

Rick grabbed the ice pick and pulled it from the newel post, splitting the solid oak as he did so. "To hell with everything. I'm going to bed and get a couple hours' sleep."

Faith found herself standing alone in the hall, realizing that she had spoken the words that Chugh had requested. What terrible things did Chugh know about Viv anyway? New vistas of Mama's pain opened in her mind as she tried to imagine Viv in her own Chugh's arms in some strange house. Nonsense, of course, but she had never had the chance to ask Chugh if he had ever in this world loved anyone else but her.

In fact, deep in her consciousness was the barely admitted knowledge that he had never said the simple words to her— "I love you." She had only assumed that he did because such deep feelings went out from her heart to his. It goes without saying, she kept telling herself. It goes without saying. Don't be so silly!

After what she had seen this morning, the idea of drinking Mama's Wine of Laudanum no longer seemed romantic. Beloved Chugh had to speak to her in order to know that she had at last obeyed. She prayed to him. "Please, Chugh, speak to me, and take me away!" But looking down at her beautiful ring, shining a steady blue on her finger, she knew that she was going with him whether he spoke to her or not.

Tiddy-Boom, forgotten, came out of the shadows of the hall and licked Faith's bare ankles. A faint smell of bacon reminded her that she was famished and that her breakfast should now be ready.

In her room, she rang the bell for Mary and got into her sleigh bed as though nothing had happened. Tiddy got back in her basket. The wedding dress, swathed in tissue paper, was hanging in her closet. The sun was high in the sky. A knock came at the door and Mary came in with the breakfast tray, decorated this morning with a bunch of sweet peas.

"Top o' the mornin', Miss Faith! A lovely day, ye have."

8

Wedding

ALL NIGHT long Guy Fitzjoy had been climbing Jacob's ladder, begging for an angel to bless him, begging for a sign! And now all the birds in the thick ivy vine around his tiny casement bedroom window were shivering their wings and chirping as the sky, suffusing with pink, presaged a beautiful June day.

Guy lay in his bed in mental agony with his arms stretched to form a cross with the rest of his body and tried to imagine how our Lord must have felt. It would be such an exposed way to die, spread-eagled like this, with people standing on the ground staring up at Him, mocking Him. He had not been allowed to curl up into a ball, crawl away, hide. But outstretched in His great surety of the Father's love, Christ had felt the nails in His hands and feet once and for all time, whereas Guy was pinpricked many times daily on the tiny crosses of nagging doubt. When he had elected to follow our Lord, Guy had naturally expected to give up worldly pleasures, luxury, gluttony, and lust, and naturally had meant to go about among the poor doing good and preaching the comforting Word. But God works in mysterious ways, and Guy's personal crucifixion was turning out to be not a natural matter of his own chosen mortifications but the conducting of the worship services themselves.

Take, as only one instance, the memorial service for Senator and Mrs. McCusker. It had been one thing to eulogize the man as a great public servant, but the manner of his death at sea—going down with the *Lusitania*—also turned him into a hero. It was an even worse matter to have to praise the Senator as a Christian, and totally impossible to visualize him resurrected in heaven, his soul going from light to light. Guy had felt like a viper as he had pretended to mourn him when, as a matter of fact, the Senator's passing had been a great relief. No more watch waving from the pew. No more chewing out on the front steps. Guy had felt himself a hypocrite as he had offered the proper funeral prayers in front of all the visit-

243

ing dignitaries, many of whom had come from as far away as Washington, D.C. Even the Secretary of War had attended. And Guy couldn't help being pleased at the honor of having had the service at St. Jude's rather than at Trinity in the city. It might even be a first step for him toward the bishopric if he managed it all just right.

Guy had come to suspect that hypocrisy was, in fact, one of the most important tools of a minister's stock in trade, the social grease without which the wheels would squeak even in a church. And so he asked himself, Am I or am I not a whited sepulcher when I perform these rites in His name which have no connection with the life of our Lord?

Not if we are all the children of God and loved equally in His sight. Even an old goat like Senator McCusker. God is love. A great ocean of love. Oh, lead us not into temptation or lust.

As rector of St. Jude's, he had already performed ten weddings this month of June, routine affairs for which he had received amounts varying from five to twenty-five dollars, all with the suggestion that he might need the money for the relief of the parish poor. In fact, being almost one of the parish poor himself, he planned to use some of it for his own honeymoon. Two weeks from now his own wedding would be taking place in South Forkville, and he would be called upon to display that special one-time-only emotion.

The last time he had been out in that part of the state he had tried to tell Lettice that he didn't think he should marry, that personal love was unchristian and unpriestly. But she, sitting in the front porch hammock, swinging in the mountain twilight, had wept and said that she was sure that the warmth generated in the palms of their pressed hands would make all worrisome problems like that melt away as soon as she came to live with him. She had knelt down and put her head in his lap and begged him not to leave her. He had raised her up out of pity, and that had settled it. He would marry. He would marry not for love in the lusting sense but for pity, and because he had pledged his word.

But the wedding coming up today between Chugh Walding and Faith Hoagland was going to be most difficult. If he could only feel the nails in his hands it might dull the ache in his heart which he had begun to feel at the rehearsal yesterday. He had long known that this was not a marriage made in heaven, nor one that Christ would have adorned with His presence as He had done in Cana of Galilee.

"If any man can show just cause why they may not be lawfully joined together, let him now speak . . ." Lawfully, as far as Guy Fitzjoy knew, nothing was wrong. Chugh had no other wife. But Guy had a sense of great harm being done: ushers and bridesmaids being shoved around the chancel by a social secretary, like puppets on a string; the bride sitting in a pew with her mother watching the rehearsal for her own wedding, the afternoon light shafting down on her head through the stained-glass window—like Mary Magdalene in the garden; a Pekingese yapping in the doorway!

"Oh Lord," he groaned into his pillow. "For better or for worse. From this day forward." Better to be scourged with the whips of the Romans than to officiate at this ceremony.

When he awoke again a cool breeze was playing in his room. A cardinal in the spruce tree outside was calling loudly, and there were delicious smells wafting up from the kitchen. He dressed in his thin black suit and went downstairs. The charlady was bending over the old soapstone sink in the dark kitchen, singing along cheerfully with the birds:

"Hey ding-a-ling
Hey ding-a-ling
Sweet lovers love the spring!"

She stopped and dried her hands on the soggy dishtowel as he arrived, and wiped a wisp of her hair up into her straggly topknot.

"I smell French toast?"

"Ah, top o' the mornin', Reverend," she said. "Bless you!" She gave him her crooked smile, half of her face having been mashed away in some accident. But in spite of her great ugliness she had given birth to eight children, and no husband visible. "Bless you!"

Instantly a great sweetness engulfed him, the Presence of our Lord. "And bless you too, Nora!"

Miraculously, all the ushers arrived promptly at the church door at eleven-fifteen, all properly tail-coated alike and each with a boutonniere of white sweet peas sent around that morning from the bride. They all seemed to know exactly what to do. The guests entered under the green-and-white awning which stretched over the walk from the arriving carriages to the vestibule. An usher greeted each guest, and then, checking a seating list in his gray gloved hand, he directed the bride's family to the reserved pews to the left above the white ribbons, the groom's family to the right; the middle of the church was for friends, the side aisles for the entire indoor and outdoor staffs from Co-Eden and Finchwicke, and some of the old faithful from the back office at Oldthwaite, Walding were seated in the rear. Opening the sacristy door a crack, the minister of St. Jude's could see that his church was rapidly filling to capacity for what had been billed as a very small wedding. The organist had just finished Bach's *Hunting Cantata* and was making a quiet shift into *Sheep May Safely Graze*. The Right Reverend P. Manigault Lee had just been dropped off in the sacristy by Bellwood Hoagland, much to Guy's relief. Now that he had the Bishop safely in the church, much of the responsibility slid from his own thin shoulders.

After cordial greetings had been exchanged between the two men of the cloth, the Bishop remarked what a beautiful June day it was. A few wispy clouds hung in the blue sky, the trees and grass were shining like emeralds, and a gentle breeze was moving the perfume from one bank of flowers to the next and wafting the sound of church bells over the valley. The Bishop said that Bellwood had remarked to him on the lovely drive over that the sparkling day had been ordered up by "the Man behind the Spotlight in the Balcony," and that, indeed, a wedding was a bit like a play because it has been rehearsed thoroughly and everyone knows exactly what is going to happen next. "I do often sense a slight bit of theatrical unreality at these affairs," the Bishop said, "but I feel very deeply about this ceremony. The bride is like my own daughter. I not only baptized her, but I confirmed her, and I have come a long distance to give her my blessing on this most holy occasion."

The Bishop's fine white linen gown had been dropped off at St. Jude's the day before so that the president of the Altar Guild could take it to Minnie Washington and bring it back. The full lawn sleeves, caught with a wide black satin ribbon at the pleated cuffs, were ironed and starched and crisp on a hanger. Guy helped him to slip into the giant white gown without mussing it. He adjusted the Bishop's black surplice and scarlet satin hood as well as his stole, fringed and embroidered in gold for him by the Indians. Now the Bishop's special traveling case, lined in cream velvet, was opened, revealing his collapsible crook. It was fitted together, the ivory top to the golden staff, and handed to the little Jaspar boy in his red choir dress. Acting as acolyte, he was to precede the venerable bishop as he carried his symbol.

Now the music was changing again, slowing down, dying away to an ending. The organist must have been warned by the sexton that the bride's carriage was approaching. And in fact at that very moment, an unearthly silvery note was heard flosting from the valley.

Tantivy! Tantivy! Looking through the side door, Guy saw Judge Hoagland's black and plum-red coach and four black horses coming smartly to a stop outside the church. Atop it was what appeared to be a living bunch of violets: all the bridesmaids with their parasols raised.

The servant in top hat and plum coaching jacket, top boots and white breeches, who had been blowing the long brass horn, jumped from the high back step to the ground and took hold of the bridles of the wheel horses. The groom, in matching livery, sitting in front beside the coachman, jumped to hold the heads of the leaders. They stood at attention, buttons gleaming, new ribbon cockades in high silk hats. Now the old coachman, Quinn himself, the buttonholes of his full-skirted plum coat straining at the brass buttons, climbed down from the driver's seat and opened the door on which was emblazoned the gold crest with the stag courant. He handed out first the fashionable corseted figure of the bride's mother, her face shaded by an enormous hat of tulle and flowers which bumped the top of the door, setting it slightly askew. Then, from the dark interior, out stepped the bride. First one small white satin slipper, then a froth of white. Marshall and Bellwood, in striped trousers and tails, stood by at attention to escort the ladies in.

On top of the coach, all the parasols had been snapped shut. The ladder was placed on the ground to the side and, one by one, Rick Hoagland handed down the bridesmaids, who descended with difficulty, having to raise their tight hobble skirts and show quite a lot of leg. Guy descreetly looked the other way until they were all on the ground. Thank heaven for the social secretary, Hebe, who was there to shepherd them all into the vestibule behind the main doors of the church.

Guy peeked again into the church. It was full, and in the back the sexton had closed the heavy doors to permit the assemblage of the wedding procession. In the front pew on the right, seated among his dead wife's relatives and next to the Bellanowskis, old Dr. Walding with his head pulled over in an attitude of eternal questioning, appeared to have fallen asleep.

The church had never been more beautifully decorated. White flower wreaths adorned the pulpit and lectern, and ribbons of flowers were draped along the tops of the pews. White candles and white flowers garlanded the altar. The sun streamed in through the windows among the people in their best hats and coats. Oh my! Guy Fitzjoy thought suddenly, but it was getting very hot in the church!

Now advancing down the aisle was the bride's mother, wasp-waisted and full-bosomed, flashing diamonds from the folds of her pearl-gray taffeta and sporting what appeared to be a black eye partially hidden in the shadows of the big hat atop her fine red hair. She took small unsteady steps, leaning heavily on the arm of her son, Bellwood, and was handed into the front, left-hand pew next to the Bishop's wife. As she knelt briefly the organ stopped playing, and the sexton and his assistant stretched a fresh white canvas runner over the aisle carpet from the altar to the vestibule doors.

There was a stilled hush of anticipation in the church.

Now Rick Hoagland opened the sacristy door from the outside, his tired young face creased with worry. "Is Chugh here yet?" he whispered to the Bishop.

"Not yet," the Bishop answered with consummate, sarcastic patience. "But at least the bride is here. And only ten minutes late."

Guy gave the high sign to the organist to keep playing. He peered again through a crack in the door into the church. The congregation had heard the tantivy, and obviously now expected that when the organ started up again, it would be the trumpet fanfare to the wedding march, but it was the waiting repertoire repeating again. There was an audible gasp of impatient restlessness.

"Just tell her to keep the music going," Rick said. "I'll stand lookout in the driveway." The organ played and played, died away and began to play again and again the insistent Bach toccata. The packed church grew hotter. The lilies began to overpower everyone with a fading smell.

Hebe bustled into the sacristy by the outside door. "The ushers are beginning to wilt. One of the bridesmaids feels faint. The little flower girl has to go to the bathroom, so thank God they've arrived! Paula Oldthwaite has just been squeezed into the front of the church with Chugh's relatives."

She disappeared, dragging the little girl by the hand, slamming the door.

Immediately the door opened again, and Chugh Walding and Johnny Oldthwaite came crowding in, looking as though they hadn't been to bed at all, filling the tiny sacristy with the odors of liquorous breath heavily masked with bay rum. They were dressed in swallow-tails and striped trousers, and pale-gray ties, identical except for the sapphire stickpin in Chugh's tie which seemed to deepen the dark passion in his lately drunken eyes.

No explanations were asked for. No apologies were offered.

Hey-ding-a-ling, thought Guy to himself, thus warding off the spear in his side as he attempted the introductions.

The Bishop shook hands with the best man, but said he had already met Chugh the day before. Guy asked the groom and the best man whether or not they intended to carry their gray toppers and gloves into church, and suggested they might want to leave them there on a shelf to be picked up later. But they stared at him glassy-eyed and unhearing, as though he were crazy. The best man was rummaging in his pockets to be sure he had the ring in his right pocket and the fees in his left. One of the gold pieces dropped out and rolled into the far corner, where Johnny, red-faced and perspiring, retrieved it from a newly spun cobweb.

"God! It's stifling in here," he said. "Let's go!"

The organist wove her way to a convenient stop at the signal. The doors were thrown open in the rear of the church. The pipes crashed forth with the fanfare to the wedding march, sending a paralyzing thrill to Guy's nerves, transforming him into the great sacred beetle waiting in suspended animation, feeling nothing. What had been set in motion would now take place.

"Right!" he said to the little Jaspar boy in his bright-red robe and Eton collar. "Go! Lead us out." And the boy went, carrying the heavy crook. Guy and the Bishop followed slowly behind him. Guy walked with the Bishop to his seat in the choir and then returned to take his stance in the center of the chancel steps. Chugh and Johnny had taken up their positions exactly at the base of the pulpit. The ushers approached, two by two, with measured steps. The bridesmaids had already mounted the step above them, their bouquets trembling, and here came the tiny flower girl, strewing rose petals from a ribboned hat in the path of the heavily shrouded bride, who advanced on the arm of her handsome brother with her eyes cast down. How small she was! Now she slipped her hand from the arm of her brother and gave her right hand to Chugh Walding, who had advanced to meet her, and they were standing in front of Guy, in the face of God and this company. The music died away.

Now, as though from a wound-up doll, Guy would hear his own voice. "Dearly beloved, we are gathered together here in the sight of God and in the face of this company, to join together this man and this woman in holy matrimony . . . an honorable estate . . . which Christ adorned and beautified . . . not to be entered into unadvisedly or lightly . . . but reverently, discreetly, advisedly . . . and soberly . . . ." Guy's voice deepened as he now sternly spoke the dreadful words: "If any man know of any impediment whereby this marriage is not lawful, let him now speak, or forever hold his peace."

A hush fell on the church. But no one rose in outcry. No one raced to the altar to rescue the bride. Only the thought in the minister's own mind echoed unheard: I know of an impediment in the eyes of God. Chugh Walding is not a pure man.

And having made this comment, in this place, to his Lord, Guy Fitzjoy crossed himself and moved to one side in the choir, giving room to the Bishop who had centered himself on the altar steps. Guy crossed himself, and turning his face away he felt the eyes of the matron of honor staring at him. Viv stood on the steps opposite and below him. In her lavender dress, holding her yellow bouquet, she stood with tears bright in her eyes.

"Save me." Her lips formed the words. "Save me."

Again he made the sign of the Cross, blessing her. Holiness went out from him into her, leaving him floating on his feet.

Suddenly Viv swayed and took a step back into the shadows of the carved arch. Leaning against it, she seemed to fade into the stone, to become part of the pillar.

Bellwood stepped back from the ranks of the ushers, and without any commotion, caught the wavering figure of his wife and offered to assist her through the sacristy door. For a moment she clung to him, and then shook her head and stepped forward to her place again.

Again Guy blessed her.

"Thank you." Her lips formed the silent words. It had been another miracle for the day, as though Vivienne had died to the flesh, Guy thought.

And by this little human interchange, he himself felt fortified to witness the part of the ceremony which he had dreaded most, the part where the couple would turn profile to the congregation, and looking deeply into one another's eyes, speaking only to each other, take their sacred vows. This was the way it happened in South Forkville, but here at St. Jude's such a display of public emotion would be considered vulgar, so the couple elected to stare straight ahead, speaking only to the priest.

"Chugh, wilt thou have this woman to be thy wedded wife, to live together after God's ordinance in the holy estate of matrimony? Wilt thou love her, comfort her, honor, and keep her in sickness and in health, and forsaking all others, keep thee only unto her, so long as ye both shall live?"

"I will." Chugh's voice rang unexpectedly strong.

To the same question, the bride's demure whisper was inaudible.

"Repeat after me," the Bishop muttered. Then loudly he said, "I, Chugh, take thee, Faith . . ."

Chugh repeated the whole vow without once inclining toward her. "And thereto I plight thee my troth," he said, facing the Bishop.

"I, Faith, take thee, Chugh"—but Faith had turned to look up at him, speaking out clearly now so that all could hear her words—"to love, cherish and *obey* . . ."

The timbre of her voice was like a magnet. Chugh had turned to gaze down on his bride.

"Who giveth this woman to be married to this man?"

Marshall handed over the small gloved hand and stepped back into his mother's pew.

There was a slight fumbling while the slit kid glove was pushed back to reveal the pink skin of the bride's fourth finger. Chugh had turned to face her, and spoke directly to her. "With this ring, I thee wed . . ."

Johnny Oldthwaite handed Chugh the gold band, which he slipped on her finger next to his aquamarine.

"And with all my worldly goods I thee endow . . ."

"In the name of the Father . . ." intoned the Bishop.

But Chugh had paused. Fumbling in his pocket, he pulled out a string of pearls. Guy gasped. In all his life he had never seen anyone pull a trick like this. "With all my worldly goods I thee endow," Chugh repeated as he fastened the double strand around Faith's neck, "and with these pearls, in the name of the Father, and of the Son, and of the Holy Ghost."

The whole attention of the congregation was riveted on this sudden breaking of tradition. The Bishop also seemed thrown for a loss, pursing his lips for a moment before raising his great-sleeved arms.

"Amen!" he thundered. "Those whom God hath joined together, let no man put asunder! For as much as Chugh and Faith have consented together in holy wedlock and have witnessed the same before God and this company . . . and have declared the same by giving and receiving a ring, *and* a string of pearls"—the Bishop spoke as a member of the family and therefore felt privileged to take liberties with the Episcopal service—"I pronounce that they are man and wife. In the name of the Father, and of the Son, and of the Holy Ghost. Amen."

"Those are Granny Chyldes' pink pearls," Edith hissed to Gee loudly enough for everyone in the chancel to hear. "How did she get them, and not I?"

Gee's bouquet shook with uncontrollable giggles.

Mr. and Mrs. Chugh Flyckwir Walding knelt together at the altar rail. The Bishop raised his thin, waxy hands and let them flutter down in their pleated cuffs like white doves as with tremulous emotion he blessed them:

> *"May the blessing of light be on you, light within and light without. May the blessed sunlight shine upon you and warm your hearts until they glow like a great fire, so that the stranger may come and warm his hands at it, and also a friend. God the Father, God the Son, God the Holy Ghost, bless, preserve and keep you, that ye may so live together in this life that in the worlds to come, ye may have everlasting life."*

Now the organ pealed forth the Recessional. The couple rose to their feet while the awkward business of turning the bride around took place. The flower girl gave back the bridal bouquet. Fat Gladys did her best to turn the heavy train. Vivienne reached up to unveil the virgin and show forth the face of the matron. The bride in her new pink pearls stood for a moment beaming and smiling at the congregation with love and happiness, seeming to burst out over the top of her satin dress.

Guy thought that her husband suddenly appeared to have shrunk by the same amount she had expanded. They had already truly become one in energy. From now on, that which left him would flow into her. That which left her would enlarge him. They were a whole, a married couple.

And Guy's beloved Faith looked like the cat that had swallowed the canary.

Why, she might even have swallowed me alive had I married her! he thought, doing his best to turn against her.

Again the organ peeled forth as the couple took their first step forward, arm in arm, passing down the aisle and on out of the church. The bride paced slowly, while the groom tried to hurry her into a run.

The tiny acolyte led the Bishop out and then returned to douse the candles one by one as the ushers took the family back down the aisle. The organ rilled and trilled. The Bishop's carriage was found, and Guy returned for a moment to pray alone at the foot of the Cross.

But already the florist's men had entered and begun to drag away the rented potted palms and the huge vases of white carnations. The sexton had made a pile of ribbon bows on the floor and was sweeping up the fallen petals with an ancient carpet sweeper which he kept underneath the corner pew.

"Sweet lovers love the spring. Dear Christ!" said Guy to himself and went out and found the boy with his chaise and drove on to Co-Eden to the wedding breakfast.

In a symbolic flight of Dr. Walding's fancy, the equipage which was to take the couple from the church back to the bride's house was to be the combination of a carriage from Finchwicke hitched to horses from Co-Eden. Now married in spirit and in word, but not in deed, it was to be a nice transitional touch before the final dizzying flight away from the maternal hive.

Therefore the elegant octagon-front coupe, which the Doctor had ordered in 1890 from Brewster Body, which had not been used since the days when he had used to take Thessaly to the theater and to balls during their brief winter stays in the city, had been dusted off and repainted in Thessaly's colors of dark blue and black. The black patent-leather harness with buckles and ornaments of solid silver had been fitted to Trooper and Corporal, who now stood by the church door. They would precede the bridesmaids, who would now be joined by the ushers on the road coach, and lead the procession of carriages and automobiles back to Co-Eden.

Sweeting from Finchwicke held open the door. Young

Monaghan, from Co-Eden, held the horses. Chugh handed Faith into the dark interior. The door shut. The men jumped up on the box.

"Sit fast!" called Sweeting, starting up.

Faith had never felt so totally alone with Chugh as in the silence of this tiny, dark-blue, satin-padded box. She seized the hanging strap of blue morocco leather as they swayed off down to the Church Hill Road. They were to be alone for a drive of two miles along these familiar roads. There was not much time for all there was to say.

The coachman flicked the horses with the tassel of his whip and they stepped out smartly. Faith stole a glance at Chugh, his legs too long for the carriage, one elegant knee crossed over the other, his godlike head leaning back against the cushions. Had he spoken to her directly, or had it been through Uncle Bishop? Anyway, it was up to him to speak now. She would not.

"At the rehearsal yesterday you were sitting in a pew with your mother. I thought you looked very beautiful." He spoke, not to her but to a fence post out the window. It was draped in red rambler roses, around which bees were buzzing.

Faith was amazed at the words. No one had ever called her beautiful, and she knew well that she was not. Nonetheless, as she was the only other person in the cab, she could only assume the words had been addressed to her. Chugh continued to look the other way, speaking out the window.

"The pew where you were sitting was where my mother always sat, and the light came down through the windows like fingers and touched you as it had once touched her. She used to tell me that it was God's blessing. Anyway, yesterday, it was as if *she* were blessing you, telling me that she was very pleased with you. And very displeased with me for ever having been angry with so lovely a person. Maybe it was only an illusion, but I felt it very strongly. If you know what I mean, the moment gripped me and made me turn around. I wanted to speak to you then and there, but there were so many people around. They might have thought it strange. I thought it best to preserve appearances."

Faith knew that this was the nearest he would ever come to an aoplogy, and in fact she didn't want him to go further. A trickle of sweat rolled down from his blond head, a sign of inner abjection. She said, "Uncle Bishop says that illusions are very important and we must preserve them if we are to have a happy marriage."

"But you are not an illusion, are you? My real wife?"

He turned his blue eyes on her, and she felt the great lumps of unhappiness melting away like cakes of ice in the summer sun. She didn't answer his question directly. There was something else she had to say, as they had now reached the end of Church Hill Road. "I thought it strange that you didn't speak to me for weeks, but I no longer think so. I should have trusted you. I should have obeyed you. Because now I think I know the truth about Viv. I understand now that you were trying to protect me and my memories of my father."

"How did you find out?" He looked so shocked and surprised that she was sure her surmise had been correct.

"Viv so much as told me herself."

"Oh!"

It seemed a subject not to be probed too much further, and yet it was not quite closed. There was one more question she had to ask. "How did you know about Viv, Chugh?"

"Everyone knows, everyone except you and Rick."

"Oh."

They had now entered the leafy lanes of the Station Road. Hard behind them pressed the road coach with the ushers and bridesmaids aboard.

"That's that, then, it no longer matters. Take the damned glove off."

Yes, my lord, Faith said somewhere inside herself. And she obeyed.

What a blessing it was to hold his hand. All the shadows of the long cold winter turned to light and warmth.

"That's better, Mrs. Walding. Remember the day you came to tea and ate the buttered muffins with your gloves on? Your mother had told you never to take your gloves off while calling on a gentleman. Well, you've handled me with kid gloves, all right. Proof of it is, here I am."

She beamed. He squeezed until the rings cut into her fingers.

"About the pearls," he said suddenly. "I hadn't meant to give them to you until now, in the carriage. But the way you said your vows ... I mean, when your uncle said that part about the worldly goods, I wanted the whole congregation to know I intend to keep my part of the bargain. I wanted them all to see how much ... well, anyway, I mean, I just had the impulse to give you the Chyldes pearls then and there. You know, Edith's been trying to get them away from me for years. Now they're yours."

"Thank you," she said in a tiny voice. "They're beautiful."

"If I'd sold them to her, the damn Baron might get them away from her. You can't tell about foreigners these days. Anyway, those pearls were in my mother's safe deposit box, the contents of which she left to me. They had belonged to my grandmother, and before that to Catherine the Great of Russia. Edith says they should descend in the female line, but I was able to remind her I might have a daughter of my own."

"Oh, Chugh! I don't know if I'll be able!"

"To have children?" He looked horrified.

"To have a daughter. I had planned on all boys!"

Faith saw Chugh look at her in amazement and she wondered if she had been indelicate again. She didn't really care.

Now they were approaching the bridge under the train trestle. "I'm always afraid there'll be a train overhead and scare the daylights out of the horses . . ." she said.

"No daylights in here." Chugh put his arm gently around her shoulder, one hand on her breast. He kissed her very gently on the lips. The tunnel rang and echoed with the horses' hooves. Faith's pulse clanged in her neck most painfully. Emerging into the sunshine around the Penngwynne Station, each was seated properly in separate corners as before, which was lucky because on the road was Minnie Washington and all the children, grinning and waving as the carriages passed by. Even though the kiss had made the blood pound painfully in her wrists, and had found an answering tic in Chugh's cheek as though he was struggling to control a powerful emotion, she managed to speak. "I was afraid that you were going to leave me standing at the church door, Chugh."

Chugh laughed. "Don't be so silly. It was the damned Oldthwaites' fault! They were late picking me up. Paula had mislaid a hatpin or something, and then she insisted on coming in for a glass of champagne. In my nervousness, I forgot to wind my watch and I didn't realize how late we were. Forgive me?"

Faith noticed a small trickle of moisture beginning on his temple as he squeezed her hand hard. She was so happy, she couldn't even dislike Paula. A laugh began in her toes and crept up like a tidal wave, and came out in a sob. "Oh, Chugh, I do love you so much."

"Are you sure you love me for myself? Or did you just plain want to get married to any man?"

"Oh, Chugh, sometimes I feel you've taken the place of God! I love you so much. I mean, one is supposed to love God first and most, but you're so much nearer. It's very hard."

"Well then, tell me why you love me. Tell me what you think of me."

She looked at him, hoping to convey her worship without words. It had been on the tip of her tongue to say it outright—because you're so romantic. But it was becoming very warm inside the cab, and her hero was beginning to perspire in earnest. Chugh, the suave, the charming, the aloof, had rolled his handkerchief up into a ball and was mopping up the liquids which were pouring from his skin in a most unromantic fashion. She did so much want to tell him why she loved him. Her excitement mounted as they turned off the Station Road and onto the Stone Mill Road, where the farmland gave way to the woods and the deep gorge of the Silvermist Creek. This was the road back to the entrance of her childhood, the gothic gatehouse set in the high stone wall that enclosed Co-Eden.

"Because you're handsome, witty, and brave." She managed these words, even though they were inadequate. Nonetheless he looked pleased.

"How do you know I don't lie and cheat and steal?"

"Just as long as you love only me, I wouldn't care. Chugh? Have you ever loved anyone else but me?"

"Never."

They were turning in at the Co-Eden gatehouse. The gatekeeper and all his little children in fresh pinafores were out, holding little bunches of wild flowers. The horses slowed to a walk going up the steep drive in order to negotiate the sharp turn by the Japanese bosky dell.

"Now it's your turn to tell me what you think of me," she said.

But he didn't answer, and she didn't press the question because Chugh had turned very pale. His boiled shirt seemed to be melting in the heat of the tiny carriage as the June day grew hotter, and great rivers of perspiration were now running down the back of his head into the thick black wool collar of his morning coat. Best not to press him. She didn't really care. All that she wanted to do was to restore him to power, as they were now arriving at the porte-cochere.

"God, how awful," Chugh said. "I'll be so glad when this part is over and I get you up into the Maine woods all by myself. My darling! I don't think I've ever told you. I love you!"

The words reverberated around the padded blue-satin walls. And even though Chugh still looked pale and sickly, there was a smile of triumph on his face that she had never seen before.

Pennants were flying from the cupolas of Co-Eden with the Hoagland crest, *Semper Superbus et Fastidiosus,* and the Walding crest, *Maintain.* The flower boxes were dripping with white cascade petunias. Co-Eden was waiting for the gay festivities of the wedding breakfast. The caterer's butler was standing at stiff attention on the steps to hand them out of the carriage, and Hebe, who had somehow arrived before everyone, was standing right behind him. They drew up at the steps, and young Monaghan jumped smartly down from the box to hold the horses' heads.

"Welcome, Mr. and Mrs. Walding," said the caterer's man.

"Hurry up now, Faith," said Hebe. "We have to assemble the wedding party for photographs before all the guests arrive." The bridesmaids and ushers on the coach rumbled up behind them.

Faith barely allowed herself a moment upstairs to freshen up before rejoining her husband, and with wild little dancing steps she proceeded on his arm over the lawns to the wedding pavilion standing among the Judge's yellow roses.

"Assemble, bridesmaids and ushers!" commanded Hebe, marching along with decorum.

Here comes Mama, Faith noted—a strange glitter in her eye but she's on the arm of Mr. Welch Seabreese. He's so devoted to her, maybe she'll make it for one more hour without sliding off. Her black eye looks very sore but we've said she bumped into the corner of a door by mistake last night. Too bad. But what a good sport she is. Dear Mr. Seabreese, taking care of her. Of dear, there was the Baron Bellanowski waiting importantly to be the first to kiss the bride—truly a royal pigeon in his cutaway . . .

A cloud of dust had been raised on the Co-Eden driveway by the cars and carriages of the guests who had arrived ahead of the rector for the wedding breakfast. Guy Fitzjoy sneezed as he handed over his old chaise to the boy waiting on the steps. "Hey! Ding-a-ling-a-ling and thank you, lad," the Reverend said festively.

A manservant in evening livery stood by the front door. Piles of little white boxes of cake were on the oak credenza. The suit of armor sported a white satin bow on his spear. Violin music sifted down from the great hall. Bowls of white flowers adorned every table. The wedding party lined up in the round garden in front of a screen of yellow roses. Hey ding-a-ling-a-ling! The minister begs permission to kiss the small, plump bride. Guy Fitzjoy found a seat at a little round table in the dining room with strangers, the Walter Josenthals. Crab gumbo. Boned squabs on Virginia ham. Garden peas. Champagne. Please call me Erlene. Strawberry meringues.

Now the bride is going up the staircase. She pauses on the long landing in front of the stained-glass window, throws her bouquet to Mariette Pardue, who catches it. Good for Mariette. The only one of them left, you know. Little Rosalie is passing bowls of rice and confetti. Did you know they're going away in a Pierce Arrow? It's his wedding present to her. Hey! Ding-a-ling! She hasn't seen it yet, they just brought it up under the porte-cochere.

Look, oh look, what's out there beyond! Standing like a statue in the grassy circle among his hounds, in full hunting pink, Old Charlton Seabreese on Militiaman and Ham Birdgrove on Iroquois. One of the boys laid a drag down the drive for a wedding hunt! It's a surprise.

What's that deafening noise? An aeroplane? Good God! He's coming down too low. He's going to take the chimney off. No, it's just Slim buzzing Chugh. He knows what he's doing.

Here they come! They're coming now! She's kissing Hebe. She's kissing poor old Mademoiselle, whose tears are streaming down her wrinkles. They're both kissing Becca. They're both kissing old Horace Walding. Good-bye! Hey ding-a-ling-a-ling! Someone said they're going to New York on the train now and then up to Boston tomorrow and then they're going up to Heron Bay on the Chyldes's yacht. Look at the plane waggling its wings. Thank God, he's flying off. Dreadful machines.

Guy found himself standing outside the front door to

watch them go by—next to Johnny Oldthwaite, who shoved a twenty-five-dollar gold piece into his palm.

Just then, Rick Hoagland called out for all to hear. "You're an interloper and a goddamn foreigner." Apparently there was an altercation going on between Faith's brother and the Baron. The two men stood toe to toe about to hit each other. But Johnny quickly moved in between them just as Chugh came running by, pulling Faith by the hand.

With her head bent, her hat tied down with a motoring veil, dressed in a long linen duster, and pelted by rice and confetti, Faith rushed by. She managed to stop for a moment to hug her forlorn little dog, with a white satin bow on her collar. Chugh stopped to shake Johnny's hand. "Thanks, old friend," he said as they jumped into the car.

In their hurry, neither took the opportunity to speak to Guy. He stifled a sharp twinge of hurt feelings. Next to him the Baroness was lighting a thin cigar with great nonchalance. He would like to have asked her for one—to be nonchalant too. But he had another wedding at five. And ministers could neither smoke nor drink in public without creating a bad impression. "Good-bye, my love," he said silently, as Faith waved in that direction.

Now in a mad melee of backfiring engine, squirts of gravel, calls of good-bye, good-bye, the Pierce finally pulled away from the waving crowd of people on the steps.

Mr. Charlton Seabreese moved into the drive in front of the car as it circled the turnaround and cast his trusted hounds onto the fox's scent. Warrior and Desperate gave tongue and took off down the winding drive as the Master raised his horn to his lips and blew the long and echoing notes. At a canter he led the Waldings off on a hunt for their life. His horn could be heard floating back from the Stone Mill Road.

"Goooone awaaaay Awaaaaay . . ."

About the Author

Eloise R. Weld grew up among the people and the settings she captures so perfectly in EN-GAGEMENT. She learned to ride and hunt as a small child, and went to Virginia's exclusive Foxcroft school. She graduated from Bryn Mawr at age 40, the same day her son graduated from boarding school.

Miss Weld is devoted to her greenhouse, with its collection of rare orchids. She divides her time between New York, Philadelphia, and a cottage in Maine, and is currently working on a sequel to ENGAGEMENT.

More Big Bestsellers from SIGNET

☐ **AGE OF CONSENT by Ramona Stewart.**
(#W6987—$1.50)

☐ **THE FREEHOLDER by Joe David Brown.**
(#W6952—$1.50)

☐ **LOVING LETTY by Paul Darcy Boles.** (#E6951—$1.75)

☐ **COMING TO LIFE by Norma Klein.** (#W6864—$1.50)

☐ **FEAR OF FLYING by Erica Jong.** (#J6139—$1.95)

☐ **MISSION TO MALASPIGA by Evelyn Anthony.**
(#E6706—$1.75)

☐ **THE BRACKENROYD INHERITANCE by Erica Lindley.**
(#W6795—$1.50)

☐ **MAGGIE ROWAN by Catherine Cookson.**
(#W6745—$1.50)

☐ **TREMOR VIOLET by David Lippincott.**
(#E6947—$1.75)

☐ **THE VOICE OF ARMAGEDDON by David Lippincott**
(#W6412—$1.50)

☐ **YESTERDAY IS DEAD by Dallas Barnes.**
(#W6898—$1.50)

☐ **LOSERS, WEEPERS by Edwin Silbertang.**
(#W6798—$1.50)

☐ **THE PLASTIC MAN by David J. Gerrity.**
(#Y6950—$1.25)

☐ **THE BIRD IN LAST YEAR'S NEST by Shaun Herron.**
(#E6710—$1.75)

☐ **THE WHORE-MOTHER by Shaun Herron.**
(#W5854—$1.50)

THE NEW AMERICAN LIBRARY, INC.,
P.O. Box 999, Bergenfield, New Jersey 07621

Please send me the SIGNET BOOKS I have checked above. I am
enclosing $_____(check or money order—no currency
or C.O.D.'s). Please include the list price plus 25¢ a copy to cover
handling and mailing costs. (Prices and numbers are subject to
change without notice.)

Name_____

Address_____

City_____State_____Zip Code_____
Allow at least 3 weeks for delivery